BOOK TWO OF THE ORATA
WRETCHED IS THE HUSK
BY ALEX CF

Copyright © Alex CF 2021

www.artofalexcf.com

The Author asserts the moral right to
be identified as the author of this work

Edited by Gary Dalkin and Lesley Warwick

Printed and bound in Great Britain by
Pureprint

www.pureprint.com

All rights reserved. No part of the publication may be
reproduced, stored in a retrieval system, or transmitted
in any form or by any means, electronic, mechanical
photocopying, recording or otherwise without the prior
permission of the author.

For Lesley

Bestiary

Ardid – Crane
Arn – Kestrel
Athlon – Horse
Aurma – Cow
Ayat – Lion
Baldaboa – Pigeon
Baobak Gorehorn – Elk
Barara - Goat
Blood son/daughter – Robin
Caanus – Domesticated Dog
Cheon/Speakers – Parakeet
Cini – Wolf
Corva – Crow
Corva il/ Collectors – Magpie
Corva Aefi – Jay
Creta – Mouse
Crepic – Crab
Effer – Sheep
Embaq – Orangutan
Evarin – Bearded Vulture
Fologuw – Coot
Grim – Bear
Gruor Tak Rorn – Non-avian Dinosaurs
Hagi – Oxpecker
Hanno - Gorilla
Harend – Song Thrush
The Heft – Friesian Cattle
Impasse / Flat teeth – Gazelle
Ingui - Slug
Inni – Donkey
Lanfol – Starfish
Maar – Pine Marten
Malor – Pheasant
Mesupun lafa - Armadillo
Morwih – Domesticated Cat
Muroi - Rat
Naarna Elowin – Gull
Necros Anx – Hooded Vulture
Nighspyn – Hedgehog

Norn – Whale
Onto-Athlon – Zebra
Orkrek – Frog
Oraclas – Elephant
Oreya – Deer
Pax – Highland Cattle
Rauka – Big Cats
Reveral – Leopard
Runta – Pig/ Wild Boar
Sabel – Wild Cat
Schev - Kingfisher
Sqyre – Squirrel
Startle – Starling
Storn - Owl
Tarkae – Otter
Tasq – Rhino
Throa – Badger
Toec Woderum – Mole
Toron – Chimpanzee
Tril – Rabbit
Trungru – Bison
Ungdijin – Fish
Vardi – Capybara
Voin – Bee
Vulpus – Fox
Wrickt – Bat
Wroth – Human
Yad Golhoth – Moose
Yoa'a/Drove – Hare
Yowri – Lark
Zev – Cheetah

Language

Ora - The Sun
Naa - The Earth
Seyla - The Moon
Gasp - The place after death

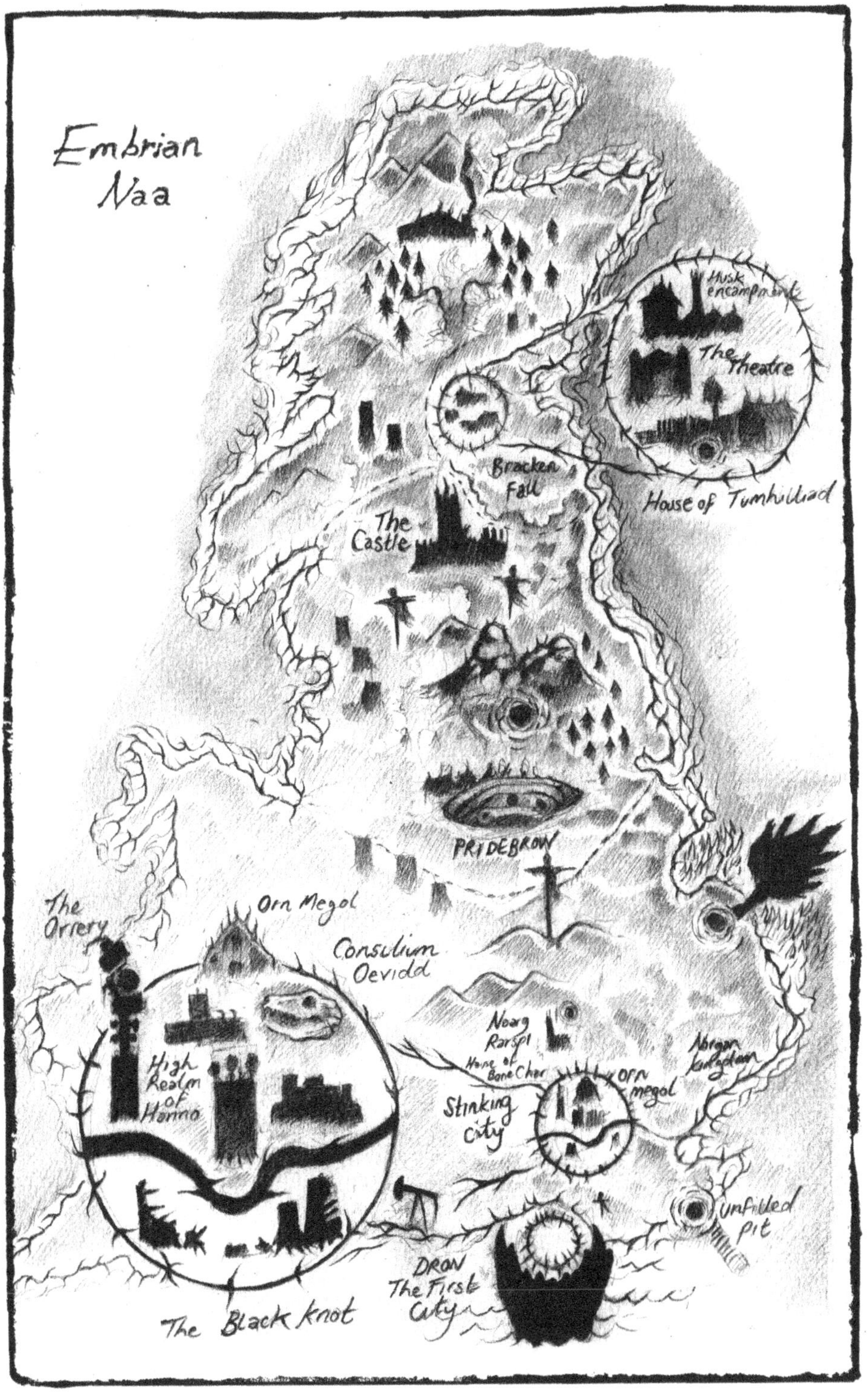
Embrian Naa
Husk encampment
The Theatre
Bracken Fall
House of Tumhilliad
The Castle
PRIDEBROW
The Orrery
Orn Megol
Consulium Oevidd
Noarg Rarspl
Home of Bone Char
Orn megol
Stinking City
High Realm of Hanno
Unfilled pit
DRON The First City
The Black Knot

From the Treatise of the Tempered Guild

Since the fall of the Wroth and the return of Dron, the First City, so too did aspects of the Umbra come to all living things. The shared tongue of Ocquia remained in use, yet for many, will alone could once again be read, and with it the elucidation of feelings. In the world before, those who could see the Umbra were Shadow Starers, forever seeking the light in the darkness. Their vision was far broader and more nuanced, and in some cases a burden.

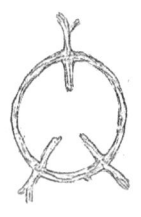

Prologue

This was his fortune. Each day much the same. He would stir and rouse himself in the gravel hours between midnight and first light. He ignored the whine of his nagging limbs as he dragged them from beneath his bedclothes and into the bitter nook that was his home, a tiny stone-built cottage set in the land like a troublesome sore. He never spoke with words, for he had no one to speak to, but he would mutter things, incomplete sounds, irksome thoughts. There was much hate in the old man. Yet there was also a little love, a love of dreadful things.

He threw a sack over his shoulder, lifted his shotgun from the table and went out into the bare night. There was a frost. His footsteps crunched on brittle blades of grass like crushed glass, up from his dark residence, on to the moor.

The highland was his bounty. He would stand alone amidst the heather, his hands outspread, brushing the very tips of the gorse bushes. The pain of each barb was resolute, and with its sharp truth he would allow the black flood to fill his vision, and in the dark a garland of light would bloom.

This light spoke of meat, of a vital living thing. He sought it out wherever it might run and he was never hurried. He would trace the meandering gossamer thread of his quarry and snatch its beating heart. Not always a hunger to sate, often another kind of want. It was the life itself that summoned him.

Soon the morning would rise and mark his slow return home, for no street lamps or other bothersome light lit his stride, just the low claret dawn, heaving the burden of night upon its back. But for now, the lithe lights of a bounty rose in his eyes, taunting him to follow.

He crept wide of the copse where they dwelt. He covered his head with a hood, so that he might shadow his colourless skin from them. The lights jostled like insects and he batted the air as if to ward them off but their glow was within him. He knew nothing of their enterprise, nothing of their biology. He had once feared a tumour or disease, yet it seemed unlikely that a sickness would provide him with such second sight.

In the crook of the land he knelt down, felt the sore creak of his body, cursed himself. He saw their breath. A herd of deer, all salubrious and strong. He was not sure why, but he called them *Oreya*. Their red fur seemed to shine for him. It was carnal, a longing that clogged his pores, made his heart palpitate.

He aimed his rifle.

Crack

The lights roiled. It was his favourite moment, the broad low stomach quake, the jitter of panic. He revelled in their epiphany, the prick of realisation as the barrel dislodged the shot, as a body fell and seethed, as the others pranced with willowy grace away from him, away from the beast.

And then the blank land. Nothing stirred. The cold drew in the ephemeral sound, sank icicle teeth into the air and swallowed time and consequence. He walked away from his hiding place, toward the shivering body, quickly shedding life. The moon offered him a splendid light, and he kneeled beside the Oreya, placing his hands on its warm body, feeling the quick thrum. He drew from it, intravenously.

He became giddy, tipping on to his bad leg, yet he cared not, for he now lay beside the animal, and the warmth was delicate and smelled sweet and earthy. He scooped at the blood that poured from the wound in its flank and wiped it over his face, the metal note on the air, and for a moment, it too held a quality long denied to him.

There was joy, and then the joy was gone. The Oreya died quickly. He had not planned for this — he had been too keen. A killing wound gave him so little time, and again he chided himself. He hugged closer to take of the warmth, his eyes closed tight, searching for its wandering spirit which sought escape. Soon the body was cold, and the frozen ground seeped up into his legs and made it difficult for him to get back up. He tried to lift himself, only to roll flat on his back. He raged, shouting his frustration.

His shout was heard, and the response came in a low snarl. The throaty rattle appeared close to him, and he lay completely still. He shut his eyes and searched the dark for the source. The scarlet aura of the dead Oreya clouded his inner eye, its death diminishing the spark that had once spoken of its life. The red swell dissipated, and at once, an orange glint bloomed and then passed through the veil of death like roiling flame. It was not alone, as other lupine presences moved, pouring either side of the Oreya.

The glen had been chosen for its remoteness. Very few farms bordered the steep cut in the land, it was rocky and the base of the gully wet. There were forests, unmanaged and deep that lifted from the green shawl. Animals lived there, herds that might aid the survival of such a predator. The wolves had taken to their reintroduction, left alone in this wide countryside. He had seen them only once before, as he sharpened his tools outside his house. They had watched him, learning his place in the land.

He had felt their desire, for it reminded him of his own. It was quite a thing to know those who craved flesh, for it gifted him with the sight of his own quarry, and despite the cruelty he already honed, treasured even, it somehow broadened the depth of his own appetite. He believed the wolves could see his power, that they too shared in his clairvoyance. They saw his majesty and knew not to trespass upon his territory. A truce, an understanding. He had even entertained walking amongst them, deific.

Their esteem would stave off their desire to eat him. He coveted this delusion as he lay silent. Perhaps the scent of the corpse had overwhelmed them, breaking their pact. Perhaps they had not seen him beside the kill. If he crawled away from them, left the Oreya for them, they would be thankful for the bounty. He cared not for the meat.

He turned to one side with great effort, the numb mass of his thighs almost immovable. He began to drag himself, hand over hand. He did not hear the wolves, so he continued on, grasping at tufts of grass, gouging the cold ground for a hold.

The snarl was now beside his ear. Liquid in its movement, the paw fell on him with excruciating slowness, a pointed weight of pain, shifting its body mass on to him, pinning him stomach down on the hard earth, the peculiar scent of sweet decay upon its breath. He lay completely still.

The wolf nuzzled his cheek, its heavy head knocking at his own. Its muzzle was wet and cold, he felt the dribble of saliva, the slip of sandpaper tongue. He acknowledged with sobering lucidity the china clink of teeth against his own as it dragged its snout against his soft flesh, all the while the low rattle quivering in its gullet.

It then withdrew. He cried, infinite relief poured from him, urine yellow. He sobbed to the empty night, for nothing would come to his aid. He wanted to get up, he wanted to find the knife tucked in its sheath and defend himself. Yet his limbs betrayed him, for they did not share his motivation.

He felt a tug on his ankle. Glancing back, he saw the expression of a demon, inconceivable but for its teeth around his lower leg.

The puncture of skin came with a singular pain as it began to drag him back towards the Oreya. He choked, catarrh caught in his throat. Finally, his arms agreed to his protestations and flailed around, as if to ward off his attackers. The wolves replied with teeth, each arm ensnared. He would die soon, he knew this, but it was still make-believe, only resignation. He flipped over against the raw bite in his pelvis.

Their leader was huge. Its head low, the wrinkled brow and withdrawn lips bore a grin that tapered to its devil ears. It moved so slowly it was as if time refused to interfere. He yelled at it. Time reeled itself in with a lunge snap of the wolf's great head, a single serrated bark that brought its face mere inches before him.

It clamped his neck with its wide bite. Catching his breath, he felt his whole body turn awkwardly against the earth, the jagged discomfort of the Oreya's hooves in his side. He could not make a sound, for the wolf's jaws had compressed his oesophagus.

He began to asphyxiate, forcing his weak fingers between the wolf's teeth, attempting to free himself of it. As he did so, the other wolves gave into their own hunger and leapt for him, pulling at his old coat, drawing away his rifle as though they understood its use.

Exposed skin glowed luminescent, a beacon, summoning mouths. They bit incessantly, pulling, shaking their heads in violent throes, and soon skin gave in and the black fount of his blood brimmed and poured as they pulled him apart, piece by piece. His belly gave easily, and he watched his innards thrash between clenched mandibles.

Finally, the lickerish swell behind his eyes submerged his dwindling sight and he fell into its embrace, dragging him into death. The curtains of life drew in as with the batter of moth wings upon a lamp, casting grandiose nightmare shadows.

Beyond was the bleak unknowable. He bore witness to the tower clouds that blistered into endless vaulted skies — alien winds whipped him, torpor crowds of sunken faces, incomplete and coagulated, rushed beside him in violent cavalcade. Their wail held a human quality, an anguish palpable, touchable. *Go back,* they cried.

He rotated his astral form towards the ember of his former life, a hole in the grey folds. Stars orbited it, orange and red, valorous and splendid. He was all but consumed by a fog of ennui. He reached with unseeable limbs for the brightest light. There was a warmth, it was faint, yet a vague quality drew him in. It was far more attractive than his own light, which diluted now like ink in water. He would soon be washed away.

The will to live was a muscle memory, to pull himself back from the dark nether, to engage unused tendons and draw into it. The window of light began to retract, and he knew his time was short, so he flung himself forth, into the diminishing swell. This time the flutter of wings was coarse, resisting his return.

A sea of silence and black.

THRUM thrum

THRUM thrum

The beat beat beat was raucous, blistering loud in his ears. Even the rough grate of movement seemed deafening.

He dared not open his eyes, the slightest hair of light burrowing deep into the sinews of his brain, a perforating inorganic sensation. He coughed through the quiver of saliva, running free of his mouth in great frothy gobbets. He tasted blood, smelled the rancid flavour of faeces. A white hot pain billowed between his organs, and he began to convulse upon the frozen earth. He felt the viscous groan of living, wet and fecund.

He was curled foetal-like in the hot runnel of a corpse, amongst snapped rib bones and the gelatinous red of torn fat and muscle tissue. There were others here with him, others he could not see, but he felt them, and he sensed their worry, these shapeless souls, shimmering effigies, eyes bright and sorrowful. He had once known this before, its splinter was deep in the architecture of his being, a tweaked nerve that offered a singular memory. The moment of his birth; he had felt his mother's warmth — so quickly snatched from him.

He wrenched open his eyes. His neck was stiff, it would not parley with him. He looked down upon himself. He could see black hair, thick and wet with blood. He tried to lift himself but found muscles and limbs that would not yield, that would not bend how he wished them to. His shoulders were narrow, he could not lift his hands to clear his eyes, for he no longer had hands.

His heart drummed. He struggled free of the Oreya carcass, pushing himself on all fours, short tight legs and arms that seized and spat at him with every effort. Bursts of pain hummed and exploded across his forehead, cascading auras that clustered and atrophied in his eyes, blinding him.

He saw the smoke of his chimney, weak and willowy in the distance. He felt his companions coddle him, reach for him to offer kindness. He snarled at them, bared his teeth, and then he collapsed.

*

When he awoke again, he was inside his cottage. He was alone. He lay upon his back, and he rolled to one side so that he might lift himself. The pain in his bad leg was gone, yet remained taut. His body quaked, as though attempting to wake him from a dream.

He heard a wiry drone. He quieted this incessant whine, banishing the needle voice in his head. He dragged himself slug-like to the door, resenting the morning light.

Beside his house were collections of found objects, broken things, unwanted and left to ruin. A large sheet of glass sat against old oil drums, where he looked upon his reflection. The crescent of white around dark pupils, the rising horns of his ears. He peeled back his thin lips to reveal his dagger teeth.

He was the wolf who had murdered him. He had stolen its body.

The wet cloying of his new form was sordid, involuntary. He felt himself a skeleton coated in clinging muscle and skin and fur, half suffocated by it, this filthy thing, stinking of wet dog and putrefaction. Each movement was mannequin-like, limp strings that attached to his struggling thoughts, so loose he had to coil each thread around his brain in hope of better purchase, of better control.

He loped back within the cottage, looked about his shabby room, the floor covered in blood. He pulled himself against a wooden chair — again, his body did not give easily. He was a quadruped.

He rested his quick chest against the lap of the chair and tried to calm himself. He lay like this for a while, half propped up, sprawled out beneath the edge of the table, hind limbs on the floor, panting to cool his blood-matted, hairy body.

In time he found some strength, and he hobbled out on to the moor once again, to find the Oreya. It was a mass of bones picked to the gristle. Beside the Oreya, the remains of a man, his former reflection, dismembered and spread-eagled, clothes torn and sodden, his face missing.

He was surprised by his lust for the grubby red morsels and eagerly devoured what was left of himself. He vomited, perhaps revulsion at this act, perhaps the consumption of raw meat a learning curve, hacking ungainly into the morning mist — yet ate what he had regurgitated without a thought. He was no longer a man. He was a flesh eater, capable of devouring raw and decaying meat. His corrosive stomach acids would quickly dissolve this food and he would feel all the better for it. This slight boon seemed to lessen the sheer magnitude of his rebirth, the old man now the young wolf.

*

Sharp bursts of thought plagued him, dizzying clots of desire and love and lust, ideas never conceived or perceived by him. With each revelation he was scolded, the true owner of the body concentrated deep within, lashing out at him with recollections, memories and painful utterances focused on encouraging guilt and regret, to drive him out, the unwelcome spirit. He fought back, for his own mind held far less pleasant visions, all of which had been retained in his transference into the wolf. He sent cavalcades of violent, spiteful malice, hurtful encounters, terrifying ideas in retaliation.

He felt the animal retreat. As its defences weakened, he felt its living strength, its compassion. He saw every apology for every kill it had ever made and every pup ever conceived.

He felt the death of a cub, and for a moment he dwelt in this memory; for it was a love he had never known. He quickly disregarded it, finding it too painful, and moved on, another memory – a smell, a scent of a mate – he felt his body brim with desire, and her fleeting shape before him.

Eventually he found his host's name. Emeris. He crept lightly about each clarified shard of remembrance, markers in this beast's life. He learned the names of his pack – *Ruthe-va Unclan*, brought together from disparate families of wolves – of his own clade, Vulpi, and their word for wolf, Cini. He saw the vast and sheer face of Emeris's inherited memory, that which was written into his blood. It held formations, primeval gods arching in vague relief, worn down to the faintest trace. He was taken aback by such impressions, of a creed hidden from man. The very idea of his own kind raised a flurry of nauseous thoughts. For man held a wolf-name too, the gagging cough, the ever present vileness.

Wroth.

And this wolf, this Cini, had a prehistoric hatred for the Wroth.

In this foray into Emeris's past he found some semblance of calm. He stood on four shaky limbs and left the cottage. He paced the cold earth and scanned the land. His vision was clear yet muted, the colours he could perceive were lessened, yet what he lacked in vibrance he gained in comprehension.

Sensing the virulent notes of recent birth and stale rot in the air, his olfactory abilities painted a potent vista. Synaesthesia blossomed in his nasal cavities, drawn across his line of sight in glorious browns and blues, the decaying presence of the Oreya, and of his Cini kin.

The family of Cini hovered around the tree-line — as he had lifted himself from the corpse they had perceived something out of place. They had gone to him, as he had dragged himself across the land, collapsing and recovering, snarling in jagged fits. They feared sickness, and had pulled back, watching him from afar, following his feeble crawl from the heathland and into the cottage, confused by his silence, all watching his unfamiliar movements, the graceless gait of a stolen body. They did not know how, or why, but their brother was different.

How right they were to stay away

They had betrayed him, killing his Wroth body, murdered by this clan of scruffy dogs. He would smite them for not recognising his prowess. He would be cruel and unusual in his vengeance.

He was cunning, and from that grew an inkling - to walk amongst those who thought him brethren, to manipulate, to deceive. This was his will. Yet he feared himself too weak to overwhelm them. For now he would rest, recover a sense of self and consider what he had become, what he was capable of doing.

When he closed his eyes, he felt a wealth of possibilities. He had no way to know for sure, yet he surmised that his second sight had been an aspect of some untapped potential, the same gift that had offered him this new lease of life. He had seen beyond death itself – the vast inebriated catacomb, brimming over with souls – and he had returned, carrying with him some sense of that lightless place.

As he stood under the moon, a language began to manifest. This was the voice of the body he now inhabited, the muscle memory, detached from its landlord. The tenant had claimed squatters' rights, and this house held an abundance of knowledge, of both the living world, and of what lay beyond life. For the Cini knew much of life and death.

He looked again to the moon and saw the vague apparition of that other place. In his attempt to recall its name, he mouthed the word *Seyla*, the cave mouth to the *Gasp*. Other words replied as echoes - *Lacking Sea, langYis, Hoerain Orblong, the Biting Will.*

He had crossed the threshold and returned, he had stepped amongst the twisting boughs of black forests, straining like a mockery of men, stretching out toward him with willow fingers, desperate for him to free them. He had sensed the weight of their torment, their wish for deliverance.

Might others be freed from death, like he had been? They too could be subjugated, made to bow to him in return for that freedom. He was a student of a new creed, and he would be a dutiful pupil.

*

The She-Cini, Noraa, stood at the edge of the forest, watching her beloved. His eyes held indifference, a cruel amnesia had claimed the memory of her. She went to him time and again, yet he remained unwilling to break his frigid gaze with the sky.

Emeris did not return to their den amongst the bracken in the forest. He did not show her the affection that had grown between them. In the pack, few had paired, for this alien land was a far cry from that into which they had been born. Those who had never hunted would surely starve without such skills. Survival was essential, finding a willing mate was not. Yet, in Emeris she had seen a strength that rivalled hers.

One last time, she stepped between him and the sky. 'Emeris, come rest with me. It has been so many turns since you slept.'

Her lover did not respond, yet he lowered his head, and curled his lips to reveal the glimmer of teeth. A low, almost imperceptible growl grew in his gullet. His eyes held menace.

She felt fear, an emotion she had never wished to associate with Emeris, and she turned away from him, hesitantly, looking back once to see that he had returned his gaze upon Seyla.

Where others spoke of sickness, she could not shake the sense of unfamiliarity. Like a thorn in her paw, her attempts to ignore Emeris became a nagging sore. He would not speak a word. He would not sleep.

All who approached him received the same cruel glare. Every turn, Noraa would go to him, with meat, with delicate stones, beautiful objects in which he had once found so much joy. All fell before him without the vaguest interest, without the slightest response.

The pack drew away from him, abandoning their den which he once shared with them, seeking shelter beneath a rocky overhang deep within the forest, until eventually his presence was little more than a dull ache. They mourned their loss of him and comforted Noraa as they would a widow.

Noraa busied herself with honing her skills in hunting with her surrogate siblings, stalking the feather-green foliage, contemplating trails where Oreya ran. She curled up upon soft moss in the warmth of her mother, Geffen. Each night, she invented a different death for him — a lone Wroth with a weapon, gored by an Oreya stag, a fatal fall. Taken from her again and again in every manner of absolute death.

But Emeris was not dead.

*

The consciousness that nagged at him was growing tiresome. In his attempt to further oppress the true owner of the body, he decided creating an identity and a purpose would cement his dominion over Emeris. A vague plan was forming, fuelled by his belief that this had all happened for a reason. He had reflected on his human life, on that which had led him to a fate inconceivable, and it brought him nothing of any use. He lacked the wherewithal to recognise the futility in seeking merit in a meritless life, yet nonetheless made grandiose assumptions.

He would have to forfeit his human name, it lacked the significance that his current state deserved, perhaps was even comical given his current form, and in the spirit of reinvention, he felt it only correct to bestow himself a new and distinguished title.

He mouthed names to the wind, the epithets of leaders, despots and dictators. He gurned and coughed up syllables uncomfortable in a canine mouth. Herrod, Alexander, Khan. A hotchpotch of half remembered artefacts, vague characters of fiction, yet none held the strength and resplendence he desired. Consonants blunt and rigid passed his lips as he spat the glottal sigils of antiquity. The stagnant byways of his memory coughed up lithographs from old encyclopaedias, Greek titans and the crumbling effigies of Egyptian deities.

He withdrew his lips, placing his tongue against his front teeth, and wrenched his jaw to trigger some withered neural stem, a crumb of knowledge wedged between the scintilla of Tutankhamen and the lofty pyramids of Giza, the fading relief of a jackal god, the tall astute ears and prominent snout.

Thoth

He was wrong, of course, for the name he sought was Anubis. Thoth – a feathered god of wisdom and truth – had been an ibis. The irony would almost certainly be lost on him. Regardless, the sound itself was sharp, short and commanding. Through his muzzle it was little more than a bark. Thoth would be his name.

He had not fed for days, ignoring the emptiness, lost amongst the ephemera of inherited memories, ideas he digested, gleaning their meaning. In his possession were the fundamentals of this animal's belief.

For his second sight had a name — Thoth was an *Umbra*, the shared will of all life, a connection with the very consciousness of Naa, the name this animal called the Earth. In lesser paws this might be nothing more than a boon, to him it was a weapon.

*

The Gasp, the place beyond death, became ever more tangible. In addition to his own preternatural abilities, the Cini carried in their blood a natural inclination to see the Gasp, a skill he would exploit. The benefit of thieving a life was that it came with everything hardwired into the grey matter. The only downside was that each sojourn into those dark regions was accompanied by the splintered screech of the Cini within, the true owner of this receptacle. Emeris. It was a vivid reminder of what he had done. He partook of it sparingly.

At first it induced nausea, a shrill sickly whine that caused him to wretch. This was but the first step; for him to achieve his goal, he would need to cross over, and yet this was a skill he would have to learn himself. The Umbra would be his vehicle and it would be bent to his will. For now, the rolling buoyant swoon of its presence resisted him, and as much as he tried to steer his glare upon the Gasp, the more it fought him.

Soon, hunger overwhelmed him and he left his watch. He was clumsy on his limbs, his frame cumbersome and peculiar, and yet with a little concentration, his stolen musculature came to understand him as master, and he galumphed out over fallen trees and grassy hillocks, following the scent of prey.

The Umbra enveloped and showed no reluctance, for this was its true sight — to perceive the weave of life. It was fluid, the trickle glint of fire hues lighting up the land with humming life.

There were no Oreya, driven south by his estranged Cini pack, but he cared not. For there were Effer, beyond the valley, left to graze for far too long, their fleece encumbering them, making them slow.

He soon crested the adjacent hill, and saw with clever eyes the dirty white mounds that were his quarry. He lowered himself for he felt this was correct. For now, he was simply mimicking how Cini might hunt, and was surprised to find his muscles leading him.

He considered that his hunger might be starvation to Emeris, who was keen to see his body live despite it being stolen from him. So Thoth let Emeris take the lead, just enough to see a kill.

He stalked in a wide semicircle, flush with ferns and gorse that hugged close to the stone-built walls which enclosed the Effer. He felt his throat spasm, felt saliva gush in his mouth, and the urgent snap of tendons wishing for him to leap forward. So he did.

Once his prey fell, he regained all motor function and writhed in the coronet of blood. The Effer struggled for far too long. Thoth was a child, a blunt instrument, unable to do his own dirty deed.

Deep within, Emeris revelled in Thoth's failure. Thoth could hear the cackle of satisfaction reverberate around his skull. He snarled with humiliation. The Effer wounded him with its hooves, kicking back at him as it bled out. It died a staggered, drawn out death and he lay exhausted in the welter of a life. He felt no remorse, only embarrassment. The Effer let out a gurgled bleat before finally giving up her ghost. As it passed into death, Thoth could see the rising revenant effervesce from its corpse.

He snapped at it, dissolving and reforming above him, its marrow slowly dissipating out of reality, finding its path to the Gasp. It looked down upon him with vehemence, a palpable hatred. The Umbra had gifted him this sight many times, and yet he had never seen it like this, for the frail wall which parted life from death was thinned ever further through the Cini's eyes, and the black beyond was now wholly visible to him. He felt assured by this. He sat upon his hind limbs and pawed the sky, feeling his claws pass beyond the rim of the sullen beyond. He smelt the cold oily draught leak from it, coil around him, at first reject his living meat, before embracing him as having a place amongst the dead.

The revenant of the Effer began to condense, filling out in ghostly form in the hereafter. Soon she was a recognisable shimmering effigy of her former self, and her eyes widened with panic as he hesitated, before reaching a long black arachnid leg into the Gasp, revelling in his power, a wide grin accompanying his unblinking stare.

She drifted further out into the great atrium, joining the coagulate current of spirits high above the dread, dead land. Thoth smiled to himself and stepped through.

At once, the bones that were not truly his ached, for the strain of gravities unphysical rallied against him in an effort to reject him like a transplanted organ. He felt suffocated by the very substance of the place, the air stale and dry. A billion eyes turned to him at once, mournful watery globes that glowed with a particular wanting. They smelt his life like a mosquito to blood, drawn in by the reek of him. They flocked with gusto; thick and greasy they glided over his fur with ease, leaving trails of ether. But their attention soon turned to revulsion, for they could sense the Wroth within. They withdrew in frightened congregation.

Yet he was not alone for long. A vast clot moved surreptitiously toward him, extending a curl of black, a hundred thousand sinuous arms reaching, soot black appendages, whisper digits that clawed and cut like cord. It swayed and bowed under its own wish to reach him, a proboscis of many hands, opening like a charred flower head to reveal a single Wroth-like face.

A tragedy of dim likenesses fawned at him with greedy eyes. Particles separating from their babel tower, skeletal nails upon immaterial hands grazed his vigorous fur. He felt the snag of their loss on him, as though he might hook them and reel them back beyond the veil, back to the living land, along with him. They were shunned here, in the dark, unwelcome in the unliving chorus, for they had been Wroth. Much like the animal revenants who had fled his presence, they too could see him within, curled up foetal-like, a Wroth in wolf's clothing.

'How?' they hissed.

'I'll show you,' he replied.

A grey and muggy dawn awoke the pack. Upon the path they had worn to their den, against the bloated clouds, a silhouette appeared, large and unnatural. It moved without grace, awkward and broken as though decrepit with age. They did not recognise its movements — it held no familiar quality. They snarled cautiously until Emeris's face emerged in the light, eyes peculiarly pale and huge. Words came forth, heavy, slow and crude, mouthed painfully, as though it did not come naturally to him.

'My family.'

Noraa swooned with joy, for her love had returned to her, be him broken, it mattered not. She went to him, to feel his muzzle against hers, to know his warmth.

But there was no such warmth. Her mother beckoned her back, but she wanted him to be hers again. She looked at him with fear and love and confusion, for his face held nothing. Eyes vacant of kindness, filled with a cold indifference. She appealed to her loved ones, who could offer her nothing.

His head jarred alarmingly, his jaw slack and wide. A vile odour poured from him, and with it lengths of mucus that wheeled toward her. She stumbled back, against her frightened pack, who cowered from the mucilage spurs that whipped and lashed, seeking prey.

Noraa felt an unquenchable cold, a raw bite as one such limb punctured her flanks, and she was at once overcome, her eyes clouded, the seizing brittle ache of violation. Something forced itself within her mind, and she collapsed against the ground, straining to see her loved ones writhing beside her, stricken by the same malice. She howled with a strangled whine, dragging herself away.

She looked to him, Emeris, whose stare was cruel and smug. He shuddered with a particular glee as blasphemous folds of plasm curled about him, tugging free of him, sending out serpent secretions toward her. She could perceive consciousness in these clots of consumption, revenants hollow with want — ghouls, Gasp-stuff, violent and hungry.

As a pup, she had known the dead well. Her mother was born wild, had learned of the tethering of spirits. The Gasp was taught as an ever present thing, and through it they had stayed the flame of their lineage, so easily snuffed out as their kind was hunted by the Wroth.

The pack learned to dilute the wall between Naa and the Lacking Sea, and coax the dearly departed to remain with them, anchored them with songs and prayers, gave them the purpose of tutelage among the living.

Noraa knew her overmother despite her death long before she was born, had seen her glib eyes in the dark, strong and terrifying. She had known the touch of the hereafter, the adoring current of familial love, and she had learned to resist the insatiable presence of wanton ghosts. She resisted now.

Feverishly, the dead attached themselves, latching each ghoulish proboscis, attempting to flay her living essence from her body. Seizing and wheezing with exhaustion, the revenants had little time or energy to do their foul work. Yet it was all she could do to tear their dread lips from her, and the eyes, glowering with a carnality, growing strong as they drained her.

Vomit rose in her throat as each jaundiced face licked at her with limpet tongues, seeking entrance. They wreathed her, a shallow shawl of many milk eyes and greasy fawning, sliding through her wet fur with slow precession. They would have her soon.

She dug her claws into the hard earth, becoming her anchor. With one last heave she pulled herself free of them and she howled into the empty air, panted the patter of old invoking verse.

'Yaga Vormors, Pale living! Overmother! Grant me tiding!'

Silence snapped.

All sound was admonished. All eyes, dead and living alike, turned to its source.

At the centre of the clearing, mere feet from the ground, a lightlessness manifested, a hole, an opening, a place where light dare not exist. The pine trees within its orbit groaned against an unseen stress, the *split crack* as shards of bark rushed to its inescapable maw.

A deep resonant throb sounded, some distant nebulous bell, strung above a palsied land. The air thinned, a taut inhale, wrenching the skin of Naa in on itself before retracting violently.

Where the dark had once been, a raw thing now hung.

Noraa knew this gnarled presence well. The crooked visage of a Cini, its face gaunt, eyes deep chasms, pins of putrescent light hovering at each centre. Her overmother lacked a countenance that imparted any feeling or love; skeletal, as though scorched black, her hackles raised behind what remained of her ears, thick with the gloss of ectoplasm. She was not encumbered by the real; she was the Gatherer of Putrefaction, lost in the din of tiny deaths.

'NO!' she shrieked.

She moved uncannily, scything the sea of ghouls with liquid wrath, a scimitar of inverted light, cutting pendulum wakes — those not quickly snuffed out baulked in her presence as she sheared their tongues, tearing with multitude limbs.

The violence made for Emeris, drawing from the dead on a wave of detritus to aid her advance. She reached him, bearing down in fits of chitin shards. The rattle pop click of her death-form lowered a fractious face before him, tar oozing from bone fractures.

His gaze was unmoved by her, a vague curiosity in his calculating eyes. She sent out her own exploratory tendrils, black stylus of unliving vigour. He smiled with an arrogance, cocking his head ever so slightly as she explored him.

She peered inside his husk, at the poor lingering soul of Emeris caged up in the ganglia of his stolen mind. She looked to the pack, who began to rise, passive, unflinching, coddled by the smoky clog of the Gasp. They were no longer Cini, held in the grasp of dead gravities.

'What are you, *husk*?' she spat at him.

The black Cini looked back at her with cold indifference.

'Know me, hag.'

The overmother withdrew in a flurry, black ghoul matter arced and sloughed.

She snarled at him, her suppurating maw venomous, yet he remained unmoved. She could feel the tumour within the Cini. Inside the strong brother of her kin was a crouched, wizened thing, emaciated, thorny. It contorted itself within him, wriggled under her children's fur. She recognised the scent of it.

'Wroth!'

With all her preternatural might she held him low. He snapped at her with his living mouth, the unshakable cold of her presence upon him, yet she would not yield.

She threw her head back and screamed to her underdaughter.

'Flee my child! Flee!' she wailed, and the asp hiss cut Noraa's muffled resignation and at once she ran, as fast as her limbs could carry her, turning one last time to see her overmother, a writhing mass, fend off the frenzied bodies of her bewitched family — her mother, her siblings, gone.

Through the veils of coagulate that restrained him, Thoth witnessed Noraa escape, and he laboured to raise his head. He let out a gargled, phlegmy bark, 'It is hopeless, dog! I will find you!'

*

She ran far from the forest, leaving the valley, up its broad bracken side, beyond which lay a wide sparse moorland. She was alone.

The ground was moist underfoot, the frost had not come that night, and a deep wet mist hung about her. Not far from here was the Wroth dwelling. She had seen him once there, greeted by skin and bones, barely a meal to be had. The pack had turned back to the forest with disappointment, in search of the musk of Oreya.

The little stone house lay empty now. She loped beyond, through coarse scrubland. An urgency grew within her, to seek help, but she did not know anyone beyond her family.

She did not know anyone at all.

The rock my bed through which I gather
And time the lulling soporific
Grit and gravel carried up;
In quaking continental agitant
I briefly see the present tense
The sweating, rutting confidence
The never ending, zealous sun
Whose path passes my meridian

All is well in living Naa
I gather up those gone a wander
And yet, what's this?
A stray, a seed
Like me, it wants beyond its means

So now I listen
now I stir
Oh, little seed gone a' wander.

Chapter One

It was early evening, and with very little else to do, Ivy had gone to bed. She lay restless for many hours, anxiously awaiting the shriek that had come every night. She was almost thirteen, but the night brought with it many unknown sounds that frightened her. She kept a candle lit beside her. The sound eventually came. It was a sad, harrowing yelp that had reminded her of her brother, plagued by night terrors.

Her brother was long dead, and she knew the culprit, so, begrudgingly, she made for the window. She pulled back the curtain and looked out upon the garden. The cold moonlight bathed the fox, casting her fur in bluish hue. She sat in the middle of the lawn, lifting her head to blink with patient acknowledgement.

Ivy knew she was a female, not through her knowledge of foxes, no, nothing as simple as that. The fox had *told her*. She even knew her name, Vorsa, although this understanding had not been articulated through speech.

The fox had appeared before Ivy every night for a week. She knew that Vorsa was aware of her apprehension, of her confusion, was aware that Ivy had suffered a great loss. Ivy knew this through means unknown to her, and yet many nuances and clarities had been shared with her, none of which she was ready to accept.

Finally, with a silent blink of goodbye, the fox left, and Ivy returned to her bed. Then she managed to sleep for a few hours before hunger got the better of her. She wandered wearily to the kitchen, seeing the tin of soup, which had stared reticently at her since she had found it amongst the other items she had recently scavenged. Always choosing anything else but it, even the entire jar of gherkins. She wasn't a fan of this particular flavour. But needs must. She removed the lid and with dissatisfaction, drank the contents cold.

*

The sun broke and she prepared herself for a hunt. She had ransacked a number of shops close to her home and feared that a few more weeks would render her local cache empty. She would make for the ruins further afield, locate the buildings that still stood tall.

Her small house had survived the catastrophe. Next door also stood, yet much of the terrace had burned after a gas explosion, exposing the innards of people's sanctuaries.

She had seen only one or two frightened humans in the following months, still overwhelmed by the tens of millions of dead. Thankfully, the rancour of their presence had waned. She knew little of the diseases that had risen from the charnel piles, but had heeded her strange inklings, odd visions that steered her free of sickness. She could not fathom what guided her, but she listened, until the weather had reduced the fat and skin of the unbridled dead to withered strips over yellowing bone. She was no longer upset at the sight of so many. It was awful to admit that her saving grace had been that very few had survived. It meant there was far more to scavenge.

Water fell free of damaged guttering, trickling into rubble piles. She paused to drink for a moment — its taste vaguely earthy.

Much of the debris that had once been a suburb was covered by plant life, leaves spread upon the warm red bricks. Like with a fresh fall of snow, the ugliness of this skeleton city was blurred by foliage, all knotted up with vine and weed.

She let her hand grace the tall wheat-like spurs of grass as she continued along the quiet street. Once in a while, eyes would peer at her through the rubble, knowing eyes of rodents that seemed to carry a greater understanding of her than she had ever perceived in them before. She would turn her gaze away the moment their awareness became too visceral, when movements seemed far more considered than before. It had not evaded her attention that they were also wearing things — strange contrivances of wood and stone and shell. Sometimes these visions upset her, for she feared she might be unwell. She worried that her loneliness had turned into something harmful.

Office buildings stood like cliff faces, the outer wall torn down, the traces of their former inhabitants now rain-soaked rubble. Colonies of birds had made roosts amongst the exposed floors, desk drawers filled with soft grass and discarded feathers.

As she walked at the foot of one building she could just about make out her goal — an open fire escape to a courtyard, a former warehouse for food storage. The outer walls and burglar-proof barbs hindered any other entrance and so it was with trepidation that she began to climb the breeze blocks which jutted teeth-like from the wall, a haphazard staircase. She clambered up, leaving crumbling cement in her wake.

Eventually she reached the summit, the second floor. It was safe to stand, the building still retaining some structural integrity. Here and there, furniture remained, office equipment mouldering where it was left, damp, rusted or destroyed with mildew.

She traced her fingers over staplers and clipboards, the final hasty messages to loved ones, weeping into an inky void of meaninglessness. She checked drawers for useful trinkets and found sweets and alcohol, she kept both, one would sooth miserable evenings, the other made a good antiseptic.

She looked out over the green hillocks and burgeoning copses of roundabouts and collapsed shop fronts. In the distance, the fractured skyline of the city. Fragments of skyscrapers leaned precariously under the weight of a vast arboretum, far taller than anything she had ever witnessed before. It frightened her, how such flora had grown so quickly, unnaturally. The land she had once known was disappearing under a rug of ferns which coiled nervously, awaiting the sun to beckon them out. She sat on a swivel chair and buried anxious thoughts, made a note to visit these places that instilled such irrational fear, perhaps in an effort to quash ideas of madness.

Her stomach grumbled loudly. She smiled, for the sound was real, necessary, and mildly amusing. She turned back to her task at hand. There was a door that led to a flight of stairs, inside the factory proper. She stepped into the dark, greeted by a flutter in the rafters.

Before her was a staircase that led to the factory floor. There was a walkway that extended to the right, which appeared to allow her a route down to huge shelving units stacked with sacks or heavy looking goods.

She crept along the catwalk. It seemed safe, yet like so many buildings within the city, what might have appeared safe was often hazardous; the dexterous giant roots that had burst from the earth and pulled down the city spread still, their presence beneath the earth only noticeable by the cracked tarmac and the great fissures in solid walls.

With this in mind, she stepped precariously along the galley until she was level with the stacked goods. She climbed the railing and stretched her toes until she felt something solid beneath her. Down she crept, carefully plotting her course.

She could see cans of something below, the labels were bright, surely food, not paint, like so many false hopes.

Her hunger got the better of her, increasing her pace downwards. Beneath her, she could make out a portion of a logo on a large sack, enough to tell her it was oats. Her father had made her porridge and bananas and a spoonful of peanut butter every morning before school.

She set her course for the sack, placing a careful foot on the corner of the hessian, only for it to split, pouring its contents, and the solid bulk to hold her weight, away.

She fell.

There was a whirl of sickening black, the tearing jolt and smack of her body against the floor, and then stars. There was pain eventually too, a deep nagging in her leg and head that made her swoon.

She lay upon the concrete, jostling consequences. If her leg was broken, that was it. She hadn't even considered something so drastic. She wanted to cry, felt like the child she was, but she was still very much alive, and despite the glorious nausea of the dizzying flecks of light above her, a fact remained, this would be fatal if she'd done serious damage.

She lifted herself up, felt the sticky matt of hair and blood and porridge oats that stung as she pulled her head away from the shelves. It didn't seem to be that bad.

She investigated the cut by prodding it. She could feel a small ragged wound, and thought best to leave it alone as it wasn't bleeding any more. She focused on her leg. There was no blood and the bone wasn't sticking out, but a yellowy purple bruise had already begun to form around her knee, and it was swollen. She tried to move it and she groaned when she felt a grinding sensation. She pulled herself together and looked around her for anything that might help her.

The traitorous sack above had stopped spewing out its stream of oats. The cans she had spied sat neatly on the shelf behind her, nonchalantly observing her, unaffected by the myriad disasters that had befallen the world. She turned one toward her to read the label. Chickpeas. Hundreds of cans of chickpeas. So it had been worth it all along.

The day waned as she considered her options. There were empty sacks to cover her in the creeping cold, and as she scooped the protein rich beans into her mouth she thanked the world for ring pull lids. The brine was no good to her and she savoured the little water she had left in her bag.

She adjusted herself a number of times until she found a position which gave some relief to her knee. Then she tried to forget her predicament. As dusk gave way to darkness, she closed her eyes and fell into dream-laden sleep. She saw rivers in the streets and the flailing arms of the dying, unable to reach for branches, doomed to be swept from the city.

*

Commotion awoke her. She heard a scamper, the brush and tumble of cans on the ink black factory floor. Fearful, she covered herself as much as possible, feeling her warm breath close beneath the sacks. The silence embraced once again and she chided herself for being such a scaredy cat. She removed her covering, staring into the darkness.

A pair of eyes peered back.

Vorsa looked at Ivy with a level of concern that was strangely comforting. There was a thought that perhaps the fox could see this injured prey, these easy pickings. Yet she could not ignore the lilt of the animal's face.

Vorsa moved, only slightly, cocking her head to one side as if to say, *are you ok?*

'You are hurt.'

The voice was clear, yet lacked an accent — if anything it was Ivy's internal voice, usurped by this animal. She moved her jaw, invoking rough whispered sounds, the wet slap of tongue against the roof of her mouth, the clash of teeth. In amongst this was a code, a rhythm that her mind understood.

I'm losing my mind, she thought, and in response, Vorsa took a few steps forward, now more visible in the moonlight. She looked strong, there were scars and a peculiar armour that appeared to be made of bone. Attached along the spine were shards of broken glass.

'I assure you, you are not losing your mind. You are Umbra, you speak Ocquia, the shared tongue. I believe you live because of this, you were spared.'

'Spared?'

'The Umbra. It gave you an advantage.'

Ivy strained to place Vorsa within the vocabulary of her surroundings. She had seen urban foxes play in her garden since she was young. A vivid memory cried for attention — the chance encounter of an albino fox, seen from the window of her school nurse's office during her rubella vaccination. It had bewildered her, amidst the fear of the injection, the sight of something so infinitely beautiful. She had felt the swoon of blood rushing to her head, the precursor to fainting.

The fox had looked up at her through the window with a particularly deliberate stare. She remembered feeling something, some odd elucidation, some soothing conveyance from this animal to her. As the memory crystallised, other memories vied for attention, remarkably familiar and yet obscured by logic.

She had heard Ocquia before.

'How is this even possible? I've never heard a fox speak before?'

Vorsa cocked her head as if offended, and again Ivy found her perception of this fox's intention fascinating. It was uniquely human.

'Vulpus,' Vorsa said sternly. 'I am Vulpus, this word you use for my kin, discard it.'

Ivy realised she had caused offence.

The Vulpus cleared her throat, considering her words. 'It is perhaps a very complicated story, the results of which are all around you. Suffice to say, the Stinking City and the Wroth who dwelt within are gone, all except you.'

The *Wroth*. Ivy did not know the word, but rightly assumed Vorsa meant humans. 'Are all the Wroth dead?'

Vorsa pondered. 'All but a few. I knew of you. I could feel you and your good intention, and we come to you for this reason. Much has changed in Naa. Your kind no longer holds sway, yet there is something dark, growing in distant lands, and I feel its intention too.'

'They have bad intentions?'

'Yes.'

Ivy shifted. 'I'm afraid I can't help you. I think my leg is broken.'

Vorsa looked at her leg, 'Yes, I believe it is. It will need to be healed. I know someone who can help you.'

Ivy wasn't convinced. 'The bone, it will need setting, I can't do it myself. Someone will need to put the bones in pla—' She stopped herself. 'A wound like this would surely kill a wild animal. You cannot know such things? Animals die of such wounds.'

Vorsa smiled. 'You see us for what we are, you hear us. Yet you still think of us like the Wroth. I am a flesh feeder. In the act of taking life we see it for what it is, the bones and muscles, how they support and sit. The bough of a tree cannot hold its fruit if broken, it will wither and die. We bind the bone and the wound will heal.'

'But who amongst you is strong and gentle enough to move the bone? We need hands … fingers, and I cannot do it myself.'

Vorsa padded away from her, leaping upon the shelving and out through the fire escape. Ivy could hear her cackle as she went.

*

The first morning light brought with it the rousing dawn cries of the many flocks, amongst them the venerated word of Gromkin, the love'd Umbra. The Yowri made their splendid prayers to the Sisters, no longer apology but filled with the soubriquet of thanks. They heard the yelp of the Vulpus and chirped their own interpretation, adding volume to its request. Soon it reached the vast ears of a particular beast, and at once the treble call was joined by the warm rumble and trumpet of Oraclas, washing themselves in a parkland lake.

Their morning bathing now complete, the yap and yelp of the Vulpus carried with it a request, and the Oraclas answered - Matriarch Eda, sending out her young daughter, eager to prove her worth within her herd. Yaran strode hastily along the remnant roads, the only vestige of the Wroth still maintained. She followed the Vulpine cackle out along the rivers that had once been canals, to the outskirts, where she found her goal, the old warehouse.

Vorsa returned. Ivy struggled to make sense of her calls, throaty yaps that could not so easily be deciphered. 'I cannot understand these sounds, who do you call to?'

'I spoke in my own tongue — you will have to learn to use the Umbra. It will give you insight beyond the visible. I call to Oraclas, Moving Stone.'

'Moving stone? I thought I'd seen it all. Talking foxes, I'm sorry – Vulpus – moving stones? Whatever next?'

Vorsa frowned. Something large shifted beyond the perimeter of the factory. The rough graze of something heavy dragging against the stonework. Ivy pulled herself back against the shelving unit, and Vorsa withdrew into the shadows.

There was a terrific thud. The great wall that separated them from freedom shook violently, agitating palls of terracotta dust. Something was trying to get through. Again, a great heavy quake, and the wall moved, again and again until finally, it gave way. The light flooded around the perimeter of an ominous silhouette against a neon sky.

It stepped through, ungainly.

'An elephant!' Ivy exclaimed excitedly. 'You brought an elephant!'

Vorsa looked perplexed at the excitable wrothcub and turned to greet the Oraclas. 'Yaran Moving Stone, daughter of the Clusk.'

'Vorsa Corpse Speaker, I come to aid you in your plight ...' She trailed off as her eyes adjusted to the dark and she saw the crumpled body of a Wroth. She narrowed her eyes and stood strong. 'Living Wroth! It's a Wroth! Should I crush it, if this is what you wish of me?'

'No, Yaran,' Vorsa spoke curtly. 'I call you to help me tend to this Wroth and her wound. She has broken her hind limb and needs your virtuous trunk to bring the bones together and carry her to safety.'

Yaran was nervous as she neared the little creature. She lowered herself onto her front knees until she was somewhat level with the Wroth. Vorsa sat beside her.

'Yaran, she is more afraid of you than you are of her.'

Yaran grumbled, 'Her kin imprisoned my family their entire lives. I feel it is wise to be cautious, even of such a ... small example.'

Ivy swallowed hard as the Oraclas unfurled its trunk. She shuffled herself away from it and Yaran harrumphed, 'I cannot help you unless you let me.' Ivy acquiesced and pulled back the cloth sack. The leg was purple.

'This looks painful, and I am afraid it will only be more painful, but once we move the bone, it will hopefully heal and allow you to walk again.'

Ivy nodded. 'Wait!' she said, rummaging in her bag. 'I need something to bite down on.'

She removed her hand from the rucksack, clutching a pen and a flimsy plastic spoon. She discarded the spoon, placing the biro in her mouth. The two animals looked at her with bafflement as she prepared herself for the worst.

Yaran wrapped her trunk gently around the leg. The slightest movement was excruciating for Ivy and yet this great animal appeared to sense each muscle spasm, each grating pain, as with nimble trunk she felt beneath the flesh.

'This bone is not broken. This bone,' she gestured to her kneecap, 'has simply lost its way.'

'Dislocated?' Ivy asked.

Yaran considered the word and deduced its meaning. She nodded and gently pushed the kneecap back in place. Ivy bit down hard upon the pen and tasted ink, and soon the welling pain consumed her and she passed out.

*

Ivy awoke a little later. Yaran peered down at her with a look of worry, until she realised her concern was noticed, and she turned away, feigning disinterest.

Vorsa smiled knowingly at them both. 'How do you feel?' she asked.

'I feel okay, it's just very sore.' Ivy removed a roll of bandages from her bag and bound her knee, adding a little pressure and support. She would need to find something more substantial.

'You're very lucky, wrothcub. A few days rest and I am sure you will feel better,' Yaran said sternly. The Oraclas then stooped as much as possible and begrudgingly offered her back. 'You will not be able to walk upon that limb, so I will carry you.' Yaran hoped Vorsa had seen her act of charity.

Ivy pulled herself up with her good limbs, letting her legs dangle.

'Where are we headed, Vorsa Corpse Speaker?' Yaran said, shifting her weight until she was comfortable. She had never been ridden before.

'To the Bastia,' Vorsa said.

Ivy began to acquaint herself with a world once obscured by a particular short-sightedness. It was not a question of seeing more, but shedding the prejudice in how she saw. She found herself adopting words and phrases with ease, discarding Wroth words which suddenly felt uncomfortable in her mouth. The words could be recalled easily, but their use began to weather away. It wasn't conscious, perhaps some inward restoration, an ancient mammalian impulse to know these families by their own appointments. By granting them that courtesy, each animal took on facets she had not seen before.

Yaran gestured eagerly at the various reclaimed structures and vast green acres now ruled by the wards of the fallen city. She made out familiar landmarks beneath the foliage, the long dark advertisement boards that once shone with temptation, fountains and entrances to subways all but consumed in the matt of leaf litter and root. This was not her city anymore. Atop the Oraclas, guided by the tough yet tender vixen, Vorsa, she imagined what her parents would say of her now, how excited her brother would have been to see such a sight, striding through the lush green streets of the capital.

Between the sprigs and new shoots she could make out the paths of animals, no longer forced to seek treacherous journeys at night, avoiding foot traffic and the unyielding war of motor vehicles. Now they made their own paths, leaving trails between the worn tread of larger beasts.

Great nests hung heavy on pylons, bound with decorous vines. The folded masses of steel and concrete, collapsed battlements of the Wroth, were now great roosts and dens. For her, the city appeared far more splendid, but it also carried a pang of sadness. For this world to be, her kind were all but gone.

'Where are we going?' she asked Yaran, interrupting her recital of the great odyssey of her herd.

'Oh, we travel to the Bastia, the speaking place, you will soon see.'

Ivy listened dreamily to the excitable pachyderm, the tales of her family and their great liberation from a place called the Moterion and the journey north, seeking the distant trumpeting of another herd, who had torn the gates asunder to their own prison — upon the arterial motorways, where cars sat like immobile blood cells, the ancient family divided by the whims of the Wroth were finally reunited.

Elderly sisters who'd known the distant plains, whose children had been dragged from them, hauled across Naa, trussed up in wooden crates, to only know from then the sedentary life of incarceration. A lifetime of being watched by gawking onlookers through bars and beyond concrete moats. Yet here, amidst the cold climes of an island in the northern ocean, they would recognise one another despite the decades apart, and be drawn by their familial voices. Like so many, they had followed the jubilant throngs seeking a new home in the remade world.

Vorsa stopped intermittently, yapping to the wind. The sounds seemed to hold authority, and as expected, replies came in staggered howls from distant places. Ivy guessed she was commanding her wily garrison.

As they approached the Bastia, Ivy recognised its former use; the iconic column at its centre now severed in half, the upper portion and its proud peak — the statue of a famous ship captain - now crumbled at its feet. A mass of giant roots, the same that perforated the city, splayed up and out from the ground, ending abruptly some metres away.

She asked Yaran to stop so that she could dismount, and using the Oraclas's trunk as a balance, hopped towards the ruin. She bent down and lifted up a piece of sandstone — a rough eye peered back at her. She considered it a possible keepsake, and then thought better of it.

The huge bronze lions that flanked the ruin remained clear of growth. The museums and art galleries that stood beyond some broad broken steps had, too, retained their form, yet damage was visible. Slumping roofs meant she dare not enter for fear of falling masonry, but imagined the treasures that must have awaited eyes inside, frescos rotting into painterly oblivion.

She pondered whether her mammalian friends understood art, yet feared offending them further, so did not ask. She pointed at the lion.

Vorsa said, 'Rauka. I believe these are Ayat. They live in the northern territories of Embrian Naa. They were freed from the Moterion along with Yaran.'

Ivy frowned, 'Embrian Naa?'

Vorsa nodded and tapped her paw against the ground assertively. 'Embrian Naa.'

She climbed upon Yaran once again, this time with a little more grace.

'There are lions … Ayat, living in this country?'

'Yes, the She-King Carcaris rules the Pridebrow.'

Ivy was a little bewildered.

There were other animals here now, flocks of Baldaboa, Athlon and Oreya. Their bodies were marked with dried mud in patterns, and some wore headdresses of sticks, bones and vines tied up in meaningful arrangements. This cortege stared with wary eyes at Ivy. They ringed the root structure that sprouted from beneath the concrete. At its zenith a cluster of fungal growths — greyish stalks twisted around one another, and leaned, top heavy towards the ground.

A Vulpus lieutenant skipped toward Vorsa. 'As requested, Sister Vixen.'

Vorsa thanked him, nodding politely to the Baldaboa who sat perched on a rusting car.

To the ungulate and equine presences, a little more encouragement was needed. 'Marin Storvin Brusk, Highmast Broon of the Athlon, Sethlitaysevin of the Oreya. I ask for your patience.'

'Patience is heartily required,' Brusk whinnied. 'Why bring this Wroth here, Vorsa Doom Sayer?' The large stallion eyed Yaran, drawing himself up, suddenly aware that he was dwarfed by the Oraclas. He spluttered with feigned disgust. 'You let this Crawcleaver ride you? Do you have no shame?'

Vorsa frowned at the disparaging words but yielded to the Athlon. 'Come now, Highmast Broon, I do not wish to cause distress. The Wroth is a Shadow Starer, we can trust her. She is injured, and Yaran has graciously offered to assist her. We have far greater ills to deal with. But do not take my word for it. My lieutenant called you here to act as witness. The Bastia will convey my word to the First City. It is here that the word may become final. Do you all agree?'

None defied her, for it was Vorsa who had ended the war. She approached the Bastia, a writhe of fleshy trunks. There were offerings here, ribcages and skulls of the long-dead, decorated with flowers in eye sockets and orifices, yellow and grey-blue lichen mottled a mass of moss and leaf. The broad cap of the fungus was distinctly alien, for it had elements of a flower bloom. At its centre, a churning mass of spores, which reminded Ivy of an object that had sat on her father's desk at work — hundreds of blunt pins you could push your face or hand into and leave an impression. Such an impression now emerged from amongst the cells. It was Vulpus, like Vorsa.

'Ora bring peace.'

The voice was gruff and dry like the sound of dry sticks rubbed together. Ivy asked Yaran to move a little closer so that she might see it better. The face oscillated to greet the curious eyes of the Wroth.

'I imagine *this* creature is the point of this communique,' the face uttered with a reticent lilt.

'Threthrin! Come now, old log, you are Eroua Vas, you know better than most not to judge a nut by its shell. This is Ivy, she is a Shadow Starer. Do you not feel her gnaw?'

The face frowned with reluctant acquiescence, 'I do.'

Vorsa continued, 'I wish to ask the city for a parley, I believe this wrothcub is important in our plight.'

'*Your* plight, Vorsa. No such disquiet had been brought to our attention. However, we have sent word to She-King Carcaris upon your request. We await her reply.'

Vorsa grimaced, 'I assure you, dear Threthrin, I do not speak false words. I fear we shall know its face soon.'

Threthrin fell away into the gyre of moving matter. Vorsa looked to Ivy affectionately, while she awaited his return. Ivy could read much from the Vulpus's kind dark eyes.

The face finally returned to the Bastia, a rising glower. 'You have your parley, Corpse Speaker, the city will accept your wrothcub, but don't expect a warm welcome.'

'Good, thank you, Threthrin.'

Yaran looked to Vorsa, 'Will we travel to the sea?'

'Yes, Yaran. If you will be so kind as to carry the cub.'

Yaran huffed, 'Well, we cannot ask her to walk on that purple limb, can we?'

*

The undulation of Yaran's stride and her gentle chatter had soothed Ivy into a daze as she lay upon her back. She lay like this for a while, drifting in and out of sleep. Now she roused herself to find them walking along the towpath of a canal. Ivy and Yaran waited whilst Vorsa commanded her lieutenants in her absence from the city. The locks that had stifled water flow were all open, reverting the waterway to something like a river. Up ahead, she saw the vast aviary that had once housed a myriad of exotic feathered.

Yaran was hesitant as they approached. 'Must we travel so close to this place?'

Vorsa looked up at her. 'It is no longer a prison, Moving Stone. Whatever the Wroth did, they have paid for their misdeeds.'

'But you did not live within its walls, your world was not a prison.'

Vorsa acknowledged this with a submissive nod.

They continued along the bridleway, Ivy peering through the stiff netting of the cage. It still served a purpose, as flocks nested within, the Oraclas having torn wide holes in the wire mesh that enclosed the air and gave freedom to all who wished it.

Above, she heard chatter and saw a rainbow of beaks and feathered bodies. Vorsa stopped for a moment to make a blessing. 'Your kin once imprisoned our gods here. It was the act of freeing them that hastened the end of this city.'

Ivy felt a little shame for having visited the Moterion on a number of occasions, recalling a rather poignant moment between herself and a female gorilla. Behind reinforced glass, the ape had sat and looked through

Ivy. Ivy could feel and see that this animal knew she was there, but was so hopeless, so resigned to this existence, that any sense of connection with her was utterly pointless. Ivy had sensed this in a wrenching, burdensome way. That moment had been integral to her own burgeoning philosophies, even at a young age.

'The Wroth did whatever they wished with us,' Vorsa uttered with contempt. The others said nothing.

The canal swelled beyond its banks, boats listed here and there, hulls rusted through, berthed against deteriorating levées now bursting with reeds. The water was clear and home to many Ungdijin, insects hummed around pollen-heavy blooms, seeking dance partners in the afternoon glow. They rested here for a while in that golden light, until Vorsa raised her ears and sought direction.

They continued south, through wide thoroughfares, vast Victorian establishments diminished by their silence. Verdant havens sprang up where the mammoth roots breached brick and mortar, pebbled pitch split like ruptured skin and spilled a carpet of grasses and fungi. There was animal life here too— Athlon made stables in the windowless frontage of gastro pubs, shopping precincts now trading posts for a plethora of Guilds' crafts.

Ruins made good refuge for rare seeds to settle and take root, and Ivy wondered how many species had reclaimed ancestral homes here. The great river that divided the city was a broad and robust marshland, depositing the silt along its muddy course. Bridges served as guides for powerful vines, the concrete fractured in their grasp, the tombstone walls of standing buildings flanked by burgeoning forest.

Flocks of feathered flew above the urban jungle, and the sounds of rustling leaves and hooting call of some distant creature were all that broke the silence. It was so peaceful that just for a moment Ivy forgot herself and all that she had lost. This ended as her eyes traced the weave of dark foliage below her, the gleam of ivory white.

Wroth bone.

'Have you seen other Wroth?' she asked.

Vorsa looked up at her as she loped beside Yaran.

'Yes, in the turns after the fall there were others. Some had avoided the sickness, some may have been Umbra. Most soon succumbed to the plague and those who did not die embraced the Umbra and found refuge elsewhere. My brother, Petulan, listens for them, his ear is keened to their song. It's how we found you.'

'Oh! You have a brother. Does your brother live in the city?'

Unflinching, Vorsa replied, 'My brother is dead.'

Ivy frowned, 'Oh, I am sorry.' She paused. 'My brother is dead too.'

They wound down through suburban streets, some intact, others demolished entirely. Rose bushes budded and flowered, their bouquet caught by the breeze. The hum of life occupied her and she felt the swelling pain in her leg subside.

The land beyond the city itself blurred with its borders of terraced houses and shops, their gardens reaching beyond their designated spaces into one another, exchanging seeds and proclaiming through colourful blossoms to the Voin. Playing fields of redundant schools grew wild, ember poppies peaked between golden grasses.

They continued on throughout the day, at length pausing to rest. Ivy found a stick to act as a crutch, and she hobbled into corner shops and supermarkets to search for food, whilst Yaran grazed and Vorsa disappeared into the undergrowth in search of prey. Ivy returned with snacks to find them both sated, and soon they continued their journey.

'You share a language with all animals. Is it difficult to kill who you understand?' Ivy asked bluntly.

Vorsa was taken aback. It was not a question ever asked of her before. 'I am a flesh eater, I kill to survive. This is how it has always been. To kill that which sustains.'

Ivy found this answer lacking. 'But these creatures you eat, they also look to you for guidance. The Vulpus rule, but they also kill.'

'The Wroth ruled, and they also killed? Did you eat the flesh and mourn the animal that it was taken from? Did you bite its neck and claw its innards for your supper?'

'No. I don't eat animals. I saw how they were mistreated. Lots of Wroth didn't eat animals.'

'Yet many did. They may not have known Ocquia, but they understood fear. They understood it very well, yet many continued to kill. I see your teeth, your clawless paws. You have none of the tools for catching prey. Yet your kind were very good at killing. Our kill is quick, and our hunger is just as nagging. There is no right or wrong. There is an order, it is a fine, a fragile thing.'

'Yes,' Ivy replied.

'Words are unnecessary, our bodies speak for us. I know that which I wrought, and I accept it,' Vorsa sighed. 'The Wroth wielded an arrogance that bestowed them with the idea that they were above all of this, above Naa, and yet their clever eyes still wanted for the gristle and guts of my kin, *my* Ocquia. This world is earth and stone and tree and water, and yes, blood.'

Ivy considered this. 'I'm glad I don't eat meat.'

Yaran trumpeted, 'This I can agree with wrothcub!'

Vorsa rolled her eyes.

Wide fields opened as they began to trek across fallow farmland. Stray wheat still grew amidst the wildflowers. Ivy picked some and examined the grain, 'We made food from this. But I don't really know how. I will have to learn to survive off the land soon. I can't live on cans forever.'

Yaran laughed, 'The Wroth ate the strangest things, you will find much nourishment in Naa!'

The waves of grasses swayed before them, as they continued south.

Drip drip drip
Little beads of dew
Percolate through
I see you

Chapter Two

He had watched these foetal, feeble souls squirm upon the forest floor, the vomit and spittle drooling, the quick pant and Wroth-like cries from canine snouts, the whimper, the sob, the pain of a second birth. He had known this adjustment, this slick shit-soaked thing, the hot damp pant, to want for nothing but to live, only to rise inside the sodden weight of a body unwilling.

He groaned and struggled against his own shackles, for his stolen frame was stricken, bound in the sinewy roots of a dead tree, brought up from the soil black and stinking, wet leathery strands that lashed his limbs together. He would eventually free himself, he had no doubt, but that dead thing, that atrophied Cini bitch who had left him here, was more formidable than he had first assumed. She had stalked the clearing, scolding him, casting an array of abracadabra abrasions upon him, chastising and chiselling him for what he had done.

Eventually, she had gone back under the rock she'd crawled from. Once again his landlord, the owner of his body, the ever-present Emeris mocked him from within, and once again Thoth replied with vitriol, ploughing fertile memories with sickening jibes. Thoth would not be made a fool.

He recovered, pulling himself free of the root mass, finding his teeth to be useful where fingers would have been. He sat patiently before his flock, as the amniotic mire of their possession dried in the morning light, finally dragging themselves sluggishly toward him. They pawed at him like weak infants for succour, of which he offered none. The old hag had been right. They were little more than empty husks, blank stares and dribbling incontinence.

'Get up!' he snarled, and they wobbled on stalk legs, collapsing and recovering, snapping at one another until, much like he had, they found balance.

The previous night, he had finally nestled into the crux of his plan. The veils of the Gasp had not resisted him as he waded out beyond life once again. It was there he felt a strength of will like nothing in Naa; he commanded the very firmament, in all its bleak variety, the coiling ivory smog, a billion Wroth faces vying for his attention. He did not forbid their keen hands upon him for they withdrew just as readily — his fur was a fiery thing, life so vivid it burned their immaterial limbs. They revered him. He said to them,

I will give life to the most deserving, a body to dwell in. Who here will do my bidding?

The strongest pneuma – poltergeists and certainties whose cause had always been to live again, who had gone so far as to perforate the pelt of the Gasp to haunt the living – now barged past the less passionate. Unhinged, violent and terrible, they flooded to his word.

Come, he said.

And now they were alive in the world, a pack of stolen bodies. Where they had been the playground bullies amongst the dead, they were now little more than shellshocked veterans, handicapped by their awe of the real. They had forgotten just how *living* everything could be, the saturated, pungent, hideous sight of it all, optic nerves absorbing every stray photon, sending sharpened spears of experience towards harrowed clusters in their sensory meat. It reduced them to staggering pups.

He was impatient, one of his many flaws. For him to forward his schemes he would need to leave the glen, leave the place that had once also been a prison, driven there by those who thought him unfit to live among them. He was now beyond recognition, beyond any chance of further chastisement. He would gather them up and descend into the world, and revel in the furious consequences he now wrought.

'Get up! Come now! I have given you this gift and you writhe around like infants!'

A young Cini, who appeared stronger than his cohorts, gathered its strength and stood. It shook itself and lumbered toward him. Its eyes were curiously milky, as though it were blind.

'You see me, pup?'

'Yes, sir. I see you.'

'Good. I am Thoth. You will serve under me as a soldier in a coming coup. Tell me, what befell you, how did you die?'

The Cini spluttered a lie, his death had been somewhat of a pathetic thing. 'Uh, I died like everyone else, in the great plague. But death wasn't so simple a thing, it turns out. We were in that dark terrible place. You freed us from that fate.'

'Yes, yes I know. A plague you say? I have lived a solitary life upon the highlands, free of the abundance of humanity. I knew nothing of such things.'

'The world of man is gone, the animals have it now.'

'Ah, yes. The animals. It seems those animals were not so vacant and feckless as once imagined. They have culture, would you believe! Dare I say, intelligence! But like the cattle and the dog, they will come to know obedience once again. Your name, pup?'

'Roger Engleworth, sir.'

Thoth smirked, 'And once again our human epithets don't sit well with these lupine semblances.'

'What?' Roger scowled.

'Your name is a bad name for a wolf. Much like me, you will need to take a more fitting title. Did you have a nickname, a moniker other than your Christian name?'

'Nah, no nicknames. My dad called me a right little gobshite.'

'I assume that was well deserved?'

Roger grinned, 'Oh aye, I was a right scab.'

Thoth nodded, 'Scab, perhaps not the most threatening of titles, but far more fitting than Roger. Scab it shall be. When you have fully wrestled with your senses, gather these pathetic excuses for wolves and we shall begin our God-given ascension to the throne once again, savvy?'

'Yes, sir.'

His misfit congregation followed him up from the dale, toward his former home. It was a derelict, and he felt a modicum of embarrassment. Yet despite the shifting tumour of Emeris sensing every morsel of humiliation, Thoth took this opportunity to make a point. He strode out before them, his fur far darker, his ears more diabolical. He played the part of a leader far more convincingly than he had imagined.

'This was once my dwelling, for a good twenty years. I was a forgotten thing, amongst forgotten things. Yet I had a gift of foresight, a clairvoyance that allowed me to see the world in a particular way, and when

I died I saw the opportunity to view my former life as a dress rehearsal, where my choices as a human were perhaps rash, headstrong, less than ideal. I decided in this life I would be more considered.

'I took from that place beyond death, like I took you. I found myself a strong body, and I took it. Took what was rightfully mine. I gifted you with that choice too. The world we left is gone, replaced with this infested place, ruled by rats.

'If I am not mistaken, you will have all found yourselves aware of notions unconsidered, customs and traditions forged in the dirt, in painful birth, in the bloody jolt of the life you now own. Our words for things are shunned by the minds we occupy, words we once took for granted are forfeited for theirs. This wolf – this *Cini* – had a name.

'Emeris.

'He had a family, members of which you now inhabit. We will be the same, smelt in the caustic flames of our ambition. Listen to the voices of those you have conquered. Learn their ways, understand this place they call Naa, but human notions will have their turn again. You are my Husk, my canopic jars, filled with the ghosts of the dead.'

Scab paced forward, sheepishly lowering his cloudy eyes in supplication. 'Forgive me, but before we engage in any daring plans, a more pressing issue must be addressed.'

'Yes?' Thoth spat.

'We must eat, and drink. Far be it for me to question your intentions, but some of us have not eaten for a very long time, and such a hunger has befallen us all.'

Thoth begrudgingly agreed. He took a moment to allow the Umbra to slide unseen into his vision, the constellation aura of lives spread before him. In the village below, the herd of Effer he had frightened away stood idle, grazing the parish green.

'You will learn to hunt. Easy pickings await us in the place below. Let us find our footing with our first taking. Those we do not eat, we might turn to our cause.'

They whooped and hollered and howled to his words. The heady froth of self-congratulation filled him up, reminiscent of that which he took from a kill. With his mob in tow, they leapt the kissing gates and hedgerows, cascading in a filthy snarling wash in the paw prints of their buoyant leader.

*

Noraa sought shelter as rain began to fall. She had travelled southwest, beyond the green of the moorland, avoiding the pine forest which hindered swift travel, wandering the regular trails scattered with pebbles that became more frequent the further south she trod.

Eventually, one of the unavoidable black paths, the true sign of the Wroth, appeared, and she placed a hesitant paw upon it. It was hard, but unusually smooth. This road led south, offering her a clear route beside the endless fields and gatherings of trees. Hedgerows atop muddy banks hemmed her path, the thick reek of slowly evaporating fuel hampering her senses as she sniffed out signs of life.

The road eventually led her to collections of Wroth dwellings. She explored a little, having never entered such dens — damp, angular places. She paused at the foot of a staircase, where an elderly Wroth lay in the hall. The corpse was old and withered and no longer exuded much odour beyond a vegetal mildew scent and the vague metallic tang of blood. There was a large black stain beneath its head.

She climbed the stairs and found a pile of mouldering bedding. She slept for a few hours, never knowing such comfort. She woke whilst it was still dark, her heart pounding. Dreams of the creature that had taken her beloved, her family. She chastised herself for sleeping so long. Dragging herself from the bed, she loped down the stairs.

She glanced once more at the dead Wroth. Felt a pang of sadness, a feeling she could not place. She exited through the open back door, stepping over shards of splintered wood.

There were Vulpus out that evening, hunting Muroi, play-fighting amidst curls of hot breath. They ceased as the cackle-call rang out, cocking heads and responding with their own shrieks. Noraa knew a little Vulpish, and listened carefully to each line uttered.

Since her first year in this land, the Orata, the spoken scripture of their culture, had altered somewhat. Their prophets, the inimitable Vorn, Vors and Alcili, had lost their singular importance in acknowledgement of the Sisters of the Flock. For Noraa, the old gods of the Cini too had seen change, saturated by visions of the Umbra.

She approached the Vulpus cautiously, shrinking herself so that she would not scare them, but they fled, too young to recognise the signs of goodwill. She was left alone once again.

A fresh kill lay on the ground, a large Muroi. She sniffed it, and devoured the morsel, having not eaten for a while. She found a puddle and drank heartily and continued on alone, aware of eyes watching her. She did not wish to scare them, but hoped they might distinguish her from what might follow, the horrors she now fled.

To Noraa, the morning sky was all rich yellows, reds and browns, her lupine eyes unable to register the full extent of its fluorescent orange, yet she marvelled in the beauty of it, a constant she carried with her, now far from her home.

As she continued south, the more urban and regimented her environment became; so, too, did the amount of skeletal remains, consumed by weaving stems and leaf litter. Eyeless sockets peered from squat vehicles, devices and contrivances for which her vague memories provided morsels of reference — she had been caged within one as a pup; that time, she had slept too long and awoken to a world that smelled quite different. She had known Wroth before this, Wroth who fed her, who seemed kind. Wroth who freed her and her kin up in the valley. She wondered whether those Wroth had also died with these hapless souls.

A scuffle alerted her to a presence in the bushes beside the path. She stopped and watched a large Throa waddle out before her, its armour old and tired, its black claws clattering against the road. It came to a halt and turned a sleepy face to greet her. It frowned, huffed, and wheeled its cumbersome frame in her direction.

'Hmm, I don't recognise you, so I say to you, good morning madam, you are either far too late or very early for orienteering. If you wish to come back at a more reasonable time that would be very much appreciated. I myself am headed to a much-needed nap.'

Noraa cocked her head. 'Sir, I am new to these parts and know nothing of this orienteering. What is it?'

The Throa lifted itself with a sense of pride, 'I am TumHilliad of the House of Brigan, I am the captain of the Roughclod Infantry of Reconditioned Caanus!'

Caanus, it was a word somewhat familiar to Noraa. 'Tell me Captain TumHilliad, these Caanus you speak of — you are their teacher?'

'Yes, teacher would be a fine descriptor. I am their liaison with the Tempered Guild of Erithacus, and the revenant brother Tor of the House of Ror and the Living City of Dron. So many poor pups lost after the big death, so many sad faces with those big lulling jowls! Oh dear. We rounded them all up, we gave them purpose once their Wroth masters had passed. Tell me, did your master pass on?'

Noraa smiled, 'I am Cini, the Caanus are — were part of our clade a very long time ago. They parleyed with the Wroth for food ... and were lost to us. We have not known their kind in a thousand lifetimes.'

'Cini, you say! I thought all the Cini were dead? Gone from these shores. You are heralded in the Vulpine Orata no less, in the annals of their Sister-forsaken caterwauling! I have to listen to it every day, keeping me up, should never have learnt that Sister-forsaken tongue, won't get a good day's sleep ....'

He trailed off into grumbles and expletives until he collected his thoughts.

'Your name, Cini?'

'I am Noraa, of Ruthe-va Unclan.'

'Noraa of Ruthe-va Unclan, what brings you to the borderlands?'

'I am here to seek help for my family. There is a darkness. Something terrible is coming, and I need help. I believe we are all in grave danger.'

TumHilliad sighed, '*I* believe I shall never get a good day's sleep again. Well, if you promise not to eat me, and can wait until nightfall, we shall round up the troops and help you on your way. Would that be helpful?'

'Yes, captain. I believe it would.'

He escorted her beyond an overgrown garden, into an equally overgrown allotment. It was a maze of fruit-laden vines and twisting creepers burdened with swollen green and red vegetables. The strict margins that once hemmed each patch were now lost in vigorous eruptions of crops. Near the hedgerow was a potting shed, beside which was a bank of earth beneath two huge oak trees. The sett seemed relatively new.

'I'm afraid it's unlikely that you will fit in my sett, so I propose you rest in here,' he gestured to the shed. 'In this shelter thingamy, some Wroth whatsit, and rest up. You Cini folk are day sleepers, like myself?'

'Yes, although I have rested where I can until now. We will be safe here?'

The old Throa pondered, 'Is anywhere safe? Safer than before I guess, safer than before. Wroth loved to kill Throa, loved to kill Cini, killed all the Cini, except you? Loved to kill for no reason, took many of my loved ones, horrible old things they were, not my family mind, the Wroth ....'

He continued muttering to himself as he slid on his stomach into the sett and disappeared. Noraa looked back to the road, hidden from her now behind trees and hedgerows. She pulled open the door of the shed with her teeth and stepped inside. It was musty, but bone dry, and she found a pile of old potato sacks to rest on. She closed her eyes, before thinking better of it, and promptly stood up, pushing the door closed behind her. She went to lie down again, and spied a large wooden box. She pushed it with her hind legs against the door to offer a little more security.

Before she slept, she whispered her summoning. 'Grand-overmother, grant me tiding.' There was silence. To exist in Naa, and to expend so much in defence of her underdaughter, Noraa knew it would be some time before she would appear for her again. She curled up and fell into a dreamless, restful sleep.

*

Thoth had caught the scent of Noraa, but cared little. His desire to take her was a small and spiteful thing, but it was an old habitual need, to crush that which wronged him. As the pack entered the stone-built town he gave it little heed beyond his cursory wishes. He directed the Husk towards the Effer, leaving them to their devices. He wondered if they would fare any better with their first kill.

He crept through the town like a spider stalked her web, weaved around the cars that had found new use as homes for wandering creatures. Shop doors wide with invitation, a million objects useless to him, yet he savoured their delicacy, appreciated the Wroth's initiative in their design. He couldn't place the feeling. Nostalgia, perhaps. It had been so long since he had lived in this world, in the lap of humanity. He wanted to dismiss such frivolous sentimentality, but he looked upon the knickknacks, souvenirs and trinkets with a kind of longing, recorded each item, for he had always thought he would one day return, after he had been forgotten, and be amongst the heady vim of it all. No chance of that now.

He had not long been Cini, and despite everything he had gained, it was the soft and familiar that was most noticeably absent. Was he longing for creature comforts? He coughed a laugh at the irony of that phrase. If anything was a creature, it was him. A diminutive word, a word to describe something unwanted or lesser than oneself. Yet he felt glad of the title. He would find his comfort as a creature.

An Oreya fled the snarls of his pack, and as it passed him it came to a jarring halt. It was paralysed in his presence. Thoth furrowed his brow, what was this? What quality of him was able to hold its gaze? A low rattle emanated from his gullet, it surprised him — a little of Emeris seeping through. A thought came, could he take an Oreya, could he bring some foul thing from the Gasp into it?

The rattle became a quaking hack, a vomitous jerking choke until the miasma of soupy grey poured out of him, the vessel of the desperate dead. It spilled and flopped and crept toward the enchanted Oreya, climbing willow legs, a rising horror, the insensible, comatose fear as her beguiling was broken and reality tore through her amygdala far too late, flight response consumed, chewed up and regurgitated.

A fawning human in an adult body, a snivelling, spasmodic thing, insanity in its eyes, and a woeful cry becoming a garbled string of sputtered words. *Free!* It said finally, stumbling, collapsing, recovering.

Thoth considered this development. *He could take whoever and whatever he wanted.*

The Oreya, now possessed by a Wroth, looked to Thoth for guidance.

'Welcome back friend. We've plain run out of Cini for you to occupy so we've moved on to these fine fillies. Introduce yourself to the pack, make sure to make your voice heard or they'll mistake you for dinner!' He dismissed the quivering animal and continued his sojourn through the town.

A petite little theatre stood as a focal point of the square. Its red and gold facia was attractive despite its shabby state. He skittered towards it, lifting himself upon the ticket office counter, stretching his hind legs to look within. The doors were wide, the brass post of a rope barrier jammed the door open. Within, the musty smell of damp cloth, vast curtains sodden with black mould. Soiled art deco motifs adorned the walls.

He paced beyond the reception into the theatre itself, a great auditorium, rich scarlet seating, and a tattered stage. There was waste strewn about the aisles. Wroth had come here, after the great death, had found shelter between the rows. There were tents on the stage, an encampment of sorts.

Shards of light played upon the floorboards, water damaged from leaks in the glass roof above. He climbed a small flight of stairs to the right of the stage, paced out, imagining himself the actor. But no one was there to see him. No one ever saw him.

He tucked his head into one of the tents, the sweet greasy stench of rot filling his sensitive nostrils; two Wroth, lying beside one another, their frames collapsed in on themselves much like the tents that marked their graves. He sighed briefly, backing away.

His ungainly recruits slunk between the rows. They, too, enjoyed the familiarity. They curled awkwardly on cushioned seats, sniffed at chocolate bar wrappers and empty tin cans. Soon they were hushed by the silence of the place.

Thoth scanned the stage for anything of use, descending another short set of steps into the backstage. A dark corridor greeted him, veering off into a room with mirrored tables and filthy stage props. Rows of costumes hung from rails, others were scattered upon the floor.

Clothing was a loss that hadn't dawned on him until that moment. He walked between the racks, the pearlescent pink of a fairy costume and a deep forest green of an elf. He tugged at the sleeve of one particular garment, an old naval jacket. Something fell dully to the floor. It was a cheap, plastic pirates hook. 'Peter Pan,' he growled with recognition. He pawed at the tunic, dragging it with his teeth along the rail and into the light. The costume had golden epaulettes with tassels, dark blue cloth with brass buttons, and a broad military hat. He dragged the coat from its hanger.

He had very few fond memories of his childhood, but books had been his sanctuary, an escape from the malice that lay beyond his bedroom. The house was filled with books, yet none of them were his. Peter Pan had sat amongst those cherished titles.

Between the neglect and abject rage his presence spawned in his parents, he would smuggle choice titles from the lofty bookcases scattered about the house. There was something delightfully vindictive about taking the books. They would not be missed, having not been read for years, but it was the fact that he had taken them against their wishes.

He would lie under the bed, leaning the book towards the crack of light that spilled from the window, and let his sorry life fall away. One such book had been George Orwell's *Animal Farm*.

He lay the jacket on the floor and shuffled a forelimb into the sleeve, dragging it up by his teeth. He lay exhausted with it half on, panting between wheezed curses, before swinging the coat over him. He pulled his right paw tight against himself until the sleeve flopped down, teasing the lapel so that he might manoeuvre his foreleg into it. Finally, the coat was on. It was a horrible fit, pinching him in several places and loose in others. He determined that, if he wore it long enough, perhaps it would stretch and surrender to him.

He found a full-length mirror. He looked ridiculous, like an unfortunate dog with an overbearing master. He leaned his head to one side, taking in his countenance. He wished to see the tunic across his narrow chest.

He pulled himself upright.

He staggered onto his hind legs, drawing in his front limbs against him to find his centre of balance. He tottered around like a performing circus animal. With time, his muscles might inherit the memories of a lifetime spent bipedal, yet his anatomy was not forthcoming. His tiny paws struggled with his weight, not built for such acts. If not for the comical absurdity he would look quite frightening to any who saw him. He fell back onto all fours. He was quick to temper and thought to abandon this frivolity.

He walked before the mirror once again and hauled himself upon his back legs. Again he tottered, losing balance easily. He considered some kind of crutch, a third limb to balance upon. His paws were simply too small, without an ample surface area, to support his body weight for long. His body was quadrupedal. His spine would not have it. *Damn it.*

He looked about the room for some aid, scampering out beyond the dressing room to find a small workshop where sets had been built. He examined tools and materials, pushing them aside with his snout. Plumes of dust erupted with each frustrated exhale.

He lifted old wire brushes and screw drivers, unwieldy in his mouth. They swung wildly and then clattered to the floor. He found two pieces of wood, the length of his back limbs. They were wide. Again he searched, pulling a collection of oily rags from a drawer.

He began to bind his ankles with strips of the cloth. It was hard going — contorted into a peculiar position to allow him to wind the cloth, his mouth replacing his once dexterous hands. He found his tail was of increasing use, and with its support, he placed the wooden pieces behind each back limb. The binding took far longer. Once complete, he lay upon the ground, fatigued by his labours. When he had regained his strength, he stood upon all fours. The wood now ran flush with his back legs. He stood up, rocking back against the wider surface provided by the wood. It was painful, unwieldy. But it worked. For a moment he felt pride.

The binding tore. He cried out in exasperation.

He lifted himself once again and tugged at the rags until his failed experiment fell away. He remained upright, feeling for his centre of gravity. He could feel the skin around him, hugging him like his jacket. Yet the jacket had already begun to loosen, its pinching seams giving as he moved in it, as the fabric adjusted to flexing muscles.

Just like the jacket, it had become apparent that he was now very much in control of this stolen body, his synapses cajoled into a tug of war against the animal's musculature and bone. It was a war he had all but won, and he wished to reap the reward. This body would succumb to him.

He felt the ligaments in his ankles, in his thighs, stretching to the point of dislocation. The host Cini screamed at him from beneath layers of suppression, almost as if Thoth experienced the pain secondhand — and, deep within his brain, the true owner of this flesh was driven mad with his excruciating misuse.

He pushed his chest out, his forelimbs held close for balance, his neck forced forward, angular, wrong. His ankles stubbornly refused to carry him, and yet he battered them into subservience.

Finally, he stood, joints swelling, muscles torn. But, in his dishevelled uniform, he stood.

A man once again.

He looked in the mirror, letting his upper limbs fall to his side. No longer the performing animal at the zoo awaiting a treat. His black silhouette was a menacing aberration. Like a scarecrow. This particular thread took root.

Man.

He mourned the death of this word. In his youth, he had learned from his father the subjugation of all others under man. Man was God; man put food on the table, man worked to clothe his wife and children, man punished if they did not follow his doctrine. Thoth knew that power first-hand. But man was dead, and the Wroth were its shadow.

He imagined the image of the Wroth would be the stuff of nightmares to the creatures that now held sway over the earth. What better sign of his occupation, nay, his ordained rule, than that of the Wroth?

He glanced around the room. He tugged again at the debris around him — broom, assorted scraps and twine. Again, he struggled without the use of dexterous fingers, and yet his determination was more than capable of making up for these shortcomings. In time and with much effort he completed his task.

He descended to all fours and hauled the fruit of his labour up the short staircase and on to the stage. He dropped it from his mouth before his captive audience. They looked to him with maudlin admiration.

He stood upright, stalking out like a villain from a gaudy pantomime, stretching his forelimbs low, pulling against muscles which did not wish to move with such a simian gait. His spectators rocked with surprise and awe. He leered in a lance of light from the glass roof, glowering at them. Some attempted to mimic his peculiar stance with little success.

'Animals! This land is nought but stinking animals! Our kind are all but finished, and yet here we stand. Killed dead and yet here we stand. Pulled back from the brink. In such a brief time our kind has been reduced to fairy stories, the Wroth they call us. Have little nice to say about us. But I see something I didn't understand in my former body. This connection to all of them, all those little lives. There is a pattern to it all. Humans were murdered, see. Murdered by some evil power. It's heresy, blasphemy. And I will not have it!'

He hemmed and hawed about the boards with increasing enthusiasm.

'I smell the spit of their courage, it drools from a place that glows, out there in the south. This Cini tries to hide this truth from me, but I feel it, the glow of it. It is a temptation, a voice — like a black fog we will slide over the land casting our shadow with deft and vicious paw. And we will snuff it out.'

He returned to the side of the stage and toppled to all fours, pulling his creation with his mouth before them all. At the base, he took it and lifted it awkwardly upright. The broom was now a body, a snapped length of pipe two arms, each hand rags and spurs of wire, and the head, a mop.

'This form speaks to their fear of us. Scarecrows will mark our territory, will be our calling card. We will take the land and fill their bodies with our legion.'

His snarl was lascivious. He hobbled across the stage, tripping with little grace. It would take time to find his footing. *Two legs good*, he thought, *two legs good.*

'You will not eat all that you catch, some you will bring to me, to add to our ranks! Now go!'

Whooping with excitement, they left the theatre, some attempting to imitate his walk in a restless eagerness, others skittering through the streets in search of prey.

He slinked bipedal, widening his gait with each step. He looked unnatural, a grotesquery, sickly slender, stomach pulled tight, forelimbs held low, teetering. His fur was damp and slick, and he bared his teeth so that they gleamed yellow against his coal black fur.

He paced out into the street, and closing his eyes tight he invoked the Umbra. 'Come now Emeris, don't be shy, show me your secrets.'

A shard of memory — the Cini's first encounter with an animal of the land. A Storn, who flew down to greet them, and the conversation that ensued.

The First city.

Another light bloomed, far in the south, on the coast. All he had was a vague notion. Here was a power he saw in the Umbra, thick enigmatic lines of light converging in a glorious panacea. The Gasp spoke of it, the seed of consciousness, or conscience perhaps. Kernel of empathy. He loathed the sensation it invoked, a warmth never known before — what was its function? Why had it been hidden from the Wroth?

A vague recollection wished to speak to him, the men and women who would come on his land, their faces covered, arguing with him to stop his killing. He had screamed at them to leave him alone, and they had left, throwing a handful of leaflets at him. He had shouted some more, bending to pick up the mess.

He had sat in his little stone house and looked at the images emblazoned on the glossy paper. And he did indeed try, tried even if just for a moment, to understand a single word they were saying. All he saw was the blood, the dominance, how easily something that lived, breathed with dogged persistence, came to an end.

These people were weak, their compassion served no purpose.

He had only wanted silence.

And now he had this.

His compatriots returned to him. They were eager, loyal. In each of their mouths, held by the ruff of a neck, or under foot, a quaking life.

'Quite a bounty!'

These pathetic creatures dared not run, ensnared in the crescent of teeth and claw.

Thoth submerged himself in the interim glaze of the Gasp, beckoning greasy eyes to fill his need. Bile sour, gobbets of phlegm rose in his throat, hocking up the viscid waxen froth of the dead, seething towards these paragons of the living, these lights in the dark. Seeking entry through orifices — clenched teeth, tightly shut eyes, ear canals, all became betrayals as the fluid of unliving want entered their bodies, and snatched them away. Inelegant they might be, comedic in their variety, small rodents, waterfowl, a spasming Vulpus, the colour leached from their hides to a sallow grey. But they were his army.

His.

So they continued on, slowly gaining girth in their ranks as they stitched their way towards the sea.

*

In a quiet cove in the south of Embrian Naa stood the First City, a chimera of living colonies, of fungi, plant and stone. Within its interior was the Hall of Receiving, where the dead came to commune with the living. At its heart, the Sisters of the Flock.

Erithacus, a large grey feathered, his face scarred by his former captors, stood before that sandstone slab, clutched in perpetuity by vigilant branches. Upon the rock three dainty fossils, three tiny feathered creatures. To him they were the Sisters, but they went by many names.

His eyes were shut. When Ora was at its peak, a shaft of light would fall here, through the roof, a focused warmth that filled him with a calm he rarely found elsewhere. In these quiet moments, when the only sound was the ocean beyond the walls of Dron, and the gentle whispers of the acolytes of Anx, the Old Grey Ghost would spread his wings wide, the tips of his feathers brushing the surface of the stone. This was where he searched for them, crystalline aspirations in their remnant bones, the timpani in immemorial time, echoing out from their death many millions of turns past. He had sought their song for a lifetime, had fought with beak and claw to proselytise, to encourage Ocquia to remember their word, and with much help he had finally succeeded.

The Sisters had rewarded his stubborn determination by once again bestowing the beloved Umbra upon the peoples of Naa, and thus restoring their cherished unity. This gift had confirmed every inkling Erithacus could have imagined — the crucible of instinct, fashioned in the loss of life and the commemoration of three tiny fleeting minds. The Sisters had left the world of Naa, become entangled in the germinating seed of sentience, in the fulcrum of the Umbra itself.

And yet, he wondered.

So here, before their rocky remnants, he asked the Umbra to show him the Sisters. He had asked this question a thousand times, he had plunged into the fathomless slumber, into the stratal folds of slate and silica, the coprolite and calcium innards of sleeping dead, sent out radiating branches of intention, voices in the dark. It was true, he had heard replies, from things absent from Naa for millennia, had communed with ancestral entities old and black and wise, had seen the scope of memory written in the weft. But the Sisters were nowhere to be found.

Audagard finished his sermon and joined Erithacus. 'Any luck, my old friend?'

Erithacus let out a thoughtful sigh. 'I wonder, could it be that I have grown so old I cannot tell my desire from my delusion?'

The Corva cackled, 'That might be two of us, grandfeathered. I, for one, have come to embrace my senility! I am told it adds character!'

Erithacus furrowed his brow, 'Malargoragor Audagard, you do not need any more *character*.'

They chuckled and hopped toward the path that led to the chancery, spiralling upwards on immense truncated roots. In the wake of the city's re-emergence, the Grand Atrium and galleries, the myriad spaces, halls and arcades had become the byways and places of worship of a hundred creeds. Then the gradual acceptance that their fragment of belief was one part of a greater truth led to a slow but steady coming together. Some were stubborn, yet with the Umbra returned the lighted ways traced a liturgy of togetherness and a wondrous and somewhat obvious shared ancestry.

They flew up and out, onto the wide balcony that held the Regulax, the receiving font of the Bastia. Resembling a huge fibrous flowerhead, similar fungal blooms grew as the First City sent out its mycelium, propagating throughout the land where the clans and flocks might need the ear of Dron.

The Regulax emerged from the floor as a ravel of branches knotted into a wide blunt capitulum, the surface of which resembled a corpseflower stripped of its colourful petals. At its centre, an intricate collection of spores that rippled with peculiar verve and around its edge, a fringe of short, stiff woody leaves. The *Eroua Oaza Vas* – the Starless Vulpus – debated with Corvan clergy, carrying collections of marked stones and spiny fabrications of sticks in their jaws with which to clarify the will of the city.

There was light here, from the same shaft that illuminated the Sisters below. Once in a while, an Eroua Oaza Vas would hop up to speak to the Regulax. There would be conversation, barked orders and requests, and the Eroua Vas would take any entreaty or appeal to Lendel, the gigantic caretaker of Dron.

The bustling veranda ran the entire diameter of the upper circle. From this vantage point, Erithacus marvelled at the balustrades, incredible pillars that grew vertically, crowning in a lattice in the high vaults of the cavernous arcade, the largest space within the city. Above them still, a plethora of warrens, caves and water channels, a honeycomb of tubules. Dron was so large that at its summit, in the mountainous crags that crowned the city, it had its own weather — its inhabitants, plant life and, most importantly, itself, were all interdependent. For Dron was alive, a mind made up of minds, the living and the dead, grafted upon each other.

Audagard spoke with his clergy before rejoining Erithacus. 'Vorsa is bringing a wrothcub here.'

Erithacus widened his eyes. 'My word! And who is this wrothcub?'

Audagard replied, 'I am not sure. Vorsa is not a Vulpus I would ever second guess again. But she now speaks of something cancerous, something wounding, moving in the northlands. I have not been alerted to any threat, either by the Ebduous Clax and the Orrery, or by the Kingdoms in that realm. Yet we dispatched Baldaboa to She-King Carcaris. Perhaps she will provide us with news.'

Erithacus thought for a while, 'It has been a very long time since any Wroth entered the city. I wonder how it will respond.'

Audagard sighed, 'If I were a betting feathered, of which I certainly am, I would say I have not a clue. Much in this place is still opaque to me.'

'Ah yes, I almost forgot. The clandestine vaults of Dron — still no sign of a way in?'

'No. The city has facets that are dormant, like parts of a mind that are not in use. I fear Dron has returned to us incomplete. Yet I cannot find an answer to this question, for there is no one alive now who lived the last time it rose from the soil, and the dead, Lendel included I might add, are silent on such matters.

'Although, something tells me that is for a reason. Our visitor might be an omen, and you know how much I love an omen, Grey Ghost.'

Erithacus smiled, 'And a riddle!'

Many hidden hollows and burrows were closed to the scholars of the city. Dron was not ready, or not able, to give up all of its secrets. Despite this, Audagard felt there was no harm in trying. The Umbra was particularly receptive to his eccentric mind. In the bronze gleam, faint images of what those rooms might hold were just out of focus, their reluctant presence only making him more determined.

Often, he could be found tracing the pattern in the rind of the walls, the etymology of larvae carvings, secretive tells in the grain. He knew where the partitions were weakest and pecked at them tenaciously. He even coaxed a Toec Woderum from the earth quarters to attempt to tunnel under, but to no avail. Eventually, his efforts were overshadowed by his need to teach the fledglings of the Corva Anx.

After his father, Azrazion Borgal Pelt had died, his was the final burial in the coal. It was a wish that he might join those of his family long passed. Vorsa had attended the funeral, as did Petulan, who stood beside her, the shimmering semblance of emulsion, pearlescent in the grey light, a perfect white skull held above the static tide of his Vulpus body.

Once Azrazion was interned, Petulan drifted to the grave, teasing the revenant of the old feathered from his tired corpse. A wisp of wavering light swelled from the black soil, taking the form of a younger Corva. No longer plagued by a broken wing, the spritely spirit looked to his son with love and whispered, *Go to the city, make it our church!*

So this is what Audagard did.

Worship of the Gasp had dwindled in the presence of the love'd Umbra. Dron had become a place where the dead could commune readily with their living relatives, so for the Dominus, the Umbra was a far more complex puzzle to solve. And it was no longer a cause he fought alone. The hierarchy of the Corva Anx had been a testament to harsh and dogmatic orthodoxy, mired in ritual sacrifice and corrupt scripture. Nevertheless, its potent magic had brought about the return of the First City. Yet in its wake, the Gasp became part of a greater whole, and with it a more egalitarian approach to their study. Except for a few fractious and zealous enclaves – the Ebduous Clax, Necros Anx and the Stiivin Dire Blight – the Bishops of Bone Char found new purpose. The Corva retained their title of Anx, yet its meaning became that of a teacher, tutoring fledglings in the art of shadow staring. Once the student matured, they took the mantle of clergy, and the clergy became spiritual caretakers. Where the Startle held court over the physical trials of the land upon which the First City stood, the Corva, and their compatriots, the Starless Vulpus, advocated for the metaphysical.

Erithacus would join his old friend in these teachings. He felt it was important to impart the natural alchemy of Naa to young impressionable minds, to act as a counterbalance to the more esoteric notions of his reverent friend. Where Audagard saw divine, Erithacus saw consciousness, much like the hyphae of mushrooms, connecting life by the marrow. So Dron, the First City, became a place of learning — in all matters.

They continued on into the hollows, veinous passages lit in part by luminescent fungi, alive with chatter of young mammals, fledglings chirruping and pecking in delight, suddenly silent as the Great Grey Ghost and the Dominus passed them by. Eventually they reached the burrow of Old and New, and their students.

Dominus Audagard stepped before them. Erithacus loomed large yet stood silently to one side. A flock of young Corva sat attentive.

'The Umbra brims in all of us. For most it brings a sense of belonging, a connectivity, and for that majority the sharing will be enough. But for some, and I assume all of you, there is far more to it than a mere sense of balance.

'For the Umbra has many facets, one of which is Dron, the First City, and, in turn, the city is a part of all of us, for when we die, our bodies become one with it. This,' he stamped his foot against the earthy floor, 'Dron is the gristle of the Umbra, the place of its birth, the tether to the real. Just as the city and all living things are connected in Naa, our collective thoughts and aspirations, our living consciousness is what the Umbra is made of.'

Erithacus interjected, 'It is an ecosystem in of itself, it thrives on our presence. A cycle of life and death and new life. I posit: The First City is an extension of our collective will, and our ancestors willed it to withdraw from all, to save all, to spare us the might of the Wroth in possession of such a tool, and it returned once that threat had gone. The City is nomadic; with its return to Naa, and with it the Umbra, it will seek to help all life. I believe, beyond its work as a forum for the nations of Embrian Naa, there might be other reasons for it to stay put.'

'Is it because of the Wroth?' someone chirped.

Erithacus flapped his wings in congratulation, 'Yes! Yes indeed. But why, if they are all gone? You are young, but perhaps not too young to remember the Wroth. They too were animals, not nightmares or angry revenants. I, for one, learned a great deal from them, despite being held against my will.

'They were spoiled by their unwavering dominion over Naa, over all other creeds and clades. They did not consider our place in their world, and for that, they suffered the ultimate price. But as much as we all hold animosity toward them, we must also offer pity for their young, innocent of their elders' deeds.'

'But the Umbra killed them all?' a diminutive Corva croaked.

'There was a sickness, some say the sickness had its own mind, to take the Wroth from their throne — and, indeed, some say it was the Umbra and, in turn, our ancestors who willed their death. To take a piece of Naa and destroy it was always the very last option. So I say this, not all events in Naa are intentional. The sickness came, and it destroyed the Wroth. But many animals died too. So, I wonder. Does Dron stay for other reasons?'

'Unfinished business?' another squawked.

Audagard leaned in, 'Perhaps. Or we have unfinished business with it. We are not free of guilt. We are capable of selfishness and greed. The Umbra *is* us, it is the collective will of Naa. If the Umbra destroyed the Wroth, then we, the nations of Ocquia, willed such an end into being, and we must live with the consequences of those choices.'

'So why does Dron linger?'

Erithacus spoke heartily. 'Because there is a piece missing. A loose thread. There are still Wroth alive in the world. I wonder if they play a role in this imperfection.'

'They are an imperfection!' A cackled laugh rang from flock.

Audagard cleared his throat, 'Students, please. We must practice humility. Mocking the Wroth only shows our fear of them. Fear serves no purpose if we are to find the answer.'

Erithacus nodded in agreement, 'They live beside us, not over us, we must offer them kindness for they have experienced a catastrophic change in their world. We are yet to see what will emerge from that shift, perhaps something we did not ever expect.'

I was once bright and brilliant!
Oh how I was.
My eminence spread oceans
Continents were trivial interruptions
But my ambition was the undoing
Of so many.

Chapter Three

The Maar ran amongst the tall pines. He leapt granite boulders and bracken thicket, following the turgid mud, the trail stomped by heavy beasts. He was soon deep within the impenetrable forest, beyond the cliff face where the white roar of the waterfalls masked what little sound he made, and the swollen river guided his descent to the track that wound through the glen. He ran with all his might towards a place he'd been before, a divide in the rock, the Grey Cleave, the gate that framed the blanched sky.

He found a collection of logs, damp and slippery. Homes had been made here once, and it offered him respite. He crawled down in the pulpy timber, sobbing, his mouth bloodied. He tended his cuts as best he could, yet he held no healing craft. They had taunted him, fought about eating him or using his body for some foul endeavour. His sleep was little more than momentary throes, waking each time to panic.

He crept from the hiding place to a dewy morning. The ample banks of pine forest loomed beside him, and across the loam he saw their shed needles and woody fruit. Every cramped dark crevice held a malice. He could not tell if *they* had passed, the rain having diluted any scent or mark. Their presence was felt in the anguish of their victims, all who dared to resist or hinder them ... and those who did not.

The path continued south, and despite the predatory shadows of Storn and Arn cast from above, he didn't meet a soul. The land was waterlogged. It had rained for many turns and made all tracks treacherous.

His feet found less treacherous ground as he descended an incline towards the lowlands, leaving the craggy hills behind him. The tree line finally broke into a wide meadow, hemmed by the infinite forest. At the far end of the grassland, his goal - a clean split between two sheer bluffs of granite.

He felt elated, and skipped across the scrub towards it, towering shoulders looming vigilant over him. The thwack of feathers alerted him to signs of life, lofty sentry towers of woven sticks. There were watchers in the rockface. He saw a distant speck of something flying toward him, too wide and graceless to be dangerous.

Ungainly yet determined, the drab grey and violet-green ruff of a Baldaboa came in to land. It noticed him straight away, the jerking bob of its head and a bright yellow eye focused on him.

'What say you, Maar!'

A commanding, yet friendly voice. The stout feathered carried armour riven with folded leaves and rune sticks. The Maar recognised his occupation. 'You are a Baldaboa of the Carried Word?'

'Awfwod Garoo of the Windsweepers! Long haul, from the wide sea of the south to the Kingdom of Carcaris. We fly in the stead of the First City. And you?'

'I am Little Grin, I am ... yet to be employed. I seek sanctuary.'

'Sanctuary?' The Baldaboa looked cautiously at him. He grumbled and spread his wings, tumbling with some sense of skill toward Little Grin. Awfwod sized him up.

'You *are* little. What do you run from?'

'There is something wrong, a sickness. The Keep Lands and the Bracken Fall have fled the grasp of it. It turns our kin cruel, something gets into them, something I do not understand.'

Awfwod cocked his head. 'Yes, I see the fear in you. You tell the truth. We have flown north from the Western Kingdom of the Hail. We have seen no sickness. You say others are fleeing?'

Little Grin nodded, 'I am a loner, I do not run with a clan, but I have seen the hoof-fall of a hundred Oreya, of liberated Effer and Aurma, and never have I seen such power and yet so much fright. I escaped their stampede only to run into the jaws of some foul thing. It chased me, teased and laughed and snapped teeth at me. I turned only once to see the black bulk and beady eyes of it.'

'What did you see?' Awfwod leaned in, 'Come on boy, tell me, what did you see?'

'I saw — I saw the Wroth.'

Awfwod Garoo withdrew. He spluttered, and a loud and hearty laugh erupted from the old feathered, 'Wroth! In the stead of the Rauka clans! Ha! No chance, young Grin. The Queen would not have it! Have you seen her cubs? Young Maro has a healthy mane, and her daughter, Esit! Under her tutelage she has become a wise yet powerful Rauka. No Wroth would dare!'

Little Grin did not have the words to describe what he had seen in the clearing beyond the place that had been his prowling grounds, where the Creta in the long grass were his bounty. He had not known Gasp-spoiled things, did not live in the advent of death like so many flesh feeders. He had strayed from the worship of Cran Insesi and Flock Sister avatars that had risen with the First City. He liked the embrace of a setting Ora and the wide smile of Seyla.

'It stood on its hind limbs, and it spread itself out in a mist that wished to take me. It stole bodies, stole them right away!'

A chorus of hoots alerted Awfwod Garoo. Above, the Windsweeper sentries had become agitated. Little Grin felt the emerging rumble below his paws. The Baldaboa flew back up the rock face, 'What is all this fuss?'

His lieutenant spread a wing toward the path from which Little Grin had appeared. The usually silent hillside of thick conifers was suddenly alive with motion, the scatter cry of roosting feathered, the rhythm pound of many bodies thundering down the thin trail. Mud and leaf litter signalled the explosion of animals at the brink of the holt, stricken huddles of disparate creatures, their howl and holler lifting with their breath.

A charge of lithe Athlon, the wide heads and white eyes of Aurma, ruddy red locks and violent horned Pax, and the stark black and white of their brethren the Heft, scattered flocks of Effer and Barara, guileful Highmount Vulpus, Proud Frown stags and their mates. Smaller creatures hung on to antlers, or were clutched in the gentle feet of willing feathered. Billowing tides of earth barrelled toward the granite gates that opened to the wide lowland plains. Little Grin climbed the crystalline stone crags to once again avoid their feet.

Awfwod Garoo blustered with consternation, 'We will do this properly, a single file, names and clan allegiances. Come on grunts, we have work to do!'

His lieutenant looked to him with disbelief. 'But sir?'

Awfwod Garoo sighed deeply. He snatched the rune stick from his subordinate's claws and descended to the ground. He cleared this throat. 'I can see you're in a hurry, but we must do things by the scriptures! Please form a—'

He barely missed the calamity of limbs. Frothing mouths threw raw cries of *Run! They come! Run for your life!*

Catapulted wide by the sheer force, he caught the wind and steadied himself, affronted by their lack of concern for the rules.

Within moments, the fleeing beasts were far from the rock bluff, leaving behind them a wake of slurry and the scent of sweat and urine.

Awfwod Garoo landed upon a large stone, at first a little shocked, and then an urgent thought came to him. Something was very wrong here, and his garrison atop the Grey Cleave, held in service to the First City, command post and messenger relay for the Windsweepers, had witnessed something truly odd. He looked to the Maar, who appeared vindicated.

'See!' Little Grin exclaimed.

Awfwod Garoo flew to him, 'Tell me again, what do they run from?'

The Maar pondered for a moment, 'I have heard them be called the Husk.'

Awfwod Garoo returned to his compatriots and agreed to take the word to She-King Carcaris and then on to the First City and to the Quorum of Ocquia. Before he left, he invited Little Grin to join him and his kin for a meal of insects and seeds. Little Grin ate heartily, for it had been a long time since he had fed. They rested in the lap of a hollow within the rock, away from the wind that howled outside.

Little Grin awoke to the flitter racket of wings, of armour laden with food stores and leaves inscribed with the events that had befallen them all.

Awfwod addressed his guard. 'Troo troo, you will stand as commander of this tower as we fly once again. There will be much word to spread so expect a fair few flyers in the coming days.'

'Yes sir!' The younger Baldaboa replied in earnest.

Awfwod turned to Little Grin. 'And you? You are welcome to stay here, but we cannot carry you. Whatever those folk were running from will soon be upon the land, and you cannot fly out of their reach like my soldiers here. What will you do?'

Little Grin frowned. 'I will stay wide of their path and seek a new place to call home in the lowlands. I want for little, so I am sure I will do well.'

'So be it Little Grin, good luck to you! Windsweepers! To the sky!'

They jettisoned from the rock mouth in a jostle of loose feather fluff, and up into the grey-stirred sky. Little Grin gave thanks to the sentry guards and began to climb down the rock, looking once again to the forest edge. The Husk would be upon him soon, and so with a deep breath, he passed between the crags and out into the wide plains, taking a sharp left and heading west.

*

Yaran, Ivy and Vorsa walked for four days, resting for the night in any space large enough to accommodate them all — the hothouse of a garden centre, still capable of retaining the warmth of Ora; the open garage to a semi-detached family home; a bed and bath store with no windows to obstruct them but plenty of mattresses to block the wind.

Ivy ate well, for the shops remained stocked with canned goods. She offered Vorsa some tinned Caanus food which she accepted begrudgingly when hunting was not an option. Yaran would feed on tree bark, those leaves that she found edible, rich grass and any fruiting vegetation. The Oraclas had adapted to wild foods after their emancipation from the god prisons, but it had come with some difficulties in adjustment. Between mouthfuls of wild garlic she assailed them both with tales of projectile vomit.

'And as you can guess,' she swallowed, 'we didn't eat that again.'

Ivy continued to feel much more stable on her leg. It shone with an impressive mauve bruise, but she gradually spent more time walking, shifting her weight on to her left leg. The grunts and trumpeting of Yaran were no longer an obstacle to her comprehension: she heard her voice in the spaces between sounds, in inflections and twitching ears. She read the humour and excitement in the tiny muscular movements, tells and inferences.

Despite this nuanced interpretation, Yaran chattered endlessly, about anything — growing more and more comfortable with her little Wroth friend. They exchanged stories of their youth, and Ivy learned of Yaran's mother, who was very much still alive, the matriarch of their herd.

They walked through smaller Wroth settlements whose buildings were intact, where the corpses of the dead still lingered, lost in the scrabble of mulch.

A few more turns passed; resting in the afternoon and travelling in the evening was easier for Vorsa. Ivy eventually abandoned her walking crutch and found herself increasingly capable of nimble hobble; scouring convenience stores in search of protein bars and dry goods, nuts and seeds that she could save for another meal.

On the morning of the sixth day, they reached a wide heathland, a blanket of elfin heather, rich violet and hardy green, the smell of salt in the air. Athlon galloped toward them with greetings, above them a flock of Naarna Elowin, who watched warily at the approaching caravan.

'Ora bring peace,' a large mare whinnied.

'And to you Grendim Efin Gladd. We will travel down to the city. Please pass on our best wishes to our flying friends above.'

Grendim smiled wryly, 'Ah, don't mind them, they have become very jealous of our good Dron. They mean well!'

'I can see the sea!' Ivy grinned.

They reached the clifftop, below them the wide azure ocean, and the coast arching to either side, stark and sure. To Ivy's surprise, the skyline was interrupted by an uncanny sight, a vast black form against the ascending sun, and for a moment she thought it might be the remains of an eroded outcrop, perhaps once attached but now separated from the cliff by millennia of weathering. Shards of scintillating light moved across her eyes as she blinked against the prism colours, trying to fit the peculiar form within her perception, for it was far taller than the cliffs it dwarfed on either side.

'What ... what is it?' Ivy asked.

'Why, that is Dron, the First City.'

As they moved into its shadow, stretching up from the shore below, Ivy began to make out its form. Great fascias of stone, a panoply of waterfalls threading amongst the sheers of root structures, a vertical garden knitted against expansive sheets of granite and slate, a topiary of laced vines wriggled in calligraphy. She could just about make out its peak, and its shape, something like a vast flower head, opening tentatively to the sun, each petal an escarpment of rock dressed in forests, each mountainous peak falling into rolling grass plains. Trunks like blood vessels fed amongst the rocky exterior, sharp and thorny structures jutted like defensive javelins.

Above the city, a flock of feathered danced in curious formations. She watched the amalgam of bodies thread and weave, amorphous and elastic. Vorsa watched Ivy with knowing delight, sharing in what the First City conjured in all who stood in its presence.

'Come,' she said, gesturing toward the cove below. They began the slow descent of a single road that led to a town, and to the ruins of a theme park. The Naarna Elowin remained above, squawking at one another.

Ivy felt she knew this town; its silent streets held the signs of dilapidation long before the fall of the Wroth. 'To Let' signs sat in dusty windows, a place that once might have had a thriving tourist trade in its fleeting heyday, a prize lost so easily to cheap foreign holidays. It had invited in the theme park attraction with desperate open arms, only to watch its gaudy façade bare in the winter months, hollow, starved of hordes of screaming children and exhausted parents. Soon, it too had felt the deprivation of Wroth life, and the sea rose to claim its rollercoasters and hot dog kiosks.

The waterlogged town had a stale, briny aroma. They wandered through the empty streets, wakes of sand and rotting seaweed drawn in from the beach against shop doors. Ivy looked through the windows of Victorian-built houses, the tables laid for absent diners as Yaran asked her questions - what had these strange objects been, what was their purpose?

They decided to walk around the theme park and found themselves on the beach, now woven within the wide reach of supportive roots. The animals of Ocquia busied themselves at the entrance, the feathered in jubilant song, mammals bartering seeds and insects, scurrying Muroi with shards of metal slung over their backs, the angry squawk of a dissatisfied Aefi. Above her, the towering city and its vast entrance, the dark and woody void beyond. She felt exhilaration and fear, but below this frenetic anxiety also something like familiarity, something deeply personal.

As they grew closer, the flock of Startle began to coalesce in the dimming sky and settle upon the lower climes of the city. They watched with benevolent curiosity in the presence of the Wroth and her huge companion.

Ivy dismounted and stood awkwardly on her good leg, her hand upon Yaran to support herself. Vorsa stepped forward and cried up to the city, 'Is there any among you who wish to come greet an old Vulpus?'

A dark fleck leapt from the rocky terrace above.

'Vorsa Corpse Speaker!'

'Rune, my dear!'

With deft wing and perfect grace, he flitted down and landed upon her back. Rune's feathers had darkened, with inflections of gold, emerald and amethyst, his eyes black and sharp. His armour carried new sigils marking his station in the flock.

'And your flight chief, Ara?'

Rune lowered his head solemnly. 'Ara is one with the city now. I am flight chief in his stead.'

Vorsa made a blessing and offered her sorrow. Rune thanked her and hopped to the ground to approach Ivy. She felt him; a chord struck in her — it was muscular, a twitching nerve under the skin. He was frightened by her; she could feel the unpleasant hot itch of his skin, the quake from his stomach through to quivering beak.

'You are a Shadow Starer,' he said defiantly.

She cocked her head. 'I think I am. Vorsa believes so.'

'I can see it in you, so many strands of light. All can see the Umbra but, for us — this sight grew with us, it is … demanding, is it not? It shows us so much.' He walked elegantly toward her, his dark eyes darting this way and that. For Rune, the light was a host of frantic threads that burned and died and shone again, an oscillating melody.

Ivy watched him dance, and for a moment, in the low dusk hue, saw that with which he danced.

Rune abruptly turned his head to Vorsa. 'I see him.'

Vorsa grimaced. 'Yes.'

Ivy looked perturbed, 'See who?'

'There is another such as you.'

'A Shadow Starer?'

'Yes, a Starer. But there is something else, another quality.'

'A human?' she blurted. 'Is he a Wroth, like me?'

Rune looked at her as though he were staring at Ora. He flinched and strained through half-closed eyes. It pained him to see that which lay beyond her physical self.

He looked to Vorsa with something like concern. 'I have spoken with your brother, in the Hall of Receiving. He is correct to be fearful of this. Have you petitioned the city for an ear?'

Vorsa nodded, 'Yes, but they are sceptical. Without news from the north they do not wish to cause panic. But we have little in line of defence.'

Rune scoffed, 'Little? We have no line of defence. We will need to call on the Oraclas, Orn Megol, the Pridebrow, and the High Realm of Hanno. We will need all the gods to come to our aid.'

'And they will,' Vorsa said.

Ivy asked again, exasperated, 'Please, what do you see?'

Rune flitted to her shoulder. His little chirps and whistles conveyed an algebra her mind could readily translate.

'The Umbra lets us see life, it allows us to witness the path others take, before they take it. It shows us the interconnections. These lives glow with differing strength, colours, movements. I saw your light long ago, but it was Vorsa and her brother Petulan who found you.

'There is a faint line drawing another Wroth toward you. He is not alone, he brings with him something old, something misshapen and dangerous. Petulan speaks of a disquieting in the Gasp — many of the dead have stepped back into Naa, freely. We do not know how. I believe, as does Vorsa, that it has something to do with the Wroth.'

'Come,' said Vorsa.

Ivy entered the great reception hall of the First City. Yaran and Vorsa remained at the threshold, allowing the wrothcub time to accept her peculiar surroundings. Rune darted off into the dim light in search of something.

She stood for a moment. The city stirred in her presence, a resistance. She felt its apprehension, apparition eyes manifesting like willow wisps, cold incandescences suspended, watching her with calculated intensity. There were things here that were no longer alive, old things that stirred in the ochre brume, ancestral tones performing symphonies of unrest in the arboreal scaffolding. She was painfully aware of why this sacred place might resent her presence.

It has been so very long since a child of the Wroth entered here.

Arcing along the rough wall beside her and all around, the chitinous crackle of something moving — she watched with fascination as shapes appeared and dissolved upon its surface. On closer inspection she could see that the walls were like that of a forest floor, and that they blanketed the colossal hall.

Limbs of plant matter began to extrude from the soil beneath her feet, a gravity of sorts, collecting nomadic morsels, specks and slivers, bone skelfs, seed chaff, spiralling into a whorl of debris before her. It was frightening and she turned to flee, shielding her eyes from the rush of dust-laden air, the rasp of dry tinder colliding into a massive shape, a skull of many skulls, wide and blunt.

Two fearsome tusks, wrought of a thousand ribs, rattled into existence. The head was animate, drifting and recollecting, a transient formation, each piece a magnet for another. Flecks parried in its orbit.

She pulled herself into a knot, crouched low on the floor.

'I mean no harm! I will leave!'

Harmful

The voice brought with it a flurry of emotion, anger, but most of all fear. The cluster of elements shook violently, like a rattlesnake — this was a warning. The face grew, spread wide, far larger than Yaran, far larger than any Oraclas. It looked down at her with one large nasal cavity that resembled a single gaping eye.

'I know my kind ... the Wroth ... I know we caused so much harm! But I am not like that, I'm just a girl!'

As torrents of wood litter were drawn into it, the looming simulacra swelled.

We see a corruption through you. You may well be benign. That which stalks you is not.

Ivy sobbed, 'I don't know what to do! I don't know what it is!'

It is like you

'If that is so, I will go to him, I will explain to him why we must all work together! There are other Wroth in the world, other Shadow Starers, they have found their peace with the world. This one you fear, he will too!'

We see his intention even if we cannot see him, and his will is poisoned. Like all who seek more than their share, it will come with pain and suffering for all.

'So we must defend the city from him!'

Dron is alone. It cannot hear its Sentinels, those who might defend it. Our hyphae no longer sense their presence. The city is vulnerable.

'Sentinels?'

The mass splintered; trailing effigies became erratic fractions, some drifting away on whispers, others clattering to the floor, a consciousness not in charge of all its faculties.

Vorsa appeared beside her.

'It's okay, wrothcub, it means no harm.'

'What ... what was that?' Ivy shook uncontrollably. She wiped the tears from her eyes, resting on her knees, head in her hands.

Vorsa placed a paw upon her knee, 'Breathe, wrothcub, no harm will befall you. That is Lendel, the caretaker of this city. He watches over the Hall of Receiving. He is the heart of Dron, the call of innumerable exclamations, cries, tears, deaths and births. He feels all of this, it is a searing pain that he bears, that steels him to protect this city.'

Ivy searched for any sign of the strange formation, now one with the architecture of Dron again.

'He said he cannot hear the Sentinels? What are they?'

Vorsa shook her head. 'I do not know. But perhaps others will. This place is a receptacle of knowledge. Its walls are made of memories.'

Ivy hesitantly reached out and placed her hand against the wall, feeling the flurry of twigs and shoots beneath her fingertips, boisterous flowers and the spirits that animated them. Beyond the corporeal, the Umbra allowed her to perceive the exhilarated ghosts beneath. She could feel the infinite vibration of the millions of years of life held in snug assemblage. She closed her eyes and breathed, feeling each dainty movement.

Something small and warm against her ankle woke her from this moment of reflection; she glanced down to see a small grey Creta. It sniffed at her before continuing on towards the wall, where it reached out a forelimb. Sure enough, the wall reacted to it, offering out an appendage of flotsam and jetsam. It placed its nose upon the limb. She could see the spirits beneath, loved ones, family members and lost siblings, jostling enthusiastically, sharing their stories with their living descendent.

'This city has many names, The Epiras, Mom'oridi, Crestfallen, Dron, the Place of Bones. But all understand its purpose.'

Rune returned, landing upon her shoulder. 'You can see them, the dead?'

'Yes, I can ....' she said.

'The living come here to learn from their ancestors, so many stories cut short in life; here each and every tale is made complete.'

They moved on, further within, muscular trunks whose silver bark split on swollen branches arched high on knotted arterial abutments, where a thick fog swirled beneath a canopy of stone. The hall was lit by shafts of scintillating light which radiated a kind and thoughtful glow. There was a warmth in this strange environment, and she searched for the word that her father had once placed upon the scrabble board one Christmas, *petrichor*, the aroma of woodland after rainfall.

There were many animals here, cold and warm-blooded creatures and the feathered above, drawn towards a convergence of herculean trees. Vorsa sat at a distance, observing Ivy as she approached cautiously, recognising that this was a shrine of sorts, and before it, its congregation. In amongst the branches that collected like gentle gripping hands was a large slab of sandstone, seemingly lifted from the floor of a long-eroded escarpment. There were tokens: colourful stones, found objects, seeds and petals from pretty flowers. A Muroi rolled a bottle cap clumsily to the foot of the rock, bowing before scurrying away. Rune gestured on, guiding her carefully through the attentive audience.

Ivy understood immediately that this was the fulcrum of the city. She closed her eyes and sent out inquisitive questions, asking the Umbra for its vision. She kneeled before the stone, taking care not to rest on anyone. There were fine lines upon the rock, skeletal impressions, drawn to one another in a misshapen star.

She could clearly see tiny feathered-like forms. She studied them; their delicate heads drawn toward each other, their little limbs held like wings, the finest traces of fluffy down hemmed their bodies.

Ivy was delighted, and Rune felt it.

'Tell me what you see?' he asked.

'I see three dinosaurs. We learned about these in school. A very long time ago, the world was ruled by giant creatures called dinosaurs. There was a meteorite, a great piece of rock that fell upon the Earth, upon Naa, and killed all but a few of them. Those who survived, evolved into… the feathered. They evolved into you!'

'Evolved?'

'They changed to survive. They had to find a new way to live.'

'*Much like you!*' A croaking voice emanated from behind her. It struck her with such shock she fell on to her hands, scattering trinkets and animals alike. She hastily gathered the gifts and placed them where they had been, making her apologies to the parishioners, her eyes tracing the dark for the sound of the voice. It was not Ocquia, not a collection of sounds her mind recast in English, this was a human voice, human words.

Wroth Tongue.

It had been so long since she had heard her own language being spoken by anyone but herself that she felt a flurry of opposing emotions; fear yes, but also anger, and an iota of hope.

The voice seemed old, decrepit. Ivy pulled herself into a defensive stance, concerned by the mere thought of seeing one of her own kind. She became very aware of herself, of how easily she had, what — betrayed humanity? How quickly she had insinuated herself with the other creatures of Naa. Would another Wroth look upon her with pity, or with disbelief?

Her eyes blinked against the dark, searching the gloom for the wrinkled frown of some elderly Wroth. Promptly, a large grey parrot ambled before her. He pushed his head towards her, examining her.

'You evolved from a line of primates. You called yourselves *Homo Sapien*.'

Ivy blinked, it was a parrot. It was large, the largest parrot she had ever seen. It had scars along its face, long healed yet deliberate.

'I—I am sorry to stare. I heard Wroth words, and I thought—'

'You thought I was Wroth! Well, I shall take that as a compliment. My English is strong, stronger than my French.' He gave her a wink.

'How? How do you know my tongue so fluently?'

'My dear, I was a victim of, what did you call it? Animal vivisection. I was studied as part of their sapient cognisance initiative — the debate over whether nonhumans should be given agency over their own bodies. I was the subject of a substantial exploration of bird intelligence, and tutored in the art of symbol recognition, speech, mathematics, but also the recipient of some invasive surgery to explore how my brain stored such information. I must admit a lot of my learning came after the death of the Wroth, but I grasped the written word, and with that I was raring to go! I have my limitations of course. But I do my best to grasp the basics of the natural sciences.'

Ivy lowered her eyes.

Erithacus sighed, 'Wrothcub, none of which is your fault.'

Ivy sat upon the ground and the parrot hopped toward her. She looked up as he lowered his head to meet her gaze. 'May I ask, what do I call your kind? I have met so many, but I have not met a ... we called you—'

'The great Grey Parrot, *Psittacus Erithacus*. I was always very keen on your language. I learned as much as I could under the watchful eyes of your kin. They took much from me, but I did not come out empty clawed.

'I was born without a name and the name gifted to me by my captors was not particularly becoming, and so I took that which represented my entire flock. You may call me Erithacus. My clade are known as Cheon, although my brood was Claff Tacouw Cheon.'

'Cheon,' Ivy muttered. 'Erithacus is a beautiful name.'

'Thank you. And yours?'

'Ivy Esther Akinde.'

'Ivy,' he softened his voice, 'I do not hold the same prejudice towards the Wroth that others might. This world is full of animals that have been cruel, have taken what is not theirs. Given that same power, any one of us might have abused it. There are those who will always hold that hatred, which is well deserved, but that time has passed. Now we must find reconciliation in this new world, we must all *evolve* a little more.'

He looked at her with exuberant eyes, eyes filled with kindness.

'I am very glad you are here, Ivy.'

Ivy was not so sure, 'The city fears me. It sees me as a threat. Speaks of defences against my kind.'

'Dron has witnessed the rise and fall of your species, made choices that would render the Wroth unable to cause the harm the city foresaw. Naa was dying. Even the Wroth knew this.'

Ivy felt frustration. None of these questions, or indeed, their answers were adequate. The first of many perceptions of a world not made for her.

Erithacus turned to Vorsa, 'So good to see you again, Vorsa Corpse Speaker. I have been made aware of your concerns. Have you learned anything more?'

Vorsa approached Erithacus, 'Greetings, Grey Ghost, we have not. I am hoping word might have reached the city by now. Petulan is ever more insistent. I feel whatever is coming is dire.'

'Then it is all the more urgent that we discover what it is you fear and make plans to defend against it.' Erithacus bounced youthfully towards the slab of stone, offering out a wing as if to guide Ivy to it. 'These are the Sisters of the Flock. Dron grew from these three tiny forms, a grave that became a monument to love and loss. Some say that in their death a true sense of consciousness was born, the first true mourning. Naa was drawn to this and, around it, knitted this cocoon, both the physical city, and the Umbra, the sap that holds us all together, the tendons of thought. Through it we are all connected. It is why Rune and Petulan were drawn to you. But there is much we do not understand, and through you perhaps we might learn more.'

A steady thwack of wings came from above, alerting them all, and a loud and precarious landing was performed by a Corva wearing an elaborate headdress. He adjusted it, the adornment having become lopsided, straightened himself, puffed his feathers and strode toward them with an air of feigned calm.

Ivy looked a little taken aback.

'May I Introduce myself, I am Dominus Malargoragor Audagard, former Anx of the Corvan clergy, Tutor of the Umbra. I welcome you to the First City.'

'I was just telling her of our beloved Sisters,' Erithacus said.

'Ah yes, one of the many mysteries of the city. I have another you might assist me with wrothcub, if you would be so kind.'

*

Noraa awoke to the snout of a Throa close to her face. She snapped, but his substantial claws held her teeth at bay. He hushed her, and they lay in silence. Noraa considered why this daynight was so insistent they stay quiet, and then it dawned on her. It was very quiet. There was a deafening lack of sound.

In a low whisper, TumHilliad spoke, 'They are here, many of them. I watched them from my peeping hole; I have a few amongst the tree roots.'

What did you see?' she hissed back.

'I saw many of your kind, Cini, but there is something very, shall we say, *unusual* about them. Their eyes look sightless, yet they see and move with peculiar gait. There is a wash of something unnatural around them, and they walk beside prey, who share in this doolally behaviour.'

They waited until Ora broke, and TumHilliad crept to the back of the shed, disappearing down a hole. His head popped up moments later. 'All clear!'

Noraa pulled her doorstop back and exited. There was no sign of her pack, and their scent, although present, stank of sickness. TumHilliad dragged himself from the sett and accompanied her on to the road beside the allotment. There were dead here. A Morwih, torn in half, and a dying Vulpus cub. Noraa ran to its aid. 'What happened?' she asked it.

The young Vulpus bled from the mouth, 'They took our mother and father. They took my sisters. They left me to die.'

The cub had been born with a malformed back limb. His flanks were bitten open, wounds inflicted which would surely kill him.

'I can try to treat the wounds?' TumHilliad uttered. 'I have some skill with healing?'

'Yes, please do.'

'Clean water and apple root. There is a whatchamadoodle near my sett, filled with water. If I can get him back there I will clean his wounds and treat them with a mash of herbs and roots.'

He sat back on his rump and with his teeth unlatched a shiny tube from his armour. He placed it in his mouth and blew. The sound was shrill in Noraa's ears, and pained the little cub, 'TumHilliad! What is that?'

'Oh! I do apologise my dear. This is my Guild-patented, one of a kind invention, worthy of the Great Tor, and favoured call to arms for the Roughclod Infantry of Reconditioned Caanus! My Caanus signaller!' He leaned in and muttered, 'I didn't actually invent this, I found it, nice shiny bit of wroth wear, but don't tell my boys that!'

The hooting howling tumble of eager feet, flailing jowls, and the clang of pots and pans descended from the hill beyond the town. There were a dozen of them, in every shape and size possible. Their armour was a disarray of found items — cutlery, saucepans, and a collection of small plants, strapped to one another with all manner of twine, rope and bicycle tires. Some of the smallest were pulled along on little carts, skateboards and anything else they had collected, scrounged or pilfered. Tongues lolled and tails wagged with enthusiasm, galloping to the sound of their captain. They clattered to a halt, a gamut of confusion and glee upon their ramshackle faces.

'Roughclod Infantry reporting for duty. Sir!'

They all raised their left front paw. They turned to Noraa with what looked like vague recognition. Paws fell. The largest, and seemingly the highest ranking in their group, moved forward. He was almost as big as Noraa, with dark brown fur and a prominent snout.

'You are kin?'

Noraa nodded. 'A long time ago. I am Cini. You are my distant relatives.'

TumHilliad ambled toward them. 'Yes yes, Cini and Caanus, separated by the Wroth, a long time ago, no need to open old wounds! Noraa, this is my trusty Lieutenant Bresh! He alone has gathered together all the Caanus before you who were abandoned in the great death. He took the word of Tor, and his protégé, Rex, and went into the world looking for those chained up and starving, those shut inside those awful Wroth dens. He has saved so many I have lost count. Some have left to travel in search of other packs of Caanus seeking a safe place to rest their heads.'

'Good to know you, Bresh,' Noraa added.

TumHilliad was lower to the ground than the Roughclod Infantry and they stooped to hear his word. He grumbled, 'Say, where were you this last eve? A clutch of scoundrels came into the town, horrible things they were, have injured a young Vulpus and murdered a Morwih. Did you hear any tomfoolery?'

Bresh shook his head, 'No sir, we were scouting the Wroth dwellings to the west for Caanus to join our cause. We have a new grunt! May I introduce ....' It was clear Bresh had quite forgotten the creature's name. He cleared his throat. 'Come forward new recruit!'

A small red furred animal appeared beside them.

'I tried to tell them that I wasn't a Caanus. My name is Little Grin.'

The Maar stepped out of the small wagon that a large shaggy Caanus had been pulling along with his mouth. Little Grin was exhausted and shaken.

TumHilliad looked him over. 'Oh Bresh, we must fashion some sort of guide for you, to distinguish Caanus from other creatures of Naa. This Maar has no need for an army!'

Noraa went to Little Grin and licked his wounds like she would a pup. At first he was resistant, until the coarse warmth of her tongue began to ease his aching muscles.

'I think we are all in need of an army,' he said between swabs. 'I fled something terrible, these scoundrels you speak of. I have seen them before in the north. I travelled west in hope of avoiding them, but their sickness spreads. Soon I fear all will be lost to it.'

Noraa interrupted her cleaning, looking down at him with an air of apology.

'They were my pack. My family. Something desolate came into the world and took them. I am Cini, we are close with our gaspkin. I recognised their hunger for life. But never have I seen such barren things infest the bodies of the living. I have been searching for some assistance, but I am new to these lands, brought here by the Wroth. Perhaps one of you can help me in my quest?'

Bresh became alert. 'It is our sworn task to help those in need!'

TumHilliad was filled with pride. 'They are a good sort. Ready to come to the aid of those in need of assistance. Perhaps some of them can escort you south, to the She-King's court. We have good relations with the Rauka, they will give you no trouble. They, too, are kin in a new land. Perhaps Dron, the First City, could be your port of call? Much of Naa leans to its word. I have never been myself, far too much of a journey. But you're all young and spritely. But be warned, you now trail these cretinous creatures.'

'The Husk, they call themselves,' Little Grin added.

'Husk. A hollow name if I ever heard it. So be it. Naa has a new foe. I will stay here and help the survivors of these attacks, whilst you travel together. Bresh! Escort Noraa and Little Grin to the She-King.'

He turned to the remaining troops. 'Infantry! Much to be done, quick march! One two, one two!'

'Thank you, TumHilliad. I hope we meet again.'

The old Throa nodded and returned a kind smile, then he trundled off towards the Caanus, who were sniffing at fence posts. 'Come now! One two, one two!'

Corvan Omency

The fat of Naa rots and wriggles
Exasperated burps beneath us
Croak in riddled expletives
Hard luck tales and woe-is-mes
The wants and whims of sediment
One on top of one another
Squash the tarry firmament
In which the oldlings toil
And seek their strategies of misrule
Once kings, once lords of all they survey
Reduced to nowt but bitumen
To glorious oblivion

Chapter Four

Sat stubborn upon a sour moor, a castle. Its windows, long missing their lintels, cast rib cage gashes in the stonework. On the surface, it was a ruin, a fallen giant doubled over, yet refusing to submit. It had suffered many wounds — the killing blow had been its obsolescence. As societies abandoned such folly, and embraced more democratic approaches to governance, the need for battlements diminished until all that remained was a pile of rubble. It had waited for a new occupant, blemished by soot and lichen, blanched in the stark light of Ora, a fragmented head held high.

Like a sluggish tide carrying a weight of rotting seaweed, the Husk crept in oily procession across the floodplain. Thoth had spied the silhouette of the stronghold from afar, entertaining new and exuberant flights of fancy; a throne, a court to hold, serfs to do his bidding. He revelled in it. They snaked up the hillside, seeking entrance.

A vault lay beneath the castle. Above there was little shelter. Down below, the walls tapered into mud, they seized the dark as though to covet it. It was here, in this bare hole, that Thoth began to construct his seat. Gradually, his appetite for this endeavour grew and, with it, his skill in exploiting the dead as a resource. He was only limited by the consumption of living, and with each day that passed, more were pulled from nests and branches, hedgerows and thickets, carried in saliva strewn jaws, torn and disfigured and then desecrated with some wicked Wroth spirit, the light dimming in their eyes as another facet bypassed the rightful consciousness and made a mockery of it. He cared nothing for those he stole, and even less for the Wroth he gifted that life to. All in service to his cause.

One evening, he climbed the masonry and looked out upon the land. He craved a cigarette. He hadn't smoked in thirty years, but a memory brushed by. A pub, recognition, a drunken brawl, escaping the heat and stink of spilt beer and sweat, the sharp air, the ritual of lighting the fag, the draw, the light headedness, the exhale.

He found these moments difficult. It was rather like missing a friend who had died, knowing that you will never converse, never laugh, never be close to that person again. But he had never cared much for anyone. And so, he missed smoking. He raised himself on his back limbs and patted the pocket of his jacket as though feeling for a lighter. He smirked, placing his paws on the turret wall. He peered over.

Below him, a moat, now little more than an overgrown depression in the earth. He imagined a legion of Husk, digging furiously to empty it of grass and scrub and restoring it as a divide between his seat and the peasants of the land. Though there would be no repairing the walls of this castle, no great feats of engineering would ever occur again. Another prescient realisation, another fork in the road. The limitations of this dog-like body were boundless. He returned again to his daydreams of crocodile infested waters.

Something caught his eye, a movement, a dark form directly below him. He skittered down the steps of the tower, through the fragments of the portcullis.

His Cini eyes were profoundly more accurate than his former human eyes and he soon found the source — a Husk, the Oreya fawn he had turned. It was still alive, though its neck was broken. Dark blood oozed from its chittering mouth. It had thrown itself from the battlements. In its flanks were old, rusted screws, seemingly twisted into the skin on purpose.

'Why?' he demanded.

'This ... this isn't a life! It's wrong, all wrong!'

Thoth seethed, 'This is a life! More life than you had known in that stinking hell! How dare you shirk my gift!'

He raged, a feral bestial thing. He bit hard into the fawn's throat, tearing it open, the sanguine eruption painting his face with arterial blood. He shook the corpse with vehemence — the nerve of this feckless fuck. How dare he question the validity of this existence? There was no better choice, some floating mote of nothing, or breathing and shitting! What more did this cretin want!

Thoth fed on the corpse until he'd had his fill and dragged the remnants back into the tomb, casting it before his hungry tribe. They gorged like maggots, pale and swollen.

As he watched the squirming mass of greasy bodies, glib in fat and gore, he noticed lengths of barbed wire, jags of bottle glass, nails and thorns, inserted into their flesh. Emaciated ribs exposed deliberate wounds, healing, irritated. But self-inflicted.

'Scab!'

A head rose from the feast. His second crept toward Thoth. In his forelimb, close to his shoulder was a piece of razor wire, wrapped taught around his limb. Thoth gestured to it.

'What is this?'

Scab bared his teeth, not in defiance but embarrassment. He sniffed at it, clearly infected from a hundred tiny cuts.

'We don't feel. Don't feel alive. This helps us to feel.'

'You don't feel?'

Scab tilted his head. 'We have lived before, we have fond memories of living. This is something else, something uncanny. Do you not feel different in that wolf suit?'

'We are not human anymore. We are something else — I have birthed a new world, a new way of living. You have no need for these flagellations.'

'Flagger ... what?'

'Harming yourself like that, it is weakness!'

'Aye, Thoth. You have your ways, we have ours. We ain't denying the good deed you've done us. We are just getting used to this, so we have our little tricks to hold us together. This helps us feel, so we do it. You made a new way of living, fine. We have to live it.'

Thoth sniffed dismissively, waving him back to the bloody pile at the centre of the crypt. Scab slunk away, turning to admonish Thoth under his breath.

But Scab was right. None of them had known this way before, and was it living? Renting space in the mind of some inefficient body, unable to build, to farm, to engineer a world. In this appraisal, another vagrant thought revealed itself to him. Were the Husk limited to these feeble animals? Were there other options? Could he inhabit the mind of something more worthy?

Were there other Wroth?

Emeris

Emeris was half present, echoes of Thoth's ventures dripping into his hampered mind, swallowed by figments of his life, inelegant retellings of almost forgotten memories. He laughed manically at the farce of it all. He fought for any sense of clarity, finding himself inhabiting Thoth as though he were the Wroth.

He woke in a room. He had only seen such an arrangement of walls and objects a few times, always under the influence of some consequence of the Wroth, leaving him stricken with confusion, lethargy, and a dreamless black sleep. Always upon a cold surface, a sharp pain in his forelimb and then nothing. Confinement was not a feeling he ever asked for, and after the trauma of being caught, and moving across the ocean, he never wanted it again.

Yet, here he was. He could sense claustrophobia. He was lying on a soft surface, he felt warmth. There was light falling here, in a single shaft from an opening in the wall. He lifted his paw to let that light fall on him, and he was appalled to find that in place of his paw was a limb he only ever attributed to a Wroth. It was then that he rose, upon his hind limbs, and caught his reflection in a mirror. He was a wrothcub. He wore Wroth coverings, stiff and hugging. His hair was missing from most of his body, except for his head.

The room moved in shuddered blurs, each blink of his eyes would skew a new facet, a new perspective of the room. The very nature of this experience was discordant; threads of light split and sauntered incorrectly, projecting off surfaces in delusional paths. He was in a memory, but not his own.

He was pulled towards the door, suddenly aware of actions and denominations, titles and designations replaced each unknown. It was sluggish and incomplete but soon he had made sense of his clothing, his shoes, the soft covering on the floor — carpet.

He was twelve.

He lived in a large house, with his mother and father.

Emeris moved through the memory, abating the motion sickness with steady footsteps, observing as much of his surroundings as possible. A dappled mottling seemed to dither into his vision as if the recollection of that particular part of the house was incomplete or faded beyond recall. There was a landing, many doors, and a staircase.

He descended the stairs, where he could hear a warbling sound. In the kitchen was his mother, who was crying.

'Have you washed your hands?' she sobbed.

He glanced at his hands. They appeared clean. 'Yes,' he replied. The sound was not his own, and he did not speak it. He was now inside the retelling, as a passenger.

His mother moved toward him, drying her hands on a cloth. She grabbed his wrists, shaking them, 'These hands are not clean! You little liar!' She slapped him across his cheek.

Emeris experienced not only the sharp raw sting of it, but the humiliation, the shame and the anger, a reserve of which was filled to bursting within the boy.

He ran, crying, out of the back door, and into a brilliant light, a garden, well maintained, and a man, his father, walking towards him.

Emeris felt a graven, absolute fear.

*

Chapter Five

Audagard cleared his throat, 'I have versed myself in the language of the Umbra, yet this city holds many unknowns, most notably those parts of itself closed off to us all.' He turned his head to one side, his pearlescent black eye upon Ivy. He was afraid of her, she could tell, but his feigned confidence was impressive.

'The city may listen to you, wrothcub.'

Ivy shook her head, 'The skeleton face, the—' she looked to Vorsa.

'Lendel has appeared to her,' Vorsa directed her reply to Audagard.

'Wonderful! Just as I expected. What did he say?'

Ivy winced. 'He said that the city fears me, and will raise its defences.'

Audagard flailed about, 'This is terrible! I assumed you would be the key to breaching the depths of this place! Did he say anything more?'

'He said the Sentinels – he can't hear the Sentinels – that the hyphae cannot sense their presence.'

Audagard's eyes darted as he considered her words, 'The heralds? The Sentinels? Could it be?'

He hopped to Ivy's feet. 'Permit me, there is a place in Dron that will not listen to us. But perhaps that is not the right approach. The city fears you. I wonder if … ?'

'You wonder what my old friend? Speak plainly,' Erithacus replied, a little irritated.

'Follow me!' Audagard said with glee.

They ascended into the higher echelons of the First City, Ivy watching her footing, the steep braid of vines coiled close to create a pathway, held up by a fretwork of enormous stems. There was no barrier — to call it a path was a reach. She feared falling again and, without Yaran, she was by far the largest in the group. Rune flew ahead with the Dominus as Vorsa and Erithacus walked with Ivy.

They passed the Regulax, Ivy noticing its similarity to the Bastia, and wondered whether this was what Vorsa had spoken with. Enigmatic black Vulpus and Corva watched knowingly, bejewelled with High Wrought armour and spindly coronets as they passed by, further into the cartilage depths of the city's innards.

Seeing passages that towered above her, corridors mottled like that of citrus rind, she began to realise that the city was a living entity. It was organic, yes — but beyond this, there were various things she recognised from biology classes. She could see botanical forms. Although they resembled trees, the vast woody systems were more like veins — an immense fabric of veins, and each opening was a ventricle, a cavity inside an organ. Doorways behaved more like valves, muscular ribbons that retreated and contracted. They were inside a beast.

Audagard brought them to one such doorway, an arched hollow, blocked by growths of vegetable flesh that resembled mushroom caps.

'Beyond this wall there are, perhaps, some answers, though the city seems unwilling, or unable to allow us to pass. I have an idea,' he gestured to Ivy.

She went to it and placed her hand against the door. She felt it shudder. Clearly, it was reacting to her presence.

'Doors don't open to enemies?' She looked to them for guidance.

Erithacus looked to Audagard. 'They might if opening triggers a defence. I remember reading of how many living things have a facet of them that attacks infections and sickness from within, Ivy?'

'Antibodies,' Ivy muttered.

'Yes, antibodies! Am I correct in thinking this is your own line of thought Audagard? You want the city to react to Ivy's presence?' Erithacus rested a wry eye on the Corva.

'Ah, well. It is indeed a hypothesis. The city is known to take up arms against things it deems a threat.'

Vorsa let out a low growl, snapping at Audagard. 'With all you have learned of the folly of arrogance, will it ever occur to you to not exploit others for your own gain?'

The Dominus considered this. 'She will not come to any harm, it is simply a catalyst.'

As if on command, the wall contracted, fibrous rings pulled into wrinkled folds. Audagard, unable to help himself, uttered some feeble excuse and flew through without a thought.

The cavity was lit by fluorescent fungi, much the same as that which propagated the city interior, yet far more prolific. Strands of organic light pulsed across arcing ganglia — feathering white mycelial lattices spread eagerly, interacting with a confluence of pulpy growths, some hardened and brittle, others new shoots. These disparate germinations of fungi and flora were symbiotic, entwined in a perfect coupling, like that of the city as a whole.

Ivy carefully stepped between vines and over verdant polyps. There was a stillness, a cautious awareness of their presence.

Audagard glided towards a burst of fruiting cysts at the centre of the mass. Infinitesimal movements could be seen in the pale filaments that blossomed from fungal strands, seeking out each other with blind tenacity.

'It is a mind,' Erithacus said softly, in awe of it all. 'It is reacting to our presence, searching for something.'

Ivy could see the cilium reaching towards root systems long abandoned. Protruding from the wall was a stump, healed over with course bark, the faint presence of dried sap. She thought of it like a loose wire. She began to pick away at the scar tissue, although her fingernails were useless. The mycelium continued to progress across the organ walls, eventually reaching the stump. Tiny digit-like proboscises searched the rind, failing to find living flesh.

'Here!' She called to her companions. 'I think there is a severed connection. We need to peel off this bark!'

Rune landed upon her hand. Fungi growths had begun to form on the cleaved limb. 'I see!' He hopped from her outstretched arm and onto the bark, beginning to chip away at it. Soon Audagard accompanied him and, together, they tore that which heeded the union. Once green fibre was visible, the mycelium began to root into the pith. In a short time, pale, doughy mushrooms had completely encased the stump.

There was no flourish of lights or apparitions.

They stood in silence, watching the steady progression of the tendrils establishing themselves into the old growth.

Audagard sighed. 'What did we accomplish?'

Rune cocked his head. For a moment he could feel a swelling light in distant lands. Ivy felt it too. 'Something is changing.'

'Changing?'

'Not here, but somewhere. Something like the city, something old.'

Rune nodded, 'Yes, the Umbra is alive with lights. Like Dron, they are vivid.'

Audagard ducked his beak close to Rune, 'I do not have your depth of vision! But please, will it help us?'

Erithacus flew down beside the Dominus. 'We will go to the Sisters, their sight will broaden ours. Perhaps we shall find answers there.'

Ivy swooned. There was a glimmer, fractal helixes, and then blinding pain in her head. She fell hard, her hands reaching out to find some kind of purchase before she fainted, but she was too late, the flood of empty black engulfed. She lay in the crook of tumorous toadstools, her fingers buried in the mulch that had collected over eons as old life seceded to new growth.

Panicked, Vorsa ran to her, licking her face, cajoling her back to consciousness. Then they were all by her side, calling out to her. The hyphae also gravitated to her, felt her alien in their sanctuary. The pollutant, the foreign body. Tiny saprophyte hands, reaching for her to begin their slow dissections, their consumption of her for the good of the city. But her skin was warm, and her body living, and they could sense her good will, and rather than digest her, they wished to bond with her —and so they did.

She could see.

She could see everything.

It was a dream, she imagined, however real it seemed. No longer in the city, she was lying in tall grassland. It was frigid cold, and an icy rain fell. There were others here, she could see their hot breath over the heads of what looked like wheat. The bellow of a huge hairy beast broke the silence, it lumbered beside her, falling back on its hind limbs, lips flaring as it hollered with a groan. Its armour was all torn branches and stone. A bear, what she now knew as a *Grim,* towering above the frozen land. Other animals too, vast horned Oreya, and huge Morwih, with dagger teeth. They came together in the midst of upheaval. Feathered and mammal alike had gathered to welcome Dron, The Epiras, Mom'iridi, The First City, risen in this cold land to further its cause of unity. Ivy could sense the presence of Wroth, her ancestors, far away, not yet ready to enact their separation.

But it was that sensation, an awareness which spoke of something far more visceral, a tether to not only all life, but all time. Coiled up within cortex fronds, a library of every notion, every decision, the repercussions of every moment of compassion and malice. Forever living, forever aware beyond life, and in life.

Ivy perceived this labyrinth of connections, elegant plumes beneath the earth, transient epiphanies bursting through stone and mud, through fallen corpses, rifling decay to supply a conveyor of nutrients – yes – but also recording the infinitesimal convictions of every single mind.

Above the rot and agency of this collection of conscious cells, she recognised the city as like a colossal fruiting fungi, the blueprint of which was held in the feather appendages of its mycelia. This was the foundation upon which the Umbra and its city thrived, a primordial intelligence gathered up in the slime mould and fungal growth, forging cognitive decisions, anchoring animal and vegetable, consuming death and coaxing new life. She was part of this, a very real link in a chain that had started millions of years in the past, in the simple organisms that would one day give rise to all manner of conscious beings. But that diaspora was sewn closely, both in the matter from which it was hewn, but also in all perceptions of reality, of Naa, of the Gasp and the Umbra itself — all were aspects of this interdependency. What her animal kin saw as alchemy, she now saw as the movement of knowledge through cell walls, an osmosis of empathy that brimmed in the minds of thinking creatures. She was one with the First City, and she sensed its acceptance of her.

From this vantage point she now saw what Lendel had called the Sentinels. The First City had emerged when the nations of Naa willed it to do so. Once their difficulties were resolved it would withdraw, and it was in their unspoken fears, an existential shift in the safety they felt, that Dron recognised a need for something enduring, a permanent line of defence. The Sentinels were its answer - aggregations of living and dead things, microcosmic cities bound by gangliform colonies of itself and folded into autonomous minds — golem giants, caretakers and guardians. Long would they watch over their protectorate. Generations of animals would look to them for neutral governance, and in doing so they would come to be worshipped, held like saints of the Sisters.

When the Wroth finally turned against the nations of Naa, it was the Sentinels that were the last line, in this cold land, where the Cini were herded and killed or made servants, mounting their final stand as the vast Sentinel of their clan fell under the sheer number of warring primates. They retreated into the earth, like the First City itself, leaving only the memory of their towering residence and the religion fashioned in their image.

A belief that only lasted as long as there were those to believe it, and soon, that also died, as the likes of the Cini, Rauka and Grim were hunted to extinction. Vestigial gods left to sleep in the earth, severed from the city by their silence.

And something else. Something older than the city. It had no shape, or feeling, in fact it gave her no sense of purpose or function, just an endless dark. It was deep below, serving neither the Umbra nor its peoples.

Ivy had awoken them.

Awoken them all.

*

He had not stirred for some time now. New sediment layers had formed, a new era lost. They came and went so fast! He could taste lime, the bitterness of solvents. Chemical run off, he could taste himself, dredged up from his depths to sate their unusual thirst.

He knew why, of course.

He burned so bright.

He could be polymerised, made into a trillion useless trinkets. Much of him was now a layer of plastic, so near yet so far removed, catatonic, skeletal oil.

He would brush his liquid limbs against car tyres buried above fissures, where he bubbled close to the surface. He mourned each severed extremity, each shard lost. He wondered if, in countless turns of Seyla, he might watch those receptacles, angular and clear, rot down into him, become one again.

He roused himself— a head, a body, a trailing gown five hundred thousand miles long, seeping like coiled intestines throughout the world.

The pumps were all silent, the intravenous wells were abandoned.

He heard the death knell, the chime of his estranged mother, Dron, his house closed to him.

An orphan by choice, he hoped that the Umbra had respected his wishes, yet was not too stubborn to hide the song from him, in case he'd changed his mind.

But it wasn't the invitation to the great levelling, the toppled cities and the extinction of the Wroth that woke him. Within his loins were Wroth, those who'd willingly joined him in the dark. At first it had been a scratch, a little tickle, something he could not reach.

With time, the tell-tale spasm of something erroneous, something out of place. He knew this irritation well, for it was his call to arms. A soul had slipped out of that pale excuse for a death, out of the Gasp, and into Naa. It was an outlier, an unwanted, and it was in his domain.

He began swimming through voids and vacancies, up through sand, through the clarifying sediment, from the lowest petroleum lakes and up to the surface, to where he would find his bounty.

*

Lucille sifted through a bank of silt that had collected at the foot of the trench, her fingers sliding over the sand and grit, feeling for the little tickle in her fingers, that tell-tale find. On her shoulder was a Creta of the field she had named Makepeace. His name was Olu Remsedia, but he didn't mind Makepeace.

'Here! Look!' she said. He ran down her arm and examined that which appeared in her fingers. She was right — she always was. A very worn piece of metal. It had been hewn by Wroth hands, not Muroi, although lain out on the large flat rock were a hundred like it, and some were High Wrought from long ago. Muroi craft, before the molten forges, hammered with stones, perhaps hidden under the furs of those who had come here seeking shelter, considered this a special place, drawn to it over the centuries.

She had felt that draw too, had studied Bronze Age archaeology, had written her graduate thesis on the barrows and cairns of ancient Wroth endeavour. She had become an archaeologist — carrying out painstaking excavations in the field. In the years before the plague had taken her family, and everyone else she knew, she had come to this plateau, high above the countryside, in search of things of consequence.

There had been a fateful day, between two immense slabs of stone, when she had felt something sharp and keen, a bright entanglement, unravelling in her mind's eye, something below her, a vast presence, slumbering underneath her. For a moment she dreamed its petrographic dreams.

She had returned to that site a hundred times, hoping to feel that connection again. Cross-legged on the black rock, her long silver hair tied tightly in a single plait, her eyes closed, a pushy wind nudging her, grounding her. She could feel and hear through the gritstone oblongs and weathered gradients, a thunderous roar of water from the falls, spray lashing with seemingly deliberate force.

She would listen, fingers outstretched, grazing the stone, the cold, the wet, the weight of it under her. Here, away from others, she felt a mind far older than any Mesolithic finds. This mind was not even human.

For a long time, she managed to hide her discovery, and her ideas, from her colleagues, eventually proclaiming such burial sites to have significance beyond mere ritual. They had found her declarations strange, foolhardy, and eventually she was shunned and filed with the fringe scientists seeking aliens and fairies. But her belief was not founded in any human faith, no half-baked conspiracy. It was the idea that the land had agency, that nature itself was aware.

When everyone died, she had sat beside her husband's corpse and felt a hollowness that could not be filled. She awaited death with a stubborn resilience, that some cloaked figure would enter that musty room, that there would be a stand-off. But death didn't come. Just the warm glow from that cold blustery crag in the hills, a sensation that she longed to feel again.

The days turned to weeks, and she had collected together her camping equipment — a life spent in the wilderness had prepared her for this. She raided the local outdoor living supply store for non-perishables, filled her Land Rover with jerry cans of fuel and food to last for months, and made for the Peaks.

The roads were not strewn with bodies, the few abandoned cars were easily avoided. She had not seen a single living human, but she was aware of how quickly the animals had taken advantage of the silent streets, their watchful presence always on the periphery, always salient, always at the cusp of telling her some hidden truth.

It was not long before one spoke to her.

She had stopped at a petrol station to collect useful items. In the store, there had been spoiled food. Other food appeared to have been eaten by mice or rats. She had stepped carefully within, proclaiming her presence in case other survivors had found shelter there.

She had approached the counter, where two pairs of beady eyes had stared back at her, perched with morsels in their little claws. She had shooed them, but they did not move. She stepped forward and waved her hands 'Shoo!'

Nothing,

'Shoo!' — she threw a bottle of windscreen washer at the floor.

'Please, stop!'

The words manifested in her mind. They were not her own, yet they drew from her own internal voice.

'My god!' she had exclaimed.

'Please, we only wish you to stop. We mean no harm — we found this food and there was no one else to eat it. If you wish to share, then you are welcome.'

She had at first baulked at the idea, but there were a lot of firsts that day, a lot of comprehensions. The first day she learned of the Umbra.

Creta. She met a few who had lived in the petrol station. They had led her to a Nighspyn, who had begrudgingly taken her to a Vulpus named Harithoin, guardian of the ward. Under his authority, were a clan of Acrathax Vulpus. He had explained the Umbra to her, what she was experiencing and that it was extremely rare to meet a Wroth who was also Umbra, that a place called the First City – which she should not confuse with a *Wroth* settlement – had withdrawn it from all, and only returned it once the Wroth were gone.

Lucille had found this very difficult to accept, but having spent an afternoon in the garden of an old manor speaking with a fox, which she now knew as Vulpus, she realised she had either lost her mind, or there was indeed a connective tissue between her and these animals that allowed her to perceive their intention. It was not a far cry from her original hypothesis, that the natural world was not passive.

'Vulpus. In what you called *Wroth tongue*, or one of the many wroth languages, Vulpes Vulpes was the Latin term for Fox. Fascinating. I do wonder if our term for your kind was derived from this sharing of minds, this Umbra. Maybe our terms for you, and visa versa, are more closely related than one could imagine!'

Harithoin had listened politely to her rumination, before asking her if she would be willing to see Naa through the eyes of another, to help clarify her belief. She didn't understand this, until the Creta, Olu, the first who had ever spoken to her, was brought forth.

'I have volunteered to be your eyes. If you will allow it, we shall cover your face, and I will describe Naa to you. I will teach you our ways, how our cultures coexist. How we know the land, what the world is beyond what the Wroth made of it. Do you agree to this?'

At first she had been reluctant, still lost in the bewilderment of her position — a lone survivor of the apocalypse, now able to hold conversations with animals. It was the stuff of bad fantasy fiction. Nevertheless, she had agreed to allow the little Creta to join her on her journey to the stones, where she would engage in the ritual.

Tent erected in the shelter of the rock face, supplies secured in her vehicle, she strode to the top of the tor and sat on the stone where she had once sat before.

The Creta had disappeared into the crevices, gathering together various agile roots, dock leaves, sticks and such, pulling them before her. She then watched this creature begin to construct something. Her eyes tried to follow a hundred tiny tears, fastenings, braids and ties. Periodically, it would run up her arm and march about the circumference of her head, before scurrying back down to make other adjustments. Eventually, it sat beside the contrivance it had made, patiently waiting for Lucille to engage with it.

'It should fit over your eyes, these two long stems are supple enough to be knotted in the back.'

Lucille hesitantly lifted the mask, expecting it to fall apart. It did not — in fact it felt tough, flexible and strong. She laid it over her eyes and found the two long roots interlinked perfectly. She could see nothing but the rich green of the leaves that made up the bulk of it, and they glowed with the little light that filtered through. The vegetable scent of the leaves was heady and earthy and familiar — she had spat on such leaves and rubbed them into nettle stings as a child.

She sat and listened. The warm rustle of the Creta beside her ear was ticklish, but comforting.

'In time you will adorn the crown with your own memories, your own constructions, but for now, please listen.'

Lucille wanted to tell Olu that she had sat here and listened before, that she had felt something here, something of his world. But in her impatience to finally talk about it, she would not be listening. She had agreed to this, and she never went back on a promise.

'Creta have lived in this land for a very long time. Our lives are very short, yet we inherit our history from our forebears, held in our blood and in the Umbra, and also in our mark on the land. So much of who the Creta were became wrapped up in the causes of the Wroth. Not many wish to admit it, but we relied on your kind for shelter and food. You provided dry, warm spaces where a thousand thousand families were forged. This is why I wished to spend this time with you, for there will be many who do not appreciate you, who wish you had died with the rest of the Wroth. I hope I can convey a sense of the Naa that I know. It will serve you well as you ingratiate yourself into Ocquia.'

Lucille nodded and sat patiently. Olu perched upon her shoulder and cleared his throat.

'How we see, is determined by who we are. There is the need to fend for your life, to find food and water, safety and a mate. The Wroth made it so that survival was above all other things, but for us to truly live we must have time to see beyond what is there for survival alone.

'From here I see the wide land, I see the great piles of stone, the water falling in an endless torrent down into the gully. I feel the brisk wind, the rain is lost in the spray from the stream. But there is so much more. I can hear the Toec Woderum digging low in the soil, searching for worms. I hear a young Schev hunting flies over the banks of the water. Beneath us, there is the vibration of endless insects, germinations, the wriggle of roots. There is a procession of Athlon, making their pilgrimage across the plain to a particular spot, where they like to feed. Oreya discussing the festival of Tosk, in which their fawns will be marked with the symbols of adulthood. The Rauka, fresh to this land, have established a new kingdom in the south, and one of their young is hunting lame Oreya who travel to witness this rite of passage. There is magic in the land few understand.

'The wide tendrils of the Bastia travel north in search of lost things, rooting the ground with uncanny vigilance. There are the flocks of Corva Anx, whose erstwhile dogma has been altered by the return of the city, no longer death spells, for now they worship the Umbra, although I feel their ways and means will always be a little peculiar.

'There are shrines to Ora and Seyla in the sparse trees and scrub bush, runes in the bark and upon the rock face. There is so much life in this bleak land, I hope I can share it with you.'

Lucille was lulled by his words, to feel for the almost inaudible, the crush of dead leaves under paw, the wake caused by an Ungdijin's tail. There were sigils of sounds, a complete orchestra, all discernible, none decipherable. All but one. The old mind, below ground.

Hesitantly, she spoke, 'There is something else here. I came here many years ago and felt it. Something alive, something deep down. I wanted to know what it was. I came here so many times to try and find its song again, but to no avail.'

'Describe it to me?' Olu said.

'I heard its dreams; it dreamt of a place, huge walls — a fortress of some sort, and the clatter of bones, the sound of maggots marching through its veins. It dreamt of spreading its many limbs out under the plains, looking for something. Its dreams were in sepulchral loneliness. It wanted to be needed, to be valued, but it was lost entirely.'

Olu had stepped out onto the rock and huddled down against its smooth surface. In time, he began to hum, a single note. It stirred an odd resonance in her.

'Yes. Something here.'

Then he disappeared under the stone, seeking entrance. She had left him to search, removing a small gas burner and a cup, to make a little warming tea. She finished her final sip as he had returned.

'Tea?' She had offered him the lid of her water bottle, filled with some jasmine tea.

'Delicious, and hot! What a delight!' He had drunk eagerly.

'Come,' he said.

They moved down the rock, until an opening appeared. She had never seen this before, hidden from the main path, above a sheer fall. The earth was wet, held in place by tufts of rigid grass.

She stepped gingerly into the mouth of the cave. Olu ran ahead, awaiting her. She lit a torch, keeping her eyes on the tiny mammal at her feet. It was moderately dry, the floor solid gritstone, and descended into a slim fissure that at first made traversing the space difficult, yet after a few feet it widened up.

She came to a shelf overlooking a wide cavern. The floor was a few feet below her and it looked as though water periodically filled and receded from the interior. Collections of loose sticks, rotten vegetation and Wroth detritus sat in neat piles here and there. The ledge was climbable, up and down, and so, with Olu holding on to her plait, she began to inch into the chamber. The earth under her feet was sandy. She strode out into the dome-shaped hollow, breaking a glowstick to provide a little more light.

'What is this place?'

Olu whispered, 'Something is here, maybe the thing you seek. Some of the markings on the wall speak of revenants in the rock, those unwelcoming to any seeking shelter.'

Lucille closed her eyes and listened. Besides the drip of water further on into the cave system, it was very quiet. She sat down, and placed her fingers into the soil.

She felt it immediately.

It was almost disconcerting, a wave of panic moved through her entirety, followed by fragments of differing emotions.

'It's under here.'

With her tools, and step ladders, and multiple halogen lights from a generator trailing wires into the innards of the earth, she began to excavate the cavern. Olu would sit atop the edge of the dig site and sing to her. His nickname, Makepeace, had arisen from a conversation about how they came to know one another in the petrol station, in his tiny voice offering to share his scraps of mouldy pastries with her.

Makepeace was his name from then on, and he remained with her, as she removed layers of silt and earth, carrying buckets of it out to the entrance and tipping it onto the slope below.

A few weeks passed, and in that time she constructed a series of crude ladders to aid in her descent into the pit. She found endless trinkets, skeletal remains, bones of cattle, Roman brooches, soda ring pulls. She fastened these scrags to her hair, to the veil that Makepeace had made her.

In the evenings, she would pull it over her eyes and let him describe the world to her, the significance of Ora, the Sisters of the Flock, his own gods.

Lucille worked out that Makepeace was seven months old, and yet he held a wealth of knowledge inside him. She never questioned the brevity of his life, and had already prepared herself for when he might not rise in the morning to greet her.

Her veil became adorned, as did her clothing. An old shawl wrapped tightly around her head and neck helped to keep her warm under the earth.

She came up to bask in the midday sun and refuel the generator, before re-entering the cave mouth, taking advantage of the handrail she had erected, tearing up old pallets she'd found in a local village.

The excavation continued, and she soon made a fascinating discovery. There were graves, a purposeful burial of two wolves, or what she somehow knew to be called Cini, in the tongue of Ocquia. These Cini were huddled in a circle, beside armour made of bone. There were trinkets — perfectly round stones, splinters of Wroth femur chewed into particular shapes. One skeleton was missing its skull.

She had sat with the other skull clutched in her hands, gently running her fingers over a large intentional hole in its brow. This animal had died from blunt force trauma, and its body had been dragged here and buried with love. She could feel the intention behind the grave, and this powerful act brought her to tears. She placed the skull back where she'd found it, an impulse to not desecrate the tomb any further.

The dugout was now two metres wide and two metres deep when finally she felt what she was looking for. Encased in clay and sediment, a carapace, leathery to the touch, hardened against the ravages of time. Her hand upon it, she felt the vigour of a living thing, and she felt compelled to free it from the earth.

This freeing of the ancient thing in the land consumed her. It had been a blessing, masking all that had befallen her. She was resilient, to a point. There was a darkness to this beautiful view, on the hillside, successions of clotted bruised clouds against a fiery magenta sky. She began her mourning that day, feeling the loss of her beloved, the loss of all, her loneliness eased by Makepeace.

One evening, she filled some litre bottles with water from the waterfall, carrying them up to the Land Rover. In the reflection in the windows she saw herself. She was covered in earth, and her shawl was festooned with toothy jaws, Anglo Saxon bells. Oreya horns arced atop her head like they were her own, knitted into the fabric with resilient strips of sapling. She was becoming something. She was feeling more with every day, every moment, surrounded by the earth, by Makepeace, by the other mammals that came to watch her work.

Many felt the same draw to the cave, that which she felt, and soon her comprehension and acceptance of the world became intimate, it was in her skin, imbedded under her nails, in how these tiny fragments of her own species' endeavour intermingled with those of other animals. She knew she was changing. Perhaps, Lucille thought, she was even healing.

*

Noraa, Bresh and Little Grin had travelled south toward the She-King Carcaris. She did not know who or what a Rauka was, although Bresh did his best to describe them as rather like Morwih, but much bigger, and far more agreeable. This did not help her in garnering a better idea, but Little Grin seemed nervous, so she decided to be as cautious as possible.

Their journey continued on through silent Wroth settlements, rigid skeletons as if posed, toppled at bus stops, fallen from gurneys, abandoned occupied body bags now makeshift homes for rodents. Blocks of flats and office complexes, to her eyes monolith configurations of glass and stone, cracked and heaved with new growth.

It was not long before the uniform road assented to grass, and they found themselves at the base of huge fells, rugged broad swathes of open land, sparsely broken by exposed rock face and huddled trees. It was less sheltered, yet it reminded her of home.

They followed a river that flowed through the centre of the valley, toward more craggy rock faces, and a wide vale, flooded intermittently with warm shafts of light that struggled through the windswept cloud cover.

They hunted the Tril on the flat land, and Ungdijin from the river swollen with them — Noraa providing for both of them as Bresh struggled to learn the art. He improved, patience and stillness not coming naturally to him. Little Grin needed morsels in comparison, and did his best to catch his own food.

They were fortunate that their path led beside this river for many miles, and only when they eventually drifted from its course did they laden a few catches upon Bresh's armour. Fashioned of pots and pans, it made the perfect receptacle.

Four turns passed and Bresh became excitable. He could smell a particular scent, one that both Little Grin and Noraa noticed yet could not place. It was familiar, yet at the same time, carried with it an ominous note. It was earthy, musty, warm and acrid. It spoke of something large and carnivorous.

The day became far more clement as they approached a gully, exposed crystalline outcrops, softened with lush green grass and healthy trees. Ambling paths and drystone walls crumbled into clumps of keen shoots. The ravine provided a great deal of shelter from the wind, eventually culminating in a woodland path. The trees were dense, deciduous growth, pockmarked by rusting metal. They continued on, the sound of feathered amongst the trees was calming. Eventually, the forest came to an abrupt halt.

They were standing at the precipice of a tremendous crater, seemingly Wroth-made, but dug long ago, its pale exposed stone bright and warm in the midday sun. There were gigantic, regular steps cut into the rock. What may have once been a passage for the tools of their industry was marked with peculiar piles of rocks, colourful motifs, sapling tree growth, grottos cut into the cliff face, and steep pathways. The epicentre held a deep freshwater lake filled with lily pads and thick rushes. Swarms of dragonflies hovered daintily about bright flower blossoms.

'The Wroth understood how to make in stone, they made their own shelters from it, clawed it from the guts of Naa,' Noraa said as they walked towards a collection of structures that perched on the edge of the chasm.

Collapsed corrugated sheds hid the wreckage of stationary machines, corroded conveyors, and piles of aggregate now miniature hills. The shadows of former Wroth activity cast fleeting cries. Noraa noticed a little sadness in Bresh, who perhaps lived in hope of resuming his former life beside his Wroth master.

There was that presence again, the faint musky chord of the living. It was apparent they were being watched.

They walked beside the quarry, finally reaching a road that descended within. At the threshold, piles of stone and discovered bone, silver barked branches stripped of leaves and held up like teeth jutting inelegantly from the ground. Deliberately bent trees, intertwined with spurs of metal, arched over them. Either side of these were large sandstone slabs, cut crudely into effigies of various creatures.

'Do you have an appointment?'

The low rumbling voice drifted melodically toward them. It was soft, yet Noraa knew it had come from lungs far larger than hers. She looked upwards to find the source, which was lain upon the sculpture, nonchalant, yet acutely aware of them.

His fur was a ruddy orange – a pale yellow to Noraa's eyes – interspersed with striking black stripes. His muzzle was ringed by white fur, a set of impressive canines shone yellow and slick. He was a powerful, muscular animal, his flanks marked with chalk in huge slashes that went against the grain of his hide. His armour was bone held together by cartilage and withered sinew. The dappled silhouette of leaves and light masked him perfectly.

Noraa braced herself. 'We do not. However, we have grave news for your kin. You must forgive me —I know very little of this land and its etiquette.'

The giant feline leapt gracefully before them, a plume of dust an accent to its sheer weight.

'I am Vign, of Clan Cuspid. You are safe here, we adhere to the doctrine of Dron. We only feed when we must and we follow the creed honourably. We expect the same from all who come here. If you would like to follow me, I will escort you to our monarch.' He slunk forward with muscular sway, his striped tail whipping behind.

Noraa was far beyond any sense of comfort. Bresh, seemingly unaffected by the great Rauka, his attention fell on a fly that had been drawn to the same heady scent of the beast before them. He swatted it futilely with his paws.

'I know this old mutt, but where are you travelling from?' Vign purred.

Bresh grinned at being recognised, 'I have parleyed with the Rauka clans for many turns!'

Noraa interjected, 'I have come from far north, at first fleeing the danger I speak of, yet finding help in TumHilliad and his infantry. Little Grin has also escaped a similar fate to mine. We are seeking guidance and wish to share our knowledge of this threat.'

Little Grin ran ahead to walk beside Vign. 'Have you heard anything of the Husk?'

The Rauka shook his head, 'No, I do not know of what you speak; however, we are rather hidden here. Deliberately so. A lifetime of servitude under the Wroth has taught us to be wary. We are a clan of many kinds, a family of sorts, our bodies may be similar but our habits are not.

'It was under the tutelage of the Vulpus and the Tempered Guild that we learned how to survive here, how our presence might be a help, not a hindrance. These fells are rich with herds of many clades, yet their feeding was held in check by the Wroth. Our presence has returned rivers to their former glory, allowed forests to regrow that would have been stripped of saplings. It was the Speaker Flocks of Cheon who spied this cut in the land, which we now call the Pridebrow.' He gestured to the quarry.

Little Grin was drawn to the effigies in the rock, simple carvings of recognisable forms, some a hundred times his size.

'Did the Rauka make these?'

'Ah, no! Erithacus told us that the Wroth made them. This was once a mine; they cut the rock to lay in hard angles upon the soil, as if in defiance of nature's thoughtful curve. Some went against this though, some were artists. When the quarry outlived its usefulness, those who still saw beauty in the stone came here, made of it a reliquary. This stone is soft, and it relents to our claws. You will find a few amongst our clan that mimic and maybe improve on these carvings themselves.'

Eventually, they reached the bottom of the pit. Fallen trees had been dragged from the forest above and placed in pyramid formations, the spire of each splaying out in jagged repose. Large boulders broke the surface of the lake creating stepping stones from one bank to the other. On the far side were abandoned mine shafts, some eroded to form a natural amphitheatre, where a myriad of Rauka lounged in the midday sun. Two stocky black felines, resplendent in bloodstained bone armour, flanked the walkway. Vign approached them, 'I have a party from the north who wish to speak with the Court of Carcar.'

Their fur was almost iridescent, exposing the faintest presence of patterns amidst the black. They silently ushered the quartet across the stone bridge, Vign ahead of them.

Noraa held her head low, acutely aware of the almost thirty formidable carnivores before her — most notably an enigmatic female atop her crescent outcropping, three younger felines beside her.

There were engravings upon the walls, further filigrees cut in decoration and veneration for their queen. Her crown was dissimilar to that of her courtiers' head ornamentation. It bore the mark of Muroi and Vulpus craft, as did her family's armour.

Vign approached her and spoke. 'I present to you Noraa and Little Grin of the Northern realms, and our friend Bresh of the Roughclod Infantry. They bring grave tidings, I am afraid.'

She nodded her formidable head and turned her attention to them, blinking into the light, 'You are welcome here, and it is good to see you again, Bresh.'

She boomed, 'I am the She-King Carcaris, and this is my daughter, Esit, and my sons, Prauva and Maro. We offer you welcome in the Pridebrow. You will find shelter here, and food if you need it. The lake is full of Ungdijin, and if my sisters will it, we shall hunt this evening. Now, tell me of your ills.'

Little Grin nodded to Noraa to speak for them.

'Thank you for agreeing to see us. There is a sickness, it is consuming all who encounter it. It began with my mate, Emeris, and spread to my entire pack. It is a Gasp thing, riven with the dead.

'I do not know its cause, or wishes, but it consumes, kills those it has no use for and infests others it then adds to its army. All clades and clans will fall victim to it. They call themselves the Husk. I come in hope you might help us, or have the knowledge to defeat such a threat. I am new to these lands, brought here by the Wroth before their death.'

Carcaris rose upright, a look of concern upon her face. She leapt before Noraa.

'We have not had word from Awfwod Garoo of the Windsweepers in a while, though they fly this path every few turns. We assumed foul weather might have altered their course.'

Little Grin stepped forward, 'She-King Carcaris, I saw Awfwod recently. I brought my news of the Husk to their post in the north. He and his squadron have flown south to alert Dron and the Quorum of Ocquia.'

Carcaris pondered this news. 'Is there any protection against this plague?'

Noraa shook her head, 'It is not a sickness of flesh and bone. It is Gaspstuff, rot craft, I do not understand how they have managed such a feat, but I know someone who does.'

Carcaris exclaimed, 'Then you must bring this someone to us, they must teach us! I can send a scout to bring them. Where in the land do they live?'

Noraa frowned. 'That's a difficult question, they don't exactly *live* anywhere.'

*

'She is awake!' Rune flapped above her as Ivy lifted herself and balanced against the fungus stalks. She wiped herself down and rubbed her eyes, gaining a little focus.

'What happened?' Vorsa sat beside her patiently.

'I saw … I saw the city, a long time ago. There were lots of animals traveling to it. It was a place where they all met. They wanted Dron to stay, but it could not, so it left a part of itself here, for protection.'

'I had a very similar experience, the city likes to explain itself this way, to share with you how and why,' Rune replied.

'Heralds! Sentinels of the First City!' Audagard exclaimed.

'Yes, they were left in the land and hid from the Wroth. When they…when *we* finally turned against the Umbra. But these Sentinels are still here, and they woke when the Umbra returned to all. But their connection with Dron has withered away. What we did, by removing the old scabs and exposing the raw wood to the hyphae - those connections with the Sentinels are now growing again, and they will reestablish that link. There is something else too, something that has risen with them, it has its own intentions. Not evil, but different.'

'Different how?'

'Old, older than the city,' she replied.

'If the Sentinels are the city's defence, we must find them, we must bring them here. It's our only chance against this threat!' Audagard fussed and flustered.

'But how would we find where they are?' Erithacus asked.

Rune landed upon Ivy's shoulder. She looked to him and nodded. He said, 'We can see them. Their light is bright, we don't know exactly where, but the closer we get to them, the clearer it will be. One of us must stay with the city, we each can see the other and their movements. It will give us at least an idea of how we are faring.'

Ivy looked to Rune, saying, 'I will go. It will be a long journey, but whatever the enemy is, they travel by foot too. Are there others we can ask for help?'

Vorsa pondered, 'Yes. Our journey will take us north, back to where we found you. We shall call upon the High Realm, send word to the Rauka clans in the Pridebrow.

'Erithacus, if you would be so kind as to instruct the Speakers to call on all in Ocquia who might assist us — Orn Megol, The Drove, Concilium of Oevidd, The Ungulate and Athlon. Yaran will bring the Clusk, and any who wish to join her. There will be others, and we shall parley with them all. We didn't live through the Wroth only to die by another's paw.'

Ivy had a thought, 'Speaking of the Athlon, how likely is it that we could convince them to ….'

Vorsa gave a wry smile, 'Carry us? Not a chance. They have very strong feelings on such things, as you well know, but I am not past trying.'

'It's either that or we walk. Or we could even try and find a working car. That would get us there much quicker.'

'A ... car?'

Erithacus chuckled, 'A *scithar*, my dear friend. The vehicle of so many deaths.'

Vorsa frowned, 'The metal beasts? Inside such a thing? A circumstance I had never considered. I am getting old, but I am not beyond adventure!'

'So be it!' Audagard chimed in impatiently, 'Much to do. I will go to the Regulax and instruct those at the Bastia. I will send out squadrons of Baldaboa to those kingdoms hard to reach, and I imagine the Speakers will cover the Wroth settlements and gather the clades that dwell there. Ivy. Thank you for helping us. I had not met a Wroth before, let alone trusted one. I am glad to have met you.'

Vorsa snarled, 'Of course you're glad! Without tricking her you wouldn't have got your way!'

Audagard reeled, 'Now, Vorsa! I only wish the best—'

'Ah, the best, is it? Well. We shall see, old beak.'

Erithacus sighed and cajoled the Dominus away from Vorsa, 'Good luck, Ivy, and to you, Corpse Speaker. We will speak more upon your return.' He nodded politely and escorted the exasperated Audagard back to the Regulax.

*

Vorsa, Rune and Ivy descended the tunnels and pathways that led back to the Hall of Receiving. In the golden light that fell from the shaft above, Ivy could sense disquiet, a knot of distress in the tenor of the cathedral chamber. A squall of particles hung in the air above the fossilised remains of the Sisters.

She broke away from the group and skipped over to the stone. 'We will go find the Sentinels and bring them back to the city, I promise.'

Strands of Umbra-glimmer hung like a child's mobile, flecks of shell flexed in pearlescent rotations, shoots emerging and unfolding with origami precision, each crumb a reference point in a grand face, the face of Lendel. It held so much sorrow.

'Our city must live for them to be remembered.'

Each fragment gently settled on the stone, every piece an offering from a pilgrim.

'We will do all we can.'

Beyond the walls of Dron, the sun was setting. Yaran chewed on some sea grass and was happy to see them once again. She agreed to travel back to the Stinking City with them, where she would gather up her herd.

They walked across the sand dunes until they reached the village and there they rested for the night in a former surf equipment shop, Yaran on a pile of wet suits and Ivy and Vorsa on a sofa in the office upstairs. It smelt damp but was mostly dry.

When Ora rose, they began their trek back up the coastal road toward the Downs. Ivy collected a few cans of food from the kiosks and stores in the little village for the journey. Water wasn't always a problem, but seeking fresh sources had become more difficult. She refilled her water bottle from a stream that fell from the cliff face.

Signposts remained upright as they reached a main road. Ivy knew there was a relatively straight route to the Stinking City, and explained the signs to Vorsa, who was very patient with Ivy's descriptions of the world she had known. So much of Vorsa's world had been the Wroth, yet almost all of it had been alien to her.

One turn became two, and with it a rainstorm. They were tired and hungry, and although Ivy's injury was all but healed, it often felt a little sore. They huddled under a bus shelter as Yaran played in puddles, deftly stripping trees of leaves with her trunk. Yaran would sing to herself a lot, and trumpet loudly with excitement. Despite her size, she was an agile animal, twirling as she stomped in the rain.

Vorsa sat beside Ivy on the bench, hunched to retain heat. For a moment, Ivy thought to offer the Vulpus shelter under her coat. It was with that idea that she turned her attention to the animal beside her. She studied her armour, thick plates of bone and bark, bound seamlessly together with intricately knitted lengths of cordage and hardened sap. They moved as she moved, pliable and intuitive. Pieces of broken mirrored glass stood upright, held in place by a thick black resin, which would make it impossible for Ivy to offer shelter without harming herself. There were little pictograms etched into the panoply — claw marks, indentations, jagged and intentional, beside those lain down by violence.

Upon Vorsa's brow and snout and forelimb were long healed scars, darker furrows of fur, boundaries of hairless skin. It was in these moments that Ivy couldn't quite believe the world in which she now lived. The armour was old, there was dirt and dandruff and tufts of shed fur in-between the panels of the armour. There were darker patches of blood soaked in which spoke of battle, playful yet decidedly crude fretwork in a soft metal that adorned the edges, tarnished with years of use. Ivy could smell Vorsa, it was a familiar earthy warmth, like her aunt's dog, Chester. She smelled of home.

For a moment, an odd sensation moved through her, something like the moment when you realise you're dreaming and strain to free yourself from it. That memory, in her kitchen at home, the scent of her mother's perfume, and that dog — that very certain, very real sense of normality.

She shivered. She turned her attention back to Vorsa, a powerful female Vulpus, someone with a definite sense of self, stubbornness, a determined spirit. She dwelt on what she had seen, what was now her life — the First City that they called Dron, the animals whose cultures were as defined and precious as any Wroth belief. But this sensation was not novel, she had cried every night for weeks after her family passed, after they were lost to her. Now she choked it all down, all the gobbets of sadness and self-loathing, that grave and empty hollow that craved attention — she would not give it a moment to take hold, because it might never let her go.

Yet, there were ideas she had learned that now blurred that explicit end, that full stop on life. She had seen the dead in motion, had seen their benevolent intent. What answers might Vorsa have for her? What had they called her? A corpse talker?

'What is a corpse talker?' Ivy asked as she chewed on a snack bar, pulling the hood of her Parka jacket closer to her face.

Vorsa broke from her reverie, deep in thought. 'Corpse Speaker. I am a twin, my brother is called Petulan. We grew up knowing each other's minds — we shared dreams, predictions. We both saw a time when he would no longer be in Naa, yet his presence would remain. He died soon after.

'The Corva Anx have a litany of rituals and invocations, spells to conjure unseen things. One such mantra allows the deceased sibling of a twin to share their living body. I trained under Audagard, and together we coaxed Petulan out of the Gasp. If he wishes, he will join us and you shall meet him. He is our avatar beyond life, and busies himself with the dead. Whatever this adversary is, Petulan will have a role in defeating it.'

'Is he scary?'

'Petulan? To some he is a totem of death, a thing to fear. It is true that his form can be a little ... cadaverous. I only see my brother. But you are a Shadow Starer, so perhaps you will soon see beyond his lifelessness, and know how wise and good he is. Yaran!'

The Oraclas abruptly stopped her singing and plodded toward Vorsa.

'We will leave now. The rain is subsiding and we must make good progress this day and make the Stinking City by tomorrow nightfall. You will go to your mother and ask her to gather the Moving Stone herds. Escort her to the Bastia and await instructions. Ivy and I will continue on to the High Realm and parley with the Hanno. Is this agreeable?'

The Pachiderm nodded. 'It will be done!'

In the late afternoon of the following day, they passed over the remnants of a bridge whose ornate towers remained standing yet groaned under the weight of foliage. Through quiet streets and wide thoroughfares they traversed, until they reached the vast parklands within which Yaran lived. At the entrance, a pair of wrought iron gates, gilt obelisks that spoke of queens and kings and their gift to the people. Yaran turned to Ivy with a frown and a smile, and an inkling of sadness.

'Thank you, Yaran, for carrying me, for allowing me to rest my leg. You are a brave and strong Oraclas, your mother must be very proud.'

Yaran trumpeted, 'Wrothcub! What a turn of events. I hope to see you again soon so we might conclude this journey. I have many more stories to share, and my herd will be intrigued to hear my tale of our exploits!'

Vorsa smiled up at Yaran, 'Ora bring peace, Yaran Moving Stone. We will return as soon as possible; bring all your peoples, and your allies. We have much to lose.' And so, before Ora set that day, they made their farewells, and parted ways.

*

Vorsa continued to defy her nocturnal habits and slept at night, hauled up in a once expensive, now dishevelled, apartment overlooking the river. Ivy lay on a huge bed, feeling overtired and restless. Sleep had become resistant to her need, for she could feel an anxiety in Vorsa which worried her. She closed her eyes, listening to the gentle breathing of the Vulpus at the foot of the bed, and eventually she drifted into sleep.

A pale light woke her. She raised her head to peer over the edge of her pillow. At the end of the bed sat Vorsa, facing toward the windows, little more than a silhouette caught in the light of Seyla, and yet the light was not moon cast — girdled around her was a coil of translucence. It was difficult to focus upon; the more she looked the less she could see — it overlaid her eyes as though it existed outside of her perception. The veil of light extended above Vorsa into an aqueous halo, at its centre the skull of an animal sheathed in fugitive pieces of matter, like a snake shedding its skin. Vorsa, whose mouth moved slowly, emitted a low murmur, seemed to be in conversation with this presence. It terrified and fascinated Ivy.

Both Vorsa and the skull turned to her.

'Ah! The wrothcub has awoken!'

It released a whisper hiss of glee, darting toward her in a flurry of enthusiasm. It halted inches from her face, specks of itself hung in gyrating rhythm, its skeletal grin was absurd, almost comical, yet the more she looked, the more she began to see — a face, the patina of fur, the hollow eye sockets suddenly appeared to have eyes, cold blue irises. It was a Vulpus.

'Petulan?'

She could feel the Umbra at work here, that same fluidity of movement as in the rhizomes and roots of the city, the same sharing of nutrients – energy – this was mirrored in his form, albeit not a physical one. There were faint entanglements, laces of photons that peeled from him into nothing, and she traced their course into quavering spheres too small or far removed from her to ever understand them. She could see his former living body like an afterthought, it frothed around the withered, articulated bones within, an animated X-ray, becoming more focused every moment. He danced and jigged with jester excitement, for she had accepted him.

'Yes, my dear, I am he! My sister has spoken fondly of me I hope? I am a fragile soul, so be kind!'

'Brother, don't scare the girl,' Vorsa raised a paw to calm him. He settled, his legs hanging below his body, cantering on the spot.

'I ... I'm not scared,' Ivy said apprehensively.

'My brother has come to tell us what he has learned of our foe.' Petulan bowed his head to Ivy.

'I have seen him! From a distance I might add. I dare not get close, but he is an Umbra, in the old parlance, a Shadow Starer, a very unique one indeed.'

'What makes him so unique?' Ivy asked.

'Ah! Well, a revenant in the Gasp that wishes to return to Naa is called a *certainty*; a spirit with enough determination and willpower to seek an answer amongst the living will draw upon the Umbra and free itself. Most gravitate to the city and live within its walls. In some rare cases a revenant will be free of any tether, and drift hither and thither in Naa. This is all hunky-dory — yet for a living thing to step into the Gasp is no mean feat. Vorsa herself knows this well, to put a limb within the gyre of grey is a painful and risky choice. However, this Shadow Starer does it with relish — he seems able to move between Naa and the Gasp effortlessly. In the Gasp, he is besieged by the dead, but they revere him, perhaps even worship.'

'Why?'

'That is the wrong question, the correct question is *who* flocks to him.'

'Who?'

'Why, the Wroth of course.'

'So he is Wroth, like me?'

'I cannot see his form. To me they are all soot motes, black complications, tortured faces. But for him to have such a bond with one particular Seethe, is very peculiar.'

'Seethe?' Ivy asked.

'Ah yes. In the Gasp, revenants exert a magnetism on one another, they form into columns of themselves, clustered tides of feelings, thoughts, needs and wants. Many lose any sense of self entirely. We call them a Seethe. These tides might form new consciousnesses, new imaginings. In a billion turns they will coalesce into aspects of the Umbra, their energy finding new purpose. Some refuse this, and separate, rogue collections of angry thoughts. Or, like the Wroth, they are shunned, spat out, refused. Not all, mind. Some Wroth mean well and join their animal brethren. But these Wroth, now — these Wroth want only for revenge.'

Ivy shuffled to the end of the bed, beside Vorsa and her brother. They looked out over the water, at the apartments on the other side of the river. From this perspective, little of the destruction was visible, beyond the signs of neglect and plant growth.

'I do not understand their anger, but then I still have a body. I survived. Maybe they are angry at me? For living?'

Vorsa sighed, 'Perhaps they are angry because they can see the world is better off without them. Or maybe they are jealous of the living. That is not a feeling unique to the Wroth!'

Petulan whirled before her, 'Whatever the reason, this creature has ill intent. I come to tell you his sojourns into the Gasp have become more frequent, and the Seethe that is drawn to him is diminished.'

"Diminished?'

'Scores of revenants have left the Gasp.'

*

His power grew. Each crossing brought with it encounters with those who had died at that very moment; their residue, that viscous enigma, the waxen phlegm of living flowing out of Naa and into the Gasp, where it would reconstitute as an echo of its former life. His skill lay in the harvesting of this energy, to draw on it. Whatever was left after his feeding would manifest, withered and incomplete, and evaporate into entropy. He felt nothing for their fleeting cries, their second death. This boon allowed his physical intelligence to expand so that he might hold Naa and the Gasp in the same vision, plucking the Wroth revenants and forcing them into luckless living bodies.

From the castle, they began spreading south. He marvelled at how easily everything bent to his will — how, in a short breath, his minions strip-mined the woodlands, fallow fields, hamlets and villages of the living animals, thrown before him in quick succession, a conveyor of adorcism, to annex the cerebral will of fear-stricken creatures, to proffer up a body for the willing dead. Thoth wished to master all living things, and if he couldn't bring a creature to bear he would snuff it out. The filthy slur of blood and earth before the keep was his chosen aesthetic, the marl of war.

Mannequins were dragged between the slathering jaws of his Cini soldiers from store fronts and across miles of land to stand in the mud. Vagabond likenesses of Wroth, crudely strung up to slake his desire for a particular vision - that those who had shunned him, those cowards and back stabbers who had driven him out, were wallowing before him, peering up at him on his battlements, king of his castle.

Yet this served a greater purpose beyond his vanity. This was a blasphemy to all living creatures in Naa. The turned earth, this unnatural tilling spoke of Wroth machination, and these Wroth effigies in the land were scarecrows, a warning, a marker. To say, *we are still here.*

*

Scab stood below the tower, looking up at his leader. He followed his line of sight out to the field. He wasn't convinced of the reasoning behind this display, opposing the use of resources for such pointless exercises. He wondered privately if Thoth was mad or just lonely, longing for company.

Scab also entertained a greater idea that his master was showing weakness in these performances. That the taking of the land did not require such theatrics. If *he* was in charge, he would be a show of force, not making bogeymen out of them. But he felt a profound loyalty, something he had not recognised in himself before. He wanted Thoth to see him, to admire him.

You should be in charge

No, that is not my route. Scab chewed at his flanks. The wound he had created was infected. He did not feel the pain of the infection, the consciousness within had the pleasure of that, but he wished he could. He would bathe it and clean it and care for it, but it was nothing more than an itch. So he dug his teeth into it, and drew fresh blood, and felt for just a moment.

A thought manifested with the pain, like a gift for his effort. His mind, along with his body was often quiet, thoughtless, a vacuous cave that offered no reflection. The pain was like a dam breaking — he was flooded with thoughts and emotions, many of which he no longer recognised.

He will betray you

The words were bright and true. He hadn't considered this before. Would he? No, he may have a peculiar way of achieving his goals, but the world he wanted for them was one where the Wroth were on top. He wouldn't betray us, he needed them.

But you've seen how he looks at all of you, he despises you. To him you are a tool to gain the upper hand. Once he gets what he wants he'll kill you all. He may be a nonce but he's stronger than you. There is an endless supply of willing soldiers in the Gasp, waiting to be plucked and brought forth.

So I have to show my worth? Perhaps if I can show initiative he'll keep me around.

Keep me around ...

... long enough for you to kill him and get all the glory

Kill him? No! I haven't considered killing him before. He dragged me from that hellhole. I owe him a debt.

You have —

I want to kill everyone. It's a habit. Doesn't mean I don't respect him. He can put the spirits of the dead in the living!

Or take them out

Take them out? Why would he take them out?

You could kill him, or you could pluck his soul from that Cini. Without that huge animal he's nothing. You would be lord. You could take that body. His soldiers would be none the wiser. You will learn his skill and rise in his opinion of you. When he least expects it, you will turn on him.

No! I don't want that! And in any case, I can't do what he does!

I'll show you how

In this way, Scab began to have long conversations with himself. In these quiet moments, skulking the tumbled walls on the far side of the castle, he looked for insects — his inner voice had taught him how to feel the Gasp. *Take a life*, it said, *and watch for its revenant.*

He had turned a stone to find a beetle, and with his paw he crushed it. Sure enough there was a distortion, a red ribbon of something that rose like carbon wisps in a fire. He bit at the air, chasing it as it lifted. Above him, his eyes caught the light of distant stars, yet they were obscured — he tracked the course of the soul as it flickered, coalescing with some abstract film, as though he could see another place overlapping the heavens.

You are seeing the Gasp. Now, hold the phantom of it, aim your focus on it alone and follow its course.

His first attempts were fleeting. His fear was very real — after all, he had died once before. He cringed at the memory of it. In a prison cell, with a knife made of some sharpened plastic plunged into his abdomen. Killed for little more than a show of strength by his cell mate. He had bled out on the piss-splashed floor, the scent of unwashed clothes, sweat and fear. He had felt himself lift into a haze, a lightheadedness that crept through every inch of him, out from the wound in his side. It was a lightness that wrapped him up, so that he no longer cared.

He never passed out, he never lost consciousness, he simply moved away from his body, cosseted in the albumen between living and death. For a moment he was glad of it. Life had been cruel and disappointing. Those he hurt were little more than an irritation to him, and he knew that it was probably guilt, yet he dared not think on it too long. Then he died, and his essence clarified beyond, amongst the ceaseless futility of the Lacking Sea, where any feeling was absent. The cold of death was like no other, for you could not escape it, you could only endure it.

Choosing to re-enter that place was so antithetical that it became a hindrance to harnessing the necessary skill. Yet his inner voice would not let him fail. He was driven by it, by this incessant encouragement.

Each creature crushed, each revenant released, he inhaled their suppuration, glimpsing those black vaults and... fled, turning away at the last minute.

You can, you must. I insist.

And so, eventually, he emerged in the Gasp.

It was not like before.

There was pain, a wrenching agony, his limbs dragged by forces that knew what he was, the violation, the living flesh and the stolen body — the infesting ghoul. Yet he steadied himself, and in this, he found his strength. Immediately, the Seethe of Wroth dead sank low in the bitter firmament, and with frigid hands they pawed him, seeking entrance back into Naa.

Below him, he could see the lights of living things, glorious oranges and yellows and deep red. He sought one particular light, that of Thoth. He did not dare take him now, for he could not be certain of his abilities, and so he let his eye drift back towards the lands beyond the castle, far from those already taken.

There! A lone Muroi, low in the grass. He courted a single Wroth revenant, and pulled him out of the Gasp. Then the tinnitus shock, ear-rendering muteness, eyes streaming, corpuscles exploding, and suddenly his body flung back to reality.

Scab lay awake, his chest rising and falling, aware of the pain in his wound. When he'd regained composure he rose on his haunches. Beside him, the Muroi, spasming corkscrews of ectoplasm lifting from him.

'You live?' Scab nudged the rodent.

'I…I do. I live.'

The Muroi rolled onto its side and lifted its head. 'What am I?' It looked down at its body, at its diminutive size.

'You're a rat. What they call Muroi in this world gone mad. It'll all come to you, like it or not. Those who live, know.'

'A fucking rat?'

'You get what you're given, son. Now, you will come with me. You're my bargaining chip with the governor.'

*

The courtyard of the castle was little more than an abattoir, slick with ichor and throngs of fat, black flies. With devilish gluttony, makeshift packs of Husk Cini and Vulpus chewed on gristle and licked marrow from the bones of slain Aurma.

More disturbing, even to Scab, was the gaunt façade of Athlon, Inni and Oreya, fur stained with black blood and foul smelling mud, shards of metal and barbed wire twisted about their horns and manes like hellish cheval de frise. They fed on carrion too, their bodies similarly buckled to serve a new condition.

Eruptions of squabbles that led to violence peppered the yard. Thoth's army grew each day as more were brought under his heel. These animals were becoming something ever more aberrant, a perversion of flesh.

Similarly perplexing, Scab found Thoth atop a low inner wall adorned in his filthy tunic, barking orders to his underlings while stood on his hind legs. He was now very much adept at this absurd stance. For Scab, it was both humorous and grotesque, a certain wrongness to it. Thoth no longer faltered as he walked, as though he wore stilts, an anatomical oddity.

Thoth fell again to all fours as Scab lowered his head in subservience. Recognised as a lieutenant to Thoth, those most sycophantic to his cause parted to allow the Cini and his Muroi companion through the crowd.

Scab cleared his throat. 'I took a page out of your book, didn't I? Decided I'd show some initiative. Took myself round the back and taught myself how to dip my toes in the Gasp.'

Thoth grimaced. He swallowed the bile that rose in his gullet. It was a fury only betrayed by his silence.

Scab had not considered the eventuality that his act might be considered seditious. Yet he quelled any thoughts, urging the Muroi forward.

It spoke, 'I am told I have you to thank for this second chance?'

Thoth shuddered. He remained passive, unmoving.

'This is fine work, Scab, fine work indeed. You can add necromancy to your list of accolades, for my plan was to teach you all to usher the dead into Naa. You deserve high praise.'

Thoth relaxed and moved toward the Muroi. 'Welcome friend, a paltry body perhaps, but you are among the living once again.'

Thoth raised his paw and signalled for the animal to be escorted away.

'Scab,' Thoth hissed, 'come.'

Scab awaited his admonishment, which never arrived.

'I see I have underestimated you. I need loyalty, yes, but I also need ambition. As long as you understand who is in charge, we are good. I want you to gather a group of Husk and go south ahead of us. Take any you find, convert them to our cause if you will. Find the places of value, the places that the wretches of Ocquia covet. Leave our mark — fear is our greatest weapon. We will follow in the coming weeks, flowing like blood across this wide and verdant realm. Savvy?'

'Savvy sir, it will be done.'

Thoth retired to the crypt below the castle; left alone in the dark, lit by the wreathe of his own ghoulish gasp-light, he shook with malignant hatred. He staggered around on hind limbs, woozy with the indignity. *How easy*, he thought, how easy this little shit had mastered the skill that he had honed, had made it his own. Had Thoth been so arrogant to assume he would be alone in this ability? Was it wise to keep Scab alive? Had it crossed his mind to teach others the act? It was the impudence, to think he could do it *without* Thoth.

It was then that he hit upon an idea. In his first acts of possession it had been him alone who had pulled the revenants forth, spilling them out like carcinogens.

A particularly crooked Husk answered his call. A large Vulpus – emaciated, ravaged with mange – skulked before him, sniffing the earth in search of food. Its armour was fastened to its haunches with slithers of glass plunged into skin that oozed with pus. He was feverish with sepsis, held at bay by the revenant already within him.

'Your name?'

'I were Keith, the boys call me Wrong'en. You got any meat?' He jittered, like an addict in withdrawal.

'No, I don't have any meat. I do, however, want to try something, help you deal with those shakes a little. Are you willing?'

The Vulpus eyed him with caution, 'Go on then.'

Thoth summoned the Gasp. His perception piqued, the drone of blue bottles, rending of flesh, seizure curl of larvae in decaying flesh — stomach-turning odour of sour blood, curdling above him, seeping into the culverts that drained into the mausoleum. The din of death, the void rattle he knew all too well.

He waded out into the swampy quag of the Lacking Sea. As if on command, the Wroth were upon him, and he spared no time in snagging himself to as many as he could manage, and with a quick and painful yank, dragged them with him into Naa and plunged all of them into the shuddering bewildered Wrong'en.

The sound was hideous. A snapping wet agony, dissolving into whimpering.

Thoth turned his eyes away.

The whimper became a slow clicking groan.

The groan, a low humourless laugh. Then a laugh of a dozen voices.

Thoth returned his gaze. The Vulpus shuddered, yet this was no alcoholic's tremor. Its face was in flux; myriad eyes populated the animal's countenance, glossy orbs of arachnid malevolence.

The laugh expanded to fill the tomb, a dissonant organ, a piping migrainous refrain.

Thoth rose once again, towering above the bedevilled creature. With vision adjusted to such qualities, he could see the ghoul matter leaching from its muscles, sporous clouds of it expelled as it walked.

'How do you feel?'

'*You*? Ah, but there is no mere *me*. We are good. We are many.'

Thoth laughed, how very biblical. He stalked like a lycanthrope out of his shadowed recesses before his fermenting army, who had gathered before him. Damp with scarlet grume and gore, under the tin grey of a rain strewn day, he raised his paws, stretching them out against the tension in his muscles, separating each toe until the ligament quivered with strain. He eased his head back into the soup of the Gasp, and swallowed whole the Seethe of the Wroth, the squall of ignoble rogues, the turbulent dead.

The dam failed, and with it, Thoth became a conduit; a torrent of ethereal sewage found its course — through the pineal corridor, the gelatinous photoreceptor, calcified with age, shattered now and made a conductive path, a hole in his brain from which foul cadavers now crawled.

He ushered in the deluge before the shocked congregation, which recognised these slurs of slurry pouring forth and into their stolen bodies. For a moment, privy to the pain they had inflicted, they were soon lost in a hundred voices, and a hundred screaming intelligences, little more than septic receptacles.

'Dominion!' Thoth howled. 'You are now livid with infections, you are plague bearers, lich folk. You will be divided into parties. The core of you will march with me south, the rest will be dispersed amongst the land. You will establish military camps, fortresses like this, where you will await our victory once we take the strength from these wretched creatures. Then, one by one, we will topple their seats of power. None are safe, take what you need to eat, and riven the rest with my virulent word. Savvy?'

A guttural roar arose. He now held sway over the living and the dead.

*

Oh, for the love of Dron. The chattering, the endless babble, he was conscious of every prayer, every invocation — and ignored most. He never considered himself vain or self-centred, the very nature of him was an accumulation, and yet, if they asked more than a beakful of times, he would go to them, in the bottom corner of a landmass he used to shun.

This was a place where the Wroth had fed from him readily. A coastline that some of his ancient black anatomy feared, and others struggled to recognise, having lived when Embrian Naa had been connected to another continent, millions of cycles of Ora before, when the Gruor Tak Rorn were gigantic lumbering beasts, not the little nimble feathered that screeched and squawked at him today.

He oozed through the calcified wet corridor of a failed attempt to reconnect those two estranged land masses, a bore hole below the seabed. He cared little that they had eventually succeeded, many turns later, for all Wroth successes were much like their pitiful tunnel, a muddy dead end.

Above him, a shaft. Like a coiled spring he rose in spiral, pulling more of himself from the earth, an unpleasant slurping that he hoped went unheard. He gathered himself in an ugly concrete mouth, by a rotten door festooned with warning signs, evidence of this engineering folly.

Before him, a congregation. A hundred Black Feathered, his loyal disciples, whose vigil in this hole and the hope of his arrival consumed them. He felt a physical inhalation from them, dressed in carcasses, the markings and accoutrements of the pious.

The Stiiven Dire Blight, jealous of their god, shared little with their brethren, the other corvan denominations. They wanted him all to themselves — and yet, he could hear her, the outsider, standing on the periphery, hidden from the gaze of his flock.

He wanted to know her.

*

Chapter Six

As the day drew to a close, the Pridebrow took on a very different timbre. Seyla was clear above, only partially obscured by cloud. Dozens of large predatory felines had appeared, some having slept in the mine shafts with their cubs, others returning from hunts, dragging Oreya carcasses with them. As more had arrived carrying news of the Husk the She-King had forgone her own hunt.

Three lithe Zev, their flaxen fur dotted with bold black chevron markings now stood before Carcaris and Noraa.

'We hunted Tril in the uplands. We have seen Aurma galloping from the west. They were aimless, some carried wounds. We parleyed with the head of their herd — she told us there was a foulness, it has taken their calves. They had to abandoned their elderly for the risk was too great.'

'It's true,' a stocky Revaral loped down from a ledge. 'We were far north, almost at the border with the Vulpir fiefdom. We found a wounded Effer, an easy kill. But there was something off — you can tell when a kill is sickly, but this was a deviance. It was choking on its own vomit, yet it had something hanging over it, like a morning fog. Yamini broke its neck to end its suffering. We both saw the fog disperse as it died.'

Carcaris turned to Noraa. 'Who might help us understand this threat?'

Noraa nodded. 'Yes. But please,' she addressed the crowd. 'This is Gaspstuff. It will appear as your colleague described, but the Cini, of which I am — we have a very old fastening with the dead. We live beside our ancestors. Some of you might fear the dead but I ask for patience and courage in the face of such things'

The crowd nervously accepted this as she closed her eyes.

'Yaga Vormors, Pale living! Overmother! Please, grant me tiding!'

Hushed by her words, the Pridebrow waited.

Air snapped. A deafness. Lungs became laboured and ears rang shrill. An outward breathlessness, oxygen starved, morsels of life that drifted with air currents pulled inward, organic processes ceased in chemical entropy.

All focus was suddenly drawn before the Cini, at first to a void, which became a something, a palsy, an arrested point, and all the sandstone groaned, as though pulled against its will, winning its stationary tug of war with an exhalation of gritty dust.

A deep guttural throb announced her coming, stippled hordes of chaff rose to greet her, the inky thrall, a twisted mass of limbs, prickled and chitinous.

Her overmother hung reticent, encircled by the panicked crowd, who began to back away.

'Overmother, it is me, Noraa. I call on you for guidance!'

The entity bristled, sending out shards of abyssal dark, cinder eyes flaring and dimming.

'Yooou aaarrreee saaaffffe?'

'Yes, I am safe, these are my allies. They wish to know what it is I fled from.'

Yaga Vormors recoiled. '*Wroth spit! Venomous things are leaking out! Cretinous, insidious! All are poisoned with avarice and vengeance. You are right to run, all of you!*'

She aimed a barbed paw toward them, rotating so that all could understand her threat. Carcaris padded before the spirit.

'I am the She-King of the Pridebrow. Your underdaughter is safe with us here. Tell me, you speak of the Wroth, surely, yet all but a few are dead. How have they come back?'

'*Come back! Yes! They are wriggling like worms, like flies on faeces. They are drawn out of the suppurating wound, out of their graves — my dear underdaughter, her family, all offered as living burials.*'

'I don't understand, who has done this?'

'*Emeris! Loved and loving, all pulled out of place, his body is now a tomb for he who calls himself Thoth! Emeris is all locked up inside — he can see every cruelty and do nothing. The thing in him has control, crumpled up within,* cancerous and full of hate. Thoth will drive his Husk through these wild and vital lands and devour it all.'

Yaga rushed towards her underdaughter, 'My dear, dear child, there is little to be done, but there is a smidgen, a little thing of hope. This land was once filled with Cini; we ruled with clear and fair intention. We were blessed by the First City, it gave of itself to us, a piece of it in the land, a steward, a little god. It will answer to you, and perhaps only you. You will need to listen! You will need to heed your studies, blood craft, bone craft, livid entanglements and necromancy. Only then will you find it. You must, you must! This thing, this Husk, it is something foul!'

'I will, I promise.'

Yaga shook. 'It took something of me, spilled my guts, it has claws that cut even the dead. I am weakened by it. I have beseeched my Gaspkin, but we are all spent and wrapt with impotence. You are strong, strong with life! You are more than a match for this enemy. I love you.'

Ensconced in shivering garlands of shadow, she bowed toward the queen.

'You have lived through the clenched teeth of the Wroth. Do not let their simpering revenants best you. There are defences — my underdaughter shall teach you. Good luck, kin of Carcar.'

With that, the embolism burst, an implosion of fraying flaying blubber strands, pulling itself inward, back into the hereafter. Dismayed, the court looked to one another, and turned to their Queen for guidance.

'What defences does she speak of?' Carcaris spoke with a sober authority.

Noraa composed herself. 'When we were cubs, we were tutored in Gaspcraft. Elders who died were encouraged back into Naa, but they held in them a yearning for life, like the urge for meat. The dead can draw from the living, and even love cannot sate their thirst. So we rendered ourselves ... unpalatable.'

Noraa made for a pile of discarded Oreya bones. She chewed at the neck, pulling away a vertebra, lengths of leathery flesh trailing as she lay it on the ground. With canny claw and tooth she began to braid the ribbon-like muscle, her eyes darting around for other objects.

"May I borrow from your courtiers' armour?'

Carcaris agreed. A splint of glass here, a jag of metal there. She placed these amongst the meat, neatly ingratiating each object with the tissue around it. She then bit her forelimb and spat the bloody saliva on the talisman.

'Some of you may have seen Anx fetishes before. The Corva honed their skills to a fine point. Cini understand this rot craft with a different desire. For them, it was closeness with the Gasp. For the Cini, it was closeness with our kin. Like you, the Wroth took away our lineage, our families, left us as orphans. In the dead we found lost family, learning of our ancestry through them. But to quell the desperate need of the dead, we made these, we wore them until the revenant we summoned could see us, beyond their hunger.'

Noraa held up the bone hex in her mouth. She walked up to Carcaris and dropped it before her. The Queen lifted it with her claws and placed it upon her diadem. Little Grin gingerly climbed her flanks and knotted the totem to the crown. She thanked him as he returned to Noraa.

'In the Corvan tongue, they call it *Nash Aka*, the will to remain alive. Without the ceremony of the Anx, it is nothing more than a trap. The spirit will be drawn into it, held in perpetuity, and its strength used in ritual.

'I can show you how to make these. The inanimate flesh is the tether to Naa, the reminder of their own forsaken skin. We will need glass, or polished metal so that the revenant can see itself. This repels them back to the Gasp, they cannot stand the sight of themselves. All will need one, and many of you will have to learn how to make them, and spread the word to all your compatriots. If we are to have any chance against them, then everyone must carry such a thing.'

*

As Ivy slept, Vorsa slipped through the balcony window and out onto the veranda. It was an easy leap to the ground below, via a series of similar ledges. Once upon the ground, she called out, a high yelp, which offered up a quick response. A Vulpus soon appeared before her, carrying in its mouth a dead Muroi. Vorsa swallowed it down and thanked her soldier.

'Is there any news?'

The soldier, Varieon, was noticeably fatigued, 'There are refugees, fleeing from the northern lands. Word has travelled quickly of a plague, yet no one can speak of its source. Some fear it might be the same thing that killed the Wroth. Orn Megol has taken in clans from many territories. Your father asks after you. He wishes you to return home.'

Vorsa shook her head. 'There isn't time. We must travel north, the wrothcub has awoken a defence against this enemy they call the Husk. If we have any hope we must rally all who are able to fight it. We need to petition the Concilium of Oevidd. The war against the Morwih was all fur and fang. Our advantage was Petulan, and the Lacking Sea. The enemy now has that advantage, we must speak to greater minds.'

Varieon agreed, 'I will go to the Oevidd personally.'

'No,' Vorsa said, 'I will go. I need you to watch over my father. He cannot be left alone.'

'Please, Vorsa. You must go to him. He will not last much longer, you must see him before he passes.'

Vorsa sighed, 'Return to Orn Megol, gather the clan chiefs. Tell them the threat is Gaspstuff. Perhaps the only defence will be to seal up Orn Megol, hide like our forebears did when the Wroth hunted them. I will return with whatever I find. Until then Oromon remains the overseer of the city.'

'Yes, Corpse Speaker.'

'We will survive. We are not idle.' She wished him safe travel and returned to Ivy in the apartment. There, Vorsa took the opportunity to sleep, and was awoken by Ivy who had boiled some water on a camping stove she had found to make tea. She offered a little to Vorsa in a saucer, who stared at it with a mixture of aversion and bafflement before realising it was warm and subtle in flavour. She lapped it up.

Ivy had dug through the cupboards of the apartment, collecting together the few useful items she could find. 'These people ate takeaway food a lot I guess.'

Vorsa didn't even ask the meaning, loping up onto the counter beside Ivy. 'We will travel to the Concilium of Oevidd, it is north from here, so we will not need to deviate from our path. They are prescient. They hold the sum of all things. They might assist us in our future decisions.'

'The sum of all things?'

Vorsa considered this. 'Yes. Like the Orata, it is a living collection. You will see for yourself.'

North of the great river they picked their way through expansive slabs of concrete that lay across torn streets. A blanket of crushed glass coated most surfaces and eager weeds punctured the paving. On a derelict building site, steel girders stood like masts, trailing garbage like rigging.

All the city was alive with greenery. Vorsa pointed out an odd tower that dwarfed the ruins of a famous cathedral which had lost its dome to a burgeoning leafy canopy. The skyscraper was remarkably intact, modern and ugly, one of only a few that had survived the collapse.

'High Realm of Hanno. They share much in looks with the Wroth. I am sure Hanno Gahar herself will want to meet you.'

Wide boulevards opened to the remains of a modern train station, flattened by the red brick hotel which had stood beside it. Horsetail reeds rose in great banks around a former entrance to an underground station — now filled with dark water, it became something unfathomable. She imagined the endless sunken platforms, Atlantean ticket halls. She wondered what lurked down in subterranean halls, what strange things might find sanctuary, now that the city's lungs were flooded, drowning in nature's vigour. Her eyes fell out of focus, and recollection surfaced, the vision of the Sentinels, and another, the consuming dark beneath them, somehow distinct from the others. She shuddered.

They continued northwest, toward the Consilium. There were older, uniform buildings here, an avenue of distinguished grey stone edifices, a university campus courtyard, now a prospering wood. It was quiet, feathered song lifted from heavy buddleia drooping in shawls over border walls. A blue plaque spoke of a man named Charles Darwin, a naturalist, who had lived there. Ivy recognised the name, *something to do with evolution*, she thought. She wondered what he would make of all this.

Vorsa skipped beside her. Another fallen tower, its ruddy entrails strewn across the street. They clambered over them, where they found an unassuming building.

'The Consilium of Oevidd,' Vorsa said, gesturing towards the broken door.

'Oh,' Ivy said, feeling it was a little anticlimactic.

'With such an impressive name, I expected something more ....'

'More?' Vorsa predictably dismissed her and carefully manoeuvred herself through a shattered pane, disappearing into the shadows. She returned a moment later, sticking her head through a hole in the glass, looking impatiently at Ivy. 'Are you coming?'

Ivy put her hand through a higher broken pane and turned the latch. Within was an empty corridor. Vorsa disappeared to her left through another door. Ivy followed.

It was a museum. The dark wood panelling and cabinets held within multifarious skulls and articulated skeletons, artefacts and illustrated diagrams. The smell was curiously comforting; a dry and bookish warmth, teetering osteology leered from every shelf, a wunderkammer of lost and found complications of bone, dusty edifices of long dead mammals. Briny glass tombs of formaldehyde magnified the lidless milk-eyes of serpents, Ungdijin and assorted embryos. The exhibition was small, yet brimming, angry, sad and soulful faces, glowering, glib or gleeful final moments, held in repose, in forever stares. Upon a plinth a familiar skull, an Oraclas, old and brittle dry. It looked at her much like Lendel had done not so long ago.

A balcony ran the entire circumference of the room, and watching silently were distant relatives, ape-like hominids, flanked by the orthopaedic carcasses of Athlon.

Ivy heard the raspy chirp of something close to her, and felt an impatient bump against her leg. She looked down to see a small, predatory feathered, what she had known as a bird of prey, striding beside the cabinets, deep in thought, completely oblivious to her.

'Excuse me,' Ivy said.

The feathered stopped and turned. It eyed her up and down, a peculiar contrivance of glass shards clasped by the claws of two withered scaled legs that sprang from its head dress.

'Hmm! Wroth! This is highly irregular. Do you have a catalogue number? Iglebock! New entry!'

'New entry!'

There was the sound of clattering objects and objection.

'New entry!'

Half a dozen large feathered upon a rolling library ladder squealed from behind a display cabinet. They were being pushed by a stroppy tusked Runta, who would have looked more at home on an African savannah. Upon its back were a series of small erratic feathered, Hagi, who made little rustled caws and flitted about carrying tools constructed from sticks. There was something beautifully theatrical about it - the Runta was directed with shrill rasps from the six haughty, razor-beaked raptors upon the rungs of the ladder.

Ivy saw they spent their time bickering with one another, or else pulling objects from cabinets which they tossed hastily, yet deftly, to one another, examined them closely then replaced where they were found, marked as observed with a sharp scratch of their tremendous claws upon sticks. Then they would argue again over the placement of said marked stick, which was finally tossed to the Hagi upon the back of the Runta.

'New entry!'

The congregation of raptors shot surprised and disconcerted eyes towards Ivy, each sporting apparatus upon their heads, magnifying their pupils to comedic effect.

'New entry!' burped the Runta with inebriated certainty.

'New entry!' chimed the Hagi.

Finally, the feathered all stopped whatever they were engaged in and they descended the steps in a disarray of stray wings, inelegant and disorganised, before preening themselves and straightening their ornamentations. They walked awkwardly over to Ivy, staring up at her with delight and curiosity.

Before Ivy could speak, Vorsa cleared her throat. 'We are here to ask for the reading. Vorsa Corpse Speaker, daughter of Satresan, speaker of the city of Orn Megol.'

The largest of the flock stepped forward. 'We know who you are, Vorsa, daughter of whatever his name is. But who is this?' He extended his wing toward Ivy.

'I am Ivy.'

The feathered stood proud and exclaimed, 'Iglebock Nefered Balktorn, Chancellor of Oevidd, Keeper of the elegant aforementioned, mentioned and soon to be mentioned. These are my scribes.'

He gestured to the feathered beside him, a variety of imposing yet ageing characters, the oldest of which was Sentevis, a quiet, yet powerful presence, her dark pennaceous feathers stark against her white head and bright yellow angular bill. Iglebock himself was remarkably prehistoric, a ruff of broad white feathers about his neck, two defining black dashes from his blood red eyes, that culminated in two tufts of down beneath his dagger beak. Various smaller, dusty yet graceful feathered stood beside them, and a large Storn, who stared with wide-eyed interest. The Runta rolled on his side and scratched his belly. A single fly buzzed around him attentively. 'I am Flonterwowhist of the Wooden Sea, fifth Duke of the Runta Regalia, heir to the ...' he trailed off into a stupor.

Iglebock rolled his eyes. 'He ate too many spoiled apples. He is our chief pusher. The Hagi are his royal courtesans, we aren't quite sure how he ended up here, but he's very good at pushing.'

Ivy bowed to them, 'It's nice to meet you all.'

'Polite! Not a common attribute in your kind. We have one or two examples here you know.' He gestured to the skeletons above. 'Wroth that is.

They are always polite, being dead you see. Maybe Vorsa can have a nice corpse speak with them.'

They all sniggered.

Vorsa frowned.

'What is it you do here?' Ivy asked.

'Do?' Sentevis replied. 'Why, we record, catalogue, make note of, examine, ponder. What the Wroth kept here, we have continued to add to. Each and every item has a story. It is in the details that we find each tale.'

'The Oevidd gather up the history of Ocquia that was taken from us by the Wroth. There are many places here in the Stinking City that held our kin, and the vestiges of their cultures,' said Vorsa.

Iglebock added, 'When the Wroth were dead, these crafty Vulpus freed us all! We were left to starve in chains within the Moterion. This young vixen and her compatriots worked to free us! It is our duty now to rescue every morsel of truth. None of us can fly you see, they cut our flight feathers so we could not return to the wilds. Our eyes are very good, but we had no use for them tied to the ground, and so we found a new use for them. We could perceive in a way others could not, we can read the tiniest imperfections in things, the stories in decay.'

Another feathered, Epidid Gwoss, raised his wing. 'The scars of seasons long passed became a language all of its own. Every bone or pelt or scrap within this trove has a tale in its blemishes. It just so happened the Wroth liked to gather up such keepsakes, place them in these halls. We were drawn to them, intrigued by how your kind would display our corpses in places such as these, our skin removed and stuffed, in reverence? As a keepsake? Perhaps even a trophy.'

Sentevis concluded, 'Now we exploit their spoils to fill the great gaps in the histories of all of Naa — we find the hidden eulogies in the bones of our ancestors. They have told us many stories.'

'We need one of those stories now,' Vorsa said.

The absent minded feathered, Gleet, who had first walked into Ivy, poked his head out from behind the flock, 'Every item has a story, which do you want?'

Ivy cast her eyes over the museum's collection. She traced her finger across plaques, feeling the indentation of etched letters. She stared at the gawking eyes of animals she barely recognised, microscope slides that spoke of tiny universes. She came to a cabinet close to the entrance. Behind glass stood the skeletal remains of a large animal that reminded Ivy of a Cini. She was drawn to it.

She read the plaque — Thylacine. A photograph of the animal was beside it, an unusually wide jaw and tiger-like stripes upon its back.

"Tell me his story.'

The raptors conferred. 'Gleet Threshix, would you care to tell this story?'

The little hawkish feathered hopped toward the cabinet, motioning to Ivy, 'Would you be so kind?'

Ivy slid the glass window aside. Gleet stepped within, gently flitting upon the skull beside the articulated skeleton. He cocked his head abruptly, and a pince nez apparatus fell before his eyes. He gazed upon the bones, examining each surface, every imperfection, each notch and weather, the sprain-wear and bruising written in the patina of the bone.

'Its kin were few and far between, it wears the tax of a withering stock, having bred within its own family. Here, there is a wound upon its spine where an object grazed it, yet it lived, knowing cubs of its own.

'Yes, there are fractures, fragile ankles, this individual ran, ran to escape the wound that might kill it. It saw its own family die, clothed in the smothering sadness that this loss would surely invoke. It was taken from its homelands, it suffered a long journey against its will.

'I smell cut wood, burned wood, dust of the Oscelan to fan the flames of Wroth machines. There is sea salt too, this animal crossed an ocean. The bones speak of an epoch of poor nutrition, the very substance of them diminished. It died not by the hands of Wroth and their violence, but of imprisonment. The abrasions on its claws speak of a wish to be free. I know that feeling all too well, we all do.'

Ivy felt responsible. She pointed to the sign that hung before the beast. 'These words, they talk of trappers, those who took the fur of animals for the Wroth to wear. These animals were hunted and caught and displayed in zoos. I believe the same zoo you call the Moterion. We passed it on our way here. You were all held there. But this animal was there a long time ago. They're all gone now. These Thylacines were hunted to extinction.'

'Extinction?' Gleet asked.

'There are no more left in Naa. The Wroth murdered them all,' she replied.

Gleet shuffled his feet and shook his head, 'Don't be so hasty, wrothcub.' The skull upon which he stood was also a Thylacine, and he peered down into its eye socket. His voice rattled about inside.

'The mind, it leaves its own marks, its own signature, in the shell it languishes within. There is a graffiti of ideas in the lacquer, thoughts that etched their importance here, thoughts that wanted to be heard. Maybe not physical marks, more of an echo. But it is a shared echo, one that resounds from past to present and future. Please, tell me their Wroth name?'

'Thylacine,' Ivy spoke almost phonetically, enunciating each letter.

'They called themselves *Laoonana*. They lived on a landmass of very particular mammals. There are fond memories in amongst the ravages of feast or famine, faded but full of life. They feared most Wroth. Many of them died, almost all of them. They ran from every footstep, every cracked twig. They hid in caves and dens deep under the red earth. They were helped by the Wroth who still understood the land. They learned to hide like this, and they waited, waited for rest. Rest came when the Wroth who hunted them were all gone.'

Gleet looked through his cracked bottle looking-glass, 'This echo is shared with the living. I can hear them, see them. Your Thylacine, the Laoonana — they live, somewhere in the world, protected by those Wroth who leaned towards the creed of Ocquia.'

Ivy staggered in amazement, 'This is wonderful! How do you do this?'

'As I said, we have very good eyesight,' Sentevis replied with a wry smile.

Vorsa rolled her eyes, 'Now you have shown us your admirable skills, perhaps you have an object to serve us in our plight.'

Iglebock looked apprehensive, 'And what pray tell *is* your plight?'

'The First City, before it departed Naa long ago, left parts of itself in the land in its absence. They were called Sentinels and we believe they were summoned in times of peril. But the connection between the city and these Sentinels was lost. We know where one might be, but we have no means of knowing how we communicate our intention to it. It may see Ivy as a threat, like it did all other Wroth.'

'Yet you travel to meet it?' Gleet said nervously. 'You are brave!'

Sentevis became wary, 'Why do you require one of these Sentinels, what possible peril do we face? The Wroth are dead, bar this little one, and we have found some semblance of order in the stead of Dron.'

'We are yet to face it, but it has risen in the north lands, and moves south. It is a plague, fuelled by the Gasp.'

Sentevis ruffled her feathers, 'Gaspstuff! For that you must talk to the Clax, not the Oevidd!'

Gleet interrupted, 'No, no — there is a precedent. Catalogued under Gasp - section, ah, Necromancy, Archaic Lore, First City, Appendices, Ritual and Rite.'

The little feathered took to wing in short fitful bursts, unable to maintain flight for long. He landed here and there, staring at items, dismissing them, scuffling through sticks that lay in ordered piles. The Hagi, who had taken to pecking parasites from the Runta, were dismayed and began signalling their objections with raucous shrieks. Eventually Gleet alighted on top of the Oraclas skull. Beside this was a bell jar, a small clump of matted red hair, and a sculpture of a Mammoth. Ivy moved the glass dome that housed them, picking up the statue. Gleet placed his claws upon the fur and closed his eyes.

'This is an old Oraclas. I can sense pine sap and sweat, the oils in the skin. The hair is dense, they lived in the coldest time, when Naa was cloaked in ice. The presence of their clan, hundreds huddled together, walked a pilgrimage to the sheltered forests.

'Their elders died quickly, for the shadow of them is more fleeting, the young nestled in the refuge of their parent's bodies. When all was lost, when a blizzard blinded them from their path, they lifted their trunks and called to the Epiras for aid. The city heard their call, and rose amongst the ice fields, shepherding them to safety within its warm halls.

'Their dead were pulled from the snow drifts, imbued with the zeal of Dron, and made a moving reliquary, a Sentinel who would watch over the woolly Oraclas as they made their journey south, answering to their clarion call — it was a colossus, striding unhindered across the tundra. For generations he watched over their descendants, until none were left in the land.'

'Lendel?' Ivy asked.

'Yes. He remained in the city when it withdrew from Naa, when all such leviathans retreated into the soil.'

Gleet let go of the fur. 'Your Sentinel may not answer to all. It might only listen to a particular clade.'

Ivy remembered her vision. 'When Dron showed me what became of the Sentinels the only remaining defence against the Wroth were the Cini.

The Grim, the Rauka, they had all been hunted to extinction. When the city disappeared, so too did the Sentinels, leaving what was the left of the Cini to be domesticated—'

'Or hunted,' Vorsa interrupted. 'So we must find a Cini? The only Cini I know are Caanus, and as much as I like them, they hold little of their history in their heads.'

'There were some at the Moterion, but they fled like we all did, as far as they could from that place,' Sentevis replied.

'Gleet, are there any Cini skeletons here? Perhaps you could, I don't know, see if you can find them? Like you did the Laoonana?'

Gleet hopped down from the plinth and mounted the ladder. Immediately the old Runta lifted himself, gave himself a good stretch and loudly passed wind. 'Excuse me!' he said, trotting to the wheeled steps. With a firm push, it glided along the railing to which it was attached until Gleet squawked to stop. He then instructed the Hagi, who whistled and whirled with grace, to delicately open the door, which they did with impressive skill, so that Gleet could reach a particular skull, remarkably similar to that of the Thylacine.

He looked at it, sizing it up. 'Quite old. But may still hold some answers.' He clambered upon it, measuring the circumference of sockets and cranial bones, flipping it on its side to pick at its teeth.

'This Cini died of a wound, inflicted by a sharp weapon. It had a consumption, in the blood. It wasted away. Very sad. These bones are brittle. Died in this land, one of the last. I have an impression I have felt something like it before. Have known it in the Moterion, unwashed, tired. But there is another mind, I can hear it with the wind. It's full of worry. Iglebock, can you sense it?'

The great Evarin skipped toward the base of the ladder, climbing the rungs with wings unfurled, until he reached the skull. Gleet shuffled behind it and pushed it so that Iglebock could examine it. He threw his head back, closing his eyes, 'Yes. Yes, there is something!'

The Consilium collected at the centre of the museum, where they chittered and whispered and cast assumptions. Ivy watched with mild amusement as they squabbled. She thought it would take some time for them to come to a consensus, so she found a chair and sat down, pulling her coat around her. She rested for a while, until Vorsa appeared beside her, and tugged at her jeans, leading her between the cabinets.

In a large, floor level display, was the taxidermied remains of a Vulpus.

'Oh Vorsa, I am sorry,' Ivy said in dismay and sat down cross legged before the animal.

Vorsa was silent. The Vulpus behind glass had no armour, which seemed peculiar.

'Why did I never see your armour, anyone's armour, before … before everything changed?'

Vorsa turned to her with eyes that spoke without speaking, holding in them the beginning of an answer. 'Because you never expected it from us. You never saw us as capable. You did this—' She gestured to the pelt made up to look alive. 'This was what we were good for. You asked me before, how I could eat those who I live beside. There is what Naa made of us, it is a real thing. It is a need, it is desperate and demanded, by both I, and by the life I take, who has taken lives itself, be them insects or otherwise. But then there is what the Wroth made of themselves. They took whatever they wanted, without need, without the prospect of starvation.'

'I am Wroth,' Ivy replied, burdened with a little frustration and embarrassment.

'Maybe it is wrong to think of you all the same. But there is a callousness that comes with dominion. We used the word *Wroth* to describe your kin, but you had other names before you made your choice to plot your own path. Perhaps it is time we sought that name for you. A name more fitting for she who helps us.'

Gleet appeared from behind the row of cabinets.

'Excuse me. We have identified the author of this memory. There are intimations of many Cini carried from the north. All but one stink of malfeasance. One is alone, and she is afraid, she is fleeing. Perhaps she is the one you seek? Regardless, this Cini skull appears to have an affinity for her. It's best you take it with you.'

*

Wrought with revenants, small contingents of Husk quickly consumed the countryside east and west, even as the main body of their army marched south. Some shed their load of surplus ectoplasm as soon as possible, claiming back a shard of a sense of self yet condemning all to the whims of the Husk. Few weren't eager to pursue any more work until they'd broken a little off for themselves.

To the west were flat acres, herds of Athlon and Aurma, in a past life little more than livestock, now fallow and free to roam and raise their families. The Husk were quick to tarnish their tranquillity, bartering information for protection — to be left alone for the price of a good lead. One such group, a half-dozen Muroi, three Vulpus, A young Sabel and their muscle, a very large Trungru bull, stalked the lanes and byways.

Naa was not free of aggressors. Yes, the Husk were by far the most dangerous, but the feudal lands of Heckl, the Dragger mobs and Shunned Runts of Vulpus were violent reminders that not all were beyond the temptation of wrongdoing.

The Husk party found their way to a ramshackle meeting of the heads of a number of criminal packs who were cutting up the land in the stead of the new enemy. They mostly kept out of the dealings of Ocquia, and didn't dare ruffle the feathers of Dron, whose loyal and exemplary soldiers of the High Wrought were not worth fighting with.

Low light from a dimming day cast long shadows. The Stegard Rodents sneered and writhed in a pile, almost reaching the mass of the fellow mammals who argued the details of their borders. A heavy swine of the Dragger mob was auctioning the water lands.

'I want the west fens, Ungdijin is our game, not yours! You want for too much!' a noisy Vulpus barked. 'What good is water to a Sqyre anyway!'

Their arguments were interrupted by something shadowy and silent. From the murk shifted the Husk. 'For a while we thought all you animal folk were nothing but goodie two shoes. Glad to see there is a little *Wroth* in all of you.'

Six emaciated scoundrels, covered in blood and mud, bristling with metallic barbs and glass imbedded in swollen welts. They grinned as they sniffed at the gallery of thieves. 'New authority on these here plains. The Husk will be running things soon enough, and in an effort to help that cause you'll all be answering to us. Who among you wants rule of all this sodden land? You can raid all the lakes and nests for Ungdijin and eggs from the feathered. Your tithing will be to work under us, patrons of the Husk. We'll even promise not to possess your living bodies with the dead. Who's brave enough?'

The Stegard Rodents hissed.

'We are!'

Emeris

Emeris opened his eyes and found himself in a smaller space. It was dark, but he was aware of a little light around the edges of a door. He could smell varnished wood and dust.

'And you will stay in there until you learn to behave!'

The voice was that of his father. His hands were burning. They had been caned. He was furious. But he was also scared.

He sat with his back against the wall, which was curiously carpeted. The memory flickered as he explored the space within which he was imprisoned. He knew he was under the stairs, in the small room where cleaning products were kept.

He moved carefully, fearful he would be heard. Eventually his eyes adjusted to the dark. The carpet was musty and deteriorating, and he pulled at the threads along its edges. It was curiously satisfying, watching the tufts of coloured wool separate with each drag of the hessian underlayer.

He tugged again, and this time the thread caught and he lifted the edge of the carpet to reveal floorboards below.

And a latch.

With some effort, he pulled back as much of the carpet as he could and found a door. It was small, but large enough for him to fit through.

The muffled sound of his parents fighting felt far enough away for him to gently push a little shelving unit that blocked the corner of the trapdoor out of the way, unhitch the hook latch and open it up.

Below was black.

He rummaged through the boxes and bags on the shelving unit and eventually found a box of candles for the dining room table and some matches. He lit a candle and lowered it into the space below. There were no steps, just a large, almost empty, room. He dropped down. The ceiling was low, maybe four feet, and he had to stoop a little to fit.

It was cold. He could make out boxes, a dilapidated rug. There was a rusting safe, open and empty. It was obvious no one had been down there for a long time.

He followed the slight trace of a draught until he found an opening into another space. There were a few steps, and the floor was no longer stone, but earth. There were objects on the ground. Old tools, a length of chain and a small penknife. He took the knife.

The draft drew him further in, towards the back of the house. There was an old rusted grill, which was easily pushed aside. He squeezed through the hole, avoiding the thick webs and spindly black legs retracting into nests.

He was away from the house, facing into the little bluebell wood. It was an acre or so of ancient woodland, of moss-laden boles and vibrant purplish blooms.

He picked up a long stick and hit it against the trees, thwacked it across the flowers, beheading them mercilessly. He could feel a kernel of malice that hummed with increasing ferocity.

It was summer now, and he was off school for six weeks. Usually, for a child of his age, the holiday would be paradise, but he was increasingly scared of his father. The old man would drink in the evenings and become violent with his mother. Emeris no longer felt sorrow for her, because she took out her own misery on him. So his scorn only grew towards her too.

The only thing she cared about was her useless poodle, who appeared to provide her far more joy than her son ever could.

It was not long after this that he started hurting things. At first, it began with small creatures, those entirely defenceless and unaware of his existence. He'd cut the heads off snails whilst they stretched out their necks in search of food. He plucked butterflies from buddleia and tore their wings from their bodies, letting the helpless bodies fall into the undergrowth where they would surely die.

It was under the house that he made his first domain, his first castle, the corroded tools he found there his weapons of torture. And it was in this summer holiday that he would meet her.

She was the neighbour. She lived in the farm across the river at the end of their property. He had been scrabbling around on the rocky shore, throwing stones in the water when she had appeared. She looked angelic in the warm light, the way her hair caught the sun in a tangled halo. On their first meeting they had said but ten words to one another before she ran away.

He could contend with his anger in this instance. It was in his powerlessness that he found a sickening frustration. His only relief was his castle, a place his parents did not know existed. If he ever wanted to escape their wrath, he would find his way under the house, the muffled shouts of his father seeking him, the clear yell as he flew out of the house in a rage — and when he couldn't find Emeris, he certainly found his mother.

It all came back to him in the end. Avoid one raised hand, receive another. The impact across his wrists, across his buttocks. The humiliation. He had no chance against his father, a man who was unfailing in his devotion to controlled violence. In his beatings, he would wax lyrical about his rationale, that he had been treated much the same by his father, and look how well he'd turned out.

The only light was the girl in the field. The girl that Emeris would hope to see every day, waiting on the trunk of the lopsided tree that grew across the river like a natural bridge. It was here that, in the many hours he sat contemplating how one might approach a conversation with the girl, that he began to see the dancing aura of the Umbra.

*

Scab stood on the outskirts of a city he had known in better times. It was overcast, cold for late spring. He felt little of it, and in that he was glad. He recognised a pub he'd got pissed in, smirked at a bus stop he'd slept in. There were sleeping bags curled up against buildings that might be sarcophagi for vagrants. He paid them no mind and ushered on his soldiers.

The evenings were his favourite hours to run. He found the moon a source of motivation for his new gift - snatching souls from the Gasp, forcing them into any who wandered into view. None were safe, and he broiled with the resinous bubbles of screaming afterthoughts, yawning, gaping wound mouths that fell from him placental wet, runny with formlessness, careering towards living flesh with appetite.

His sentries were at first afraid of the ease at which he mastered the skill, but soon egged him on. Thoth's message would be spread — he would stand victorious.

Three days of running, hunting Muroi and feathered, taking the odd Effer and feasting. When they grew bored of the chase, they constructed scarecrows, bare branches torn down and strung up in the likeness of Wroth. For added measure, Scab found he could bring revenants into Naa and let them roam — pitchfork totems, pronged nightmares, haunted by the dead.

Further south, a red dawn rose over the Stinking City. Another place he'd known well, in his youth. He'd done very bad things here, crimes no one had ever pinned on him.

Now he felt the thick grass beneath his feet, a hill that he'd watched fireworks from one New Year's Eve. The smell of beer and sparklers, grass turned to mud under a thousand feet. He could see the bird cages of the zoo, a gigantic Ferris wheel at the river. For a second he lost himself in memories.

This is all very nice, but what good is reminiscing when you have a job to do?

He agreed with himself, but wanted to live in the moment a little longer. Dying had never been on his agenda and living again hadn't provided him with much leisure time. He snarled at the Husk to help him collect wood for more scarecrows that, with much effort, soon stood forbiddingly over the land.

*

South towards the Pridebrow was a route Awfwod Garoo had flown countless times, shepherding information between the northern kingdoms and the southern Wroth metropolis most still knew as the Stinking City — and further afield, to the Epiras, Dron, the place of bones. They were five hardened couriers, sons and daughters of Troon, who, in the weeks after the return of the First City, saw a need to establish a network of outposts, exchanges for those remote places to play a role in the whys and wherefores of the nascent democracy, free of the Wroth.

Awfwod rose quickly to Flight Chief, he was stern but fair, a stickler for decorum. It was he who founded a new pictographic language with which the various clades discreetly shared private affairs and familial politics, all scrawled on tough leaves and listening sticks and carried in carriages that hung below each wing. They would sleep nestled into their own down on any surface they could find, huddled for warmth against the elements.

They did not divert to the She-King Carcaris. Though the night withdrew, it left something of itself threading through the land - a pack of beasts that moved like a river plotting its own course, picking up debris as it meandered, animals in their line of sight caught in the deluge, struck down, only to rise again with shaky zeal, joining the swelling armada that continued south.

They flew high, hid away out of earshot, watched the Husk snaking ever further, taking ever more lives into their fold, regardless of clade. His battalion of Windsweepers spied the castle and its torn land, and the garrison of Husk who departed, going south.

They followed.

Awfwod had watched them inconspicuously as they slept in the early afternoon and ran at dusk. He had seen them make their diabolical figures, idols that even Awfwod feared. These Cini that moved incorrectly, that hunted with blundering tenacity — and when they spread their curse it was nauseating to watch, for nothing good came of what spilled into the world.

In the Stinking City, a place Awfwod had also spent many turns, they observed the leader of the Husk pack invoke his unclean ritual, yet this time, there was no victim. Instead, pale, half-present things leached out of him, and conversed with him for some time.

None could see quite what he spoke to, cold beings that faded into the earth once the meeting was complete. Awfwod wondered if the hellish hound had seeded the ground with an unnatural fruit.

Once the Husk had moved on, the Windsweepers landed upon the scarecrows to examine their malign creations. They did not notice the hungry revenants woven into the wood, until it was too late.

*

Noraa feared the bone hexes might not ward off the Husk themselves. It would repel anchorless spirits, yes. But the flesh they wore might make them stronger. There was no way to test this hypothesis, besides confronting them. She chastised herself for having been so careless in maintaining her craft, disregarding the threat of a new land and the phantoms that might reside in those fallow, shaded places of purposeful stones and gnarled trees. Now that threat was real.

The Rauka learned to make the grim tokens with relish. The artists within their ranks who had taken to carving the soft stone of which their home comprised began to cut wards into the walls, smearing blood runes, attaching scraps of metal found between the quarry buildings, polishing the surfaces until they shone with reflected light.

She, too, took time to construct her own protections, both spiritual and physical, in the form of her first suit of armour. She followed the lithe felines up into the yards that held every dropped tool and a trove of metal fixings. She scoured the lean-tos and sheds for something suitable, coming across pieces of old tyres that could be pierced with a collection of screws, nails and fastenings and so held together. With great effort, she chewed and tore at the malleable rubber, shaping the pieces to overlap one another.

Once the main body of the armour was complete, she began to decorate it with talismans, bone spurs that strutted from her flanks and head. She embellished it with as many garlands of good fortune that she could muster, until her panoply was complete. Little Grin helped her place it upon her back, with a cord of twine and sapling bark securing it to her shoulders and tail.

Noraa revealed armour for Little Grin to wear that, together, they adjusted to fit him.

'You look fine in your garments of war, Little Grin!' said Bresh.

'Thank you!' he replied bashfully.

They appeared before the She-King once more, to thank her for her hospitality.

'The Pridebrow will send parties to our neighbouring districts, as guards and to teach the art of bone hexes. Bresh, you must return to TumHilliad and share this new defence with your kin. Noraa, if you make it to the First City, ask for Psittacus Erithacus, and please tell him that She-King Carcaris sends the promise of all Rauka if it comes to it.'

'Consider it done!'

Bresh turned to the pair and bowed, 'It was a pleasure to bring you here. If you ever return to the Northlands, you'll be most welcome to eat a hearty meal with us!'

Noraa placed her muzzle against his cheek. 'You are a good boy, Bresh.'

*

Noraa and Little Grin walked an uneasy path south. There was no flock song, each dawn a breathless quiet that spoke of more than any Yowri prayer. The Husk had silenced it all. But it was other survivors they sought.

Noraa was aware that she could be mistaken for the enemy, and she made every effort to quell that notion in her onlookers, those who hid amongst the branches in fear. Little Grin suggested they sing, for singing was such a joyous activity, none would mistake them for the Husk. They hooted and howled and taught one another jaunty tunes, those filled with merriment. They danced around one another, and quite forgot their torment for a moment. They eventually found themselves in a small clearing, a glade between some oak trees. They could smell the presence of an audience, drawn to their singing.

Noraa waited for calm, tracing the flit or rustle of hidden companions.

'Please!' she exclaimed, 'I only wish to speak with you! We are not the enemy!'

She sat for a long time beneath the canopy, and eventually a Bloodson appeared. He was hesitant, skipping up and down the branch.

'We carry warding hexes beast! Do not cross us!'

Noraa was taken aback. 'Good! I am glad! Our armour is covered in hexes. We travel south. We wish to warn all of this threat! Please! If you have any information, we ask only for that.'

The Bloodson began to warble. The canopy erupted, and hundreds of feathered emerged, adorned with chitin armour. The treetops were heavy with creatures. There were ground-borne too; Sqyre and Creta. They held barbed sticks and brandished stones.

Little Grin stood on his back legs and held out his paws, 'We come directly from the Pridebrow, under the care of the She-King.'
Finally the Bloodson relented and flew down to greet the pair. Agitated and scared, he apologised, 'We must defend ourselves you see. If you can fly, you're relatively safe, we can flee, so myself and the sons and daughters of blood have taken to escorting ground dwellers to the south — we can watch from above, see. But this plague, it out-manoeuvred us, they've taken so many of our loved ones, leaving them nothing more than spoiled flesh, hungry to kill us or spread their disease further. Sisters help us, we've had to kill those who would not leave us be. The Northlands are cursed. Few escape their necromancy.'

'I did,' Noraa said solemnly.

'You survived his hand? This is news, all who witness him are forsaken. And you travel in search of your kin?'

'They are my kin, taken by this cursed thing. We travel to a place called the First City — we are told we may find help there.'

The Bloodson hopped excitedly, forgetting his fear. 'Ah, the jubilant throne! It is in the south, by the sea. I have not been there, but I am told wonderful tales by the news bringers.'

A herd of Oreya appeared nervously in the clearing. Their quick eyes saw Noraa and made to leave, but were quickly beckoned back by the flock. They sought safe passage under the wing of the ragtag army.

Noraa bowed to the Bloodson. 'Thank you for letting us speak, we have a long way to travel it seems.'

*

Thoth grew a little perturbed by his creation. The courtyard of the castle, where most of his soldiers slept and ate, had quickly become vicious and depraved. A kind of brutal hierarchy had evolved, and in ways he could not have predicted. The largest of the Husk, the Oreya, a pair of Grim, together with a small herd of Aurma, had risen in the ranks as the muscle, their bodies becoming instruments of force. Meanwhile, the likes of Cini, Maar and Vulpus took advantage of their teeth and claws and agility, becoming savage antagonists, pitting Husk against Husk; and much like Thoth himself, in his efforts to walk upright, they too had begun to distort their form to their own whims. Eyes frothed with cataract madness, blood became the liquid uniform, smeared red and quickly decayed to a tarry black — blood from fallen victims, rejected hosts and the animals themselves, who routinely stabbed any pointed object they could find into their skin in the hope of feeling something. The emptiness craved attention.

Normalcy was lost in the fevers and infections. Unable to know the extent of the torture they inflicted on the bodies they rode, death knocked without notice, sending revenants back to the Gasp — and Thoth continued to court hosts of dead, and drive them into unwilling victims. His authority remained, yet he soon began to question whether those he had freed from the hereafter might ultimately become so corrupted, so insane, that he would lose any command. He therefore abandoned plans to teach his skills to the Husk and settled on the capture of his prize in the south.

The morning light rose tentatively, as though it preferred not to illuminate the atrocious ranks that now heaved for space within the castle grounds. They would begin the march, many hundred strong, amassing more would-be soldiers on their journey, somewhere south, a beacon that only Thoth could see, for only he was Umbra, only he had the gift. He had sent out parties of Husk to create fortifications, sentry posts in enemy territory. He was sure their ranks would grow quickly, hunger and boredom and excruciating madness would drive them out in search of ever more victims.

But something had entered his perception that had not been there before. For when he settled his eyes on the aura, that glorious focal point, a stabbing glare would dazzle him, making him look away. The more he tried, the wider its flare and the less he could plot his course. He sensed there was an intelligence behind this, a mind that could see him, and knew a fragment of his intention. It only made him want it more.

'My Husk!' he snarled. Outside the gates of the castle, they had funnelled and formed into patchwork columns; those he deemed *Legionnaires* – his vanguard – led the charge, spasming with countless rabid ghouls, chomping at the bit for new flesh. He skirted the edges of his infantry, stalking on his back legs, he bared his black gums and jaundiced teeth, reminding them of who they served.

'You have risen from the muck as a bloodied revolution! This land was once our home, and we were stricken from it. But our ingenuity, our cunning alone has given us new life! New bodies! All of you are my children. We may have shed our humanity, but that does not make us any less Wroth, the virulent word, the scarecrows of this animal land! Come! — We shall slake this thirst with blood of the feeble and reclaim it as our own!'

He had never considered himself much of a public speaker, but he was discovering many facets of himself denied by those who'd made him pariah.

He strode out, two legged, one eye in the Umbra, the other down, down towards another town. He took to all fours, running hard towards the fields that abutted empty streets, the wall of acidic bodies behind him, all drunk on the promise he'd fed them.

What are you? he ruminated of his bright antagonist. He tried to outwit it, his eye poised on that glimmer in the south, trying to catch it out. Thoth supposed there must be others like him, others who fought for the enemy. He shook his head, never mind, they would all come to know his authority.

*

Rune sat poised on the edge of the Regulax, head low, concentrating. He had honed his sight of Thoth, at first as an extension of Ivy, and then eventually as a separate light, a crimson orb surrounded by lesser orbs. He considered this colour, a dull red was always associated with death, a dimming light was sickness, was never a sign of strength, yet with the speed that it moved it was hard to decipher.

Behind him, the Oroua Vas and Corva orthodoxy went about answering the call of terrified refugees who'd fled to the First City from the north, the Bastias out in the land becoming vital routes of communication. Morwih and Vulpus were directed to act as guides to places of safety, the sewers beneath the streets, train tunnels. Anywhere out of sight. More feathered had reached the city with word of sightings of the Husk, some having lost loved ones in a bid to escape the shapeless forms of revenants free to roam the skies.

Erithacus watched over Rune. 'What do you see my boy?'

'I see he is determined. I can reflect back that at least. The harder he tries the harder it will become. All I can do is hide Dron from him. But the closer he gets to us the less I can do so. He is not feathered, so he has no guidance by Naa. He is on foot, running. He is far off. I can see the lights of so many lives taking on his hue. He is strong in this magic. But I still do not understand what he is.'

Athlon herds had come down off the heath to move remnants of the fairground. They were limited though in their ability to erect any kind of barricade, which would fall to the Oraclas once they had joined in the effort. The promenade, long smothered in dunes, became a good support for their defences, but the preparations would require strength few in Naa could muster. Those who could help, did.

*

A pair of tall ears appeared from behind a ridge of tussocks. Each movement was answered with a rutting bark of comprehension. She was dressed in High Wrought armour, and upon her foreleg was a sharp blade. Her fur was short and wore a hundred scars. Her name was Onnar Proudfoot.

'Onnar, we have word that the Oraclas are on the move and will be here in several turns. They bring with them the Brawdhead Tasq and the Egresc Horn Guard.'

Without acknowledging her Drove sister, Onnar stared out at the two steep slopes either side of the collapsed theme park. The only way to the First City was down a single wide road that entered the town. It was littered with cars and lorries, and provided enough established barriers that it would be a relatively simple task to block the gaps that remained. It was also a perfect place for an ambush.

She gestured to the cliffs. 'This path, it is the only entrance. If we block it, we will not be able to allow refugees in. Once the Clusk arrive, have them drag any large logs or trees, anything heavy that will roll, and pile them on the steeper slopes, behind a big rock or something to hold them in place. If we need to, we can spring the dead falls and block the entrance.'

Her Sister Drove agreed. 'Some Yoa'a have brought up the use of fire.'

'Wespen bless us, how on Naa do we control fire? I have seen it used once, to smoke out the Groak Maar; the fire spread to the forest and burned the whole thing down. Leave fire to the Muroi.'

Onnar had travelled with the mercenaries of four Droves out from the west, answering the call for help in shoring up defences and protecting the city. She was now Mother Drove, in the stead of DreyGlare of Fellreath and her untimely death. Onnar had not wanted such a position, but her battles had become legendary and the title had been flung upon her when no other worthy candidate would dare fight for it.

In the year since the city had returned, Onnar had given birth to a single daughter, Ether, who had matured quickly and taken to the Drove far more readily than Onnar had done as a child. She was a fierce fighter, of which Onnar was secretly immensely proud, but also a source of constant worry, which was something that she dare not let slip. However, despite her best efforts, everyone knew, most of all Ether.

As she hopped back towards Dron she observed the Startle perform their sacrament, vortices of the Umbra given form. The entrance to the city was alive with commotion as the smaller clades gathered bedding materials and foods for those seeking asylum from the Husk.

Onnar felt uneasy. She had enjoyed this period of rest, although plenty of scuffles and diplomatic envoys had ended in bloodshed – which was all too common with Yoa'a – the lack of life-altering war had been good for her. She had defied her own trajectory by having a child, something she had never considered before. She felt a responsibility that she still battled with, a fight she knew she had already lost. Ether was already a sworn member of the Drove. Danger was the language of that young Proudfoot.

She entered the hall and made for the Sisters of the Flock. The shrine was bedecked in shells and coastal flowers. She bowed to the Corvan attendant who visited with parishioners. There were faces here she knew from difficult times, those who had fought in the war for the Stinking City. To return to this state of disquiet lay heavy on all who had lived through it.

The speaking wall uttered with somber tone. She placed her paw upon it. 'Hello, old soul.'

A gentle wave of particoloured flotsam, rich red and mottled brown leaves, assortments of bone chips and twigs undulated purposefully toward Onnar, an amorphous mound that began to tease itself into shape, a snout, dark rows of ebony earth along its face, eyes of coal and two thistle ears. An ever-churning countenance of an unmistakable Throa.

'Onnar my dear, it has been some time.' Tor's voice was a dry and haunting whisper.

'I am sorry I haven't visited for a while, such is the life of the Drove. But I bring news my friend, I have a daughter, Ether, and she runs with us. You knew her father, Agellion, a good Yoa'a.'

Tor's form shuddered with joy, 'A daughter! I am so happy. My son Tordrin and his family have come many turns to see me here, to learn of our ancestry. They spoke of your visit to them. Time no longer moves so inelegantly — I do not mourn the absence of my beloved for long.'

Erithacus flew down to join them, 'Day bring peace Tor, and very good to see you too, Onnar Drove! Tor has much to be proud of. His school for the Caanus has spread far and wide in the Throa communities, giving the pups a fighting chance in this new world.'

Onnar agreed, 'We have fought alongside a number of Caanus in the outlier fiefdoms, they are a good sort for sure. I have sent for them all. We will need every fighting chance. If only we knew what we face! I cannot command just defences, we must have an offensive strategy.'

'Rune says the Husk are moving with haste, and their number is great. Vorsa and the wrothcub, Ivy, continue north, keeping a wide berth of the enemy,' Erithacus said.

'Vorsa runs with a wrothcub? Not words I would ever imagine hearing. We can trust her?'

'I believe so. But we have the benefit of Rune, and of course Petulan, who have the uncanny ability to see truths hidden from most. The child has a good soul.'

'A good soul. My Ether has a good soul, but she cannot help but get herself into trouble.'

Tor chuckled, 'I see motherhood hasn't diminished that hopeful charm of yours, Onnar Proudfoot!'

Onnar sighed with a smile, 'I apologise. I am ever vigilant. More so since Ether was born. Suddenly the world is filled with enemies.'

Erithacus sighed, 'Naa has always had its enemies, perhaps I was naive to think that with the Wroth gone we would be free of such darkness.'

Onnar frowned, 'Do we know what form this enemy takes? Has anyone considered the possibility that they *are* Wroth?'

'Rune is not sure, but he says it has a determination unlike any he has seen before, and at first he could only see it through Ivy, the wrothcub. This suggests this is indeed Wroth.'

'How on Naa do we fend off the Wroth?' Onnar shook her head in dismay.

Tor moved toward her, 'I have killed Wroth. They are very strong, but their weakness is in their arrogance. They never expected us to be more than lowly animals. That is our greatest asset.'

*

Ivy and Vorsa left the Consilium. Outside, rain fell, and they made for a small café to wait for it to subside. The door was unlocked, and they found a quiet corner next to the window. Vorsa leapt up on the tabletop, whilst Ivy explored the kitchen. She found a fizzy drink, and some packets of crisps, and a can of tuna that was still in date. She emptied the contents onto a plate, found a large coffee mug for water which she poured from a bottle, and gave both to Vorsa. The vixen ate ravenously.

Ivy removed an object from her bag. It was wrapped in a clean t-shirt. She place it on the table, gently revealing it — the ancient Cini skull, given to them by the feathered stewards of the Oevidd. She moved it around – studying the yellowing surface, an attempt to discern what Gleet had seen – until it was facing her.

She placed her hands on it and closed her eyes tight. Fractal geometries of light raced past her inner eye. Often these focused moments where she accessed this secretive plane were fleeting, a rushing plethora of images making themselves of the little light that filtered through her eyelids, coalescing with her imagination, shaping configurations in symmetry. Sometimes these patterns spoke of greater meaning — of a place, and the movements of life.

She felt nothing, there was no map in this animal's head for her to find. She opened her eyes and pushed the skull across the table

'If we are going to find this Cini, then we have to go look.'

Vorsa nodded.

Ivy picked up the skull, pushed it back into her bag, pulled up her waterproof hood and together they left the café, and headed northeast. Through the maze of Victorian terraces and modern offices, roadways losing to intruding broad and needle leaf, gardens spilling their green across narrow pavements, cobbles now flooded tributaries like Venetian waterways seeking new territory. All the while the reed beds of flooded dainty ponds belched with amphibian choruses, songs of the unity of green spaces, a tapestry of horticulture as borders and turf healed over the Stinking City, losing the meaning of its name in a floral burial bouquet.

Islands of metal remained, twisted torsos of girders, obelisks of concrete — like hands reaching from an avalanche, they dared not give up to the green sprawl. They would soon leave the city, and if lucky, Ivy would find a car.

'Ivy, stop.'

Ivy turned to find Vorsa alert, her ears pricked, her tail held tight between her back legs. The rain abruptly ended, the sun bronze on wet gleam. There was something standing between the buildings. It was tall, and it stood like a Wroth. Ivy felt her knees give way.

'Is it them? The Husk?' she breathed, terrified, unable to stop shaking.

The figure stooped, and another appeared beside it. They were large, muscular and bipedal. The first began to run, and as it gained in speed it descended to all fours, a side-swinging lope, galloping towards them. It let out a powerful scream, a scream Ivy recognised. 'It's a chimp!' she cried as it swung toward her, knocking her to the ground. She heard the nauseating crack of her skull against the tarmac, and then darkness.

Verses of the Orata

Old crag, old rock
Sitting long on the moor
You were once brave
You were once strong
Do not think we have forgotten
Your green embrace, your strong limbs
That cleared the ember floor after lightning cometh
Who licked our wounds and offered refuge
Old crag, old log
Do not lie too long,
and be lost under bushel

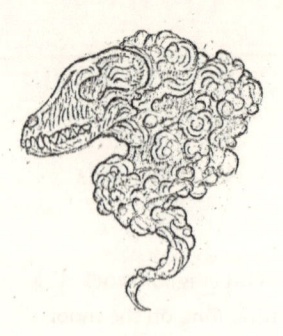

Chapter Seven

Vorsa awoke to pain. Her brother was a disorderly cloud of worry above her, 'Wake, my dear! Wake!'

She pulled herself up. She had been tossed aside like so much rubbish. She tasted blood in her mouth, her flanks were bruised, and pieces of her shard armour would need to be repaired. She was dizzy, and there was no sign of Ivy.

'Where is she, Petulan?'

Silence. He was elsewhere, his form little more than an echo, yet he returned shortly. 'Sorry, my love, lost in a sea of trouble.'

'Where is Ivy?' she asked curtly.

'They took her, up into that monstrous place, High Realm. They carried her away — they were so disagreeable!'

Vorsa padded warily to the entrance of the High Realm. It was a towering building of glass and metal. The once gleaming interior was now green with algae. An arch of handprints in dried mud and blood formed rudimentary images across the many windows; faces, angry warnings of the empire she now entered. She had been here once before, in the infant days after the Meridian.

She quietly stepped over the threshold. Petulan had withdrawn, leaving her to stealthily move through the building. What had been a well-kept lobby, complete with pruned inner borders and wide polished windows was now filled with a tangle of thick exotic plants vying for sunlight and space, taken root in the collected mulch and shattered marble tiles in search of water. The elevator shafts long dead, silent twin escalators the only path to the higher floors — this, too, surrendered to a throng of woody creeper vines wrapped purposefully around the handrails, trailing roots into the wet and nutrient rich loam that made up each step.

As she made for the still escalator to ascend the building, she was met by two tall simians, standing on their hind limbs, mouths full of bared teeth, eyes that spoke of honed rage. They brandished weapons, one with a spear, the other a club made of a chair leg. They were similar in stature to Ivy. She had not been new to these creatures, they too having been liberated from the Moterion, from where they quickly took to the streets in raucous vitriol, tearing up anything in their path. They rejoiced in the death of the Wroth with a frank and open mocking. They marched any dead Wroth they found to the river and drowned them in ritual funerals. They were varied clans, in size and shape, but all had come together in search of somewhere to call home.

From the ground, the summit of this building shone with green fortune overlooking the entire city — it remained one of the few towers to escape the First City and its vines. They took it for their own, lashing makeshift bridges to the much lower neighbouring buildings and the tree-like roots of Dron that drilled through masonry with ease. The largest of their kin, a female Hanno named Gahar, was made their overseer, and she ruled cooperatively with the other simian clans.

'Vulpus, this is none of your business.'

A muscular Toron, his fur sparse, greyish pink skin beneath, galumphed down the steps toward her, pointing his spear in her direction.

Vorsa was having none of it. 'Who fed you when the Wroth left you to die? Who freed you from those cages?'

'This Wroth will answer for what they did to us,' he spat back.

'She is a child, you fool, she is as responsible for their crimes as you are! Take me to Gahar and I will debate this with her myself!'

'You have no authority here, vixen! Be gone with you!'

Petulan emerged from her in terrifying apoplexy, a skull amongst stabs of splintered gore, a butchery of cold light flowing around the Toron like mercury — which stabbed at Petulan impotently, screaming out for it to stop.

'My brother is the Prince of the Lacking Sea, he has little time for living obstacles.'

Petulan corralled the pair away from Vorsa so that she could climb the escalator unhindered. Each level would present more guards, more barriers.

Once Petulan had scared the soldiers down into the lobby, he returned to her. They screamed from a distance yet did not attempt to come after her.

'Is there another way up, brother? I imagine there are many like our friends down there, many chances to end up flung from the peak of this place.'

Petulan's eyes widened, 'Let me explore.' With that he was gone.

Surreptitiously, Vorsa made for the emergency staircase, the doors of which had long been pulled down. An array of smeared handprints covered the walls.

Gahar shared little with the other clades– they had secured warm sheltered places where trees might be grown to provide food for her kin, becoming gardeners. They had no quarrel with Orn Megol, or the Forging sects of the Morwih, under Hevridis the Brave. They bartered a little but were rarely seen outside of the High Realm.

Vorsa bounded quietly upwards, until Petulan appeared to her. 'There are more guards above, more than I can protect you against. However, there are tunnels throughout the building. There is a path, but it will be a struggle to climb some of the passages.'

'Show me,' she said.

The ventilation shaft was almost entirely vertical until she could reach the second floor. She was a deft jumper, and could leap most if not all of the perilous metal corridors, yet one or two required her to push her back into the wall to attain a little friction, shuffling upwards until she had climbed at least four floors. By then, she was exhausted and paused for a while.

Petulan wriggled out of the vent to see if the coast was clear. He returned, nodding to her silently. She exited, finding herself in a wide bright space, filled with giant nests constructed from piles of clothes, old mattresses, cushions and blankets mingled with feathery pine branches and leaves.

'This must be where they sleep and raise their families.'

'Much like Orn Megol!' Petulan whispered in return.

She found a pool of water close to a broken window and drank heartily. She returned to the ventilation shaft and continued her climb. It was almost dusk when she reached the highest point of the building. The shaft was horizontal and ran the width of the building. She peered through a grating.

She saw a forest.

Beyond the metal grill was a glade of trees, and below the canopy, the trunks were hugged by low lying ferns, succulents and exotic palms. The ground was covered in soil and leaf litter. She could make out a little of the Wroth structure that housed this woodland domain, hidden almost entirely by sprawling vegetation.

A roof of glass allowed light from all angles, by which she saw she was far from alone. Over a hundred animals stood in monastic silence, looking upwards. Projecting from the sloping incline of the woodland perched atop the tower was a cliff-like overhang, itself heavy with trailing plants. Windows had long been broken and removed, leaving a balcony from which a variety of Toron and Hanno now sat, hung, and swayed from leathery limbs. At the centre, the seat of Hanno herself, Gahar, a nest of severed branches and fronds.

Vorsa saw Ivy. She reeled in shock. The poor cub was sobbing, blood upon her face, held by a guard.

Gahar sat with her head in her hands. She wore a headdress of bracken and silver birch. She was a powerful giant, her fur thick and black, her face broad and empathetic, riddled with guilt. She began to speak.

'I do not bear this decision lightly, but I also know this token comes from Naa — it was sent as the great redeemer, the great leveller. What we know is this - given the chance, this child will grow. She will foster kinship with other surviving Wroth. They will go to their places of power —find their technology, their ingenuity. They will revive it, in the name of progress. They will do all of this and say that it is good. But the progress that excites their brilliant minds is the same spark that leads to our suffering.'

The crowd was silent, passively accepting their leader's decision.

Vorsa began to chew at the grate, which was not obliging. She began to panic.

'Who have we had to answer for our suffering? No one. Their deaths were quick and discreet. The pain we hold is thick and choking.'

Vorsa felt the panel give. She turned and kicked at it until it buckled and she pushed her way through.

'Stop!'

The crowd turned to her; great silver backed hulks, ruddy furred Embaq, countless Toron of varying creeds, cradling young. They were armed and armoured in complexes of plastic and wood and metal. Nimble and fierce, they tensed in offensive stances.

'Please stop!'

They parted for the Vulpus and she cautiously stepped through. She sat on her hind legs. Above her the lattice of glass trapped the heat of the day, and she saw trees burdened with fruit, lithe creatures plucking the ripe harvest.

'I know your anger! I know your hurt! Long had we all struggled under the Wroth!'

Gahar leapt down from the overhang, hitting the ground with a heavy thud.

'How dare you, Vixen! The time for your kin to make decisions for us has passed! You have no voice here, we will enact our own judgement!'

'Judgement? This is a farce! Ivy is no more at fault than you! How are you any less guilty than a child who was barely old enough to have her own mind before the walls of the Moterion fell? Walls that I brought down!'

Gahar slid forward on her forearms, puffing her cheeks, her nostrils flaring, baring her teeth in a furious grin against the far smaller Vulpus. Vorsa could see a malady in her eyes that had obscured the once cogent Hanno.

'This child is an avatar of their destruction! She is a worthy sacrifice, for we have not had the luxury of vengeance that you once did — Vorsa Corpse Speaker! We are left to mourn the dead, mourn those who tortured us with their medicines, locked us up in their prisons. Tell me Vixen, what good could letting her live bring to Naa?' She sneered, pounding her hands against the floor.

'You have no idea! You cast assumptions, but you know nothing of her. You are right to fear the Wroth, but not this child. We came here to warn you of a true threat from those that wield all the cruelty you accuse her of, and they wish to break us into submission. The child you so willingly blame might be our only course to safety. Would you deny us this?'

Gahar arched her spine, breathing quickly, baring her impressive fangs. But it was not mockery, or even vitriol — there was so much pain in her. Vorsa could tell that this cause was a substitute for something far more potent.

'At least let her speak her mind, let her have a voice.'

Gahar reeled herself in. Her laboured, angered breath caught, 'As chieftain of these clans I must exercise jurisprudence. We will have a trial, for the life of this Wroth child.'

'Help me, Vorsa! Please!' Ivy screamed, as she was dragged back away from the ledge. Vorsa began to run toward her, snarling at any who forbade her or blocked her path. Her route was severed by a huge male Hanno, who grabbed her by her armour and lifted her from the ground.

'This is not the time for heroism.' He was not cruel and placed her down upon the ground.

'She is a child! How can you not see the madness in this?'

Her pleas were ignored. The sorrowful eyes of onlookers watched her slink to the corner of the atrium. A Toron guard appeared beside her. He said nothing but she assumed correctly he would watch over her until such a time that she would be called to represent Ivy. Vorsa could only look on as Gahar and her entourage disappeared into the undergrowth.

*

She looked down on the Stinking City, its aching vastness in blocks and cuboids. She had never been so high, and she marvelled at how endless Naa was. *The forest on top of the world*, she thought, her eyes following the rhythmic movements of these great simians grazing the leaves and fruits of their orchards, their cubs clambering over them, escorting them to the nests on the floor below — the night drawing in. She had known this comfort herself, at Orn Megol, with their mother and father. She had lived in the memory of that warmth on so many cold nights, in the frigid snows of winter, marching the streets in stubborn rain in spring.

Vorsa felt Petulan rush through her, but he did not manifest. She knew he had heard her thoughts and felt it best to leave her. She also knew he would encourage her to travel to Orn Megol, to see their father. Avoiding him was not going to somehow save him from his fate, she even felt that her presence would exacerbate his illness. He might die, and she would surely see him again, like she did her brother. But any warmth would be gone.

Petulan perceived each of these thoughts and felt shame for his hibernal form. He longed to offer comfort to Vorsa.

She curled up under a wide-leaved shrub and slept for a few hours, still uncomfortable to her nocturnal nature. She awoke to some food which had been brought for her by the guard – some unnameable meat – and once she had eaten it she was escorted to a place to relieve herself and lap from a puddle of rain water.

'When can I see Ivy?'

He looked down at her with a glare that seemed forced but said nothing. His silence, she sensed, was perforated by a keen frustration, perhaps even dissent. Gahar had a firm hand, yes. But she was also very fair. Vorsa had never known the High Realm to be needlessly aggressive. If anything, they had been incredibly peaceful, rising above the endless negotiations and inter-politics of the clades that shared the Stinking City.

Vorsa placed her paw on the Toron's foot. 'Please. The wrothcub has done nothing wrong. What could her death possibly achieve?'

He huffed and sniffed, and finally crouched low beside her. 'Gahar had a son, before you freed us, before all of this. She had a son, Eru. The Wroth let Dorharid, a grown male, into their cage. They had nowhere to hide. Dorharid killed Eru — so he would have no rivals. Gahar blames the Wroth for this.'

'A child for a child,' Vorsa lowered her head. She saw now it was an impossible position.

*

Noraa looked for a deity, hidden somewhere out of sight. For guidance and perhaps reassurance, each evening as both she and Little Grin woke to continue their journey, she removed the bone hex from her armour and invoked her overmother. Then the colourless entity bled into Naa, ushering a stale, cold air, tendrils of black unguent trailing about her as though submerged in water.

You are close, she would say, *close to that which can aid in your salvation.*

She would point a bony paw toward distant hills, and they would walk, sharing tales of their lives, sometimes followed by the suspended apparition of her ancestor that drew in the light like a collapsed star. Later she would be gone without a word, for which Little Grin was always glad.

His mother and father had died not long after his birth, in traps set by the Wroth. He had lived a very solitary life, having not known many of his own kind — hunted to near obliteration, he sought fellowship with any who would spare a moment for him. Within the woodlands he had once called home he would spend a lot of time in the company of Sqyre. He found himself useful in scaring off predators, keeping Muroi and Creta out of their winter stores.

'Friendship is something I value very highly,' he said to her one evening as they crested a hill, overlooking a craggy steppe. There were large predatory feathered amongst crevices, and they sat and watched them fly out against the fading light. 'I count myself lucky to have known so many good souls. I feel these Husk are everything I fear, that hollow sadness, to be nothing but a shadow of yourself. To know no peace.

'I saw the pain on the faces of those taken, it was a singular realisation of that fate. I am so small, but I wish to drive it from Naa.'

'We may yet get that chance, Little Grin.'

The undergrowth became sparse once again, exposing capacious skies filled with cheerless motion. The grass beneath their feet was coarse and resistant to the wind. They huddled behind boulders to retain heat, and strode out against it when they felt able. Overmother Yaga, would emerge and grace them with her uncertain counsel, and whilst that did little to quell Little Grin's grief, it was apparent to Noraa that much of this was a test of her own fortitude. As a cub she had been taught to never expect everything to be explained or done for her. Her earliest memories of the enclosure she was born into, where their food was given to them by their captors, always came with a prayer — that one day this might be taken from them and they would need to hunt for their supper. Just like the will to hunt and survive, so too would she find what she was looking for.

As the dawn yawned wide, they came upon the carcass of an old Effer. It was still good to eat, which both of them took advantage of, and as Little Grin rested at the base of a depression in the earth, where soft moss provided a bed, Noraa took the bones and sinew and made a conundrum of meat, a pyramid of femurs, a question and an answer, to any who might see and understand. As the day rose, so too did two shadows, one that marked the rise of Ora, the other a shadow not of this world, cast by something drawn to her prize.

She searched for a moment to find some pebbles — the prettier the better. She lay four to mark her way, and then collapsed beside Little Grin. They slept until the afternoon, the daylight invigorating their tired bodies.

Their stomachs soon grumbled and so they picked the bones clean, and she showed Little Grin her path. Three pebbles remained, one had disappeared. She smiled and thanked the dead, and then they made their way southeast, towards the highest point on the horizon.

*

The sensation began as a low rumble. A stirring beneath her paws. It soon became insistent, accompanied by a low whistle that Little Grin could not hear. The quake lasted a day and a night, becoming fuller, more melodious, neither painful nor exasperating. If anything, it felt familiar, and shepherded her toward an outcropping of doldrum stone anchored in the moor that spoke of something hidden.

But the stones were not alone. Noraa could see a fire.

Fire wasn't entirely alien to her; she had seen Wroth-made lights, and the flames after lightning strikes. But this little fire shed a comforting light, and she could see movement in the shadows cast. Something sat beside it, stoking the burning wood with a stick. She could smell it, under the smoke, a scent she had only known as a cub. It was a Wroth.

Little Grin feigned anger, which did little to hide his fear. She knew she would have little time to kill it before it could kill them, and so she ran, the sound becoming louder, grinding, screeching, the rich clang of metal ore, and it rose as she hastened, rising until she was unable to hear over it, until it drowned her in a clash of sediments, of the mantle below her paws, until its clogging heaviness suffocated her, and she stopped running and she fell in agony, burying her face in the earth, trying to rid herself of it. Little Grin was upon her instantly, pawing at her, crying for her to get up. But the sound! It was parting her skull, a clamouring cacophony.

And then it ceased.

*

She felt an unfamiliar paw upon her. It was warm, and pleasant. Noraa pushed her head out of the soil, turning her muzzle to one side, fearful the sound would return. Above her, a face, half lit by the fire, and an arm reaching down and stroking her fur, like her mother's rough tongue. Noraa was disoriented, her eyes thick with tears.

'It's okay, you have nothing to fear. I mean you no harm.' The voice was Umbra, risen in Noraa's own mind.

A Wroth, an Umbra?

The Wroth.

She recoiled in disgust, and at once was on her feet, lips riled, teeth shining, the flutter snarl in her oesophagus.

'Stay back!' Noraa trembled in adrenaline fugue.

The Wroth held her arm out as if to calm her, repeating

I mean you no harm—

'All you know is harm!' she seethed.

Little Grin stood behind her, hiding under her tail.

Noraa's eyes remained upon the creature, this fulcrum of all she had ever hated, ready to snap at that anaemic arm, to tear it off, and then—

A Creta, fat with seeds and nuts, ran down that arm, and perched upon its fingers.

'You have nothing to fear. She has bequeathed herself to Ocquia. She is an Umbra I believe, and she wants to help us. She has lost so much, her entire family. We must show her that which the Wroth never did.'

'What?' Noraa growled.

'A chance to prove us wrong.'

The Wroth lowered her arm, and the Creta ran back up and perched on her shoulder.

'My name is Lucille, and I promise you, whatever my people did to you, I am truly sorry, but I want only friendship. I am an archaeologist — I look for things buried in the earth from long ago. Makepeace and I are digging under these stones. You are welcome to join us for some food and shelter.'

Noraa narrowed her eyes and said curtly, 'What is under the stones?'

*

The mist rolled in across the marshland. It played tricks on the mind, formations like shadows with motive, mirages made of curls in the water vapour.

Ether, the Yoa'a, sharpened her gauntlet blades on a piece of flint she carried with her. It was always good to keep them sharp. Her companions were Brunthola, an older Yoa'a of a different Drove and Emig, a dear friend from birth, who ran with her sisters. Above was a Collector called Aggi, who was their spotter, armourer and general guide.

Even in this poor light, Aggi was able to see the path. It was an old Wroth route, following a hedgerow, which would lead them to the water. It was dangerous here, the tidelands were plagued with flooding, some inconsistency in the seasons, a legacy of the Wroth. Warmer winters and more frequent storms had raised the sea level and much of the former land here was bog — an easy place to drown.

Aggi landed beside Ether, clutching a worm which she unceremoniously tore apart, much to the disgust of Ether. 'Do you have to do that in front of me, Aggi?'

'Oh! Sorry, my love, bad habit. Hungry after all this flying. Path is good, down to the water, but you will need to watch your step, some parts of the fog are too dense, can't make hide nor hair of it.'

Emig was shaken, 'I don't like this. There are things in the fog.'

'It's just your mind playing tricks on you, there isn't anything out there other than water and mud. This path, however, leads straight to our goal, and those little egg thieves will be expecting us.' Brunthola stood on her hind legs and shook her haunch plates, 'And we'll be ready for 'em.'

They continued on, with Aggi flying beside them. A few hours passed and the fog became ever more impenetrable, Ora barely a diffused glow. A fretful cry could be heard in the distance, perhaps some water feathered. Even Ether, who was level headed when it came to dangerous situations, felt a sense of panic. Yet they pressed on, along the dirt track, stopping once to feed on berries they'd hung from their armour.

Ahead, the trees enveloped the path, creating a tunnel of leaf-laden branches. Of the light that penetrated the grey haze, almost none of it lit their route. They could hear the lap of water, the fleeting slosh of feet in mud. Ears twitched with each sound. They kept close, with Aggi walking with them, unable to see them from above any longer.

An arthritic snapping reverberated off the water, it appeared to be moving parallel to them. A yellow haze had grown on the horizon, yet it was no Ora, and it carried a foul odour.

'Smells like rot, from below. Maybe from deep in the bog.'

They came to a standstill, with Ether holding them back. She hopped towards the treeline. A head pushed through, long and pale. It was a dead Ardid, its body bloated with gases.

As quickly as the head had appeared, with a croaking wrench, it was pulled back. A half dozen Muroi poured out of it, having burrowed into its flesh. They gnashed their incisors at the Drove, fur engrossed with oily gore and fat.

The Drove recoiled and immediately took defensive positions. The largest of the Muroi lurched forward, hissing at them, bloody spittle raining down.

'Drove scum! I thought they might call on your lot. This scratch of earth is ours now, under our jurisdiction. We've made a deal with those who rule here!'

The body of the Ardid belched.

'Oh him? Just a disagreement on the final terms.'

Ether raised herself onto her back legs, 'You're a liar. You're holding these feathered against their will. If you leave with no trouble, it won't come to violence.'

'Oh, you're in no position of authority here, missy. This is Stegard territory now. So you can drop the pretence.' The snivelling creature squealed and a swarm of Muroi flooded from each side of the track. The Drove were forced further along, their gauntlet blades held out as they were corralled towards the water.

'Haven't you heard? Embrian Naa is under new rule. Just this past turn we had a band of those Husk through 'ere, making a nuisance. Tried to take us, but we made a deal with them too, ya see they don't have any use for this land, small pickings for an invading force. They'll barter with those who won't resist them, and we stand to gain once all you goody goodies are nothing but meat for hungry mouths, eh?' He spat, his greasy fur standing upright on his head.

They came to some banks of thickset reeds and a number of nesting waterfowl, all in distress. Five fat Muroi sat consuming the eggs of a mother, who wept silently on her barren roost. The Muroi were drunk with gluttony, and only took notice of their commander when he shouted at them. They chittered humiliation as they lined up, covered in yolk. The shore was strewn with eggshells and faeces.

'That was for all of us, you dung larvae!' He bit the flank of the closest to him, who squeaked in pain and slumped off to hide.

'We're a loose affiliation of thieves, ya see. Came together when we realised without the Wroth there were no longer easy pickings. Had to get creative, had to find a steady source of food.'

Whilst his rough and ready guards hung back, surrounding the Drove, hissing with fetid teeth and claws, he swam out to one of the nests. A number of chicks huddled next to their mother. He took a webbed foot in his mouth and dragged it back with him, a tiny Fologuw, trembling with fear. Once ashore, he threw the chick before them.

'We have meat with the newborns and plenty of eggs. We let some live of course, so we can have more egg layers! It's a thriving industry. So really, you have no place here, Drove. But as you can tell, I like to make deals. I find there is much to be gained from mutually beneficial exchanges. You can work for us, bodyguards. We'll pay you in whatever you need, we have salves, precious objects, even Drove armour we've pilfered. You can do that, or you can die, either by our paws, or by the Husk when they swing back around for their tithing.'

Ether sighed long and hard. She loped forward so that she was level with the vulgar rodent. He was large, far larger than any Muroi she'd dealt with before, and in her time she'd met many. She wondered if more would embrace this attitude.

'Stegard. Let me consider your deal for a moment.'

She moved her forelimbs with such ferocity that, afterwards, few could make sense of what they had seen. Aggi had been very particular about Ether's gauntlets. In the little time she had run with the Drove, Aggi had procured a number of whetting stones, and had perfected the art of sharpening metal with her strong beak and the blade between her toes. She had taught Ether, who was more than willing to carry the sharpening tools upon her armour alongside an assortment of implements useful to the Collector. 'If you sharpen that blade any more, there won't be much blade left!' she had remarked that morning.

Stegard looked bewildered. He wobbled a little, and then his head toppled off his neck and rolled to the water's edge. His body collapsed. Ether shook the blood from her blade and held it up before her. 'Will need sharpening again, I think.'

The Stegard thieves panicked. Brunthola strode out before them whilst Emig and Aggi helped the little chick back to its mother.

'Right, you horrible lot. Your fearless leader is dead. You now have the marvellous deal of getting the piss out of here, and never coming back, or feeling the grain of our blades.' She kicked the headless corpse before her. 'He was the biggest of you, and he didn't put up much of a fight, so if I were you, I'd piss on out of here.'

The thieves instinctively moved in one direction – to fight – before Brunthola growled. Then they quickly lost their impetus and shrieked away into the mist.

The mother and her chicks swam to the shore, 'Thank you,' she said, 'you have saved my children from them. So many lost, so many young.'

Ether bowed, 'We were so enraptured by Naa without the Wroth, that we never considered the void it left for the scavengers, the animals that had grown fat on their waste.'

Aggi appeared beside them, 'Where are your Vulpus guard? I thought this district was always Vulpus territory?'

The Fologuw shook her head, 'Not in my lifetime. There are the ruins of a city I am told, further along the coast, where the land is less wet — the Wroth destroyed it and drove the Vulpus away. Maybe you'll still find some there willing to help us?'

Aggi nodded, 'We will keep a regular eye on your breeding grounds, not to worry. We will make sure any local Vulpus clans, or indeed, Naarna Elowin are aware. We will travel back to the First City and address these matters. Ora bring peace.'

The Drove and Aggi made their farewells. Before she left, they dragged the body of Stegard into a ditch. Ether paused over the head. It would make a fine trophy to impress her mother.

*

Their journey southeast began, resting under trees to feast on browning apples, play fighting tipsy battles with one another. Aggi pecked at the decomposing fruit, finding a few treasured maggots dug in. A procession of Vulpus could be heard, singing dourly. Ether flopped around in a drunken stagger, loudly accompanying the humourless dogs and vixens who solemnly walked along the track.

'Oi!' Ether hollered. 'Where you going?'

The leader of their pack halted and turned back. 'We are traveling to Thron Awlbringa, the sunken Church of Tet. Be careful, Drove, there is danger in these lands. The Husk are everywhere. Go home, be safe!'

'I am home!' she slurred. 'The road is my home!'

*

Narna Elowin soldiers stood idle on the low peaks of Dron, pecking at loose down, squabbling over stone games and the size of the Ungdijin they'd caught that day. They exchanged tales of how they had been conscientious objectors in the war for OrauNaa, how they had defied the word of Esperer, even in the face of court martial, or death.

None had done such things; all had fought under the webbed talons of their leader, and yet now evidence of support for the dead king was frowned upon. Roak and his lifemate, Tawk had proscribed a new accord for the Naarna Elowin, one that respected the rule of the Thousand Headed King yet maintained a much desired sense of self-worth. So, they had become the Guardians of Dron.

Much of their work was identical to that under their previous command, but this station came with an earned pride; protecting this place was paramount for all living things —no guardianship such as this had ever existed before.

The Naarna Elowin faced few threats, although Dron was not without its adversaries. Some species held the city in contempt for not assisting them sooner, generations lost to the malice of the Wroth. Yet it was the Naarna Elowin and the Morwih who had picked this battle – had found such a place of purpose in the First City – that confronting those who were against its presence became almost a passion, something akin to a religion.

Morwih preached of how the First City had given them an opportunity to claim their heritage, stolen from them by their former masters. They had found and adopted old feline gods from the annals of ancestors held immemorial. The Naarna Elowin flew the banner of that same belonging, a palpable gravity in which they wished others to be caught.

And so, from their posting atop the craggy outcrop, the wind at their back, the wide land below them, they watched zealously as a cluster of dark shapes moved toward the city.

'Looks like the Windsweepers are coming in from the She-King Carcaris.'

'Yes. Shall I send message to the Dominus? They are expected?'

'Good idea. I shall remain 'ere and direct the squadron.'

One awaited the flock to become more visible, and then performed a series of wing manoeuvres to direct their descent toward the lofty valley that lay between the city's mountains. Here, the shaft to the Regulax could be found, and the guide traced their path above him, unusually silent. Their flight was erratic – wing beats lost – frantic recovery.

He called out to Awfwod yet received no response. He frowned. Something seemed a little off. He thought nothing of it and returned his gaze to the horizon.

*

He preceded the messengers, landing before the Corvan clergy gathered with Audagard and the Starless Vulpus. There was some decorum to follow - the handing of the message to the Dominus, and the deliberations of the news amongst the Quorum.

'The Court of the Clades, Dominus Audugard of the Anx of many kin, may I present the Windsweepers and their flight chief, Awfwod Garoo.'

The flock of Baldaboa appeared moments later, cascading through the open shaft. The light that brought them shielded their presence and they moved without sound, without the usual hot air that came with this particular squadron.

'Awfwod, what news from Queen Carcaris?'

'News? News I have!'

The voice was disconcerting, a sliding wet click, a jaw stretched. The tell-tale jerk of Baldaboa was absent, muscles pulled taught. The light no longer hid them as they emerged from its glare and now it could be seen that their feathers were greasy, smeared in a black spoil. There were wounds too — pecked out feathers, thorn barbs dug in flesh. Their eyes were milk white, and vapour hung about them with a particular autonomy.

'News we have!'

They skittered, fell, recovered. Unhealthy, yet powerful.

Dominus Audagard wasted no time. He screeched at his clergy in Corvan tongue and they rushed to his side, pecking at two spurs of bone dug into his head dress. A veil of tattered black plastic fell over his eyes. He dug his beak into his own skin, spitting the blood upon the floor. His clergy rushed again, accompanied by the Starless Vulpus, an array of fetishes fashioned from fossil bone clenched between their teeth. Mirror shards were thrust before the Quorum and more blood was shed. The Dominus began scrawling incantations in the ichor — as the Baldaboa watched with a mixture of shock and ridicule.

'What nonsense is this!'

Audagard began to chant in low wretched squawks. His clergy stood beside him, repeating each phrase. Finally, they stopped. Their eyes returned to the Windsweepers. They picked up the shards of mirror and held them out before the Dominus. He lifted his mask and turned a shard so that he could see the Baldaboa. The reflection showed him their true form — septic eyes, hungry mouths. These poor feathered were taken.

The Dominus stepped forward.

'I spent a lifetime in veneration of the place from which you have been freed. I know its black facets, its immutable depths. I know Gaspstuff when I see it. Why have you forsaken these innocent feathered? What possible purpose could they serve to you?'

'We are the Husk! Harbingers of Thoth! Bastions of the true King of this land! We come with sad tidings for you!'

That which had been Awfwod Garoo slinked forward, his legs in unnaturally angled repose. He shook, regurgitating something foul onto the floor. It slid toward the Dominus, whose eyes remained locked with the Baldaboa. The grey mass climbed the bone hex on a path for the Corva. The clergy whispered to it, and with that, the corruption was absorbed into the bone hex.

Awfwod wheezed, 'What is this?'

'You will not succeed in your attempts to possess us. We are masters of revenants — we control the dead in this plane. You will find no hosts for your grim enterprise here.'

Awfwod grimaced. 'So be it. My lord, Thoth, sends you word of his approach. He will take these lands, and he will seize this place. You will bend the knee to him or be food for his soldiers. His army grows with each stride, and you will be powerless against him, even with your petty spells.'

The Dominus thought for a moment. 'You come to the citadel of Naa and threaten us, and you wish us to surrender to this Thoth? Tell me, does your master know what this city is? Does he know how it tore asunder the Wroth metropolis, toppled its monoliths? How can one creature compare to the sum of all, to the Umbra and the Epiras!'

The Baldaboa began to laugh, a frantic, unnatural hack, no longer Baldaboa, a facsimile of something dead, something wroth-like. 'You speak so highly of yourselves, but Thoth will remind you to whom this world will grovel!'

Audagard smiled. 'I assume whatever you are, you will eventually find yourself the means to return to Naa, to once again defile a harmless victim, so with that in mind and when that occurs, please inform this Thoth that pride is a fool's errand. Enough of this.'

The clergy wreathed the Baldaboa, their eyes covered, placing hex assemblages at the feet of each Windsweepers, who attacked with beak and claw. The Corva parsed their revenant speech, the *Nash aka*, revealing the twisted, condensed ghouls held within their victims. They left the prayer unfinished, tethering the apparition not to Naa, but to the hex upon the ground.

'Get out!' they chanted, they cried, increasing their recitations, a lather of blood and powerful words, dragging the consumption from their hosts, splitting perversion from untainted meat, until the fetid revenants screamed into the void and were gone. The Baldaboa collapsed, wings splayed.

Audagard kicked the glass away, severing any means of escape, and slumped to the floor. 'I did not think I would need to use such magic again!' He pulled in his wings, shivering.

Pelspet Rakiq, one of his loyal clergy, leaned towards him, 'Dominus, I did not read the nature of them, I could not place the wraith, did not know its clade. But it was…strong.'

'Yes!' his fellow clerics echoed.

Threthrin gathered objects and charms of ritual and placed them beside the Regulax. He looked to the Dominus.

'So. They are Maligna, like my brothers and sisters of the Oaza Vas. But what, pray tell, was in them?'

'Wroth.'

The Quorum gasped.

Audagard said, 'I saw the cut of it, I saw how small they had made themselves, holed themselves up inside the Windsweepers. I perceived their intentions. They are what Petulan spoke of, revenants pulling themselves into Naa, like certainties, yet they are not simply wandering visitors — they are infections, they are *inside* our kin. They are like you once were, my dear Threthrin.'

Threthrin growled. 'Yes. I felt it, the unforgiving cold. Old scars pained me. But how are the Wroth freeing themselves from the Gasp? What is this Thoth they speak of?'

The Dominus ruminated, 'I dare say he was the first. Perhaps he has some natural propensity for Gaspcraft, or—'

'Or?' Threthrin probed.

'He is a Shadow Starer. A strong one.'

Rune came forward. 'He is, I have been shielding the city from him. I have not been able to see him clearly until now. Your fears are correct. He is Wroth, but he has a particularly disturbing presence, there is rage and hatred, but also a madness, and something I do not recognise, a Wroth thing no doubt. We are right to build defences, but I fear this monster will storm us on all fronts, physical and immaterial.'

*

Scab and his lieutenants walked the streets of a district he'd once thought to rob. How quickly it had all been taken from them, all the fancy things now grimy and unwanted.

He waxed lyrical about his exploits to the two Cini beside him, an older female who harboured the Wroth revenant of a young man, Khan Singh, who had never committed a crime, but had also not achieved very much in his eighteen years. The other, a younger male Lupine, was inhabited by the spirit of Carl Henderson, a man whose exploits had been so varied and frivolous he found Scab to be somewhat of a bore, but having died so unexpectedly, high on cocaine, his second chance was not to be sniffed at. So he listened, glancing at the shop windows, still laden with once expensive jewellery and clothing that circumstance had rendered meaningless to him.

'We were going to hold up one of those posh banks, the ones only rich people get to use. But my mate said they had that special security, where the cashier has no access. Anyway I got nicked, but I went down for other things.'

The *other things* sparked a morsel of interest in Carl, imagining all manner of debauchery.

They made for the river, and a bridge to cross. As they turned on a road where fortunes were once lost and gained, they saw something very unexpected. A human – a young Wroth – being tackled and dragged towards the entrance of a remarkably unscathed office building, by two large apes.

'Shit! Did you see that? Did you see that?'

'A Wroth, a fucking living Wroth! How? How come she got to live?'

Scab hushed his fellow Husk, and they backed behind an abandoned car. Scab felt his vision blur with shock and indecision. He asked of his subconscious for the right course of action. He knew this was important — a living girl would be a prize.

You'll never get up there. Those animals are far bigger and stronger than you. Even if you managed to take a few, they'd overpower you — who knows how many are up there. You'll need a far greater force.

He glanced towards the invisible river, still hidden behind derelicts and crumbled piles of long departed commerce.

He had an idea.

*

Vorsa was escorted up a path that led beside the thicket of trees and stocky undergrowth. The sleek marble steps and guard rails were chipped and coiled with greenery.

Gahar perched within a large nest held between two boughs. Beside her, and lower to the floor, were more sleeping places for the great Hanno, and Vorsa was reminded of the egalitarian nature of this clade.

Toron escorted Ivy from the ledge above. She had been washed and a paste of healing leaves covered a wound on her forehead. Her eyes were red with tears, but she was silent.

Soon, the motion of many great Hanno, Toron and Embaq, as well as a school of smaller, more agile simians, began to congregate around the arcade that overlooked the city through tall windows, their frames accented by eager green vines.

Gahar climbed down slowly, her eyes never deviating from Vorsa, 'Tell me, Vorsa Corpse Speaker. You saw me as a god once?'

Vorsa bowed. 'My dear Gahar, you will always be a god to me. In the Moterion were living beings I could not comprehend, animals far larger and more varied than any in Embrian Naa. It was not just a duty to assure your survival, but a necessity.'

Gahar looked away. 'The Wroth saw me as less than a god, less than, perhaps anything. I lived in a cage for most of my life. I was taken from the forests of my home and moved from one god prison to another. They wanted me to breed, you see. They thought I was stupid, or perhaps incapable of love. I shunned all their suitors. I refused to give them any more of myself.'

'It was your right to bear children only if you wished,' Vorsa replied carefully.

'I cannot deny that I did want a child. But I also knew that my child would be worth more to them as breeding stock than as a son or daughter to me. I refused, until the choice was taken from me.'

Vorsa frowned, 'How?'

'They gave me a medicine and I slept. I awoke and I felt my body changed. In weeks I was showing signs of carrying a child. I assumed it was some Wroth magic, but by whatever means, they took that choice from me. I gave birth to that child, and for a very brief moment I felt something I had never known before. I felt joy. I was so in love with that little cub, so enraptured, I could forget the walls that imprisoned me. Until one day, the Wroth decided I was too happy, too full of love. They opened those gates, not for me to leave, but to let a contender in. A male I did not know. Do you know what he did?'

Vorsa cowered. To deny this mother her grief was perhaps the most damning act. But she must try. She did not reply.

'That ogre broke my son's neck and carried his limp body about that cage with him, flashing his teeth and screaming his dominion, shaking my son like a trophy. You see, the Wroth didn't care about how I felt. Yes, they probably mourned their loss, they may have even felt sorry for what they had done. But they made a choice, I can never forgive them for that.'

Vorsa sighed, 'I will not attempt to placate you. I will not shower you with platitudes, but I will speak plainly. Regardless of the significance of this wrothcub, she is not a tool of vengeance. The love you feel for your son is the loudest, most clear proof of your compassion. If you were to kill Ivy, you might have a moment of vitriol, yes, but it would be quickly followed by a lifetime of regret and sorrow.'

'We existed in spite of them. We breathed in spite of them. This wrothcub is all that is left of them. If we destroy it, we are free of them.'

'And if she were your child?'

Gahar's head jarred. 'If she were my child?'

'If your child was the one thing that stood between freedom and subjugation?'

'My child was not a harbinger. My child was not stricken with the curse this creature carries in its nature. My child lived because of their greed and arrogance and died because of their careless disregard. *Oh, the child died, never you mind, the ape will birth another!*'

'But to usher in a time of peace, would you let that child die?'

Gahar bellowed, 'Your attempt to play to my weakness is laudable, but we are beyond such mind games, Vorsa Corpse Speaker. Maybe you'd have more luck with the dead with such subterfuge, but I am not so easily outwitted! This is not a hypothetical matter —this is meat and bone! Here is a Wroth, the seed of future misfortune. Do we allow her to take root, or do we pull her up and discard her, like they did my child?'

Ivy groaned, 'I know you.'

Gahar turned her grimaced face toward the wrothcub. She loped on all fours peering down at the girl. She lifted Ivy's face with her finger.

'What did you say? Speak up, let us all hear your lies.'

'I know you. I visited the zoo with my family when I was younger. I saw you in the enclosure. I heard you, and you heard me. You looked through me with such sorrow. I carried that despair with me, I made different choices because of you. I knew your sadness when my own family died.'

Gahar snorted, dismissing her words with a swipe of her hand. 'Words, just words. Meaningless. The Wroth had all the time in the world to right their wrongs, to atone for the endless acts of violence they had committed. To lock me away was one thing, to take my child,' she whimpered, forcing her voice into a venomous cry — 'YOU TOOK MY CHILD!'

Ivy sobbed, 'I didn't! I was nine years old! My mother was still alive then. It could have been a happy memory, but meeting you, changed me! I saw beyond myself. Now the memory of my mother is all mixed up with my memory of you!'

Gahar narrowed her eyes. Vorsa saw something, an inkling, a tiny shift. She could tell Gahar wanted to hear more.

'You lost your mother?'

Tears welled in Ivy's eyes. 'Yes, I was ten years old. Mum wore a headscarf — all her hair fell out. She was tired all of the time. Dad would drive her to the hospital for chemotherapy. She was doing better for a while, but the cancer came back and she got sick very quickly. She had an operation to remove it, but it was too late, it was all through her body. I remember seeing her in her bed, she was so thin and pale. So lost in pain. She died in her sleep. I wasn't there. For a long time, I was so guilty for not being there for her when she died.'

Vorsa said loudly so that Ivy could hear, 'She knew you loved her!'

'But I just wanted to say goodbye!' Ivy burst into tears, exhausted by all that had befallen her, and the assembled simians lowered their heads in shame. Gahar's eyes darted about the crowd before her — those who followed her word loyally could not meet her gaze.

Gahar screamed. 'All those who defy me will know my hand!'

It was an empty threat. She had never raised a finger to hurt anyone. She galumphed towards Ivy, grabbing her by the shoulder, wrenching her towards the window.

Ivy vomited with terror, crying out in hysteric gasps for air. She strained against Gahar's grip, tearing at her hand to free herself.

The great Hanno was incredibly strong and unflinching in her resolve. She stooped to pick up a large heavy branch and began to rail against the glass, her face crumpling with grief. The glass gave way and shattered.

Gahar held Ivy out towards the Toron guard beside Vorsa.

'Take her, throw her from this place. Now!' Gahar cried. 'Now!'

The guard, Rawm, did not move.

'Have you forgotten what they did? Have you all forgotten how we lived, what we lost!'

Rawm stood on his hind limbs, 'How can we ever forget? You ask us to see this wrothcub as our enemy, but all I see is my daughter.'

He held his hand up in the air, and moved hesitantly towards Ivy, tentatively holding out his open fingers. She raised her hand and he placed his against hers.

'I cannot kill this wrothcub, for she is no more guilty than me. I am sorry, Gahar. I love you, we all love you, but this death would not bring back Eru.'

Gahar collapsed, releasing Ivy.

Rawm gently took Ivy and escorted her to Vorsa. She whimpered in pain and they slowly made their way to a quiet corner.

Gahar sat motionless before the window. She looked down at her hands, palms facing her.

'He was so small.' A few of her attendants went to her and offered comfort.

Once Ivy was safe, Rawm fetched fruit and water, which he handed to her with her belongings. Her coat was ripped but her rucksack had survived.

Vorsa licked Ivy's face. 'I will go to her and try to explain our plight. You will wait here and he will watch over you.' She looked to Rawm, who nodded.

Before Vorsa could even move, a commotion was heard beyond the sky garden, the sound of a succession of dull thuds. Vorsa ran to the steps to the promenade, 'What is it?'

Eyes focused on the window. There was a blood stain.

Another thud, another, and another. There were feathered flying at the glass. The window suddenly shattered, and with it came a large Naarna Elowin, falling awkwardly before the startled crowd. It sloughed off a greyish film and its eyes held no life.

'Run!' Vorsa screamed, as a volley of Naarna Elowin pummelled the glass, a dozen barrelling over themselves as they breached the tower. The congregation looked to one another in bafflement, peering at the first Naarna Elowin. Its legs were broken yet it slid toward them with a determined leer, leaking blood and a black slop that appeared to reach out of its own volition.

'They are plague bearers! Run!'

Vorsa began to run, followed by a barrage of terrified simians. Rawm ushered Ivy out of the garden and down the stairs, following the path taken by Vorsa. They tumbled down, avoiding office furniture and wide holes in the floor caused by water damage, all the while their companions in flight using ledges and handrails in their agile descent of building.

*

Scab watched from afar, waiting to see if his plan had worked. They had gone to the edge of the river and parlayed with a flock of seagulls, flattering them with tales of their heroic wars, and all the while, Scab had been entering the Gasp, herding fervent ghouls into corporeality — and, like a flood, they had gushed from him, into the stunned silent eyes of the gulls, taken en masse, a squirming heap of slick feathers. Eventually they stood to greet him, confused, gangling, altogether ill at ease.

'We're bloody seagulls!' one squawked.

'We're bloody alive, that's what we are!' another retorted.

Scab cleared his throat. 'You have a job. See that ugly tower? I want you to fly to the top floor, where that greenery is, and I want you to gain entry. Inside you'll find apes — gorillas, chimps, big fuckers. They are all yours, you want them, kill the body you're in, enter another. It's that simple.'

'That simple he says. How do we bloody well fly?'

'Like this!' another had shouted excitedly, already taking to wing in little bursts.

'Comes natural!'

Clumsily, the entire flock had lifted and headed for the building. Not that all would make it through the window.

Once inside, the survivors attacked the Hanno, and were torn from the air by powerful fists, wrung by the neck and split in two — a quick release that hastened their occupation of the more formidable beasts. Once again reborn with violent spasms, they lifted themselves in unison.

'I'm a fucking gorilla!' The revenant was a woman, a former police officer. She ran her thick hands over her fur, her face, and found something attached to her head. 'What's this thing?' It was a crown of some sort, made of sticks and leaves. She pulled it from her head and stamped on it.

Ivy was outside. She stumbled to her knees, hyperventilating, desperately trying to catch a breath —her ears rang, her wrists were swollen. Vorsa knew there was little she could do to help, so instead she led Ivy away from the High Realm.

They found shelter in the ruins of a church. Once manicured borders and thick bushes of red and green leaves had hung handsomely from consecrated walls — a little oasis, hidden amongst featureless concrete buildings. They sat on a bench, and Ivy slumped against her bag. She cried a little, and then slept.

She awoke to find Vorsa curled at her feet. They talked a little, and Vorsa examined Ivy's wounds. Thankfully they were superficial bruises. Eventually, Ivy spoke of her ordeal.

'When mum died I was so angry at dad, for letting her die. I blamed him for it. I know now I was just so…so angry at mum for dying, for leaving us. I didn't know what to do. In a way, her death prepared me for this — for Dad and my brother. When they died I really thought I'd done something wrong. I realise now, all of us who survived, we all lost something, because we're the ones who lived.'

Vorsa reflected on her words. 'Waiting for Petulan to die was a pain I found so hard to bear. I feel that again, with my father. I feel like, by not going to him, I am prolonging his life, that my presence, would encourage death to take him.'

Ivy had never touched Vorsa, but felt the urge to. She held her hand out, offering it to her. Vorsa pushed her cheek into Ivy's fingers, and Ivy stroked her ears and neck. It felt like an important gesture.

'Nothing we do can stop death, but maybe we can ease their suffering.' Ivy pulled her coat around her, and stood up. 'I am alive. I have you, and we have a goal.'

She breathed deeply, jumped up and down. 'We need to get out of the city,' she said, wincing at the stiffness in her wrists.

'The feathered, were those Husk?' Ivy asked.

Vorsa nodded, 'I believe so. I recognised that foulness about them. I've seen things taken by revenants before. They're already here, which is too close for comfort.'

'Okay, well, we have a goal. I don't think walking is really an option, so I am going to suggest we drive.' Ivy awaited Vorsa's response.

Vorsa didn't understand the statement.

Ivy tried to remember the term Erithacus had used — 'Scithar?'

'Oh, well, I have no idea how someone might ride such a thing, but if it gets us to where we need to go any quicker, then, yes,' Vorsa said plainly.

*

Ironically, there were very few cars to choose from. From the first few days of the pandemic the inner city had been almost empty; those who were not yet sick cared for the dying, only to be infected themselves. No one had left the house to drive anywhere, so most vehicles remained in driveways, in garages, or parked neatly at the side of suburban roads. Any who fled were soon consumed by symptoms of the virus and succumbed to them soon after.

Ivy furrowed her brow — three large vans and a truck. They made for the nearest van, only to find a smaller car behind it. The door was open on the driver's side, and a woman lay sprawled on the seat. The back seats were filled with bags of canned food and survival paraphernalia. This woman had died fairly recently and there was little sign of decay. It begged the question, how had she died? There were no signs of illness or wounds. Thankfully, there was no odour, although pulling the body from the car was not a simple task. It wasn't the first time she had moved someone who had died, but it wasn't something you ever got used to. She hoped the woman hadn't evacuated her bowels. The relatively recent death gave her hope that the car had been in use and, therefore, still worked.

She made an apology as the cadaver slumped onto the pavement. The body hadn't soiled the seat, so she got into the car. The key was in the ignition. She leaned over and unlatched the passenger side, pulling the handle to open the door wide enough for Vorsa to jump in.

Vorsa stood outside, sheepishly staring at the car. 'I am not sure what I am supposed to do.'

Ivy had the urge to pat the seat, but instead explained to the vixen that she wished her to sit beside her. Once they were both inside, Ivy leaned over and pulled the door to.

They sat in silence. The familiar car smell and the sound muffled by the confined space was strangely comforting, distinctly normal. She closed her eyes for a moment, her head against the head rest. *Head rest,* she thought. No one would ever make a head rest again.

She sighed, and turned to Vorsa, who sat on her hind legs, watching Ivy attentively.

'Can you take off your armour for a little while? It's not wise for us to travel with you covered in shards of glass. I don't want either of us to get hurt.'

Vorsa agreed, shuffling out of the neck cuff, and with deft movements of her teeth, her tail cuff. Ivy lifted it, remarking at how light it was. She placed it behind her seat. For a moment, she considered asking Vorsa to wear a seatbelt, but thought it might be too restrictive.

She turned the key. After a few false starts, it sprang to life. She laughed, 'That never happens in the movies!' to which Vorsa could only nod. The dashboard showed her that the tank was full. She wondered what journey the woman had planned, before her sudden death.

Ivy oriented herself. She recalled the time her dad had taken her out in the carpark of a local pub. She had been eleven. It had been a summer evening. He had laughed because her legs barely touched the pedals. She had stalled, and stalled again, and burst into hysterical laughter when she very slowly drove into a bollard, leaving a crack in the bumper. Her father, who adored her, laughed along with her. But she remembered the basics, and this car was an automatic, which would make everything easier.

She placed her hands on the steering wheel and let the world blur. She searched for something, a feeling, a warmth. Her eyes flickered under her eyelids, tiny movements, chasing lights. She could feel the First City. She let her eyes wander, and then a sound. It was very quiet, but it seemed to be coming from somewhere north.

She reversed off the pavement, and very gently began to drive up the silent road. She took a moment to glance at Vorsa, who sat awkwardly still, trying to make sense of her surroundings.

'How is this moving?' she said eventually.

Ivy giggled, 'It's like us, it takes fuel, for us that would be food, and it turns that into energy that moves the bones and muscles of the machine. But the machine isn't alive, and I am its brain. I control it, with this steering wheel and pedals.'

'Pedals and wheel.' Vorsa made a face when she thought hard. 'Petulan can control me. It takes him a great deal of concentration, but it is possible. He does it very rarely, if he wishes to feel alive. I have to relinquish control to him though.'

Ivy shuddered. 'That sounds odd. But he is your twin, so I guess you guys always shared everything.'

Vorsa reflected for a moment. '*Guys.* I am beginning to understand more and more of your parlance.'

Ivy laughed again.

It was not the smoothest journey. Ivy stopped frequently, stalled, hit obstacles she had purposely tried to avoid. But the roads were clear of traffic, giving her free rein. Her mind wandered to thoughts of the High Realm, and of Gahar herself. Despite the terror that she had faced, and the violence that had been inflicted, her lasting memory was not of the anger, or even of being held in the tower under the threat of death. For some reason, the thought of that great simian, in the Moterion when she was much younger, when she looked right through her, held Ivy in the grip of guilt. On reflection, she realised Eru, Gahar's son, must have already died by that time. Gahar had given up long before the gates of her cage were finally brought down; part of Gahar had died with her son.

'We have to help Gahar,' she said to Vorsa, waking the vixen who had curled up on her seat.

Vorsa didn't move but she said quietly, 'We will.'

*

It was a few hours later when Ivy became aware of an odd sensation through the tyres and axle and fabric beneath her, a resonating hum that grew the further they travelled, until the tone was no longer a distant abstract but something she could feel.

It took Ivy a little while to find the switch for the lights, but she was so alert with adrenaline she decided to drive until sleep got the better of her. They passed a sign that read 'To The North'. She wasn't sure if a map would be useful, but made a mental note to find one at the next service station, and they pulled in when one appeared on the horizon.

Ivy checked the fuel gauge. She had half a tank. She looked around at the few other cars parked at the station, spying an empty plastic can, knowing that there was no chance the pumps would work. She found a car of a similar model to hers. She checked to make sure it was the right type of fuel, cut a length of hose she found and pushed the tube into the fuel tank. She sucked, until the acrid taste of petroleum filled her mouth. She spat it out and stuck the end of the syphon into the can. She was particularly proud of this achievement, and celebrated with a fizzy drink from the shop beside the station.

Vorsa lapped at water Ivy poured into a bowl left for Caanus, and Ivy collected a few cans of Caanus food. Then she saw a trolley, dropped the cans in and filled it to the brim with as much non-perishable food as would fit, and, of course, a handful of maps and guides. She sorted through the items left by the previous owner of the car, and found it all to be in date. She added her new haul to this and moved everything to the boot, making room for them to sleep on the back seat. She wiggled a can of food at Vorsa, 'Dinner time!'

Vorsa grimaced. 'That is not food.'

'Oh come on, how is this any worse than dead Muroi?'

Vorsa ate with little joy, and then together they curled up to sleep.

A few hours later they continued their journey. The highway was empty, save for the odd car that had driven off the road. The land looked well. The trees seemed fuller, able to breathe without the incessant presence of exhaust gases. It was still early in this new age without the Wroth, but even the roads themselves were beginning to disappear under leaf mulch, collapsing soil embankments, the creep of trailing plants and tenacious roots bursting through in tiny slow eruptions. Nature was far more powerful than Ivy had ever given it credit for.

'Orn Megol is the Vulpus capital, yes?' she asked.

'Yes, it is my home.'

'But are there other Vulpus cities? I mean, there are Vulpus everywhere, are there other meeting places for the clans?'

'Yes, there were once many. The Vulpus inherited many of our cities, left by older clades - the Grim, the Cini. Some we founded ourselves. There were once grand halls beneath the earth, the churches of Tet, and the mausoleum of Hadredg, Thron Awlbringa - all destroyed by your people, torn down, buried. Orn Megol only survived because it was below a Wroth settlement, and was not dug by paws in mud and clay but by water through rock.'

'Do you meet with Vulpus from other parts of the land?'

'More so since the Bastia grew; it is far easier to exchange greetings. We will come together when my father dies — to appoint a new overseer.'

She read the look upon Vorsa as a vain attempt to hide her feelings. She decided not to push the matter. For a little while they remained silent, acknowledging the weight of loss. Eventually, Ivy began to chuckle to herself, which broke Vorsa from her contemplation.

'I'm sorry, I just got a thought in my head. I am not sure if I can easily explain.'

Vorsa nodded, 'I am all ears.'

'I was thinking about the awkward silence and the bigger issues we are both not talking about, and, well, the Wroth have a saying for this — when there is something big no one is addressing, we would say that subject is "the elephant in the room" — Oraclas, the Oraclas in the room. I imagined Yaran here with us and it made me chuckle. Being an Oraclas and all.'

'You're right.'

'About what?'

'It's not easy to explain.'

Ivy laughed, and a smile appeared on Vorsa's face. After some time, Vorsa chose to speak of Satresan.

'My father and I have often fought. Since Petulan passed, he was very protective of me, he always forbade me from perilous tasks and coddled me. I know why, I know he loves me and feared losing his second child, but it was stifling.

'He was keen for me to become overseer of Orn Megol after his stepping down, but, when he became sick, he hastened his petition for my taking of the role. I didn't want it, don't want to be stuck below ground. I am a soldier, I serve greater purpose in defending Naa.

'So we fought, and I left. I do not shirk my responsibilities. I have a responsibility to Naa, I can't abandon that.'

'You must see him if he is dying. You won't be able to forgive yourself if you don't get to make up before he dies.'

Vorsa lowered her head. She said nothing.

Ivy looked at the road signs, maintaining her course north. She noted turnings to cities and towns she had never been to, and the further north they travelled, the more rural the land they passed through became. Wherever she could, she would stop to find supplies, and with no one else to share them with, it seemed likely she would be able to last far longer on preserved foods than she had first thought.

Driving became easier with each mile, learning the idiosyncrasies of what it was to be a motorist. She wondered if petrol went bad, if it would become impossible to travel this way. It was an unknown quantity to investigate, whether she should be driving at all. It was such acts, the use of fossil fuels and the destruction of habitat that might have necessitated the end of her own species.

Vorsa was attentive, and took a keen interest in the world around them — she had quickly become accustomed to traveling this way. Eventually they arrived at a small town which seemed like a good place to rest. Ivy reached for the guidebook and found reference to the town. 'Famous for an Anglo Saxon burial mound,' she read out loud.

It was early afternoon and she decided to have a break and take a moment to visit this oddly fitting memorial to long dead Wroth. She felt drawn to it — she found it hard to discern it as a separate presence to that which they were searching for, and yet, this place was important in itself.

The cairn was built upon a small hill, or perhaps the hill itself was the burial ground. Vorsa trotted beside Ivy as they made their way to the top. Immediately, she saw a second mound, and standing still upon it were two misshapen figures. Vorsa and Ivy both reeled with fear.

Vorsa sniffed, but there was no scent of Wroth, besides that of Ivy.

'I think they're scarecrows,' Ivy said.

They walked up the hill, cautious and slow. Eventually, they reached the first effigy. It was little more than a crude T-shape, hewn of haphazard lengths of branch, burned remnants from a fire. Angular limbs threatened the air, its face a shroud of torn refuse sack. At first, Ivy thought it might be a kids' prank, or perhaps, simply its namesake — to ward off Corva. But this was no field.

Ivy took a few steps back. Upon the earth were drag marks and paw prints, at least three separate sets. She traced the torn grass and mud back across the hill. She returned to the scarecrows. Around the neck of each was a poorly made emblem made of sticks lathered with dried spit and a little blood, as though a Caanus had chewed at it. She placed it on the ground for Vorsa to see.

'What is this symbol?'

Vorsa turned it with her paw. 'This represents the Sisters of the Flock. You see, the three sticks are the three sisters in the stone. This is the source of the Umbra, the source of our shared will.' She sniffed it and recoiled. 'The animal that made this has marked its territory on it. They mean to mock us. I think this must be the work of the Husk.'

Ivy knelt down and placed her fingers in the impressions in the ground. She recognised the shape.

She offered her hand to Vorsa. 'May I see your paw?'

Vorsa lifted her forelimb and Ivy examined the pads. 'Would you place your foot beside this footprint?'

She did so. She pressed down, leaving a mark. Once removed, they saw the similarities. The original print was far larger, yet they shared a distinct shape.

'Caanus?' Ivy asked.

Vorsa shook her tail. 'No, not Caanus. This is Cini.'

Chapter Eight

Lucille picked up a torch and, with Makepeace on her shoulder, carefully manoeuvred her way beside the megalithic stones, using the handrail where necessary, until she was within the cave itself. Noraa and Little Grin followed nervously until they entered the cavity, within which lay the dig site.

Noraa was overcome, sensing the presence within her bones; it spasmed through her with intention and it spoke without words.

Lucille ushered them to the pit, where she climbed down, and pulled back part of a large tarpaulin. Beneath, were two skeletons. It was immediately apparent to Noraa that these animals were Cini. A rush of consciousness overcame her; memories, thoughts, annotations of lives in livid colour, hues she could not recognise, a pantheon of ideas that had been born and died before she had lived herself, matted in the locks of long oblivion.

She felt the need to cry, and she found herself lying beside the old bones, the two corpses huddled close. She felt the droning rhythm quelled.

'I can see them,' she said, overwhelmed by lingering visions.

Lucille put her hand upon Noraa's paw, 'This place was important to many, but most of all I think, your kind. Makepeace has found the markings of his own kin in the tunnels that cut through this soil. Even the Wroth were drawn here, we buried our dead here too, before our religions called to other gods. We all knew this soil was sacred, but we never knew why. So I kept on digging, until I found it.'

Lucille lifted the remainder of the covering to reveal a gigantic mass of thick grey roots, gnarled and hewn tightly together. They resembled atrophied muscle tissue and appeared to be petrified, having lain there for millennia.

Immediately, Noraa was taken by it, aware of this being the source of the sound that had plagued her.

'This is it. This is what I heard.'

Little Grin cautioned her, 'We don't know these things, we have to be careful.'

Noraa nodded and proceeded to place her face against it. Like the bones beside it, she could feel its intention.

'I feel sadness.' She spoke softly. 'It failed its cause. It has lain here, unable to act, unable to right its wrongs, torn from its body like an amputated limb. It feels loss, but above all, guilt.'

Lucille crouched beside her. 'What is it?'

'It has many names. My clade called it Moorvori Groor. It is a herald of the First City, a Sentinel of Naa. Here to defend us from—'

'From what?' Lucille said excitedly.

'From you.'

Noraa nuzzled the hide of it, feeling for its voice. 'This grave was desecrated. Its final charge was to protect this burial. Like the city, it grew around a grave, but in this case as a defence against the thralls of the Wroth. But they came looking for it, dug up the earth and took the bones. Yet they did not find it, and so it lay here, confronted by its final failure, forever.' They ringed the edge of the burial, as if in mourning.

From behind came the sound of someone clearing their throat. 'I think I might be able to help with that.'

They all turned to see a girl in her early teens at the top of the ladder, flanked by a Vulpus, clad in shard armour.

She held a Cini skull in her hands.

*

Ivy and Vorsa had returned to the car, having pulled the scarecrows out of the earth and thrown them into a bush. Ivy started the engine.

It was not long before they were back on the road, the blur of pine trees beside them, the day warm and bright. With every few miles, Ivy sensed the presence of the hum becoming stronger — she even attempted to harmonise with it.

'Rune would speak of a song, the song of the city. He said he could feel it, through the earth. Perhaps you hear that song too.' Vorsa hung her head out of the window, the wind blowing her ears back, her eyes closed, which made Ivy smile.

An hour later and the landscape had changed from villages and motorways into wide moorland, the road snaking between ridges of rugged rock and short cropped grass. Sparse, low-lying trees and an array of staggering vistas of endless verdant hillocks and expanses, stone bluffs like textured reliefs rising from the earth in calloused crags. Here, the song sang loud inside Ivy, drawing her on.

They left the car in a lay-by, hopping over a kissing gate, and began to climb a particularly large hill. Ivy had tried going the wrong way to see if it had any effect on her perception of the song, and indeed it had, it becoming fainter and dissonant.

The hill was steep and there was a coarse breeze as the light faded — flaxen crowns of grass whipped ghostly against it as they followed a well-trodden route to the top of the tor. As they approached, they saw the sun set behind a large stone outcropping; but Ivy saw something else — a Land Rover, and a tent.

It wasn't the first time she'd seen the remnants of Wroth encampments, but there was something peculiar about this — a kettle over a smouldering fire, a neat pile of used cans in a box, and no signs of mould. She thought of a tale her father had told her about a ship that was found, missing its crew, but a table set and a meal half-eaten, the *Mary Celeste*.

They saw a light moving near the stones, disappearing into the twilight. They followed cautiously, and as they came closer, heard voices, recognising a Cini, a small animal that Vorsa called a Maar, and one other, a Wroth. They listened, laying low, until they made sense of the words, and then when the three descended into a pit, they moved quietly to the top of the ladder.

A burial, the Sentinel, a grave for two Cini, one missing its skull — how this robbery had tortured the herald of Dron. Ivy had felt the tingle of bafflement at the coincidence, perhaps serendipity. She removed the skull from her bag, and clearing her throat said, 'I think I might be able to help with that.'

The faces below turned in the light with astonishment.

A Wroth, a woman.

'I can't believe it,' the woman said, brushing the earth from her knees. She began to climb the ladder, her eyes fixed on Ivy with a mixture of disbelief and joy. When she reached the top she held her hands out, and Ivy backed away.

'Are you real? Are you well?'

She realised she was scaring the girl, so she moved back a step.

'I'm sorry, I haven't seen another Wroth since my husband died. I am just so happy to see you!'

She was older, she was white, maybe in her fifties. She was slim and had long silver hair tied in a neat plait that fell down her back. Ivy thought she had a very kind face.

'I lived by myself, my Dad and brother died, and Vorsa, she came and rescued me. I have been with her since,' Ivy replied, unsure of what to do.

'Who is Vorsa?'

'I am,' the vixen stepped forward. A Cini appeared beside the woman, followed shortly by a Maar.

'Ora bring peace,' Vorsa said to the pair.

A Creta ran up onto the woman's shoulder. 'I think we need to sit down and discuss this calmly, and perhaps have some food,' he said. They all agreed.

They left the dig site, returning to the camp. The woman stoked the fire, adding some logs to the embers. She made tea, which Vorsa was quite keen to have a little of, and they all exchanged names and greetings.

Noraa was far larger than Vorsa, but they shared a great deal of their mannerisms, and the Maar, although unrelated, had strong ties with the Vulpus clans.

Ivy looked inside her bag and removed a tin of Caanus food and a dish, and spooned the contents onto a plate for their new companions.

Ivy was struck by the balance Lucille had brought to her world. In her presence, she felt almost as though her entire ordeal had been a delusion, and this human, this Wroth, had broken the spell. She felt herself wanting to ask, 'Do you hear them speaking too?'

She felt a warm blanket being draped over her shoulders, and was handed a hot cup of cocoa.

'It's instant, but it's good!' Lucille said as she sat down beside her. 'So, you can hear them talking too?' she asked with a wry smile, prodding the fire with a stick, gesturing towards their animal companions.

Ivy stifled a chuckle, 'I guess so, although I feel I have heard others before.'

Lucille nodded, 'Yes, I have wondered about that. I did consider the noise of the Wroth being a contributing factor to not being able to hear them. It's so quiet now. Our ancestors made so much effort to un-see the connections we had with other species. In the past, it was religion, culture, and then all the noise! The radio, TV, internet — so loud and obnoxious, we drowned out the voices we weren't even listening for.'

Ivy agreed, 'Yes! I was talking with Vorsa about this; why we didn't see their armour? But in a way we did. I remember watching a video of a Corva using a jam jar lid as a snowboard, or Collectors using sticks as tools, and we just laughed at it, and said, "Isn't it funny, they're just like us," and then dismissing it all as a joke. It was right in front of our eyes, but we were so caught up in being "human" that we never stopped to listen or see. Those who did, they got called insane.'

Abruptly, Vorsa added, 'And neither of you ever wondered if we bothered to listen to you?'

'Could you understand us?' Lucille asked her.

'So many of my kin died by Wroth hands. But there was something. I can't speak for my friends here, but I encountered Wroth often in the Stinking City. If I ever made eye contact, it was almost always peculiar.'

'Why?'

'Because, strangely, Wroth always seemed happy, or pleasantly surprised to see me. This I could never understand.' She pondered for a moment, 'May I have a little tea?' she asked.

Lucille poured some of hers into a tin mug and placed it before her. She lapped at it eagerly. Noraa watched curiously then turned to the dish of food that Ivy had offered her, which she had ignored up until now. She acknowledged the grimace from Vorsa, but ate it all the same. Little Grin joined her.

'How did you know to bring the skull?' Noraa said as she finished the dish and began to lick the empty tin.

Ivy blew her cocoa and took a sip. It was sweet and delicious. 'I didn't. We were looking for you, for this place. We need to find a defence against the Husk, and the Umbra gave us you, gave us a direction. The skull, it was read by the Consilium of Oevidd - they can see the memories of animals in their ancestors' bones. I didn't think the skull was needed beyond that, but they gave it to me. Maybe they knew?'

Lucille held out her hand, and Ivy handed her the skull.

'What is the Husk?' Lucille gently rotated the skull in her hands.

Noraa looked to Vorsa, who nodded for her to proceed. 'They are revenants who have taken living bodies; they have escaped the Gasp, through a creature that calls himself Thoth. He infected my entire pack with these ghouls, possessing any and all who get in his way. He is spreading a plague of the dead upon the land.'

Vorsa interjected, 'They travel towards Dron, The First City. We believe that is their goal.'

Lucille held up her hands, 'Wait, wait, I do not understand any of this. What is the First City? What is the Gasp?'

Ivy cleared her throat, 'I've thought about this a lot. I think of it all like the cycle of a plant — like the Umbra is the seed, Naa is the plant growing, and the Gasp is when it dies down into the soil, and all the nutrients, all the goodness is given back to the Umbra, and it starts again. The First City is like the flower on top of the plant, it supplies food and shelter, and its ideas are like pollen, spreading these connections to all life. I have been there — it's crazy! It's this huge ... thing ... this place that's — filled with life!'

She slurped her hot chocolate, 'Vorsa, can we take Lucille there?'

'Yes. However, we have more pressing concerns.'

Lucille looked overwhelmed, 'Wow. So I am told by Makepeace that I'm Umbra, and this is how I can understand all of you, so the Umbra is an extension of this First City?'

Vorsa nodded, 'The Umbra was born of thinking minds, of the collective will to survive. Life flocked to know this feeling, and in that act was born a place for all life to find harmony. We call that place the First City, but each clade has a name for it. Dron, Mo'moridi, The Epiras. It is the physical presence of the Umbra.'

'Fascinating. It looks like I have a lot to learn. But this,' she held up the skull, 'this is my area of expertise. Now, I might not be a palaeontologist, I specialise in archaeology, but I have had some experience with animal remains. This appears to be about the same age as the skeletons we found below; however, this has been cleaned and then kept in dusty rooms for a very long time. Now, what are the chances that this is the missing skull from our burial site?'

Noraa sniffed at the skull, 'Yes. I think it is. I believe the connections we spoke of are all part of a continuous cycle and, perhaps, they also apply to objects such as these, and the unliving — if they too have a role to play.'

Lucille spoke now, 'Yes, like the mycelium of fungus, Ivy. You describe the Umbra and the Gasp like plant roots, but perhaps it is more a network of fungus, those little feathery tendrils you see in the soil.

'The mushroom or fungus, that is the fruit; the body is below the earth, connecting a forest together. In the great rain forests, it is the fungus that keeps the forest alive, the soil alone is too shallow to support that life. It's called symbiosis. All of this, and all of your fantastical things and places, they share the same system, so that death and life are intricately connected.'

Vorsa agreed, 'I have a friend, Erithacus, who spent a lifetime trying to show us all the connections within beliefs — that we all share them from a singular source. Perhaps his theory goes far deeper than we all imagined. Every system intersects with another.'

'In that case,' Lucille replied, 'this skull might just be our key. But now we must rest and tackle this tomorrow. Agreed?'

There was consensus.

Noraa and Little Grin found shelter in the mouth of the cave, while Lucille offered the tent to Ivy. Ivy thanked her and said, 'If it's okay, can we sleep in the Land Rover?'

'Of course!' Lucille replied, escorting them.

Ivy jumped in, followed by Vorsa. They made a nest of blankets in the back. Lucille watched as Vorsa stalked around by Ivy's feet before slumping down to sleep. She placed her hand upon the window, as if to draw from this warmth. She climbed into the tent, with Makepeace finding refuge in the folds of her knapsack.

*

His sense of smell was acute, and often he found it nauseating, the perfumery of rot, of faecal matter, the musk and mustiness of his filthy entourage. But it was useful. Each scent brought with it a portent – he knew the smell of fear, but he also knew the smell of a predator – and those who ate meat carried with them the sweat of it. Plant feeders, they were more subtle. But what he smelled now stirred a new emotion — apprehension.

Thoth had brought his battalion to heel at the edge of a city. Amidst industrial estates – row upon row of identical warehouses – they rested under corrugated roofs in the dusty repositories of unusable stock. The stillness brought him further ill tidings — he was haunted by the absence of the thing he had rejected, company. Yes, he was surrounded by hundreds of others, yet even through the eyes of an animal not far from a Caanus, he could only see all those sympathetic to him as little more than pets or farmyard cattle. He longed for humans, despite his mind constantly rejecting that epithet — *human human human*. The presence of Emeris was always there, no longer acting out, but watching, tutting, shaking his head at Thoth as he continued his campaign of wanton destruction, not allowing him the use of his own words.

Each moment Thoth dwelt on his actions conjured a wealth of opposing thoughts, and he wished they were just the stubborn thoughts of the owner of this body, but he knew they weren't. He was battling his own needs — in his desire to be the lord of all he surveyed, he had not addressed that annoying little sore. Alone in the land, the pariah could spurn humanity, could label it weak and useless, all the while knowing it was there, out of reach, desired but denied. Now he could have the world, but none of the people in it.

Once upon a time, he hadn't felt so much anger, so much hatred. Once upon a time, all he had wanted was love. This thought, however weakened Emeris had become, could now only make him laugh bitterly. Thoth had run out of ways to torture the animal within, so he just ignored it. His imprisonment was punishment enough.

They had left the grey buildings and found themselves at the edge of a wide river. With a bridge to their left, they mounted the road that spanned it, and began to cross, until Thoth caught the scent again.

The waft was strong, thick and powerful. He could not place it, but it made him second guess the crossing. The Legionnaires were frantic, heeding the same stink.

'What is it?' he snarled.

None could tell him. He set the vile canines free; delirious they scattered, great arcs of saliva flung from their mouths, disappearing into alleyways and buildings.

The water lapped against the supports of the bridge — he heard the tinkle of a wind chime on a small boat tied at the shore. The short sharp yelp of a Cini.

Large animals appeared on the far side. Thoth recognised them, Rauka – huge golden -maned felines. They strode confidently, blocking the width of the bridge. He was terrified. The apparent leader, a female, roared with guttural girth. Thoth contemplated two things: somehow take these animals and inhabit their formidable forms, or running for his life.

He knew he couldn't run —behind him the Husk began to jeer. Somehow, beyond all logic, they did not fear these animals. For a moment, he questioned his apprehension. There were but a few of them, and he was an army.

He strode out toward them, suddenly sure of himself. They were no match against him! Nothing would impede him!

As he neared them, he noticed they were decidedly quiet. Upon their foreheads hung black scrags of bone and glass — the mere act of looking at these stygian amulets made him feel queasy.

He steadied himself and rising up on his hind legs he stalked before them. His voice quavered, even with the hubris of his words — 'Look upon my works ye mighty and despair!'

A flood of effluent leaked from him, greyish slugs of ectoplasm, liquid and wanting, flowing in ungracious shivering columns. He snorted with glee at the theatrics of it all, how shocked they must be, how proud his soldiers must feel.

The Rauka were steadfast; the revenants swayed in listless craving motes, sending out probing limbs in search of access to their bodies. But there was a resistance, a barrier none could cross, and as they pawed at living flesh, soon they found the source of their inconvenience — the bone hexes, desecrations of meat, dawning on their spectral minds, the reality of their own death, and in the reflection, splayed on the shards of mirrored glass their bodilessness, their amorphous slime residue of a once living thing. Perhaps remembered pain, perhaps the embarrassment of the naked soul, the fragile spirit sent them shrinking away, becoming nothing once again.

Thoth heaved with consternation. His eyes wide, he stumbled, falling back to all fours. He couldn't stall, couldn't falter now. He pulled forth more revenants, more slithering welts lanced and suppurated, eager to take the bodies of the Rauka — and again, they could not.

The leading Rauka, nonchalant and polite, paced forwards on wide paws.

'I am Dynast Esit of the Pridebrow. Your attempts to infect us with your black flood will always fail. We are immune to it. By whatever means you invoke this madness, it is best you stop. All of Naa will rise up against you if you do not desist.'

Thoth pondered this.

'Dynast Esit. How very opulent. Perhaps you are right, perhaps those little trinkets tied to your heads are the means by which you defy my word, and perhaps if we were to take them from you, that smug look upon your face would fail — much like this little uprising. For as many as you repel, more will rise, and you will be overcome.'

He turned to his troops, 'Take them!' he howled, and they descended upon the Rauka in a deluge of bloodied, emaciated forms.

*

Scab appreciated the view from the roof of the High Realm of Hanno. Around him, he saw the movements of the possessed simians, revenants suddenly thrust into bodies not so inhuman — prehensile hands, able to stand unassisted. He watched their former queen, her crown discarded, stomp around, comprehending her weight.

'Feels good?' he asked smugly.

'Yes. Yes! He promised us skin, but this — this is magnificent. I feel strong, far stronger than that damn gull. Yet I feel this itch in my head, like something is pissed I'm in here.'

'You'll get used to it. They quieten down after a while. You'll forget they are there, and then just like that, they're gone.'

She stood and leered over him, 'Now that we're here, what is wanted of us?'

'You're muscle mostly, if you got the same speech I did when he sold his tale in the Gasp — but the world isn't quite how you left it. The animals are indeed running the show, and the world is full of things I don't fully understand — you'd think a bunch of guns or some poison and we'd put an end to 'em all, but sadly, there are a lot of 'em, and they have ways and means. But it seems some of us have been blessed with gifts, hence why you're standing here right now, in a fucking gorilla.'

'Hanno,' she said, with an element of mild irritation.

'Ah yes, the old word association game. Your brain isn't exactly yours. You'll find new words, ideas that you feel impelled to say. It's annoying, but you can ignore it and use their grunts and whines, or you can force out the word you want to say. A little defiance goes a long way!'

'Her name was Gahar, I can hear her screaming. You promise it'll go away?'

'Yeah, mine gave up long ago.' he spoke assuredly. He wondered if it had died, all bottled up in his head. He spared no mind. 'Anyway. We answer to Thoth. He was the first, the Second Coming of Christ, if you like. If Christ was a megalomaniac in the body of a wolf. All of this is in service to his cause.'

'And that cause is?' she reached up and tore down a hand of green bananas, gradually devouring the entire bunch as they talked.

'Why, dominion of course.'

Your dominion of him

He pondered that thought, and the more he considered it, the less he liked the idea. He wasn't one for rebellion. He'd always tried to take the easy road — he robbed old people, and those he'd killed had never put up much of a fight. Even when he died, he'd been pretty blasé about it all. He wondered why, all of a sudden, he was so hellbent on being on top.

Must all be going to my head

'So?' she looked at him as he recovered from his reflections.

'Oh! Round up the rest of your kin and go out into the world. We need bodies, prisoners of war. Bring them here – alive – and I'll do the rest. The bulk of the Husk will join us soon and together we will take their seat of power — some place of importance in the south. Thoth reckons the rest will be child's play.'

He returned to the window, where he saw a dozen Hanno and Toron descending the rope bridges built by those they'd *wronged*

Wronged?

Do you feel any remorse?

Do I what? Remorse. I feel bad about Joe. Joe was a good kid. I shouldn't have robbed him. I shouldn't have stuck a knife in his gut.

That's a start. I am always here for you

He strained to see the Hanno who had escaped his attack. There were many. He was unsure of how best to deal with them. His henchman awaited his command, seemingly impressed by his actions.

'Follow the apes. See where they go. I imagine Thoth will arrive soon, so we'll move operations to greet his arrival. Go on then?'

They nodded and began the descent of the tower.

They don't respect you enough

When did anyone respect their elders?

He cared not.

Emeris

Emeris found himself upon the periphery of a fateful memory. It wasn't that Thoth had lost control, that he had seceded from that part of his brain, but that Emeris didn't want to remember. It was a fuzzy black recollection, and he was hesitant in exploring it.

He awoke one morning and he could hear his father screaming. The slurred, long drawn-out words were typical of his father having drunk all night, and only just fallen asleep before his mother had started moving pots and pans in the kitchen. The sound reverberated throughout the house, and inevitably it triggered an incensed rage in the old man.

Emeris now sat at the top of stairs, watching his father drag his mother by her hair to the floor. Emeris felt the slightest urge to get up and help his mother, and yet a cascade of memories, the beatings he had received, stayed him.

But guilt was also not alien to him, although it manifested in his own experiments with cruelty. He left the house through the back door, beckoning the poodle with saccharine voice, who yapped in response and followed him to the river.

Emeris could not see the little girl climbing the tree on the far side of the river. He sobbed between his angry throwing of stones. The blind rage had found form, found direction. He had lost himself in it when he drowned the dog.

The little girl saw him. She saw him pick up the animal behind its shoulders and push it under the water. For a long time, Emeris only heard the deadened thump of his heart as the blood rushed to his ears in fibrillated surges.

Then he heard her scream, and the fugue snapped.

He was suddenly very aware of the limp pale mass in his hands, how wet he was, how much his knees hurt against the stones. He was acutely aware of how much trouble he would be in if she told his parents.

He started running, leaping over the branches, the rich green of their leaves, the scratchy grey bark on his hands.

'Please! Let me explain!'

He had grabbed her hand as she mounted a root mass, the impacted soil that ringed the base of the fallen tree. He pleaded with her and she tried to pull away against his protestations.

He just wanted her to listen.

Emeris felt the years of neglect and beatings and trauma in a nauseous rhythmic embrace — it slid around him like grit, sore and constant, gaining a callous outer layer that had made him numb to his decisions.

He pulled her a little too hard
Just a little too hard
The memory distorted. He was under the house.
He had stayed there for a day before they finally found him.
The little girl would remain so, and her name he chose to forget.

*

The once iconic tubular office complex and antenna array leaned precariously. Despite this, it remained one of the tallest landmarks in the Stinking City, held in place by Dron's green roots, serpentine about its waist, both performing and staying its execution. It looked forlorn and naked, having shed many of its scales, window frames empty of glass.

It was top-heavy, its crown of satellite dishes pitched to one edge, much of the cladding long collapsed, leaving a slumped array of incomplete concentric steel haloes, dangling aerials, reams of cable spilling into the wind — a great lazy eye overlooking the rubble of the city. Its pupil had been built long after its partial collapse, a purposeful orb of distorted masonry, of wire, wood and bone, daubed with a wash of dried blood — a hundred thousand offerings, a hundred thousand incremental additions of teeth, sinew, gifts bound up like little covenants into a misshapen skeletal sphere within which divinations were proscribed.

This was the Tempered Orrery, its disciples born in the ashes of dislocated religions, and in the fibre of their union. Much of the Corvan orthodoxy refocused their efforts in the causes of the Umbra alone, yet splinter flocks remained somewhat loyal to Gasp worship, albeit with an open mind to their sisters and brothers of the Anx. These somewhat puritanical Corva became the Ebduous Clax.

The Morwih, having cast aside their selfish ambition, had embraced an approximation of a god, Vormauo — *the one guided light in a prism.* Similarly, the Skulks of Vamish, Vulpus whose beliefs aligned with the Anx of older times, were drawn to this aberration of faiths.

Strangely, it was not under the auspices of superstition that this bond was formed, but in the pragmatic realism of Erithacus and his Tempered Guild, for it was he who had tried with all his might to unite the nations of Naa under the one truth – that of the Umbra, and the Sisters of the Flock – and so here, in the shadow of a giant Altar of the Black Knot, they charted the movements of the dead, and found reason to be afraid.

The Morwih, Thisel, a cleric, sat at the centre of the Orrery. She observed her colleagues of the wing, who moved tokens of influence, crepuscular ornaments like fallen stars, didactics of clairvoyance. These tokens hung from a web of intertwined lengths of chord, string and unidentifiable gristle. With ease, they could be unhitched and moved, like the markers on a map of war, each pawn a player.

Since the Umbra had returned its second sight to all, their predictions were ever more precise, forecasts that would leave the tower on the morning chorus, on the talking sticks of the Windsweepers. What was once the act of a single Startle, the love'd Grom, was now an entire cooperation of oracles. Yet since the Husk had risen in the north, their avenues of influence had been cut short, throwing their guidance into chaos. Now, all attention turned to plotting the black flood. But it was not the only unknown. Other things, indecipherably old things, had risen too, as if in reaction to the Husk.

Thisel wore a headdress of prongs, a portion of television antenna, its teeth bent upwards, skulls threaded upon them like heads on spikes. Periodically, she would move them, an abacus of death's prognosis in Naa. She stared up into the Orrery, trying to perceive the movement of a number of points, while a flock of Corva were hard at work, divining and interpreting thrown sticks, A*rnik Valish Maggrigorn* — the blood skry patterns of the former Anx, arranging talismans in gore and cartilage.

'They have moved closer to the city. Our opportunity will be brief.'

Beside her was a Vulpus, Penhalef, who wore the mandible bone of his father below his jaw.

He agreed, 'This is something unheard of, the *Nash Aka* invoking the will to remain in Naa. It takes training to master, yet for this creature to simply will it? It is power we cannot understand. The need to stop them is great, their path can only be to the First City.'

A squawk from above, an alert. Something large moved beyond the amphitheatre; it lowered itself as a sign of subservience - a female Hanno, followed by others of her tribe.

'Come forward, you are welcome here.'

The Corva abandoned their tasks within the constellation and flew down to join their fellow priests. Nervously, the simians entered the wide platform of concrete upon which the Orrery sat. Much like the Regulax, it was hemmed by piles of bone hexes, magick tokens, frippery in petrified skin, and a company of animal clerks who dutifully enacted the commands of the clergy.

'I am Gilia, of High Realm. Our home has been taken from us. Gahar is no longer in her right mind — Gaspstuff. We seek sanctuary and guidance.'

Thisel asked, 'What did you see? Tell me everything.'

'From nowhere, we were attacked by a flock of Narna Elowin — there wasn't time to make sense of such a thing, but it was clear they were not well. They coughed up some foulness that left them fitting on the floor, and those things, ghouls, they entered our kin, making them writhe in agony. A Vulpus, she told us to run, and so we did. We left them there. Oh, Sisters, we left them there!'

'Tell me of this Vulpus?'

'She was Vorsa Corpse Speaker. I remember her from the Moterion. She was arguing with Gahar over the life of a wrothcub.'

'Vorsa? A *wrothcub?*'

Thesil tipped her head back towards the Orrery, 'Clax, back to work!'

The Corva took to wing and manoeuvred within the orb. They hung from the scaffolding, nimbly orienting themselves far from the cluster of baubles that represented the Husk already present in the Stinking City.

They pointed to the cracked bones hanging loose far north. 'These?' There were a number of them. 'Individuals? Vorsa, this Wroth, and…?'

'And another Wroth, one Creta, a Maar and a Cini, we think!'

'Cini! How odd. But what is this they stand beside?'

A concentration of teeth, hundreds had moved to form star-like manifestations, a number of them far from the centre. Thesil asked, 'What is the feeling behind these?'

The Corva chittered between one another. 'They feel like Dron, taste the vigour of it we do! Separate, meaningful, these six.' The Corva gestured to the lone pieces. 'These are drawn to one, they smell its strength!'

'And this?' She gestured to a vortex of black. It was hanging low from the Orrery, which suggested it was underground.

The Corva swung towards it, picking at the shreds of bin bag that constituted its form. 'Shri Vermis! Stinks of it!'

'But the Shri Vermis left Naa.'

'Something older. Can feel its draw. There is anger.'

For the moment, these things remained opaque.

'The wrothcub and Vorsa were unharmed?'

Gilia looked remorseful. 'Gahar, she lost a child, and blamed this wrothcub. She was held against her will, but she escaped with Vorsa. Neither were taken by the Husk.'

'So why do they travel north? What is this? Something important? We must consult Rune and the Dominus — they will know the cut of this.'

'And what of the Orrery?' Penhalef gestured to it.

'We must wait until the Husk move into the city. Audagard's Black Knot still stands, but its ring of influence is small. Once they are within its grasp, then we shall use it.'

Gilia placed her hand on the strange structure, 'I know a little bone craft - the Starless Vulpus would speak of its power in the god prison. What is this?'

Thesil looked at it lovingly. 'Think of the Orrery like the mind of a Shadow Starer. Most cannot see the Umbra with such precision, so we must build the means to. But this has another use. We are Ebduous Clax, watchers of the Gasp in Naa, and when we identify a corruption, be that a violent Poltergeist or feral necromancy, the Orrery becomes something far more potent.'

'What?' asked Gilia.

'A weapon.'

*

Ivy awoke to the sound of chatter. The Umbra was still a mystery to her, how the thoughts of others could rise in her mind, a mixture of physical vocalisations and projected ideations. When Lucille spoke to her, she only heard that which left her lips, but read her body language, probably on some subconscious level.

As she lay in the car, she heard the sound of discussion coming from the direction of the campfire, where the others had already risen. She heard laughter from Little Grin, a bright wash in her mind's eyes, which was accompanied by the faint physical sound of a warbling squeak. Her mind interpreted their intentions.

She rubbed her eyes. She sat up to see Vorsa, her paws on the rim of the open door.

'I heard you stir, hoped you were awake. It's time.'

Ivy dragged herself from the Land Rover to find Noraa and Little Grin beside the fire, where Lucille was brewing some tea. The day was cool and overcast, a cold shadowless light, and a strong wind. Noraa had caught a Tril, which she shared with Vorsa and Little Grin, and Lucille had made some jacket potatoes in the hot ashes for herself and Ivy. They ate their breakfast, then Lucille stood up.

'I don't pretend to know how we proceed. But I feel your presence, Noraa, and, perhaps, Ivy is enough, and of course this skull, if it is indeed intended for this grave.'

They agreed that it was, and walked towards the cavern. They were soon standing in the cold pothole at the edge of the excavation, the two embracing skeletons below them, the thick greyish roots beside.

'May I?' Noraa asked as Lucille uncovered the skull she had wrapped in a towel to protect it.

'Yes, of course.'

Noraa took the skull gingerly in her mouth and leapt down beside her ancestors. She felt something like happiness, for she had never known a place of her own, a homeland. The presence of these ancient Cini brought her a sense of belonging.

She scraped back the earth with her claws and placed the skull in the indentation. She said a few words that none of the others could hear.

Ivy's ears popped, she felt strangely dizzy, and she looked to Lucille for reassurance, who began to yawn, to clear the muffled feeling from her own hearing.

'What was that?'

Above Noraa, and not far from her audience, a clump of *something* shuddered into being. Little Grin backed away, 'Oh no, not her again.'

They all shied from it, as a quake of shadows began to stab spider-like from the air itself, and a presence emerged. Vorsa recognised it, as did Ivy. Much like Petulan, this was a revenant.

The entity was uninterested in them, and quickly descended to Noraa. Ivy got on her knees and peered into the burial site. She watched as Yaga, the overmother of Noraa, placed a spectral paw upon the rib cage of one of the Cini.

'*Old, old, old. The debris of old souls. Come on now, sleeping is for the restful. You are both in need of the biting wind, no more lurking in the muck.*'

The bones shuddered, and their inversion, a translucent approximation of the bodies in the soil, lifted hesitantly, a pair of star-old lovers, lustrous clods of aether rolling about them, particles of themselves, fur and skin now long dirt, caught in the eddy. With every moment they became more substantial, until Noraa beckoned them to her.

'We have come to free this Sentinel of the city from its burden. Long has it lain in the earth watching over you, hoping that your bodies would be restored, making you whole. It wishes to shed this shame, eaten up by it. Will you help us?'

Wordless, sallow orbs for eyes, they drifted back towards the host of wizened roots, whispering to it in a language of purring bleats and glottal clucks long unspoken in Naa. As quickly as they had risen, they turned to look at Ivy, with something like fear, or perhaps disdain, and with gossamer motion, lay down again within their former cadavers.

Silence.

Those watching looked to one another, and then to the crawling spectre of Yaga.

'It is done.'

She enfolded the damp air around her — and was gone.

There was an absence, perhaps even a little disheartenment.

Ivy coughed. 'Well, I guess it didn't work?'

Vorsa shook her head in dismay. 'We have very few options left. I suggest—'

As if in response, the stone floor beneath them began to move. Dust and shale fell from the rock face.

Lucille grabbed Ivy's hand, 'Okay folks, RUN!'

They hastily retreated from the cave, out into the joyless light, a strong current of wind hitting them as they exited, an inhale, pulling air down into the mouth of the cavern as the moorland groaned ... and slid like a lizard sloughing its skin.

Little Grin ran before them all, quickly followed by Noraa and Vorsa, as Ivy helped Lucille up and on to the grass. There, they watched in awe for a moment as the entire rock formation began to lift, sending plumes of soil and water cascading dangerously around them. There came howls and barks of desperation.

'Back!' Lucille shouted, and they jumped into the Land Rover, Lucille slamming it into reverse, taking it far down the track, as great ribbon cavities opened either side of them. They made it to a rickety fence and abandoned the vehicle, climbing over to join the others, only to be stopped in their tracks, struck by the sheer size of the manifestation beneath the hill itself — for the hill and its weathered rock outcrop were now one hundred feet above the ground, and beneath were four titan legs, and what could only be the Sentinel's head.

It was living, growing, a clustered maze of endless thick cambium-bound roots, woven up into supportive, pliable structures, radicle tendons, splaying out to carry the mass of stone and earth upon its back. It was somehow tree-like, turtle-like, both fashioned and growing, a golem of nature. The air around it was displaced, a rushing whooping maelstrom, awakening the trees, shearing stone walls and fences.

It took one huge step forward, swaying its gigantic head towards Noraa. She looked up into a thatch-like face, branches jutted out like whiskers. It had no eyes, no nose, no mouth, yet it perceived them, and it spoke.

'CINI,' it boomed, 'WHAT IS YOUR NAME?'

'I am Noraa, of Ruthe-va Unclan! We are a damaged pack; my loved ones have been abducted, their bodies used by spirits of the Gasp. We come to you in need of help.'

'I WANT ONLY FOR THIS PURPOSE, NORAA RUTHE-VA UNCLAN.'

It shook itself, sending out torrents of dirt, lowering its head toward them. The Land Rover, which was now hanging precariously off the Sentinel's back, slid silently from its perch. They watched with hushed shock as it slammed into the ground below.

'Holy shit!' Lucille spluttered.

'I DO NOT KNOW YOUR COMPATRIOTS. I WAS RISEN IN THE STEAD OF THE CINI.'

Noraa yelped, 'They are my friends, they want only to protect the First City!'

'AS DO I.'

It lowered itself further, offering forth a great woody limb.

'I think it wants us to climb?' Ivy said. 'Should we?'

Lucille laughed, overwhelmed by all she had seen. 'Why not!'

They carefully ascended the fifty feet up its leg, helping the less able Cini and Vulpus. Acting as leverage, they found a hollow in the ring of branches that supported the land above. The Sentinel now carried much of the tor and surrounding hill upon its back like a tortoise's shell. Ivy pointed to the rhizome mass, which held each tree, each blade of grass, every boulder like an anchor, a knit in fine fractal whirls, elegantly securing the island in the sky that was once a hill. They soon found themselves on a plateau, their campsite destroyed, yet somewhat salvageable.

Ivy ran to the front of Moorvori Groor, a gnarled stump large enough to hang on to as she peered below. The Sentinel lifted itself upright. Dizzyingly high, Ivy cried out in excitement. She felt invigorated.

Noraa joined her and shouted down, 'I say, do you know the way to Dron, The First City?'

'I CAN HEAR IT ONCE AGAIN, I CAN FEEL THE OCEAN WINDS UPON ITS HIDE. SHOULD I GO TO IT?'

'Yes!' Noraa shouted, and with that, Groor, the Golem of the Forests and Plains, began its pilgrimage home.

Chapter Nine

There was blood. For as much as Esit had wanted to avoid death, death had made itself present. To save her life, and the life of her kin, those who threatened her, be they physical or the ghostly harbingers within, they had to die, she had no choice.

But she found herself confused. There was a pressure upon her, from all sides, and her eyes were swollen shut. She tried to reach out, but her limbs were atrophied; in fact she couldn't feel them at all. She felt the tug of sleep, and soon she was lost to a dreamless dark.

She awoke again, and this time, there was vague sight. Hazy, blurred, her eyes filled with tears. But what she saw was not easy to explain. She felt as though she might be swimming in the lake at the Pridebrow, looking up through the water, to see the loving faces of her brothers, or her mother, Carcaris.

But she was far from the lake, far from her place of safety.

She tried to turn to make sense of the world, but her head would not respond, her limbs refused her plea. Yet she moved; she could feel the sensation of movement, of her paws upon the ground, of the other Rauka beside her. Still they were indistinct, recognisable shapes.

But what was that? And again?

Beside her, the enemy, walking with her?

The vicious, blood-soaked Husk, their hoots and howls and laughter, nudging and knocking and bleating at her kin, who stumbled, stooped and recovered.

Their voices were fuzzy, muffled, incoherent. A face came close, a Cini, a twisted smile, a croaking cackle. 'How do you feel in there?' it said.

She went to speak, but another voice spoke for her.

'It's fucking weird innit, I'm in a bloody Lio— Rauka …What's a Rauka?'

'You are mate! You don't get to use our words for things really, we've hijacked their brains so it comes with built-in vocabulary!'

'They have a vocabulary?'

There was laughter, laughter that was not hers, laughter that was alien. Her voice, her body was not hers anymore. She was pressed against the back of her skull, imprisoned.

She screamed. 'Get out of me! GET OUT!'

'No such luck lady. You've had your go. It's my turn now.'

The voice was unfeeling and venomous. She felt a sharp vengeful pain in her phantom flank as the violator bit himself-herself. He felt nothing. She felt it tenfold.

The talismans? How had they failed?

Torn from her. Taken by force. Trodden into the ground. She had seen many Husk fall in the presence of the bone hexes, but there had been enough bodies, enough to crush them down, enough to infect and take and take … her. Through her silent tears, she watched the Husk move further on, towards their goal in the south.

*

Bresh returned to his Roughclod cohorts in the early hours, sniffing them out on the morning breeze, avoiding the stench of the Husk and their desecration. Each new glen, paddock, field and town was rife with their stink and signs of corruption.

His passage home had been interrupted by those seeking help which, as a serving guardskin, was his duty. He escorted wounded Nighspyn to seek assistance, exchanged information with Fraurora Vulpus, guided orphaned chicks to willing adoptive feathered parents.

Harend and Yowri sung the morning chorus, yet it was lacking in details. The Windsweepers, The Flap, and Breathcutter squadrons of the north, east and west respectively had halted their services, withdrawing from the threat of wing-borne Husk. What little news that got through was quickly disseminated.

He stopped at a glade in a forest as another troop of Caanus limped back to their home turf. They were the worse for cuts, bruises and savage bites.

'Jamboree, halt!'

The captain, one Lolop Hembrad, a gigantic animal with long limbs and a jowly face, saluted Bresh with a raised paw.

'Good day to you, young Caanus. We are the Jamboree of the Useful, Once Useless, on our trek back from the front. You might not want to go that way, plenty of those toe-rags skulking around. My troops and I were fighting alongside a number of other brigades of Caanus, but those damn Husk, they pack quite a bark!'

'Good day, Captain, I am Bresh of the Roughclod Infantry. How are you combating their sickness?'

Another Caanus hobbled up the line. On his back was a satchel of sorts, carrying a pile of what looked like animal bones. On closer inspection, they appeared to be bone hexes.

'These 'orrible things, they call them *bone hexes* in the Corvan parlance. Seems those blighters can't go near the things, don't like seeing their reflection! Get sucked into 'em. Got to keep it with you at all times.'

Bresh revealed his own bone hex, hung on his armour.

'I was taught the craft by a Cini no less! I did not know that news of this defence had spread.'

'A Cini you say? The Necros Anx in the west, ex-prisoners of war themselves, are fighting alongside us! Fascinating creatures they are! Hideous brutes but fascinating all the same! From foreign lands they say!' Lolop looked wistfully into the yonder before shaking his jowls and regaining his composure.

'You'll find skirmishes all the way to the Norgan Kingdom, I'm afraid. What they're calling the *black flood* continues south, but they leave their nasty recruits here and there, making new outbreaks of this disease. Be on the lookout. Keep your bone hex at paw — and don't eat it!'

'But sir, they look so tasty!' a voice perked up from behind.

'Back in line corporal, those bones aren't for eating. We'll have some nosh soon enough! Good luck to you, young Bresh, Ora bring peace! Right, you bunch of scruffy ne'er-do-wells, back in formation, left right left right...'

They disappeared into the bushes, leaving Bresh alone again.

He slept fitfully through the night, curled under a car, waking to the quick voices of Morwih fleeing a skittish horror that crept from the undergrowth. It was a Yoa'a, although hardly recognisable. A series of splinters of wood had been forced into its back, which were bleeding profusely, and its eyes leaked a foul smelling pus. It looked at him with such fury that he pulled himself from his hiding place and made to run — yet the nagging need to help almost overcame him. Already, the creature was invoking the spirits it harboured — worming vapour-mouths coughed out of its maw.

He flung the bone hex before it, drawing its attention. It sniffed at it, thinking it an offer of surrender. It let out a wheezing laugh, mocking him. The mocking soon turned to a cough, and Bresh watched in awe as the apparitions were pulled into the field of the hex's influence. Unable to free themselves, they were soon devoured.

A wet hacking preceded a dark foam forming around the Yoa'a's mouth, and with it came a vivid phantom, ropes of runny oil, spitting and seething and hopelessly resisting the magnetism of the hex. But even it, in all its maturity as a resident ghoul, was no match for the necromancy — soon even it was sucked down into the rotting marrow of the talisman.

The Yoa'a collapsed. Bresh collected the bone hex and hung it back on his armour. Very slowly he approached the animal. He could see its chest rising and falling. It was alive, in some regard at least.

'Hello?' he said.

The animal blinked. A semblance of normality returned to her eyes, no longer holding the clouded vision of the Husk.

'Is there ... water?' she uttered in little more than a parched whisper.

He helped her up and they made for a puddle. The Yoa'a lay beside it and drank her fill. She was struggling to make sense of her body once again, having been denied it for so long.

'I will stay with you, until you regain your strength.'

She slept for a turn, and it was nightfall before she was able to rise. She fed on some choice green leaves Bresh had collected for her, and with a little more rest she felt better. He carefully removed the pieces of wood from her back, and licked the wounds clean. She winced with each daub of his tongue, but soon every injury was tended.

Eventually, she spoke of her ordeal.

'I had no control, no say over my limbs. I saw what it wanted, heard what it wanted. It was driven mad by the voices, clamouring for theirs to be above all others, vying for dominion over my body. They ate the flesh of others, and I became sick, yet they were unable to feel the nausea, they vomited and laughed at me as I died a little more every day. I felt that in time, I would be gone entirely. I fought with every ounce of my mind to rid myself of them, but they clung on, clung for dear life. As I began to let go, I heard the voices of others, all of the victims of their cruelty, all half in and out of life. I have never known such pain. We must stop them, all of them!'

He escorted her back to grassland that she had once called home. Her Drove were gone, or dead. She collected what armour she could find, the precious artefacts of her sisters, strapping them to her body and regaining a sense of self. She stood surrounded by flattened grass, the dried blood of her compatriots about her, and wept.

'Tell me, is anything being done to stop them?' she asked once she had recovered somewhat.

'Yes, but I don't know how. I will do my best to help those I can. I am Bresh, of the Roughclod Infantry of Reconditioned Caanus.'

She went to him. 'Bresh, you saved my life, and for that I am forever in your debt. My name is Arophele, my Drove is all gone. If you will have me, I shall join your Roughclod Infantry in their efforts.'

'Of course! But, I'm not sure they'll believe you to be a Caanus I'm afraid. Those ears are quite a giveaway.'

She laughed, although unsure if he was joking.

They emerged in the allotment of TumHilliad later that day, where there was a makeshift triage of sorts for the wounded. Animals of all creeds gathered food and medicinal plants, Collector flocks travelling far afield to locate any who needed help.

Bresh's fellow soldiers bounded to greet him with barks and sniffs and licks, excited beyond measure. TumHilliad shuffled over to greet him, 'My boy! I assume you successfully delivered our Cini friend and her little whatchamacallit?'

'Little Grin, sir. Yes! All delivered. Teaching the Rauka to make bone hexes!'

'Bone hexes, yes I have heard about this, turning your supper into a weapon — whatever next? Perhaps we all need to sit down and have a look at making some ourselves, what say you?'

'Yes sir, they work a treat.'

'I can speak to that!' Arophele said, as she limped towards the Throa.

'Arophele? My, do you need assistance? We have salves for those wounds. I haven't seen you since that scuffle in the … where was it?'

'Battle of the Marsh! Thank you, I will need to rest and medicine is very welcome, despite the kind and healing tongue of Bresh!'

TumHilliad patted a proud Bresh.

'Ah yes, Battle of the Marsh! Back in the year of Vimswater. Your kin, are they safe?'

'No. Taken by the Husk. Much like myself.'

'You were taken? But you live!'

He peered at her, his great gentle claws turning her head so that he might see every aspect of her. 'You must tell me all you can of this affliction. If the innocent can be saved then we cannot kill the enemy.'

'I can only liken it to a fever, a nightmare of pain and captivity. Never have I known such things. I was very close to death; in fact, if it was not just delirium, I believe I was in the Gasp.'

'Yet you came back? Fascinating. Well, Arophele. I am very glad to see you alive, if a little bruised and battered.'

They walked amongst the former raised vegetable beds made with old sacks, straw, and leaves into nests and resting places for the many animals bearing the marks of the Husk.

'Nasty stuff indeed. We need all the help we can get. The enemy has positioned itself in old Wroth settlements and they only leave to hunt for prey and victims for their foul deeds. We are yet to form any kind of defence against them. Perhaps you can begin making some of these wards, make sure everyone has one, and hang them up on the trees at the entrances to this garden?'

Bresh saluted with a raised paw, and Arophele hopped awkwardly beside him as they made for the streets. 'We need carcasses. I believe we shall find some on the streets, poor victims of the Husk.'

Arophele grimaced. Even the bodies of the dead had become tools of war.

They set about dragging barely recognisable skeletons and shrivelled hides towards the allotment. Arophele glanced back at the road itself, making note of it.

'Do we know where the Wroth have their encampment?'

Bresh shook his head.

As the day progressed, more and more casualties were carried in alongside the steady stream of those seeking shelter. Athlon herds carrying dozens of injured feathered upon their backs, Aurma pushing an old trailer filled with mammals, unable to walk. Speaker flocks lined the branches above, each clasping projectiles, ready to assault any enemy who dare approach. Yet, despite the death and injuries, the sense of community was healing in itself.

Bresh sat beside Arophele in the shade of a tree. He watched the harrowed faces of animals, their fur marked with blood and dried tears. He saw burials of loved ones, Malor males with bright red faces and richly painted feathers alongside their mates making prayer circles to the Sisters of the Flock.

'I want to go find them, I want to fight.'

Arophele's ears perked up. 'Bresh, no, it's too dangerous. My hardiest fighters fell in battle. The Husk are ruthless, they care nothing about dying themselves.'

He shook his head, 'We have a defence now, we have bone hexes. If all we have to fear is their teeth we stand a far greater chance of overcoming and freeing those of the Husk. You, yourself, should want this?'

She sighed, 'Of course, but I am too weak to fight again. It's a fool's errand. Even with a hundred hexes.'

Bresh got up. 'I won't ask any to fight with me, but I must do something.'

Arophele considered his words. 'If I could offer you an alternative, would you listen?'

Bresh furrowed his brow. 'What do you have in mind?'

*

They stared down at the large metal plate in the road. Arophele had asked Bresh to drag an angled stick which they would use as a cantilever, and had managed to insert it into a small opening in the plate's centre. An Athlon, Gimblenod, was asked to put all his weight on to one end of the stick, and eventually, the plate lifted. It was very dark below.

'The Wroth build tunnels, all over. No one knows why, but ask any Throa or Woderum and they will tell you, the Wroth dug a lot of tunnels in the most inconvenient places. But these tunnels lead places, and one day I realised that these roadways usually have these tunnels beneath.'

Bresh frowned, 'How does this help us?'

Arophele smiled, 'My thought is that the Husk in those Wroth dwellings, they're hunkered down, not going anywhere yet. They await word from their master. They leave only to hunt — if we can get to where they are, without being seen, we can leave as many bone hexes as possible, and draw the damned ghouls out of them. The thing in me, it had no idea about Corvan magic, knew nothing of Ocquia. It's a little thing, but it's a start. We have knowledge of their folly.'

'The bone hexes?'

'Yes. We sneak up on them, leave these hexes at doorways, openings, anywhere they are likely to venture, and we just wait for them to come across them, and *woosh* out comes the Husk, trapped forever. Instead of going in, all teeth bared, we slip in, silent like, we set traps, and leave without them ever knowing we were there.'

Bresh turned to the Athlon, 'What do you think?'

The great Equine, from behind a lock of mane, whinnied, 'Rather you than me.'

Bresh grinned, 'Sounds like a plan!'

*

The Reveral named Nenfa awoke on the shore of the river. He coughed up water and pulled himself from the thick mud. The bone hex remained attached to his headdress. He looked around for signs of his companions, and found none.

In time, he crawled up the embankment and onto a bridge. There was evidence of the fight he had escaped, wide sprays of blood spilled between the bodies of Husk. He wrestled with his guilt for having fallen from the bridge, overwhelmed by the gnashing teeth of the adversary.

He began his trek back to the Pridebrow in hope that some of his fellow Rauka had escaped. Along the path he saw no evidence of such, no fresh paw prints, no lingering scent beyond that which they had left before. He could only assume the black flood had taken them with it.

He descended the slope down into the quarry, to be met by the sombre face of his queen and her two sons.

'Esit is taken. I survived only by sheer chance. I did not see her, dead or alive, and I can only assume she now labours under a new master. Will you let me seek her and her soldiers? I cannot live with the knowledge of her abduction.'

She-King Carcaris levelled her gaze at him, stoic yet shaken. 'These Husk have made their intention known. Send out scouts, find my daughter.'

*

Yaran liked the smell of the sea. She had trotted ahead of her mother, hoping to be the first to spot the blue of it, to introduce her extended family to something almost none of them, besides her mother, Matriarch Eda, had ever seen before.

In her youth, Eda had seen the sea briefly, through the rungs of a cage on her long voyage from the savannah. She had mixed feelings about seeing it again. As a result, she walked far too slowly for her daughter, flanked by her sisters, Preu and Gyhm, who had inherited their mother's apprehension. Yaran was an aberration that Eda attributed to her father's wilful ways.

The Clusk herd was twenty Oraclas strong, and despite their resistance to assist, a number of males trailed behind. The Crash of Tasq, known as Clan Brawdhead, walked beside them, sharing a similar herd of females, whilst solitary males coaxed into helping them straggled behind.

The Egresc Horn Guard consisted of a collection of ungulate herds, Oreya of many clades, from the gargantuan Yad Golhoth, nervous Impasse, Flat-teeth and Baobak Gorehorn. The black and white striped Onto-Athlon and other smaller families had accompanied the exodus from the parks of the Stinking City, many of whom had never travelled so far as to be able to see the glorious green countenance of Embrian Naa for themselves, let alone the wide ocean.

There was a mutual inhalation in awe as they reached the top of the cliff. Below them, the frothy avalanche of waves broke against the rockfall, sending out plumes of spray, the turquoise of the shallows plunging to considerable marine depths. The breeze was warm and invigorating as they turned their attention to Dron, the First City.

'And there,' Yaran trumpeted, 'is the First City!'

They found the coastal path and descended, through the quiet cobble streets of the village and out onto the sand.

Eda was brought to tears. Something in the shape, in the scale and purpose of it. 'I know this place. How do I know this place?'

She was drawn to the opening, felt a youthful exuberance in each step, and in the Hall of Receiving, perceived the aura of something composed in her own blood.

'Welcome, sister.'

The voice was gentle, a precursor to the formation of a face, fashioned of ephemera. A face she'd known in dreams.

'Lendel,' she whispered.

'Yes.'

'My mother spoke of you in children's tales, you are the crux of us, the tusk and trunk of us. I've told that tale to Yaran a hundred times! The shepherd on the killing day. The saviour, the Sentinel in the cold. To find you here brings me so much joy, to know the stories hold truths. We have been so bereft of hope in this place — I've lived a whole life in want of a stolen sky, of the dust and mountains. To know you are here, Lendel, I will die happy.'

'Die, my Eda? No. You will live happy, in this land. But first we must assure the survival of this city.'

*

Onnar had divided her Drove to orchestrate the defences. They helped direct the Oraclas in moving fallen timber, logs and wooden wreckage, and the ample, sturdy horns of both Tasq and Yad Golhoth, could carry the lumber up the sand dunes and begin the construction of a sea wall that ran the perimeter of the bay.

It was soon apparent that the cliffside was less than stable, and many large, fallen rocks were scattered about. It was decided to use these large boulders to funnel the Husk towards the town, trapping them behind the sea wall, with only one route in and out.

Onnar ran to the top of the cliff and looked inland towards the Downs. There were large trees further afield, where the Naarna Elowin would establish lookouts. Onnar's fastest runners would act as check points, if and when the enemy made their approach. But it was little comfort. The rumours brought with those seeking sanctuary spoke of vicious, remorseless things. Older Corva who had learned of bone hexes and gore craft in their youth were called into service, to build talismans and traps in the undergrowth and all points of entry.

She was heartened to watch the hefty movements of Oraclas and Tasq. But it was all piecemeal.

'You look tired, Proudfoot.'

The streak of black and white in her periphery was a very welcome sight.

'Aggi!' Onnar grinned, flinging her forelimbs around the surprised Collector, who looked a little perplexed by her affection.

'Your daughter warned me you might be acting out of sorts.'

Onnar laughed, 'I am becoming soft in my old age, Aggita Fenwhistler. My daughter would prefer I keep my sentiment to myself; she is after all, still a child despite her agility and training as a Drove. I have the ways and means of being a constant embarrassment to her!'

'True,' Aggi replied. 'However, she is also very proud to be your child. Ah, speak of the spirits, here is Ether.'

The rumbustious young Yoa'a, her armour covering the upper portion of her face, her back plates festooned with two Oreya horns, and gauntlets on both wrists, appeared alongside other Drove. They were soon play fighting one another and laughing.

'Mother,' Ether said, when they had finished greeting one another. It had been many turns since Ether had left on a pilgrimage to the east, to fight the Stegard thieves.

'I am good my daughter. I see the Stegard didn't fair too well?'

She gestured at the severed head. Aggi interrupted, 'Now, before you two begin one of your heated discussions, I would like to add that we did not take lives unless it was unavoidable. They destroyed at least ten nests, killed a number of chicks. Your daughter spared all but the leader, a particularly vile Muroi.'

'Yeah, Aggi saw him coming a mile off. Best spotter we've ever had.'

Only spotter you've ever had, Onnar thought. 'Well done both of you, and thank you, Aggi, for accompanying them.'

'My pleasure, Onnar,' Aggi bowed. 'I will leave you to catch up. I will go see if I can be useful elsewhere.'

She flew towards the city, leaving mother and daughter alone.

'Did you eat well, did you get enough rest?'

'Yes, mother. We also became inebriated on fermenting fruit after our success and danced and sang until morning. I am tired from my travels so, if we can forgo the usual debrief, I think I shall find a tree to lie under.'

Ether bowed cordially, and slumped off to join her compatriots.

'Children,' Onnar sighed.

A flock of Naarna Elowin flew overhead, bedecked in slate armour. Armour that had not been worn since the war for the city. The sun was high and bright and their silhouette was a powerful reminder of the past. Now they fought beside her. It was dreamlike, the warm breeze, the sea spray carried up from the water below, the scent of sturdy blossom and salt. She closed her eyes, just for a second, to will away the blights.

'Mother Drove.'

She opened them once again, to see half a dozen of her mercenaries, all alert to her call. All counting on her.

*

Dominus Audagard stepped among the luminous flesh of fungi that grew within the once hidden spaces of Dron. It was strangely reminiscent – ganglion, spongiform – like the thinking organs of the dead he splayed in ritual, in amongst the workings of this living metropolis. He was particularly taken by the slime mould that wriggled with rudimentary sentience across the tough skins of fruiting toadstools, how their filament strands shuddered out in search of food. That same pattern, that interconnectivity was repeated all about him in the fleecy mycology of foraging hyphae. Patterns, patterns everywhere. All interwoven, all sharing.

How ironic that he had retired his lifetime of service to the Gasp only for those works to be so vital again. But nothing was coincidence. For him, serendipity was like breathing, the rhythm of lungs, the patter of water against leaves, the testy storm; all was synchronous, a repetition, coordination, not in the design of Naa, but in the natural laws of Naa — for all of this had grown from a grave, a grave that bore new fruit.

For what was more real, more tangible than the viscera of death, the inanimate ingredients, lain bare? In the grotesquery of discovery, to spark something, anything in that which no longer served its primary function. This was the essence of necromancy, where blood and bone and muscle became components, machinery in a different design, one not meant for Naa, but made of Naa. Much like the fungus, that went out in search of death, to feed, to reinterpret, to share those nutrients.

So he, too, would reinterpret. The Umbra was life, a cauldron of ideas, the concentration of experience, a trillion infinitesimal choices, wrapped up in feeling, motive, motion. The Gasp fed that experience, the halfway house for the essence of a being. He had begun to consider the Gasp and the Umbra like the mycelium, feeding off the dead to make new. It was a cycle, replenishing itself.

He let his wing feathers glide over the slick dermis in hope of divining its function. He saw how the structures of plant and fungi grafted to one another, the machinery of a living ecosystem — the flora had found common purpose and amalgamated into a colony, and, in many ways, so too had the fauna.

He hopped over to the once severed limb, the link with the Sentinels restored by Ivy, however the city connected to them - the flow of spores, the intelligence shared between single animalcules in the earth, the reticulum of the soil. He let out an audible *Ha!*

Erithacus found him brooding over these thoughts, 'Old flock, what ails you?'

'All this,' he gestured widely, 'I am beginning to see its function. There was never any competition, never a secret to be found. The city did not hide this from me, it was protecting itself. I was wrong to assume the city reacted to Ivy as a defence. The city knew she would help it. All of this, it's all about synchronicity. It's all cycles, it's all inherent in us.'

'The city needed Ivy to heal this wound. It is aware of the Husk, and it is scared. Dron is not above the nature of things, because—'

'It *is* the nature of things,' Erithacus took him under his wing.

'Now you begin to see it all through my eyes. The magic is in the real. The Umbra, it is a sharing of minds, and that may be a physical thing that we, in our unbridled intelligence,' he grinned 'will never understand. The Wroth, however, they may have one day deciphered that particular riddle. But it is not hidden, it is waiting to be found. I mourn their death for what they knew. That is not to say that we will never grasp their intelligence — I myself will indeed try. But you are right, Dron is many millions of seasons old. It is an evolution, from the little feathered in the earth to the citadel of Epiras.'

'And my Gaspcraft?'

'The Wroth called it mathematics, chemistry. It is one way to make sense of it. What the dead are in Naa? I do not know. But one can hypothesise it is all one and the same. All sides of the same shell.'

'Then I will no longer be ashamed of it,' the Dominus said.

'Ashamed? It was Gaspcraft that brought back the city, that brought Petulan to Vorsa. Embrace it, use it once again. The Umbra is open to you, in all its glory —do not shy away from it. In our lessons to the Anx we have often butted heads over how we convey ideas.'

'But those ideas are always the same.'

'Yes, my friend. We cannot chastise each other for our perspective.'

The Dominus reflected, and coming to a silent decision, teased four small sticks from his headdress.

'Ah,' Erithacus smiled. 'you never threw them away I see!' The Dominus cast them on the floor. They clattered in a little heap. He peered down at them, hopping about to examine each angle.

'The Husk, I think.' He pointed to the stick overlapping another two. 'But this—' he pointed with his beak at the largest of the four, the outlier. 'This is an unknown. Something coming.'

'Ivy? The Sentinels?'

'Perhaps. It has shades of something else. Something potent, and old. My old tricks still work a treat. But they lack definition. There is, perhaps, something more useful to us than a pile of old sticks.

'I will return to the Naag Rarspi, visit my old skrying grounds. There are scraps of ideas there, old sorcery, oscelan-black chattels. I fear all the bone hexes in the world may not be enough.'

He placed his wing on the wall of the city. 'Look after the old girls for me.'

Erithacus smiled and nodded. He watched the former High Priest of Bone Char disappear in a flurry of feathers.

'There is something in all this,' he caught himself saying out loud. He hoped Ivy would return soon, so she might help him with his reading — one last piece, a Wroth shaped piece, to place in the puzzle.

*

Gahar was not willing to sit quiet. Although her limbs were not hers any longer, she was not easily silenced, not easily beaten down. Her clarity in that moment when she had been so sure about Ivy's death was quickly snuffed out, stolen, reconstituted and spat out by this invader. She had not had time to even exhale before the riddle of it gained coherence. She was so ashamed.

She could not weep, so she stayed in contemplation, exercising thoughts. She held the thought of Eru in her mind, and it was so perfect, his tiny face, his wide eyes. She had swum in the love for him, and it had disappeared the bars of her cage — he had made life worthy. But it had been, all told, a very brief motherhood. A few days. They had taken Eru's body from her, thinking so little of her need to grieve. So she had been alone once again. Alone — beside her rage.

The blame was nebulous. The male who killed her son. The Wroth who thoughtlessly let him into the cage. She knew nothing of Hanno in their own land, how a rival male might react to a son. Her memory of the forests was a smudge on a long and unchanging desolate sky, the screaming, ceaseless, mirthless faces that glowed red against the glass, the ignorant adult Wroth who chewed and whined and pushed their cubs around in wheeled contrivances of metal. How they lingered, gawping, over fed, indifferent to her. Their stink, a miasma of sharp unnatural identities bleeding into an olfactory blasphemy. They, the Wroth, who put her in a cage and killed her son.

Ivy.

Erithacus had once come to her, not long after she found the High Realm. He was full of ideas and excitement. He had speculated that the Hanno, Toron and a plethora of simian forms shared an ancestor tied in the deep past. According to him, another relative, who had migrated from the warmer south of a continent, who wore armour of shells and made painted markings on cave surfaces, had been called Thalei. They had spread across the land, sharing in the Umbra, and they had died at the hands of the Wroth.

He had asked her to travel with him to the Epiras, to commune with her ancestors. She had denied him that, for her conversations with her own past were always painful affairs. The present and future, The High Realm, her people, were all that had mattered. She had pushed her son's death into the pit of her stomach.

Until Ivy had appeared.

Until she had seen that little wrothcub running through the streets with the vixen who had freed Gahar. Had this wrothcub so easily manipulated even the strongest of Naa? It would not happen again.

She had slammed her fists against the glass in anger, feeling it shudder with her strength. She would end any chance of their return, their dominion quashed with the death of the child.

Gahar remembered Ivy. It hadn't been an epiphany — it hadn't materialised in the moment Ivy had mentioned it, between deep, tearful inhales. No, it had come to her after, when she sat upon the ground and found herself incapable of moving. To move would be to acknowledge she was responsible for almost killing that child. The memory had clarified in light of this truth.

Very few Wroth were Umbra. Yet, in her close proximity with so many Wroth from behind the bars of her prison, every hundred or so turns, a face would appear at the glass that appeared different. Their vacant stare would not curl into a grin, would not scowl at her inaction, they would not ball their fists and pound the glass. They would stand in contemplation and they would think *you are so similar to me. I can see how sad you are.* Sometimes the words would be so clear to her, she could not help but react. That face was often young, brought to this prison by a parent, and they would turn to that adult and say, 'Mummy, why are they so sad?'

The reply would always be nothing but sounds, but its intent was always the same. She would hear it again, repeated in the thoughts of the Umbra, 'They are not sad, they are resting. They are not sad, they are watching.'

Sometimes the cognitive dissonance was excruciating. 'They are probably sad because they're stuck in a cage. Shall we go see the lions?'

And they'd be gone, pulled away, the last fleeting look of the little wrothcub, and the thought that lingered in their wake, *I am sorry.*

Ivy had not been pulled away. She had stood beyond the glass and tried to catch Gahar's attention. The pain of that child was visible — guilt, shame, a desire to help, the frustration of being incapable of doing anything meaningful. The resignation when Gahar refused to look at her — humiliated, dejected, and deeply scarred by grief, her hatred of the Wroth embedded in her.

Ivy was innocent, and Gahar had almost killed her. She shivered, and she felt it, she felt her chest heave, her limbs jolt. She felt it, and so did the thief who'd stolen her body.

*

The Husk followed the carriageways into the Stinking City. The elevated roads were treacherous, those that were still standing. Thoth had been here only once before, in his youth, a very long time ago. As for his army, many of them had lived here, worked and played and died here. Now it was a shadow of its former self.

He had longed for a bastion of Wroth, the survivors of the apocalypse. He had expected piles of corpses swimming in septic swamps, a hum of a trillion flies. He found neither.

It had been a year since the city was pulled from under itself, leaving many of the high rises and skyscrapers kneecapped and crumbling. Yet despite the untold damage, there was a palpable calm to it all. Glass-fronted offices had become hot houses of lush vegetation, growing from inside and out, twenty foot cheese plants splitting concrete troughs in search of fresh soil, drifts of autumnal leaves had mounted an assault against every surface and turned to compost in their wake.

Flocks of feathered flew overhead, making nests in telecommunication towers and powerlines. Like vertical farms, multi-storey carparks held bouquets of wildflowers, sprouting from vehicles filled with Baldaboa dung and moss. It was quite beautiful, silent but for the sway of mouldering flags from hotels. Many roads were now flooded, at least by a few inches of water from broken water mains and drowned subways. It might take a hundred years to clean the city of its stains, but the water would hasten that task, erasing the mark of the Wroth ever further.

'Such a shame,' one of his more stable Husk uttered as they began to fill the streets, sniffing out any living thing, any morsel of food.

'Quite,' Thoth replied, scenting for Scab. 'Let's continue south, towards the river. We'll establish another outpost in that old castle there.'

His army was tens of thousands strong, a thick, heady reek of animal faeces, the sweet tang of blood, and a more malodorous foetid sickness, infected cuts, wounds upon wounds. They bit and cut at one another, and forged primitive weapons for their toil; found objects on the road, splinters of glass, shards of brittle plastic, radio antennas. Armour too - discarded car parts - imperfectly lashed to limbs.

Many succumbed to their illnesses and quickly became nothing more than flesh to be eaten, descending into melées of arterial spray, of organs caught in a tug of war of rival mouths, splaying hot, wet meat that was always quickly devoured. Bones were dragged along and chewed until they were nothing but spines, dirty white, dug deep into flanks and chests as an attempt to feel further grounded.

Occasionally, Thoth would consider what he had done for the briefest of moments, and was always, always punished for it by Emeris. The echo of a distant laugh, a mocking chorus line.

Means to an end

What end, he was still unsure, but the further the ground gained, the clearer the intention was. Soon his emissaries would return with information, and he would know his enemy, and his quarry.

He climbed on top of a bus shelter, looking back on the shadowed streets, his lecherous cavalcade a spillage of clay grey bodies that snapped and hissed about him, filling every nook and cranny, tearing down boarded-up dwellings in search of victims. Urban dens and earths were raided, the few who had remained immediately ensconced into the fold.

'Wretches! Crawcleavers! Good for nothings!'

A Corva appeared on a lamppost. It flashed its eye – triumphant – its head darting, squawking, jeering at them.

'Good for nothings! Ha ha ha!'

It flew to another lamppost, flapping its wings to gain their attention. Another joined it, this one far more raucous, defecating, swooping to other stoops, cackling erratically, before dive bombing those closer to it. In retaliation, the Husk festooned with revenants leaked with ghoul-fat, reaching syrupy limbs to the sky.

Thoth leapt from the bus shelter and ploughed through his troops. 'Don't let them escape!' he cried, sure that they were spies. They might have wings, but he would not be so quick to let them leave.

A bevy of plasm now lifted into the air, a malevolent swell that moved in a column, a Seethe, up towards the Corva.

'Onwards!' he howled, and the brigade marched on. Above, the murmuration of ghouls, hunting the screeching Corva, towards the centre of the Stinking City. Towards the Orrery.

*

Bresh and Arophele made their move in the early hours of the morning, long before Ora would rise. They were joined by three Caanus - Tango, Turing, and Orch. Turing was a big Caanus. He carried an old apple box on his back; the crate was a little lopsided but was held in place by a foraged belt. It had taken a host of Collectors to fasten it on, but eventually, loaded with two dozen bone hexes, they began their descent into the sewer.

After some effort, Turing and the box squeezed through the manhole without injury and they stood in the cramped tunnel. The smell was foul, yet difficult to identify. A year of disuse and natural decay had somewhat reduced the presence of Wroth waste, yet it remained a thick and unavoidable aroma. Tango, one of many Caanus with a keen interest in plants, offered them all some dried flowers — tight little purple stems with distinct and pleasant fragrance. Arophele took some and with her delicate paws rubbed them on each of their snouts. She tucked a sprig under her forehead armour. 'Better,' she said, and they proceeded along the sewer.

After a short distance, they came to a wide red brick crossroads with tunnels leading in several directions. They continued on north, avoiding the pale stalactites of congealed waste, the putrefied detritus of the Wroth. With only a basic direction to steer their course, and their path dictated by the tunnels themselves, their goal remained clear.

The troop quietly moved along the tunnel, taking the small ledge where it was accessible, wading through muck when not. Arophele replenished their flower scent until it crumbled away and they were fully exposed to the stench.

Eventually, the drain widened again as various tributaries merged. On the far side, the wall had collapsed and piles of masonry and earth formed a slope. There was a lot of water below it, but the debris was climbable. Arophele hopped across onto the raised incline, carefully manoeuvring towards the broken wall, and she felt a breeze. She poked her head out.

The Caanus below waited impatiently. 'What do you see?'

She crawled back, 'We are there. It's dark, but I can see a big space with walls on all sides, and there are crowds of them, and I ... I can smell death.'

Bresh scrabbled over to her, and carefully looked through the hole.

'More of them than I thought! A whole army dug in.' He climbed down. 'Well mates, now we must decide on how we proceed. Wait until they sleep and sneak out, lay the bone hexes and barely escape with our lives? Or—'

'Lead them down here? Trap 'em? Make this hole our snare? If we line the walls with the gruesome things, they'll have no hope of not seeing them.'

Arophele looked back up to the hole. 'I think I could run the gauntlet. I'm quick and light on my feet. If Turing stays close to that exit, I can take one at a time. Perhaps we can pull the ghouls out of them in their sleep?'

Tango perked up, 'I think they 'ave to see 'em, look into 'em, before they get walloped.'

Orch sniffed, 'Or we fight them? I don't know about you, but I'm up for a ruckus, damn Husk — need a good hiding if you ask me!'

Bresh panted, 'Orch, I think it's best we avoid them at all costs, but you may just get what you asked for. From what I've heard, they don't go down without a fight.'

'Arophele, are you sure you want to take the risk? This could be very dangerous.'

She nodded, straightened the bone hex upon her brow, and beckoned Turing towards her. 'Please stay here, Bresh, and pass the hexes to me when I call for them.' She took two in her mouth, and silently pushed her way out of the sewer.

She emerged in a wide courtyard of a former textile mill. Much of the yard was filled with sleeping Husk. She tiptoed out, achingly slowly, avoiding sprawled limbs, convulsing tails in dream repose. She was not prepared for the sight of them — for, whatever their former bodies had been, little of it remained.

Disfigured, brutalised, flayed hair and skin, blighted injuries engorged with maggots, staked with glass and wood and rusted metal stuck between muscle, slathered with the spoil of some sour film, the repulsive residue of the Gasp that had not yet fully penetrated their bodies. Their sleep was fitful, in turmoil, stricken faces, nightmarish.

Seyla was still vivid and provided enough light to orchestrate her mission. Arophele made for the centre of the pack, the remains of some poor beast, obliterated into gobbets of meat, rejected organs, gristle and gnawed pelvis. Given time and effort, these remains, too, could be fashioned into shapes that the dead could not resist, though the leftovers would be picked over when they woke, so this was as good a place as any to leave her traps. One, two, placed far apart. She hurried back towards the break in the sewer wall, where Bresh waited eagerly. He passed her up another two bone hexes. She took them, realising then she could carry more by hanging them from the horns on her armour, and whispered for two more.

Back amongst the enemy, teasing her way beside whiskers whose hair triggers would surely awake them, avoiding the gaze of open eyes – empty globes of blanched gelatine – as the dead breathed, loose serrated teeth protruding from rotten gums, an acrid bite of halitosis ringed her on all sides.

With little time, she had danced there and back, observed by Bresh with awe. She was silver in the moonlight, pivoting from one space to another, brandishing the wreathes of wrecked cartilage and glass between her teeth, leaving them like some gift-bearing deity. All but the large brute on the steps to the old mill's entrance were aligned with a hex, about its feet a number of smaller, scrawny victims. Surreptitiously, she wove herself around each buck tooth, each outstretched claw, and found a spot for her final snare.

A pair of eyes opened, little yellow lights, followed by curiosity, and finally a frown.

The shrill scream of the tiny Storn was surprisingly loud. Loud enough to wake them all.

'RUN!'

Bresh was standing on the far side of the yard, a mouth full of hexes. They dropped from his jaw when he barked, and he was already back through the hole as she began to hurtle towards it herself. Around her, Husk were waking to the commotion, at first confused and annoyed, or filled with an uncontrollable rage. And then all were on their feet, eyes aimed at her, not at the hexes beneath their feet, scuffing them, lackadaisically kicking them away, undeterred — they were on her, howling in spittle shrieks.

*

The Sentinel, an island of moor and bracken in the sky, little copses of stunted trees hardy against the wind, and a tall ridge of eroded dark rock along its spine. It advanced turtle-like, cotton wads of cloud caught in its vegetal crags and protuberances, legs like giant redwoods, it trod with care over each hill and dale, considering the landing of its limbs.

Upon its back, Noraa, Vorsa and Ivy took it in turns to watch the ground below for signs of refugees and Husk alike. Flocks of feathered danced along with them, some alighting on its back to rest and share and perhaps collect information that could be distributed amongst the clades of Ocquia. If a stop must be made, Little Grin would crawl along the neck of Moorvori Groor and relay instructions. It was not long before many animals had climbed the steep stalks and found harbour upon the Sentinel's back.

Lucille, however, had descended into the cavern that had brought her to this juncture. Much of the rock remained, only now the complex of bracing roots once hidden in scale and mud had been revealed, trusses and tethers that looped and coiled and enshrined each stone. Where once was a clogged pit of earth was now a labyrinth of Herculean structures. She pulled a flare from her bag, lit it, and threw it from the stone ledge. It fell into the dark, offering her a brief yet astonishing glance of a bifurcating endless spiral of woody struts, curled like springs, like musculature.

Her path was supported, seemingly with purpose. Her torch allowed her to continue cautiously on until she reached the site of the grave of the two Cini. Their skeletons remained, held in place by immutable stems. Below them, something she had not seen before, further graves — large skulls of animals she barely recognised, carnivores with tremendous teeth, armour long petrified into stony composites. She moved further into the maze, her lantern revealing intricate shrines to the long dead, tiny cartouches cut into stone by claws, hints of primordial language.

Makepeace ran along the roots, stopping to examine his own ancestors, great rodents curled with the vestiges of their belongings, arrangements of seed hulls, each in the palm of a curled shoot.

Soon Lucille came upon something unexpected — a Wroth. He had been lain flat, mummified, his red beard still visible, the fragile remnants of his helmet beside him. The stone beneath him held his belongings, somewhat buried in pockets of silt, yet remarkably undisturbed, despite the lulling stride of Groor. She was overwhelmed; in many ways she expected any remains of the Wroth to have been discarded, and yet here one lay, nestled in the clutch of this great earthen beast.

Makepeace had run ahead, but returned to her enthused, 'You must see!' he said. Further on, was something of a mass grave. Here, below the earth, flowers blossomed. They were archaic blooms, oddly prehistoric, grand and primeval, their petals robust white and pinks and yellows. They ringed at least a dozen bodies, intact, huddled close. A woolly Oraclas, what looked to be an Athlon, adorned in armour. There were Muroi, and large felines. Feathered of myriad species and beside them, an animal she had seen once before.

It had a broad head and a heavy brow, its nose was flat, and the jaw was extremely pronounced. Its forelimbs were longer than hers, yet it was far smaller than her. She knew it wasn't a child, and she knew it was a woman.

'Wroth,' she whispered.

'Not quite.' Makepeace scampered over the petrified corpses, examining them.

Lucille crouched down and placed her hand on its femur. She could see that this female had been laid to rest beside the other animals, not by others of its kind, but by all these clades.

'How can this be?' she looked to Makepeace.

'I do not know, but can you feel them?'

'Feel them?'

'They are at peace, all of them are at peace.'

Back above, Lucille found her friends resting on the slope of Groor's shoulders.

'Can you tell me, were the Wroth always hated?'

Vorsa looked at her, 'Hated, yes. Some we knew could see us, but most did not.'

Lucille thought again, 'Below there are graves of many animals. One such grave is a collection of skeletons, placed with love. In among them is a Wroth. It is very old, an ancestor, who lived in the grasslands of another continent. I don't think they ever came here, to this land.'

'The First City moved, to serve those who needed it. It made the Sentinels of itself, perhaps those graves were once part of Dron, and now they are held amongst the bones of Moorvori Groor?' Vorsa speculated.

'Yes, perhaps, but who were they and why were they buried alongside these animals?'

'I do not know, but there are those who do, and we shall meet them soon. I promise you will have your answers.'

Ivy smiled at Lucille, 'Maybe there was a time when the Wroth were one with Naa. Like us!'

'I can't wait to find out. I feel like I have stumbled upon an entire history of the world that was hidden from us.'

Vorsa let out a humourless *ha!* 'Hidden, no. You just weren't looking!' She grinned wide, very much aware of her sarcasm. They all laughed.

Ivy was careful not to get too close to the edge, but she couldn't help but feel elated by where she had found herself. She wrapped the blanket that Lucille had given her around herself and studied the green below, the slopes and plains and once divided pastures that were now very quickly merging, regrowing, losing the geometry lain by her former kin. There was life everywhere, rich and full and bright. She wanted so much for everything to be okay again, and from here, far above, everything looked right, far above every loss, every painful reminder. She rubbed her wrists, felt a dull ache in her leg. Bruised and battered but still alive, still breathing.

Lucille had enough bottled water and food for a few days, and many of the animals could go without food when necessary. Not all could climb upon Moorvori Groor, so a caravan of sorts trailed behind, flocks of Effer and Aurma, protected with bone hexes where possible, herded behind the step of the Sentinel, and above, Ivy and Lucille tended and cleaned wounds of those not too afraid to be approached by Wroth. It would take a great deal of time before they would be accepted, and so they made every effort to gain that trust.

Most injuries had been inflicted from fleeing the Husk, impalement wounds, scratches and scuffs. Yet some had deep bite wounds, and carried infections. Rubbing alcohol and bandages were all Lucille could offer, having lost so many supplies when her car had fallen, but she made do. When it rained, they placed as many receptacles as they could find upon the ground and asked those able to search Moorvori Groor for puddles and pools where water could be collected.

The evening came, and Ivy lit a small fire as she sat beside Lucille, 'What do you miss the most?' she asked.

Lucille smiled thoughtfully. 'My husband. He was a wonderful man, he was difficult and grumpy, but he was everything. I miss sitting with him and reading, listening to music together. What about you?'

Ivy thought, 'I miss ice cream.'

They giggled.

'I miss my Dad and my brother. I missed my mum, she died from cancer a few years before, before the sickness came. But I guess I didn't think I would be left alone. My Dad tried to keep us safe. But it was so fast. One day they had a cold and then ….' Ivy began to cry. Lucille put her arm around her until Ivy felt better.

'I wonder how many Wroth are left, how many of us.' Lucille swilled her tea around in the cup. 'I feel like a stranger in my own world!'

Ivy nodded, 'All of this — the animals, this Husk thing, I was convinced I was going mad. But recently, I have felt like all of this is just, well it's all just life, creatures living, having babies, and this walking mountain and the First City, they are living too, like a coral reef. Solid like stone but alive. All of these living things all together, all sharing in an—'

'Ecosystem,' Lucille interrupted.

'Yes! An ecosystem. We just hadn't seen one so big before!'

'I am still waiting to find some more pieces of the puzzle. Below us, where the Cini skeletons were, there is an Anglo Saxon burial site. I don't think it was put there by the animals, I think other Wroth, a long time ago, chose to place that man there, among the roots of Groor. I feel that they were, in some way, aware of the importance of it. I wonder if all the old tales of nature spirits, woodwose, Pan and the like, maybe all of those mythologies came from worshipping these wondrous animal guardians. I feel I have so many questions to ask, and so much to look forward to knowing!'

Ivy put her hand on top of Lucille's. 'I am so glad we found you here,' she said.

Emeris

Emeris awoke in another room. It lacked any character, worn whitewashed walls, scratched curse words in the plaster. He was free of the presence of his parents, yet he had found himself in a far worse predicament. He had welts on his arms from beatings. There was a healed cigarette burn on his hand.

A Borstal was his new place of residence and he would be held there for the foreseeable future. He was a murderer, and his fellow inmates both feared and admired him, and attacked him for their own self-esteem and delusions of grandeur. He heard how the press vilified him, how depraved he was. His parents feigned ignorance, of course, their seemingly happy marriage torn asunder in the popular press when it emerged his father had a mistress and a second child.

Emeris was compelled to witness the life he had lived — a series of dreary anecdotes. He grew older, and eventually was released. The world had not forgotten the child murderer. Much like his inmates, those around him feared and hated him. He was driven from halfway houses and hostels — all who crossed his path thought he should do the world a favour and take his own life. This only bolstered his anger, his hatred of all those who denied him the chance to know peace. His entire life had been a prolonged act of violence, a red smear of inherited pain.

And so he found a small cottage high in the hills, and hid himself from all who had despised him.

In all the suffocating tragedy of this life, Emeris could feel the thorn of that little girl, and the welt of gnawing guilt. A wrong he could never right, however angry he became, however many he passed his pain on to.

But he wasn't Thoth. He was Emeris, and he hadn't lived an intolerable life — and he wasn't done living it yet.

*

Naag Rarspi, its chimney felled, a brickwork shadow of its former self, appeared to Audagard, bringing him a strange sense of comfort. It was not an inviting place, little more than a ruin. No longer the Church of Bone Char, spire of a guarded doctrine, now soot stained, rubble strewn. He flew down to the entrance and took a moment to recollect. He entered on foot, the coal black floor, looking up at the empty windows that once held his parishioners, his clergy, the faithful. At the far end, his seat where he had lauded as the Dominus, an archway and its cornicing, little more now than an indentation in the wall.

Beyond this, the old coal stores, the graves of so many Corva and Vulpus alike, buried there to retain their connection with the Lacking Sea, and perhaps to coax a revenant twin or two back into Naa. Further north was an entrance to the Oscelan, which he'd rather forget.

He closed his eyes and remembered his father, the old Anx who had stoked a little furnace of piety in him, had shown him the spinous dalliances of the inquisitive dead, the mortally impaired and their endless rhymes and riddles, and the little golden flecks of profundity hidden in the contrived dung they fed him. Oh, the revenants of the Gasp, what a tedious lot they were.

He waddled through the arch and into the cloister, old rickety buildings that were once the barracks of his flock, his soldiers in worship. In amongst the rookeries, the tools of his trade: Black Knot antennas and spirit barbs, calling sticks, spines of raucous assembly, and the leaves of creed, inscribed on a thousand chips of glass and bark, in blood, the cicatrix of the Gasp. He had not expected anyone to remain here, but he could sense a presence among the frills of gore craft.

Leaves caught in a little whorl of wind, but there was not even a breeze. He turned quickly to catch whatever thing was following him. It was a Corva, her eye on him, a black pupil, an accented glare in the ivory white of her down, the Inverted One, Infal Gar.

The leaves were a garland around her, held in perfect revolution. They curled and wilted into frail skeletons, before miraculously regaining their dewy green — a cycle of life and death. She wore a crown of bone, bleached to the hue of her feathers.

An albino Corva, a casting, shunned from her roost at birth. As a result, and perhaps in defiance of her estrangement, she had risen to become a formidable practitioner of necromancy.

'Malargoragor, taking a sabbatical from your deviated path?'

He bowed to her. 'Lady Gar. You reside here?'

'Here? No. But I had an inkling you would be popping in for a visit. The Clax have done a fine job of picking up the slack, but you left us all bereft, old Audagard.'

'I had a calling.'

'Umbra? Umbra is all shiny and new again! Even I have felt its boon.' She spread her wings wide. 'You have come to pick the bones clean?'

Audagard sighed, 'I would be a hypocrite if I were to dismiss my lifetime of worship, but time is of the essence, and in this hour of need I ask only for plain speaking.'

'Plain speaking? How very dull. Well, plain speak, little chick.'

'The Husk, you know of them?'

She breathed in and stood straight, 'Yes. An abomination.'

'Then you will understand why I have come here. The First City and all its subjects are rallying together any and all defences. We have petitioned the Sentinels that once guarded the ancient clades, we have spread the word about how to make hexes as wards against the Husk. We have called the strongest of us to build fortifications. All of this, but we are lacking. The Husk is an army made of us. It spreads and gathers up its ranks. Their leader is an Umbra, capable of pulling the dead from the Gasp. No one has ever thought to do this, let alone accomplish it for evil deeds. No one knows what this leader, who goes by the name Thoth, wants. But he sets his sights on Dron, on our Epiras, and we must find every weapon we can. I learned and I keep learning from the Umbra, but I've come back to engage with my former life, to put my lifetime of practice to good use.'

Infal Gar snorted, 'Plain speaking. Highfalutin I'd say!'

Audagard scowled.

'The Ebduous Clax built your Orrery, did you know?'

'I did, it is at the centre of the Black Knot.'

'They skry with possibilities — probables and perhapses. They see like an Umbra with that great eye of theirs. Clever ideas you had, once upon a time!'

'Thank you,' he said wearily.

'Your father was keen eyed too. After his wing was broken, and thus unable to fly, we would sit for hours and talk of how one might see beyond seeing. He would dream of it, all the ways the world had left us the means to do so. But, in the end, he feared that which he sought. Perhaps a life spent in pursuit of death, only for it to be in pursuit of you, is not without irony!'

'Your point?' Audagard didn't appreciate her quip.

'Take your bone hexes, mirrors to the soul, reminders of the living. How do you terrify the dead? Remind them that they rotted away in the dirt.'

'And?'

'You can scare the dead, you can parley with them, you can even trap them temporarily in their own reflections, make use of their ghoulish energies in further spellcasting. But can you woo them? Can you entice them to follow you? No. The dead are fickle, mercurial by nature. Unless…'

'Unless?' he was exasperated.

'You can,' she slouched.

'How?'

'How, pray tell, did this Thoth character encourage them to walk in his step?'

Audagard pondered this, 'He offered them life, he offered them a second chance.'

'He has offered them more than that. For these revenants are not just a collection of unruly certainties. They are exclusively Wroth. He has offered to give them back their world. He has offered them Naa.'

He wheezed, 'All Wroth? But we are spent, there is nothing we can offer them!'

'Not so quick, my dear Dominus. The life he has offered them is distinctly lacking. You should know this more than anyone, when you willingly subjected the Starless Vulpus to the Heralds of the Oscelan.

'It is temporary. There is no staying. The mark lies heavy on the flesh. A brief moment with that burden and even now your dear Nox suffers to this day, hauled away from his people.

'The body dies under them, and they cannot feel much at all. All of the sensation they wish for, the lustful, carnal, painful elegance of life, it is but a fraction of their memory of it. Have you seen how they inflict wounds upon themselves? How they illicit feeling through pain, through self-torture, through depraved acts of cruelty? It is unsustainable. Thoth, well, he may be fine, he is Umbra, he may indeed live his life under that fur, but his compatriots will wither away, returning them once again to the liminal realm of the Gasp.'

'What can we offer them?'

'They will learn to resent him, until they are nothing but hunks of ghoulflesh floating in the forever. They have tasted the Gasp and escaped it. What they want is to remain in Naa. They want to permanently dwell on this earth.'

'Yes, but there is no magic I know of that can do such a thing.'

Infal Gar squawked, 'Old beak, you are becoming forgetful! You once pulled the Maligna, the old ones, from the Oscelan, you conjured such incantations none had performed before. Tell me, Dominus Audargard, why won't you go in the Oscelan?'

He bowed his head.

You are dead, and you will live in death forever.

He had never forgotten the penetrating cold of the Oscelan, the insatiable drag, losing his body to it, tearing him from all comfort, all sense of belonging, down into the nether.

'The Maligna, they tried to pull me down into it, into the black.'

'Yes. They felt your need and distorted it, showed you the truth of it. The Maligna were servants of the city, commissioned by the Umbra itself to act as herald, given a function in their ceaseless consciousness. But not all were willing to listen.'

The Dominus gave her a suspicious glance. 'Of what do you speak?'

'You already know. How did the sticks fall for you? I could feel your little wriggle in the dark. I knew you were practicing again. What did they speak to you? Something old, lurking in the black. You came here looking for answers. How long has it been since the First City formed above the grave of the Sisters?'

Audagard coughed, 'Longer than I can fathom.'

'And in that time, we know of one instance when some defied the will of the city, acted against the order of things?'

'The Wroth? Of course.'

'And in all the time the city has existed, in all the countless iterations of life, the cataclysms, rupture and rapture, no other has ever gone against the city's wishes?'

Audagard crowed, 'Come now, Infal Gar, plain speaking.'

She laughed, 'Oh, my Dominus, you are too quick to temper! You did not know me as a chick, did you? The fledgling flung from her nest into the dirt? I was too young to fly then, and easy picking for predators. I hid in an old Tril hole, I ate the worms that crawled on to the stone and died under Ora. Was a pathetic start to life I must admit. But I survived. I dug my claws in. I was there, hidden in the thorn bushes. While your father taught his Anx the prism scripture, I was eating out of Wroth waste and scratching runes in the dirt. I peered over the walls of this very church, and squinted at the prayer tiles cast in revenant speech. I cut myself and bled on mirror glass and invoked the dead while you all preened yourselves.

'I found other castings like me, whose magic was feral and violent. I went to the Unfilled Pit and stole leaves pocked with thaumaturgy, right from under their beaks — and I found *him*. I walked the sunken vaults of Tet and read the first rendition of the Vulpus creed — and found *him*. I puked for days in the thrall of poisoning, eating fungi that played havoc with my sense of self, sent me into an apoplexy of shock and awe, and in all that pain and putrid poetry, I found truth of him —for he surely is a him, unseen, even by your father.'

'Him who?' Audagard spat.

She paused, 'Like the Wroth, he disobeyed the Umbra. He was old, and shared a fate of all Maligna, yet when called upon, ignored the song. He craved an end, to banish the din of consciousness. No such fate awaited him in the Gasp, and so he shirked the Umbra, and the Lacking Sea, and writhed in the earth, collecting souls who sought his blessed silence, and some who did not.'

'Did not?' Audagard replied.

'Of course, it was an unspoken agreement. Think of the Umbra and the Gasp as facets of a whole; there is a balance, and thus there are consequences when the balance is uneven. This old thing filled a niche, redressed discrepancies, became the arbiter of the dead in Naa. He claimed his own quota as payment.'

'Arbiter of the dead? Does he have a name?'

'He has had many names in Naa. The name I learned was *Echid*, the Vulpus learned of him from their forebears and knew him as *Trok*. The Wroth knew him. He is the liquid dead, and he has felt the Husk, and he is hungry.'

*

Arophele sprang through the hole, followed by the jaws of a snarling beast, wet with saliva and blood. She recoiled as it snapped at her, pulling itself through the opening. In response, Orch and Tango were upon it, both baring their own teeth with feigned anger, shedding a slew of drool and throaty barks at the enemy. The Husk withdrew with surprise, and with that they began to block the entrance with bricks and clods of earth.

They listened, and soon came the gargled growl of the gigantic captain commanding Husk to dig up the enemy, followed by the sound of hundreds of pairs of claws scratching at the earth.

"We have to run!' Turing barked.

'We can't, we'll lead them right back to the encampment. We will put everyone's lives at risk,' said Arophele.

'Then we'll take a different route. A different tunnel,' Bresh implored.

Paws and toothy snouts dug ferociously at the earth, and with so much weight upon the fractured sewer, the loose earth began to subside. The group ran back to the corner as the soil barrelled its way towards them, pinning them in a dead end, burying them in a wave of rancid sewer water and earth, a cloying soupy slop that seeped into their fur. The remaining wall, already compromised, shifted precariously. Then suddenly, it gave way, bringing down the curvature of the tunnel itself.

Waterlogged and tired, they all pulled back as far as they could. The sound of hurried digging continued unabated. They made sure the last of the remaining bone hexes would be visible to any would be assailant. There was nothing else they could do.

The digging stopped, then came a wounded howl, a yelp of fear, and another. A wretched hacking cough, a bark, a myriad of painful, sorrowful hoots and hollers, and then…silence.

Bresh looked to his companions for reassurance. He whispered, 'What do we do?'

Arophele's ears were erect. She shushed him, and quietly moved towards the collapsed wall. They waited in silence, sure that something had happened to the enemy.

Bresh suggested that they dig their way out — digging was something Tango, Turing, Orch and himself enjoyed, and which Arophele took to with ease. Eagerly, they carved at the earth, showering soil into her face. She rolled her eyes and backed away, keeping her distance until finally the light of Ora was let in.

They pulled themselves free of their prison and looked out across the courtyard, filthy with muck. It was filled with the Husk, lying flat on the ground. All but a few of them were rigid in angular contortions, convulsive, tortured — they dribbled and drooled, locked in seizures.

Arophele went to one of them — a Vulpus. She was alive. Beside her was a bone hex.

'It worked,' she said. "It worked!'

'It worked too well,' said Tango, pushing one comatose Morwih with his paw.

'This is no good, we must get them water. All of these poor creatures are victims now, no longer the enemy. We must do our best to save them.'

Bresh helped an elderly Oreya up, its body covered in angry wounds. He escorted them to a trough filled with rainwater, where they drank heartily. Exhausted, they lay down and thanked him.

'You freed us. You freed us all. My body was letting go of me. I could feel the essence of me leaking out of Naa. You pulled me back in.'

'It's alright, you're safe. You must rest now.'

Tango found a group of Maar lapping at a puddle. From his collection of jars he gave them some salves to treat their wounds.

'Do you remember what happened?' he asked them.

'Happened!' one of them said. 'The Sister forsaken ghosties were ripped out of us! They couldn't help but look at those — those things! Once one had looked, all of them did. Not too bright I tell you, not too bright.'

He returned to Arophele, who was helping some Tril. She took leaves from the garden and began to treat their cuts.

'The bone hexes,' he said, 'the Husk couldn't help themselves but look at them.'

'Curiosity, my dear Tango, 'tis what killed them.'

'Maybe that's our weapon. A few we can take out with bone hexes, but we need more, we need something more powerful. I don't know much about anything, let alone this Corvan magic, but maybe they can help?'

Arophele nodded, 'I agree, and we will take what we have learned south, to the First City. This war will not be won with fighting, it will be won with thinking.'

They allowed the recovered to rest until morning, and once able to walk, escorted them back to the allotment. TumHilliad greeted them all with kindness and provided places of rest. Already, many of his former patients were strong and willing to help the cause. Collector flocks had been busy gathering objects useful for armour, Sqyre and Nighspyn digging up winter food stocks and shepherding Ingui from under rocks and logs to feed the many hungry mouths.

In the shade of great old oak trees, animals whose lives, until that moment, had been simple - rearing young, collecting food and finding safe spaces to sleep at night – were now privy to a real peril.

The Husk could be defeated, but it was not their violence that was the problem. It was their numbers. For every creature freed from their grasp, another ten were taken. Stories of roaming revenants, bodiless and depraved, came from the old woods and pathways, the places usually found to be safe.

So, armour was made, from whatever could be found, and circlet hexes woven in-between every plate. For many, wearing armour had only ever been ceremonial, never having the need to fight. Mercenaries had always been hired to defend families from predators. Now the Drove were all employed under the city, from all corners of Embrian Naa, and so mothers and fathers left their nests and burrows in the care of their elders and took up arms.

Arophele spoke decisively. 'We will travel south, to the First City. and we will send out soldiers to teach other communities how to protect themselves.'

*

Thisel sat on the precarious edge of the old antenna tower. She looked down on the main road that ran below her vantage point and felt something that, in her previous life, she associated with badly aimed leaps and subsequent falls, and with taking on Morwih far bigger than herself — fear. Fear was remarkable in that it could make or break her — either she would be frozen with it, or she would act.

She ran along the outer rim of the tower's hilt until its buckled slouch met with the floor below. Here, sitting amongst office debris and the litter of black magicians, was the Orrery.

It had been inspired by the Dominus Audagard she was told, and construction had begun in earnest while his attention had snagged elsewhere. She had not met him herself, but had learned alongside his acolytes. The Orrery was an extension of the Black Knot, a ring of Corvan fetishes that had drawn Dron to behead the false city, to raze it to the ground. That same power remained now, unfocused, erratic. The Orrery took advantage of this, becoming the focal point of a kinetic necromancy, the eye of a skrying storm.

It was a cooperative effort of sorts, the fledgling occultists of the Morwih, stretching their claws beyond mere sacrifice and blood patterning and embracing the gospels of the Corva, finding rhyme and reason, and indeed echoes of a shared root language in their scratch runes and alphabet. It was Hevridis himself, newly elected consul, who decreed that the once fractured sects and Vulpus clans could indeed find common ground, no longer divided territories.

The inner circle of the Corva Anx had flocked to the First City following Audagard, leaving behind their hundreds of thousands of believers eager for guidance. With no one to turn to, only the scriptures, Ebduous, long dead prophet of the Gasp, whose first disciples were known as the *Clax*, (a squawked cry that over time would morph into *Anx*), had become the linchpin of a reinvigorated Gasp worship. Some might have resented Audagard, but his plans had brought about an era of peace, and for this he was pardoned in the eyes of all who worshipped death.

Those same eyes focused their gaze on his former stratagems, half-finished extrapolations of his grand vision. If the Gasp would not open itself to him, if his old plan to raise the First City had been nought but wishful thinking, then he would build machines to extend his influence. The Orrery, the artifice of an Umbra, the great eye opening.

The Morwih found it half built, the Clax desperate to reestablish their connection with the Lacking Sea. With all their Bishops of Bone Char gone, all they had was their holy writ, and so the Morwih and the Skulks of Vamish picked up ribs and staves and branches, bound them together in an imperfect sphere, at its core, a great bevelled shard of glass. A conglomerate of witchery, the hex of all hexes.

Its power would only be known through use, but with little effort, one could stand in its circumference and read the tells of Naa — the wind, the striae of magnetism, every movement and intention was tuned to perfect clarity, inscribed upon its inner surface.

Yet it was a first attempt to invoke the Nash Aka, the will to remain in Naa, that would unveil its true potential. A twin and the summoning of their revenant was performed beside the great orb. She appeared in a spasm of ectoplasm, but before any could make sense of it all, what had been summoned was yanked violently from this earthly plane by the Orrery, acting as a lightning rod, threshing the ghoul into gobs of ether slag and casting it back into the Gasp.

At the time, it was ruled that the exorcism was a sign of abject failure, that their creation was the opposite of what they wished for; a shrine that banished denizens of the Gasp and recreated the mind of an Umbra seemed far more in line with those Corva Anx who had defected. It was only when the presence of the Husk was known that Thisel realised the use of such a potent magic.

What appeared now on the streets was a short distance from them, a scant flock of Corva jabbing them from the sky, gusts of shimmering entities chasing them down, and the slow march of the Husk, a hundred wide and a thousand deep, an avalanche of emaciated, feverish miscreants, tongues lolling, teeth bared, sores and gashes seeping discharge, a cancerous malady of flesh.

She had planned this moment, as had Penhalef. The great Hanno, Gilia, had returned to help them orient the Orrery, reinforcing it and holding it taut — now they rolled it to the edge of the tower.

The Corva screamed out to their pursuers, 'You'll never catch us! Look at you, so slow, so useless! Ha ha ha!'

Below, Thoth picked up his pace, flailing his snout at his cohorts, 'Take them!' he snarled, 'take them all!'

He hurdled obstacles himself, scrabbling over bodies, for he was not going to be mocked. 'Come down here!' he shrieked, 'You're nothing! Nothing!'

The streets at the base of the spire were not wide, so the Husk were forced to file into thin columns and, unable to remain in any sense of order, they began to climb over listless cars and bollards, up into trees and over fences, piles of themselves, leaving blackened slick marks where they trod.

High up, Penhalef guided the Orrery to the edge. The Corva were in his sights.

'Here they come!'

Ascending almost vertically, the Corva were now heading directly toward the crepuscular sphere, lungs burning, wings gnawing, their shadows ensnared by the ghouls that trailed them. Abruptly, they course corrected, taking right-angled dives away from the tower, revealing the looming gaze of the Orrery above.

The Seethe was lain bare before it, caught in its cataract, the silver slither that reflected all but them, all but the bodiless, the incomplete, flawed rations, disowned by their rotting meat sacks, left to the whims of a simple breeze, to be dissolved into nothing — meaningless, pathetic abbreviations of former mortality.

The Orrery tore them from the world, a muscular chord being plucked, a reset, a vortex of unseeable influence, condensed into entropy.

Gone.

Thoth felt the seismic quake, the exhale from the air. The Seethe, his column of heaven, sank back into the darkroom of the Gasp.

He could see his work undone

He then saw the Orrery

Lungs depressed

Eyes enfolded

He was vomiting himself up; a deep hollow pain, coughing up a lung, a liver, a kidney, a convulsion like a contraction, a breach

Wet

Blood withdrew

Flesh excreted him

He felt himself leave Emeris

NO NO NO NO

He pulled himself back, fingers around ribs, around hair, around intestines, tearing his face away from the circle of putrefaction, down, back down inside Emeris, the worm in the apple.

He was a crumpled heap on the asphalt. Around him, piles of motionless corpses. He strained to see others, confused, searching the skies for reason and saw—

More revenants, torn from their stolen bodies.

Don't look at it he hissed. His mouth parched, incapable.

He pulled himself free of his acolytes as they collapsed on top of him — he was being buried by his own army. He struggled, stretched and kicked until he was free.

'Don't look up!'

His Husk turned to him. The dregs were terrified.

'RUN!'

The lost soldiers bolted from the streets, looking for escape.

Thesil's gaze fell on their path. 'Heave!' she cried to Gilia, and the Hanno rolled the orb to the far left, catching the odd fleeting backwards glance, the hurried fearful gawk — one, two ghouls wrenched from their occupation.

'No!' she howled, 'they're getting away!'

The Husk were no longer in view. She strained to see beyond the edge of the wall that now hid them from sight of the Orrery.

Penhalef ran to the edge, frantic barks to catch their attention. 'We must! We must get them all!'

Gilia had an idea. She signalled her kin, 'Help me.' She pushed the sphere to the edge. It was twice her height and far wider and heavier than she had considered. Yet it was moveable.

She looked to Thisel, 'Shall we?'

'It may not survive the fall, but what good is it if they are outside its influence?'

Gilia nodded. 'Agreed. Push!'

They rolled the Orrery to the brink of the tower, and pushed it over the edge. It fell, spun, caught in a strong updraft, the innumerable scrags of cloth, old trash bags and scraps, its perforated surface a basketweave shell, filled with holes and channels. The air was not quick to let it go - some eminence, perhaps invisible hands of influence, or simply thermals rushing through its innards, kept it aloft just long enough to reach beyond the underlying concrete structures, derelict houses, and over the fleeing hordes of the Husk. Then it slammed into the canopy of a tree, whose branches recoiled and catapulted it up and out, into a quick forward tumble, gaining momentum on the gradient. A murder of Corva dove down to seize this boon of good fortune, encouraging its mindless fall towards the Husk. Rubbernecking the great black thing that pursued them, the whites of eyes exposed utter terror, their escape thwarted by blockades of cars and fallen stonework.

Thoth watched in disbelief as his minions toppled like bowling pins, their commandeered bodies falling limp as they locked eyes with the Orrery, spilling grey unguent out of mouths and ears and tear ducts, quickly sucked up by the rampaging hex, now a maelstrom of ghoul matter, plasm flumes like solar flares warping the air around it. By now, it spun with such force that the end was inevitable, and it slammed into a bus, shattering into shards of black spindles, imbedding the giant concave mirror core deep into the coaches red chassis.

Thoth once again rose to find himself outwitted as a shroud of dust and debris settled on the silent street. A whine rang in his ears, as though he'd experienced an explosion. He yawned to try and clear it, yet it would not relent. Around him, his loyal flock lifted. He had lost hundreds to the Orrery. He could not place its source or, indeed, purpose, or how it had almost torn him from his host. He shook his head.

He slowly began to walk away, shaken, but not deterred. The diminished Husk picked themselves from the wreckage and joined him, making a slow procession towards the river.

*

Thisel was on the roof of the antenna tower, from where the bright day revealed a sea of fallen bodies, not dead, but desperately needing attention. She rushed down, calling for assistance from the simians, Vulpus and

Morwih under her charge. The Corva returned, and she instructed them to seek out other allies to help attend to the wounded.

She soon found herself on the street, surrounded by freed Husk. They pockmarked the avenue, vulnerable, torpid. She had not seen such suffering since the great war, where so many of her kin, and her now allies, had needlessly died. Gilia appeared beside her, carrying old bottles of water, offering them to any who could sit up.

There were hundreds, all in various states of sickness, starvation and thirst. She helped as many as she could; some had been kept alive only by the zeal of the revenant within, and quietly slipped away on the road. There would be a funeral for these poor souls, but for now, they needed to tend to the survivors and ward the prefecture from the surviving Husk. Armed with bone hexes, Ebduous Clax Corva began to mark all entrances with runes, anticipating any return of the enemy.

Chapter Ten

Thoth had lost a third of his troops. He had no words to acknowledge how he felt, for his brief encounter with his own exorcism had left him weak, incapable of fully maintaining his own consciousness. With each swoon of pain in his head, he lost valuable mental capacity to Emeris, who was quick to dam his attempts at total dominion, clawing back neurons.

A moat, long empty of water, ringed the former castle, more recently a famous tourist attraction. Scab had preempted their arrival, his own expanding army perplexed by how dishevelled the great commander and his forces had become. Scab looked well, and Thoth hid his indignation.

'Thoth old chap, you been in the wars?'

The commander spat, 'Terrorists, usurpers. We survived nonetheless.'

Ransacked and worse for wear, the entrance to the castle grounds had been quickly breached. Now they lolloped over axe-battered wood, finding themselves within the castle walls, between former servants' houses and the original medieval fortifications. Thoth scoured the nearest house for a bed to lie in, and slunk down into a deep sleep.

Scab was deflated. If word spread that the Husk had been wounded it would hamper their efforts. New tactics were advisable, a new course. Perhaps brute force was not the best approach, perhaps there were other ways.

Take him while you can, while he is weak.

Scab wasn't sure if Thoth was worth taking, was worth the effort. This wasn't even a coup, this was a correction, a new tactic, new ideas on the field of war.

He had found a comfortable Caanus bed to sleep in, and a large sack of stale biscuits. He chewed on them for a while, then spat them from his mouth. At what point had he stooped to Caanus food? He sighed heavily and tried to sleep, finally giving up and leaping onto the kitchen sideboard and looking through the window at the hundreds of Husk who rested outside. They were an odd mix, from the largest Rauka and Grim to Maar and Muroi. A menagerie if ever he saw one.

An idea bloomed.

*

Thoth woke to something akin to a hangover. The whistle in his ear had abated, of which he was glad. He ploughed the cupboards for food and mustered little, and eventually plucked up the courage to face his troops.

He found them stoic and cold to his gaze.

'We have met resistance,' he cried. 'It was only a matter of time before our presence was felt and these lowly creatures would attempt to stop us. Their defiance is only proof of what they stand to lose. We are still here, and we are still winning.'

Scab took advantage of the lack of morale. 'I've got a suggestion.'

Thoth hissed in response but did not reprimand him.

Scab took the floor. 'Well, seems like just smashing through the land in hope of taking everything by storm isn't working — we might have more luck with a lighter hand. Those we don't catch all flee, and they're fleeing in the same direction as us. It stands to reason that the place they're going and the place you're leading us to is the same place.'

Thoth narrowed his eyes. 'And?'

'Ditch the armour, forgo the wounding, the flagellati—'

'Flagellation.'

'Yeah, that. Clean 'em up, send 'em out in small groups, infiltrate. None of the animals running away from us will know the difference.'

Thoth was impressed, and Scab could tell he was mostly angry that he hadn't come up with the idea himself.

'Yes, yes. That's a good plan. A silent invasion. Good thinking, Scab.'

Thoth didn't like his second-in-command's cheek, but he couldn't fault his strategy.

So they went to the river, climbing down the wooden steps to the beach below. It was littered with old bones, the remnants of animals used in labour, tossed into the river when eaten or unwanted. Amongst the tide's flotsam were also keepsakes, the odd clay pipe, bone china, a coin or button.

The river was recovering from the Wroth. Reed beds flourished along the banks, their roots providing stability under foot. It was here, at low tide, that the Husk washed themselves, a cleansing of wounds, of thick matted fur. They washed one another as best they could in the cold water, running cloudy with blood. Shanks and spurs were pulled out from skin, armour discarded.

Scab thought this a strange sight; a few hundred animals lined up to be baptised in the waters, to be washed free of the marks of the Husk, to be sent out and pretend to be refugees of their own making. He wondered if any might simply disappear, set themselves free of this whole charade. Loyalty to Thoth was remarkable so far in that it was unshaken.

Scab imagined this might be because so little was known of their condition — he himself had awoken on a number of occasions without recognising the body he dwelt within, that sickly claustrophobia, a symptom of his fear of being dead again, of being immaterial. Being nothing and aware. How on earth was that in any way a fair reward for a life of hard graft? He'd rather be gone and done with it all. This was enough to need Thoth, a source of comfort. Whatever his own story, which Scab was sure was probably just as bad as his own, he seemed knowledgeable of matters not even Scab knew, despite his talents in Gaspcraft. His conscience was quiet on this subject. He had gone for days without some internal debate, which he put down to having found a sense of direction.

Don't get comfy, there is still much to do.

Eventually, the Husk made its way up the flights of steps from the river beach and stood on the boardwalk. Moth eaten, worse for wear, they would pass easily for victims of war.

Scab arranged them into small groups, according to clade. They each had a story, scrounged from the little their hosts, coiled up inside, had betrayed in fits of exhaustion. Without a map, Thoth gave them directions to follow, towards the coast, where he was sure a game trail would have formed out of the creatures fleeing them.

'You will ingratiate yourself into these groups, but resist attacking or maiming them. You will do this until we have established ourselves within the source of the power they wield. Then, and only then, will a message be passed on and we will reveal ourselves. In that moment, we will seize strength from them and take their crown. Deal?'

There were murmurs of agreement.

*

Petulan hung in the gloom of the Lacking Sea. He often found himself far from the massing cloud-forms, fronts of colliding Seethes of souls, carousels of leaden vapour, dancing timidly until a final embrace, immolating in bright electric temper.

From his vantage point, he observed tiny effervescent corruptions in the shroud, the pale wall that hung between the Gasp and Naa. It was perceivable only when something passed through it, the recently deceased, or revenants with unfinished purpose in Naa, whose stubborn determination was rewarded with admission back into the world of the living — or as Petulan knew well, if you happened to be a revenant twin.

He caught a migrant current that pulled him closer so that he might investigate. As he neared, he witnessed such an event. A welt swelling, perforating, aspects of souls passing through and just as quickly retracting from the saponaceous film, gurning in agony, impossibly wide jaws, eyes dilated, and abruptly transforming into a vacant, emotionless stare.

Petulan placed his paw upon a face that strained through. It was a Cini.

'Who are you brother?'

The face was cold, drained of any colour. Petulan knew this face, for this soul was at an impasse, its body not having died. The soul seemed encouraged by Petulan's presence.

'I ... I am Emeris. I am dying. My body has been taken from me and I am losing the will to fight. I am so very tired.'

Petulan swooned with sadness.

'My dear Emeris, all is not lost. We are mounting forces against this enemy. You are not alone in this battle. Tell me, what have you learned of the thing which controls you?'

Emeris spasmed into a dissonant scream, before returning to his glassy stare.

'He calls himself Thoth, but his true name is a Wroth word, I cannot hold on to it. I have found myself inside his memories, reliving moments, tangents, formative meanings. My own sense of self is entangled in him.'

Petulan balked at the name. 'Then my dear Emeris, you are inhabited by their chieftain, their captain! My word, old log, you are harbouring *he who we seek*. Tell me, can you hold on? If I might find the means to empower you, would you work with me to rid, not only yourself, but all of us of this scourge?'

Emeris coughed, a little of his pneuma escaping. Petulan plucked it from the firmament and breathed it back into him. In this act, a little thought germinated.

'Ah! A plan.'

Petulan careered out into the nebulous murk. He began to sing; perhaps it was more of a discordant whine, yet the result was much the same. Four apparitions, urbane and fat with unlife, coalesced. Together with Petulan, they were the five pillars of Nok Langean, The Court of Torpor, the most resplendent dead. All had died very young, all the runt of their litter. Yet here, amidst the colourless vacancies, they found an uncommon power.

A portly Aurma named Briel, a giant of a ghoul, hovered beside a tiny unnamed Creta, who appeared to mimic his every move; a wide-horned Barara called Havic, who appeared rather like Petulan, her skull floating above an ethereal body; and Calibon, the oldest of the four, one of the first true mammals, whose long time in the Gasp had distorted his manifest form, strands of frail glass trailing from him like mummified wrappings.

'My wise companions, phantasms of fathoms past. I, your lowly serf, request assistance in a very pressing matter. For our beloved living are threatened by the dead! Have you not noticed the quieting of the Wroth Seethes? Where once were unruly spirits whose pillar of souls would wilfully disrupt the ennui of our other more apathetic residents, now they are drawn to corners unnoticed, plotting with ghouls who have left the Gasp, and at this very moment carve the land with their misdeeds!'

Briel leaned toward Petulan, little gyres of matter buoyant around him. 'Yes.'

Petulan expected a little more, but nothing else came.

'Well! The poor waif who is harbouring the big bad is beginning to snuff it, dying right now. I propose, if you are willing, that we bolster his chances of survival by imbuing him with a little of our plentiful power, fatten him up for the prize fight?' I have an inkling he might be the deal breaker in this affair.'

They turned to one another, and deliberated over their decision. Eventually they ceased and once, again, Briel inclined towards Petulan, 'This is not the first time you have asked us for such a thing, my little Vulpine

Prince. What was it you required our energies for in the past? Some frivolity or other?'

Petulan shrugged, 'To invoke the Meridian and return The First City to Naa.'

'Ah yes, the First City. The Ensign, Crestfallen, the Seed of All.'

'Yes, my Briel.' They were often rather full of it.

'Well, I suppose we better help you then. Show us your intended.'

He brought them to the place where Emeris had appeared to him. They didn't have to wait long for the emergence of a pained visage, so disfigured that even the dead were disturbed.

Pearlescent sputum poured from their mouths, carrying with it an artefact of creation; the fatty rigour in placenta, the mitochondria of cells, the nutrients of life passed along the hyphae, from one to another, from the have to the have-not.

For Emeris, in a prison of his own mind, it fed his withered volition, invigorating every cell that harboured him, every ounce of him. For Thoth, he would feel no boon, no shift, no better. Emeris would now live a little longer.

'You have saved me,' he said. 'What is it we can do?'

Petulan grinned, 'We shall mount a spiritual offensive against him and his Husk.'

*

Groor came to a standstill close to an estuary, the river flowing in from the west. It lowered itself with a tired groan, drawing water to feed its roots. Ivy and her compatriots disembarked, Ivy making for the river herself so that she could wash herself. Lucille and Noraa continued to attend the sick and injured who they had picked up along the journey, and Lucille handed Ivy a collection of empty plastic bottles to fill in the river. A growing crowd of animals seeking amnesty crowded at the foot of the Sentinel.

Ivy crouched by the river and began to submerge the bottles, the air escaping as she did so. She heard a commotion behind her and turned to find a group of young mammals watching her. They ran back to their parents giggling. Ivy was aware that she was perhaps still a very strange sight, so she surreptitiously stripped off, taking a moment to wash herself and some of the clothes in her bag. She was running low on all supplies, and hoped they might pass a town soon where they could restock clean clothing. For now she would take her washing and hang them to dry upon the stones and low shrubs still clinging to Groor.

In the distance, a small procession of Vulpus appeared against a treeline. They eyed Ivy suspiciously. Vorsa had successfully caught an Orkrek, which she ate with little enjoyment, and then joined Ivy, spying her kin beneath the shadow of the leaves.

'What are they doing?' Ivy asked.

'I don't know. They dress like Scribes of Tet.'

Vorsa called out to them. Her yelps prompted a reply and she slowly paced towards them, Ivy in tow, drying herself on a spare t-shirt.

The Vulpus were adorned with armour constructed of charred wood and bones. Remnants of a fire perhaps, Ivy thought.

'Ora bring peace. I am Vorsa Corpse Speaker, daughter of Satresan, overseer of Orn Megol. This is the wrothcub Ivy; you have nothing to fear from her. From where do you hail?'

The leader remained wary of them, hushing his companions. He stepped forward, 'We are the Scriven, Utterers of Tet. You are very far from your land — are you refugees too?'

Vorsa nodded, 'Some of us, yes. A group of us have raised the Sentinel Moorvori Groor—'

The chief Vulpus interrupted her, 'You have raised *a what?*'

'A herald of Dron. We are travelling with it to the First City to offer defence. Please, from where do you hail?'

'A herald? We have heard stories of such things during the great war for Orn Megol. We are the children of the Scribes of Thron Awlbringa.'

'Awlbringa? This citadel was destroyed, surely?' Vorsa replied.

'The dens close to the surface were destroyed by hunting Caanus, but deep below, the Church of Tet and the teachings of the Three survived. Our families have kept it hidden, perhaps needlessly since the death of the Wroth; however, in such dire times, we felt it right to safeguard it from the new threat. We travel there now to provide that protection. But you speak of this Sentinel, where is it?'

Ivy pointed down to the water, 'It's there.'

Their eyes followed to where she pointed below, to the edge of the river. At first there was little to see, a group of boulders nestled within a green glade near the water, and many animals. But as she withdrew her hand, the great golem rose up, a spit of land hoisted into the air on gigantic limbs sending curtains of water plunging back into the river. The Vulpus pack staggered back in awe.

'By Vorn's teeth!' Nenf exclaimed.

'We can take you with us, we shall set out a route taking us by Thron Awlbringa — will you agree?'

Nenf was still in shock. 'Yes, yes of course.'

When they were all ready to resume the journey, Groor strode across the river, raising plumes of mud from the water with each step, until it reached the far side, where it climbed up the silt beds and once again onto dry land. So the Scribes rode with them, explaining to Little Grin which way they must go, and he continued to be the navigator on this unusual vessel.

Astride the walking land mass, a panorama in vivid green before them, Ivy admired their new companions. Nenf was a large Vulpus, his fur was rather grey in places and his armour differed entirely from Vorsa's — all chipped blackened wood, brutalist in its simplicity, making use of the natural curve around knots and rings to satisfy the curvature of his own body. His troupe were younger than him, and obviously looked to him for guidance.

'Are you a teacher?' she asked, his gaze upon the land a mixture of wonder and vertigo.

'Oh, yes, these are my students. Thron Awlbringa holds a lot of the artefacts of old Vulpus culture. It is mine and, therefore, their task to preserve them.'

Ivy looked back to Lucille. She was changing the bandage on a wounded Tarkae. A thought resurfaced that had troubled her after her father had passed away — that she would not have anyone to turn to and learn from. Her mother had always been very practical in that regard. Ivy had started menstruating at twelve and, thankfully Ivy's dad had got to grips with periods and adolescence. She imagined her mum had played a role in guiding him when she was still able. It was perhaps the single silver lining to her mother's illness that Ivy had had to grow up fast to deal with helping her day to day after school until her father had got home from work. She had made dinner for her brother, had learned to navigate the rigamarole of being something of a parent.

Despite the embarrassing attempts by her school at sex education and teaching about the monthly cycle, it was social media which had introduced her to a moon cup —one of the first things she had stolen once she'd run out of sanitary towels. No one else would ever use them. She'd taken two.

But now she wasn't alone. Lucille was Wroth, Lucille was a woman and had lived through so much more of what it was to be a grown up. She could read all the books she could find, but experience, that was gold dust in a world with so few of her own kind.

She felt compelled to go to Lucille and offer her help. She remembered the water bottles that bulged from her bag and carried them over.

'Hello, my dear! Oh marvellous, you've brought me water. Tea?' Lucille said with glee.

Vorsa appeared beside Ivy a moment later. 'Yes, please,' she said eagerly.

Lucille gave Ivy a knowing grin as she poured water into her kettle and stoked the flames to boil.

'Drinking tea was quite a tradition of this land for the Wroth, Vorsa. The leaves were grown very far away from here, and what is left of it in this country is finite.'

'No more tea? That's terrible. I find it very relaxing.'

Ivy and Lucille laughed out loud, and once the water was ready, they filled their mugs and offered some to Vorsa. 'There is still plenty left for us all to enjoy!'

*

Their journey took them further west, until they reached fenland, wide flat former marsh that had been drained to make arable land for farming centuries before. The marsh had already begun to reclaim soil, and the proud call of wetland feathered serenaded their approach.

Where the ancient chalk met clay beneath the earth marked their destination. It was here that Ivy began to feel a familiar insistent tone. It was not as pronounced as the draw of Groor, yet it was undeniable.

As their new companions readied themselves to leave, Ivy found Vorsa scratching messages of goodwill for the Awlbringa elders.

'Vorsa, I can feel something here. It's the same feeling I had when we were looking for Groor. I think I felt it when we found that scarecrow, at the barrows? It's low, down there, down in the ground.'

Vorsa took note, calming her fears. 'The Church of Thron Awlbringa is an old place, perhaps it holds some significance in its great age.'

Unable to join them due to her size, Ivy waited as Vorsa, with Nenf and his Scribes, located the earth's entrance. It was not far from a muddy track, where long dead grass drooped, concealing it. A tunnel led them on a steep decline, the walls of the passageway at first eroded soil, soon turned to chalk. The chalk was riddled with holes, bored by water over the millennia, where primordial shells had erupted from powdery tombs.

As they approached sea level, the tunnel became very wet, and eventually a cavity appeared, filled with water, hampering their path. The scribes began to wade into it.

'Thron is below the water, we must swim,' said Nenf.

Vorsa was undeterred. They plunged into the briny dark, any natural capacity for sight lost here, with only the motion of the water to signal her companions' movements. She felt old things, rotting things, brush against her, things hidden low in the tawny roil.

Ahead was light, and an entrance hewn in rotting vegetation, carved from the peat itself. She watched the silhouettes of her companions kicking up towards this gap, breath almost depleted — she took one look back, to see what the light might illuminate. Things recoiled, black extremities, sentries hidden. She shuddered and swam up to the golden glow.

She breached into a pool in the floor of a chamber, where they shook their coats dry. Before them, another passage, yet this, like the light, was reminiscent – furrowed walls, grown not carven, and the scent of forests – of warm grass in the summer. She was escorted further in, lit by the faint luminescence of shelf-like fungi that clung to the walls. Sprawling frescos of coloured lichen, lesions of puffballs and soil riven with the bright threads of mycological colonies. But there was debris all around, pylons of collapsed plant matter, heavy with age and old rot. She noted that the surface of the walls were shedding this accumulation of growth, and it came to her, in their brilliant simplicity, words she had spoken herself every morning since she was a cub:

> 'Hollow old soul
> All bringer Thron
> The prize is thee
> Under turned loam
> The heart of Dron
> Interned in two
> One piece for all
> One piece to you'

'You know your verse,' Nenf stood beside her.

'My father was rather puritanical when it came to learning the cackle. "Wrestle weed, delight in thee," and so on. He was particularly drawn to the oldest verse, ideas we found scratched into stone by Grim and Cini.' She turned pointedly to him, 'Nenf, you know this place is no Vulpus den?'

Nenf nodded, 'We had no way to know what it was, and our ancestors built their dens above it, until they were destroyed. It has lived under the marshes, down in the deep. But you can feel it, can't you? It has the resonance of your giant friend above. My grandfather told us of it, that none would cross the water and find the entrance unless they knew what to look for. My first journey here, I was so terrified. I am sure you felt the presence of things hidden in the water?'

'Yes,' Vorsa shivered.

'I think they are old revenants, of things that died here but never moved on. They watch over this place.'

'Like heralds of the city. I have encountered such things before. The Starless Vulpus—'

'Yes!' Nenf agreed enthusiastically, 'The war for the Stinking City, we heard of a creature, risen in our own kin, to proclaim its return. Other skirmishes were fought outside the city, and other cities fell, but the Vulpir Fiefdoms had no quarrel with the Morwih here, and no inland Naarna Elowin. It was only when the Husk appeared did we feel a sense of change. I don't like change much, Vorsa.'

Vorsa scraped at some fallen debris, 'Was it always such a mess in here?'

Nenf shook his head, 'No, but we have not been here for a long time. Our families couldn't live here — all the dens were destroyed, the Wroth would send packs of Caanus after us.'

He escorted her beyond the halls to a second chamber, much smaller than the first. Sprawling hands of longevous wood reached from either side of them, the digits of which were inscribed with thousands of tiny etchings, glyphs and pictograms. As Vorsa moved further into the auricle, she turned to see a grandiose shrine above the archway, reminiscent of that which graced the Hall of Clans at Orn Megol. It was far taller than any Vulpus, a raised arboreal knot-work in the relief of an animal unknown to Vorsa, the head of which was a skull, held in place by a crowd of tiny tubers, themselves petrified by time.

'Perhaps the first to find shelter here, when the Wroth came.'

'I don't know this clade — it's definitely very old,' she replied.

Vorsa read the markings, recognising portions unblemished by recital or reformation, and she began to read them out loud. 'Oh eminence, oh tree fruit thrice, sing long in times of plenty and in bower rest ....' she stopped. 'These are the Homilies of Vorn, Vors and Alcali. These runes are very old. Is this—?'

Nenf nodded with pride, 'Scratched by their first disciples, a hundred thousand generations ago, before the Vulpus knew its form.'

'This is the Orata, the scripture of the Vulpus.'

'Yes.'

'And this is a Sentinel, a piece of Dron.'

Nenf sighed, 'Yes, I believe so.'

'If that is true then that explains all this debris — your golem is waking up. To think a piece of Dron was here waiting for us.'

*

The former Husk, mostly recovered, who were willing to take the fight to the First City, held a vengeance that had no one to temper it. To aim their anger at other Husk was pointless — even the one above all, Thoth, was squatting in someone else's body. So it became the only course of action for their rage — to free others.

With Bresh, Arophele, Turing, Tango and Orch at the helm, their path was long, but not fruitless, seeking the paths suitable for all — valleys similar to those Bresh had walked before, through the towns and villages yet to be reclaimed by the world. They encountered survivors of Husk raids, terrified by the unknown, cowering from their large band of animals that could have been the enemy — and then, finally, as was inevitable, they encountered the Husk.

It was dusk. A highway empty of vehicles, the width of a dual carriageway, a large barrier beside where a strip of scrubland had flourished without the spill of car fumes. Here, a natural fear was expected, for too many had died on the gravel.

Arophele made the first move, her paw instinctively testing the road for the vibration of scithar, of which there were none. She encouraged her companions to follow her, and they began to cross.

Eyes fluoresced in the light of Seyla, a row atop the embankment beyond the second road. The eyes were unblinking, yet their movements told all — they were erecting a scarecrow, its flaccid arms hanging at its side.

'Husk!' she cried, ready to fight. She scrambled for her bone hex, yet it caught against her armour, leaving her exposed and defenceless.

The leader of the Husk pack, a large Caanus, descended the bank, snarling strings of saliva. Arophele fought the desire to run, and against her better judgment, she loped out before it.

'Brave, but stupid, like the rest of you.'

Arophele knocked free her gauntlet blade, swiping it across the breadth between them.

'Fancy little poking stick you got there, but it ain't gonna cut it, little lady.'

The hound coughed up a ball of unfolding gob, it was yellow and sickly and it moved into flexing tentacles, arching towards her.

She backed away, but as she did, the rancid slither recoiled itself. She caught this peculiar reaction and leaned into it. The phlegm retracted back, back towards the Caanus, who stared with frightening realisation.

'What's this?'

Arophele thought for a second. Could it be that she was spoiled meat? She had already harboured one of these disgusting things, had already been defiled, but more than that, she had freed herself, and perhaps she carried the scent of that with her. She felt a surge of adrenalin.

'They can't touch us. They can't possess us!'

She glanced at Bresh and his soldiers, 'Hang back, you're easy pickings for them. Let us dispossessed do the work!'

The Husk looked bewildered as a horde of animals, battle worn and scarred, piled towards them, bone hexes wrenching ghoul matter from stricken faces, feathered dropping them from above in a shower of viscera and gleaming bone and polished glass, legs seizing, tongues lolling, eyes rotating into skulls, as the greyish aether of the Gasp escaped through several orifices leaving the tired victims upon the trodden soil.

Arophele launched herself upon their leader, bone hex in her mouth, forcing him to look upon it as she hung from his neck, and together they rolled head over heels down the slope, her blade retracting to save them injury, until they lay crumpled at the foot of the slope. Bresh dragged Arophele by her armour from under the Caanus. He panted, 'Are you okay?'

'Yes,' she said, turning herself the right way up. The animal beside her let out a long, exhausted sigh.

'Is it ... gone?'

'Yes sir, it is.'

Bresh recognised the Caanus. 'Arophele, this is Lolop Hembrad of the Jamboree of Useful, Once Useless.'

'Aye boy, that's us. Got the wind punched out of us. Thank you kindly for freeing us from their dastardly grip.'

'Where are you coming from, sir?' Bresh asked as the leggy beast raised himself on his haunches.

'We were taking pot-shots at their dig-ins up north, got ourselves a good little tactic going. Easy to lay bone hexes on their entry and exit points, caught a fair few. But it seems they worked out what we were doing. Didn't realise until too late that they'd ambushed us. One good thing came out of it though. We know how they're passing information to one another.'

'How?' Arophele asked.

'Oh, they kill one of their own, send the ghoul back to the Gasp with a message, and then that ghoul gets put back in another body elsewhere and hey presto, got yourself a message passed along quicker than any Windsweeper!'

'Ghastly, but efficient,' Bresh replied.

'Yes indeed. So where is this army of yours headed?'

*

The word had been passed to the Oraclas who ran the first barricade. They couldn't block the coastal road until they had rescued as many refugees as possible. Meanwhile, Yaran pulled branches from trees, shortening the wide track into a funnel that fed between two lorries. With great effort, the Clusk could move cars, and even trucks, although it was an imperfect skill.

Yaran's mother, Matriarch Eda, had found a large water trough and had begun to crush slabs of chalk in it, to create a white paste. She had asked her younger Oraclas to seek out red berries, and in the burned wrecks of houses, charcoal. This would be her palette, and the animals of Naa her canvas.

Lendel had led her into the pollen haze in the light of the shaft that played on the Stone of the Sisters, and asked her to call out to her ancestors. He had materialised the strident shapes of Oraclas that had trodden icy earth, who had sung with spring when the snow melted, when troves of yellow flowers blossomed in the warmth.

She had watched etchings in golden particles dance around her, their fur plaited by nimble trunks, tied up with shells and driftwood, and she had seen the sigils of her kin, the markings of old herds, herds that ran in her blood, in her step. She had made note of each symbol, had locked the memories in her mind and would bear them herself, on her skin, and on the skin of her kin — and on any who wished it.

So, in the morning breeze, once the wooden barricades were in place, and the sharpened sticks aimed true from the sand dunes and defensive walls, and her herd had cauterised the opening to the bay, she began to make the thick paint to daub upon their hides.

Yaran stood patiently as her mother mixed the pinkish red pigments, of chalk and black berries, and with deft skill, began to mark her skin with sharp angular patterns in red and white.

The Tasq had been making armour from old metal parts in the town, torn from car panelling and plastic housings and shaped with heavy feet so that even the largest kin now sported armour. Eda marked Yaran's helmet, with her trunk, leaving an impression at its centre.

'A kiss, my daughter.'

*

Onnar completed her morning debrief with Erithacus at the Regulax, collecting information from the Stinking City and further afield. Reports from the north were remarkable, of moving mountains and battles won against the Husk. Such news spurred hope amongst commanders of their respective regiments.

Awfwod hobbled onto the veranda, looking a little dishevelled, and began to reinstate messenger routes. The Speaker flocks, under Glaspitter, were employed as armed escorts, carrying barbed hexes that could be flung at would-be ghoul Seethes.

Onnar was happy to relay any cause for optimism to those out in the field, stationed on the sand, high up on the cliff face, on the Downs to the north that skirted the sea. She ran from the fallen theme park, up through the town, passing the Clusk hefting wood in their tusks, and onto the ascending road. Soon, she was far above the beach and the First City.

Here she found flocks of Collectors making note of the steady flow of refugees. Elderly Effer and former working Athlon, numerous herds of Oreya, and a multitude of individuals – some of the clades she had never seen before, families freed from god prisons, giant rodents – Vardi, armoured mammals known as Mesupun Glafa.

She exchanged tidings with as many as she could, promising safe sleeping spaces, food and water. The wounded would be tended to when possible. She met fearful eyes, untrusting of this kindness, and though she scanned the crowd for familiar faces, she saw none.

She hopped to the treeline, where her daughter now stood, looking out over the land, watching the distant shapes of folk seeking salvation from the Husk.

'This waiting,' Ether grunted, 'it's far worse than any fight.'

Onnar nodded, 'True. But don't will the fight to begin. We have no idea what kind of force we will face. But I have good news, pockets of resistance have sprung up — one took out a whole battalion.'

Ether looked impressed.

'This ugly brute,' she produced Stegard's skull, 'made a deal with them. They didn't take him, take his body that is. Told him he could keep the land and enslave those feathered. What do you make of that?'

'The unscrupulous will always make deals with the grave. I imagine he had a clever tongue before you cut it from his mouth.' Onnar looked at her daughter and she felt such conflict. Pride and worry.

'Mother, I can feel your eyes on me. I am okay. I have my Drove, I have you.'

'I know,' Onnar paused. 'Come, we can be of more assistance. These poor souls will have information of use to us. Let's try to find out as much as we can — and be patient!'

They hurried back to where the refugees were arriving, gently asking questions among the mammals and feathered. Many wore old armour, the ragtag remains of inherited plates, desperate attempts to offer the slightest defence. Ether provided berries to those who might want a little sustenance, and they didn't last long.

From a distance, a large emaciated Vulpus caught her attention. His eyes were piercing white, uncanny. He looked as though he'd seen the brunt of it, so she weaved amongst the crowd of animals towards him. Eyes and snouts and muzzles darted out of her way, missives of doubt, cynicism, defeat and exhaustion filling her field of vision. The smell of unwashed fur was nothing new to her; she was filthy at the best of times, but she had never known such frailty. It was a concept frowned upon by the Drove. Born into it, *born running*.

She saw her mother was speaking with a Corva Aefi, its beautiful orange and blue plumage, its sharp eyes. She turned her attention back to the eyes she sought. A glance, a momentary graze across her line of sight and—

They locked eyes.

Something was wrong with this. She felt her stomach turn. His eyes carried with them a liquid paleness, as though he were blind, but he saw her.

The crowd moved on and he was gone. She stood for a moment with the stink of warm fur and shit and shame, the brush of many lives against her, nudging her, pushing her back.

She strained to see him again, and then pulled herself free and hurried back to Onnar. 'Mother,' she whispered. 'Could the Husk—'

She thought again. The Husk were distorted shells of former living things, twisted up. Was she seeing things in the mist, like Emig?

But Emig had been right. Ether had the skull to prove it.

'Mother. Is there a chance the Husk could infiltrate this crowd?'

Onnar frowned, 'The Husk haven't made it this far south, and no one has seen them moving in the land since the Stinking City. I am sure there is nothing to worry about.'

'Practice caution, Mother Drove!' Aggi squawked, appearing as she always did with profound timing. 'Something you're always trying to inspire in your daughter!'

Onnar hopped back towards the mouth of the road, where a number of bone hexes were tied above in the trees, and upon staves in the ground. Most, if not all, were being knocked or occluded by the influx of larger animals. She tried to straighten them but they were quickly shunted aside, one barely holding on by a thread. She was suddenly aware that there was indeed little stopping those who wished to take advantage of this flaw in their defences. They had expected a fight, after all.

She ran to the edge of the cliff to look down upon the beach. Dron had the sun above it, making it impossible to see how many had made it to the glades between its peaks, and how many now made the beach itself their shelter.

'Aggi, take this news to the Regulax. I fear we have overlooked a great weakness.'

*

Vorsa began to read the etchings with zeal. Her entire life had been dictated by interpretations of what lay before her, hewn in contorted arcs of a thousand inscriptions. It was no rushed work, or by any means a small feat. This had been a place of divine worship, in a portion of the First City left in the world after Dron had withdrawn. She was giddy with the importance of the find.

'Why was this kept from the other clans?' she said pointedly to Nenf.

'To protect it. Wars have been fought over less.'

Begrudgingly, Vorsa agreed. 'Have you studied it yourself?'

'A little. When I was a pup, we were taught to read it. But when the dens above were destroyed, we fled north. We have returned only twice to ensure it was still safe.'

'Is there mention of the Sentinels themselves?'

'There is mention of old things. Other than that, I'm not sure. Please feel free to look yourself.'

She had no personal knowledge of the Sentinels, they had been omitted from the Orata she knew and she wondered why. It was possible they were so obscured by time that they would make no sense to any who read about them. The life of a Vulpus was not long, and such ancient ideas had been lost entirely. Lost, until now. She scanned the roots for a particular glyph.

Above her, a cartouche of sorts, a series of larger pictograms, clawed into the bark. Ora, Seyla and Naa in alignment, the presence of the Gasp and the Umbra, of the First City, and below this, the Oscelan.

There were six icons, three either side of the Oscelan. Five were risen, one was stained black. Each held small cuts within. It was thousands of generations old, but there, cut in old Vulpus — Moorvori Groor, Thron Awlbringa, Maligna, Carcharigon, The Sethseez, and *Trok*.

Trok hung low, and the word was almost smudged out. She followed the cartouche out in a spiral along the truncated verse. The Sentinel she stood within was Thron All Bringer. It was described as the founding forest. It was a very old part of the First City, shed in this land to protect the ancestors of the Vulpus, but born, grown, assembled millions of turns before.

She looked up again at the skeletal giant that loomed over them. She wondered what it had looked like in life, whether she might be related to its primeval form. It was, itself, a herald, the watcher in the dark, guarding this holy of holies.

'We must wake this Sentinel,' she said, eyes remaining on the beast.

They returned to the surface, passing through the watery threshold, the shadows in the deep perhaps accepting her presence and remaining hidden as they swam the brackish water and ascended the tunnel.

At the surface, Vorsa found Ivy sat on a fence, eagerly awaiting them.

'What did you find down there?'

Vorsa grinned, 'You won't believe it!'

'Groor!' she shouted, 'your brethren hides under the marsh! Will you rouse it?'

Groor swung its great head towards the water, and with four gargantuan steps, was level with it. As it leant down, it produced a tone, a sonorous reedy drone that piqued Lucille's ears — she had heard this sound before.

It came to an abrupt stop, and then there was silence but for the wind and distant feathered song.

A deep baritone yawn preceded the muddy slurp of something moving beneath the reedbeds. They were far enough away from the displacement of thick black mire, which soon was erupting in burping expulsions – and then ten, twenty – a hundred black columns emerged from the muck, spilling sheets of plant matter, revealing at the base of each, roots.

It was a petrified forest, tar black and preserved, stumps and trunks alike, and finally, the body of a Sentinel, bright anaemic cordex and taproots of lilies speckled the deep earthen brown of the golem — much like Groor, a moving landmass comprised of life, of ligaments and muscles in vegetable resplendence.

As it slowly pulled itself free of the sucking slurry beneath it, water drained from its many crab-like appendages,. It sprayed more water out of numerous orifices and stepped onto the land. A dry clicking emanated from it, the rubbing and tapping of various mouth parts ushered forth dialogue between the Sentinels.

'THRON ALL BRINGER, UNGBOR GOSH, FOUNDING FOREST!' Groor proclaimed to the clam-shaped body of the Sentinel festooned with preserved trees, each a gnarled spike that added to its crustacean appearance.

The Umbra made good on its eternal promise and translated the chitter the monstrous creature made.

'LONG HAVE I BEEN BELOW, WHERE MY LITTLE CUBLINGS HID INSIDE ME. THOSE I WAS CHARGED WITH PROTECTING ARE ALL GONE.'

Noraa scampered before it, 'I think it's time to go home.'

And so, with dozens of animals upon their backs, they continued the journey south, towards the First City.

*

Beside him, Esit, daughter of the She-King Carcaris, was a formidable animal, over twice his size, yet under the influence of a far less imposing Wroth spirit.

Thoth felt the slightest inclination toward wishing he could have wooed these powerful animals to his cause, and not rely on possession to add their prowess to his ranks. Regardless, the journey south was almost at an end.

His Husk divided into small groups, himself dressed in armour more befitting a Cini, his tunic tucked up under his belly. He admired a herd of Athlon galloping across the Downs. The land here was vaguely reminiscent of his home, and with this realisation came a pang of homesickness. How strange, he thought, to feel such a thing, so close to his goal.

Not far off, Scab and a few fellow Cini, the last of the original pack, walked together. They exchanged a knowing glance. The sun was warm, the air from the ocean fresh. Watching them, Thoth felt the tickle of the wind in his fur, and imagined again, for a fraction of a moment, what it would be like to let this need go. But he was a small man, a jealous man, and he would have his throne, and his castles, and he would dig his boot heel into all who opposed him.

His cerebral foe, the glare that had hidden his goal from him, had ceased its futile attempts at resistance. Regardless, that endpoint was still just as mysterious, a nebula of energies, frenetic lines of light culminating before him. He attempted to read these like sheet music, chords in a song that he didn't know. Yet he felt them in him, tied to him, a significance that none around him shared. It was dazzling, uncomfortably so, a vivaciousness that hinted at ultimate power.

Flocks of flea-bitten animals, some carrying the marks of his Husk, ambled beside him. His influence had spread far further than he had imagined — he'd made good use of his skills. He congratulated himself for this, a silent admiration that didn't warrant the self-aggrandising that Scab seemed so keen on. Oh, how that prick loved to show him up!

He couldn't fault Scab's current plan, even as he marvelled at his own modest strategies — he had made incendiary devices of the dead, the Husk crowded with baying souls, his *legionnaires*, wandering into some pitiful den of fluffy bunnies and detonating, turning useless fodder into obedient drones. It was beautiful in its treachery — how many he wondered, how many were out there, cleansing the earth of the inconsequential, reinvigorating the soil with Wroth – nay – human ingenuity.

Human.

The word was gaining new meaning under him.

He was full of the inebriation of deceit, of greed and terror. He looked down on the expansive grassland, rolling acres of hardy grazed grasses, bracken and gorse, the blunt shoulder cliffs before him, the thousands of Trojan horses amongst the assembling throng of those escaping him. He felt very pleased with himself.

And then, like a beacon, a wondrous perplexity, a giant hive rose from the seashore, filling the horizon between the twin cliffs — a metropolis of stone and soil and forest and life, brimming with a living dignity, composite architecture that encircled the fruit, placenta, crux of the love'd Umbra.

The First City.

It was all his for the taking.

Peripheral glances showed him where hexes waited — his gag reflex triggered if he looked too long. He was sure one or two would be caught out, but a fitting animal in a sea of underfed lost souls wouldn't draw too much attention.

He hobbled forward, doing his best waif and stray impression, pained expression and so on, looking back to see similar hackneyed attempts at acting from those Husk closest to him.

He kept his eyes low. The Rauka beside him fidgeted, the burn of not wanting to be noticed manifesting in subconscious physical tells.

'Don't give the game away, you useless piece of—' Thoth hissed under his breath. The Rauka was keenly noticeable, he imagined the sight of such a beast was very uncommon among the countless Yoa'a, Tril, Throa and Vulpus.

He almost felt relief when the lumbering megafauna of Tasq and Oraclas marched into view, their skin bedecked with vulgar painted images, armour of engine parts and gallon water jugs. In his diminutive Cini form they were truly formidable, and they drew any attention away from the spasming Rauka. That aside, he distanced himself from her, and feigning a painful paw, he stooped on his right side, thanking others for their patience with him.

He was soon a good ten rows back, beside two tall white water feathered. They eyed him as any prey animal would eye a carnivore, and his vain attempts at garnering pity from them failed. They were soon replaced by a family of wild Runta, who feared no one.

He walked beside them until the road met a pile of vehicles and the fences fashioned of branches and logs. Their fortifications were impressive. He left Esit at the top of the hill and began his descent towards the beach. They had successfully created a bottle neck between the lorries. He saw evidence of tusk marks in the bodies of the vehicles; they had positioned them so that the Husk would have had to walk single file. Above, on flatbed trailers stood Vulpus guards, each monitoring the refugees as they streamed in. It was profoundly fascinating.

Before him were ranks of sharpened lengths of timber, all pointing towards the new arrivals on either side, guiding them through a miserable seaside town with a browbeaten amusement park, geriatric fairground rides and a collapsed rollercoaster — then onto the wide beach, something of an esplanade before the enormous, phenomenal monolith that seemed washed up with the tide.

For some time, he stood alone on the brink of a sand dune. The familiar smell of Scab came to him, a kind of musty tang reminiscent of cheap deodorant, something he imagined Scab would have worn in his former life.

'So you did it, made it past their defences, made it into the heart of their world. So what now?'

'We take it, we take it all.'

He walked without a care in the world, towards the First City.

*

'He is here.'

Exhausted, Rune ruffled his feathers and walked along the edge of the Regulax. He had failed to hide the city from the enemy. The creeping will of Thoth was inescapable. He had felt the caustic presence before he could see its shine upon the Downs, the ailing red of revenants in Naa.

Erithacus raised his head, hoping he had misheard. But he looked upon the little Startle and understood consequences in those dark eyes. 'What do you see?' he croaked.

'He is strong, and he has learned how to hide himself, but I can feel him, he is very close, perhaps among those fleeing his menace.'

'Then he is hiding in plain sight, but how? Can you feel the nature of him? His form?'

Rune shook his head. 'I will try to find him.'

He hopped down from the Regulax and darted out and up, through the sunlit shaft and out onto the glades. He was soon high above the city and the beach, and closing his eyes, he felt for tautness in the weave, the little indentations of cause. Each had a colour, a sensation — it was a cacophony of experiences, both alive and dead, shrill and indistinguishable in their volume, but their shades became identities, and soon the noise was a murmur, and the prismatic colours radiant.

The cove, though, was filled with thousands of animals, all projecting their fears and despairs, an insensible array of hues bleeding into one another, cascading worries that spread like a flame, such that Rune could not decipher let alone see the conscious thoughts of a single soul. He was lost in his own delicate interpretations. He shook his head with frustration and flew lower, skimming the billow of sand and the trumpet of Oraclas.

Onnar ran beside the column of animals. She was looking for the impossible, some sign or evidence of the Husk among the innocent, and she fretted, as did her daughter. They met away from the crowd, hopeful not to frighten anyone.

'What can we do? We can't fight something we cannot see.'

*

Esit screamed — she screamed and screamed and screamed out, a silent, dry heave, so empty, so sluggish. She wasn't sad any longer, she was livid, and she would have her moment. The Husk within her was nervous — each misstep, each quiver was to her advantage, and she leaned into it. She could see whatever he saw, and he was staring at his —her feet. If she could turn his head, just for a moment and catch those hexes, she could have him. He had stalled at the top of the cliff, just before the vehicles.

The wretch was trying with all his might to defy her, his concentration split between oppressing her and trying not to show his true colours. In a fit of frustration she sent an impulse to his left leg, and he stumbled – his weight far greater than his former body – and he tumbled to the ground, smacking into the barrier.

They lay belly up against the barricade, a slew of animals knocked from their feet. Her eyes had closed against a cloud of blinding dust. In his confusion, she forced her eyes open.

Above them, hanging at the end of a branch, was a hex. In the force of the impact, it had begun to swing wildly. The revenant within was not focusing, was not attentive.

Look

The word was simple for her to roar through the numerous neurological pitfalls he'd erected to keep her at bay. That fraction of disarray was enough to catch his attention, and he looked up — and saw the shard of glass at the centre of the spokes of black rotting meat, a wheel of putrefaction, the damp click of fly larvae gorging on it, wriggling. He'd been that.

It had started with a fever, on his way home from that nightclub. He'd felt a bit too drunk, and he was sweating. The next morning he'd woken to welts in his armpits, swollen, tender. He'd started puking blood that evening, stumbling to the sink to wash his face with cold water, seeing the colour drained from him, his pupils dilated, milk white skin. He'd died soon after.

Those same sickness eyes reflected back now — just for a moment, that cold unfeeling, unwelcoming gaze within.

That was all there was of him, a paleness, a frail afterglow.

You're dead, he thought, *and you will live in death forever.*

*

Esit did not expect such an abrupt end to her imprisonment. She felt a levity, a yawn of agency, the rush of blood refilling limbs, or perhaps herself refilling each stolen part of herself, no longer chained to the futility of a limbic cell. But the violation remained, stuck in her craw, and she vomited him up, a dreadful sputum, a gangrenous clag that poured from her orifices in stringy oleaginous clumps. The plasm shuddered, and she coughed between a snorted hollered 'Stay away from it! It is Husk!'

The crowd immediately tore wide, bodies piling away.

Onnar heard the commotion and ran towards the break in the crowd.

A Rauka, stood on shaky legs, ejecting something from itself, a disgusting pool of — something moving, seeking a host.

Rune and Aggi met high above, and without a word they knew the scent of it.

Aggi dived and knocked the Hex from the branch. It dropped next to the foulness, and like a trap being sprung, it snapped around the revenant, pulling it within the shard, locking it away from any living thing.

Rune took it upon himself to haul the hex in his claws, almost too big for him, yet determined, he flew up and out beyond the shore, casting it into the ocean.

Aggi knew Esit, having freed her from the Moterion. Now she flew beside her. 'Esit!' she called out. Before she could utter another word, the great Rauka cried with urgency,

'The Husk! They are here! They are in amongst the refugees, there are hundreds of them!'

*

Thoth entered the First City. He could immediately feel the bearing of the Gasp within — like himself, it was a conduit, a permanent window. He could see beyond the physical, the elegant filaments that held the city firm, it breathed, photosynthesised, digested through its fungal interlacing, taking of the dead and sewing each organic intricacy into itself. He could even see the movement of nutrients in the veinous tangle hidden behind walls of stone and thicket — the glue that bound this all, stemming from some other finite place.

He continued on, breathing deep the fragrance of dew and moss and lichen, the soft tread on leaf strewn floor. It was monastic here, quiet, warm, safe.

Like tree rings, the closer to the centre he trod, the older the city became. Here, the foundations drew in towards a fulcrum — the First City seemed to grow from this point. Like a grave, there were dried flowers and shells placed upon it, and like many a grave, it was comprised of a large slab of sandstone.

He was taken by what he saw in its surface — he had once seen a similar fossil in a book, that of an archaeopteryx, some ancient feathered creature. Like that fossil, there were imprints of feather-like down, but these were far smaller, perhaps fledglings, barely out of the nest, their little toothy snouts reaching for one another.

A Corva leaned in without being addressed. It wore a head dress of sorts that looked a little like a grotesque bishop's mitre. Indulging in his role with queasy obsequiousness, Thoth gave a fawning sigh, shuddered as the Corva spoke.

'Beautiful, isn't it, the seat of our city, and our belove'd Umbra. To gaze upon the Sisters of the Flock is such a privilege.'

Sisters of the Flock

Thoth said nothing to the Corva, who bowed and moved on to another arrival seeking priestly platitudes.

The stone was large, but not deep. It was cradled in hardened roots. He pondered for a moment, followed by a confident nod to himself as he made his decision.

He left the city, pausing at the entrance. He looked at the plethora of animals, hopping, scratching, sniffing and defecating. He shook his head, and made for an Oraclas who was busy helping families find a place to nest or take shelter.

'May I ask for your help for a moment?'

Yaran looked at the Cini beside her. He was dishevelled. She felt pity for him.

'Yes, of course.'

She followed him back across the sand, acknowledging those she had befriended with a loving raise of her trunk. Entering the great hall, he patiently walked to a quiet corner. Once there, he stopped and turned to her. With his head lowered he whispered, but she could not make out the words. She leaned in so that she might hear him.

He choked. An odd sulphurous odour rose from him, some sickness she imagined. But the smell was followed by an almost indiscernible snarl of *something* that lifted from him — she tried to make sense of it as it floated toward her.

Thoth had sharpened his skills to the finest point, like muscle memory. He did not even see the Gasp anymore, just felt the nag of some impatient ghoul hanging on his every effort. It seeped through her tear ducts, in through the backs of her eyes.

Yaran collapsed.

Thoth had no time for theatrics.

'Get up, you shit,' he growled.

The revenant began to hyperventilate, erroneous spasms of muscles, of a frame so large. He was flung around a mind far more complex and angry than he could have anticipated, but he did not want to disappoint Thoth, he did not want to return to the Gasp. He would not. He tripped and fell and recovered, loose and inconsistent. He felt like he was dreaming, his limbs unresponsive.

'Follow me.'

Thoth guided the ungainly animal back towards the sandstone plinth. Once they reached it, Thoth ushered him close.

'This stone. It is the pillar upon which the enemy rests. Break it.'

It took so little effort. The revenant raised Yaran's forelimbs and slammed them down upon the stone. Her weight alone was enough. The stone split in two.

Within her own mind, Yaran sobbed at the profound betrayal, crying into the fathomless black of her new prison.

Thoth grinned at the Oraclas. The revenant hoped it was for him, but somehow knew it was not, a mocking hurrah to the animal inside.

Then Thoth felt for the Gasp. He could see the tethers to the city, the lines of ascent, the host of sinuous corridors that leapt from consequence to transcendence, from this living plain to the hereafter — and he cut it clean through. The city would not be aided by the dead. He felt the living walls go quiet, the shifting tapestries of revenants silenced.

Thoth tore the armour from his body and pulled out the tunic that was tucked beneath it. He flung it over his back and forced his paws through the gashes he'd made to aid his adornment, and then he rose up on his hind legs. Knocking arms half out of their sockets so he could stand with wroth-like gait, he strode out to the entrance to the city, straining his neck until he heard the relieving click of vertebrae.

He howled. A euphoric, endorphin-fuelled cry.

He had won.

Amongst the tired crowd, his Husk rose to the call. Hundreds discarded the trappings of their masquerade. Some rose like him, on shaky back limbs, and very quickly they toppled any resistance with bared teeth and quick claws.

The beach was alive with blind terror as they ran from the enemy, who marched defiantly through the defences meant for them, that stood redundant. Arcs of arterial blood escaped the necks and flanks of any who resisted, though some were far too powerful to control and were left to flee the beach.

'Where is my daughter!' Matriarch Eda cried. 'My Lady, look!'

Beside Thoth, stood Yaran, unflinching in his presence.

'Silence!' Thoth snarled. The beach fell eerily quiet. Even the wind seemed subdued.

Thoth raised his voice, magnified by the façade of the First City.

'I am Thoth, leader of the Husk. Your pathetic attempts to stop me have failed miserably. Those who defy me will be killed. Those who serve me will be taken and used as vessels for my kin. Your pitiful display of life is over.'

Then Thoth summoned as many revenants as he could, desecrating the city and its citizens.

*

Onnar and her daughter cut a path away from the rout with their gauntlets, fending off the violent mouths of the Husk. They stood raised on their hind limbs, their backs to one another, defending the few animals that had escaped the attack.

Rune and Aggi picked up stones and hurled them at the enemy. Between winded breaths, Ether cried to her mother, 'We have to run! We are no good here, no good to anyone! We need to get away from here, gain some ground, plan an offensive, we can't win against so many!'

Below, the beach was bedlam.

*

In the Regulax, Erithacus directed the Starless Vulpus out to the seaward side, asking them to jump from the rocky face of Dron, into the water. The sea was relatively calm as they threw themselves down, followed by the flocks of Baldaboa, Startle, Speakers and Corva Anx, who together guided the swimmers further up the coast to a small beach where they could come ashore and rest.

Erithacus and the Speakers then took to wing once more, flying relatively high over the bay, and looking down on scores of silent bodies, some in fits, others already possessed and ominously staring back.

Erithacus turned to Glaspitter, 'They have taken the city. We must help those who have escaped and bring them to safety.'

Glaspitter nodded and cawed to his squadron, who flew towards the cliff tops. Erithacus saw Onnar, Aggi, Rune and Ether fleeing north and he followed and overtook them, landing in their path. They balked as the shadow of him appeared from above, yet recognised him immediately.

'Are you safe?' he panted as he collected himself.

They all nodded. Aggi was hysterical, 'They took Dron, they took our dear Epiras!'

Rune tried to comfort her, 'We will overcome this, I promise.'

'But how?' she wailed. 'Where are these saviours, where are these Sentinels that I have heard of, why do they not come now, in this time of need?'

The band of survivors ran and flew away from the coast, and Ora betrayed them by shining brightly, offering no storm clouds, no sympathy. It remained a beautiful day even whilst the crux of all their purpose withered into corruption.

A long time ago, in a land not so far from this one, a plague had claimed a little Wroth settlement. I could sense the fortune of this disease, its grave entitlement, carried on the bodies of Muroi, in the tiny blood feeders upon their fur. I felt the finite life, the infinite suffering, and wished to offer my wares. I went to the town, took a form not so dissimilar to them, and I said, I will relieve you of this infestation, if I may have your dying and alleviate them of the pain of death. They agreed, and with my song, I led the Muroi away. I returned to claim my prize, only to find them unwilling to part with the mortal sick. They dug graves for them, sealing a fate beyond their agony. The dying begged me for succour, so as an act of kindness and no small boon for me, I raised them up from their death beds, and I led them to my bosom, with my song, so that they could know the silence evermore.

Chapter Eleven

Lucille had excavated a number of artefacts in her attempts to understand the nature of Groor. Beside her now was Ivy, who had taken a keen interest in what Lucille had discovered.

'It is, in many ways, a family tree. The further down into the depths of the body of the Sentinel, the older the graves are. I started here, close to the entrance, with the bones of the fallen Saxon. Further back, we come to this skeleton.'

She had lain out a tarpaulin and placed a number of items upon it, little trinkets, bones and tools. The skeleton was huddled on its side.

Ivy studied the skull. It was not noticeably different from any Wroth skulls she had seen before. Ears of wheat, growing in the dark, had interwoven themselves through the body. Ivy ran her fingers through the stalks.

'Why is this growing here?' she asked.

'Around 10,000 years ago, Mesolithic Wroth began to domesticate and cultivate wheat. Perhaps she was buried with some seeds as they would have been important to her people. They sprouted and, like everything else, Groor maintained it, allowed it to prosper, supplying it nutrients. Again, this burial occurred long after the Cini were buried here, long after Groor went to sleep in constant vigil of their grave.'

'These Wroth had their own beliefs. I wonder why they practiced them here?' Ivy asked.

'I think they could feel the importance of this place. Many Wroth religions stemmed from the same root, in fact they shared the same religious sites and wars were fought over those places of importance. This place, I don't think they knew what it was, but they felt a need to bury their dead here.'

Lucille lifted a large flint. It was delicately cut into a point, with sides chipped to give it an edge.

'This is far older. I believe it was buried here thousands of years before this Wroth. I think Vorsa was right, Groor must have crossed seas in the past. There is evidence of prehistoric animals from north Africa.' Excited, she beckoned Ivy further into the rooted cave system, leaping across little chasms, until she reached the mass grave.

'This skeleton,' she identified the hominid amongst the other animals, 'I believe is Australopithecus. Our ancestor. This grave was made before the schism, before the Wroth diverged from the rest of Naa.'

Ivy very carefully placed a foot between the various skeletons. Clutched in the hominid's hand was a long staff, like a walking stick. There were markings carved into it. With some effort she rotated it towards her. 'There are drawings on this, like letters. I think ... I might be able to read it.'

She closed her eyes and saw the inversion of the sigils burned on her retina. Her mind took these, feeding from the Umbra, the well of all collective thought. Their meaning offered up — Oad.

'This person called itself an Oad, and this was a burial after a forest fire. The bodies were bought to Dron and lain together. This happened in the First City.' Ivy looked up to Lucille. 'Before Groor separated. So Groor carries with it part of the First City.'

'Yes, and there is more!' Lucille said eagerly, ushering Ivy onwards.

They descended further, sometimes climbing hand over hand into winding culverts and passages, spirals of millennia-old wood that felt much like stone and yet still lived. Here the roots clustered, the former bramble-like countenance lost to a sandy soft rock.

'This is the heart of Groor — the oldest part. This rock is sedimentary, and there are old fossils in it. Big ones.'

She lifted her head and let her head lamplight pass over the rock face. The rock was ever so slightly slanted, a layer of sandstone. Within it was a huge skeleton, a feathered dinosaur, crouched with its head pulled in towards its chest, and a long fantail slightly bent towards the body. The impressions of the feathers were immaculate.

'I don't know the species, but it's a carnivore. Look at the detail! Even all the little tufts of down around the body, and these are pennaceous feathers. It couldn't fly though its descendants would. But look at its head.'

There was an aberration of bone above its skull, a complexity of fragments, crushed flat by millions of years, yet retaining, like the skeleton itself, a degree of form. It was a crown.

'This animal wore armour. How did we miss this?' Lucille dabbed at the stone with her brush.

'Again, like Vorsa said, we weren't looking for it,' Ivy replied.

Below the fossil, a large piece of rock was missing. Ivy couldn't be sure, but it seemed as though she had seen a slab of stone that would fit perfectly.

Ivy hazarded a guess, 'I think this was their mother. The mother who made the first grave, the first to make a shrine to mourn the dead.'

'Whose mother?' asked Lucille.

'The Sisters of the Flock.'

*

Infal Gar stood at the centre of the yard behind the Naag Rarspi, scratching sigils in the coal that smeared the surface of the ground. Audagard carried shards of marked glass from the listing sheds that housed them, placing them gingerly at the foot of each of her markings.

'Without a revenant twin, this will be difficult.'

'Don't be so pessimistic. I am sure he will be more than willing.'

Once the work was complete, they exchanged glances and stabbed their beaks into their chests. With the blood, they smattered the four corners of the orchestration, and uttered incantations of revenant speech.

The tell-tale shudder of the air was a relief, as a split of dark drew itself between them, stretching itself into something with too many arms and legs. It slinked out of the gloom realm and chittered, climbing invisible silk. Another followed, an arthropodal form in ferrous liquid. They hung either side of the void, until a disembodied skull trailing an emaciated body followed.

'Petulan,' Audagard bowed.

The dead Vulpus lacked his usually mischievous manner. There was no quip, no humour.

'Dron is silent, the Husk have taken it. Their leader, Thoth, has withdrawn its eminence from the Gasp. We are losing ground to the enemy.'

Audagard stuttered, 'Dron? What can we do?'

Petulan sighed, 'The body Thoth inhabits is a Cini named Emeris. Those he has taken are dying, their essence is leaking into the Gasp. Half in, half out, they are withering in their brain meats. We are channelling the love'd Umbra into them, to sustain them. We believe we can outwit Thoth, if we have a plan, though you will need to discard your petty differences. The Gasp will work with you to succeed.'

Infal Gar held a look of concern, an emotion Audagard had never seen in her before.

'He is far more clever than I gave him credit for being. How did he manage to take the city?'

Petulan glided toward her, 'His Husk have killed many. They passed over with their stories. He hid his soldiers amidst those escaping his tyranny. Regardless, no one thought to suspect the innocent. He holds the seat of Umbra in Naa, and all who fled to its safety.'

'It has come far quicker than I anticipated, but my plan still holds,' Infal Gar replied.

'Plan?' Petulan asked.

'In these times of struggle our positions are formed in the extremes; the Husk are the enemy, our disagreements amongst ourselves become inconsequential, all black and white, good and evil. But as disciples of the Gasp we have always waded in murky waters. We exist in the grey, we are useful to Ocquia when it has suited them. But once again, in times of need, even our excommunicated high priest returns to scratch in the coal with us. I suggest we take advantage of such contemptible things. Embrace the in-between spaces.'

Petulan twisted about himself, 'I'm listening?'

'You know of the Echid? I believe the Vulpus call it Trok?'

Petulan grinned, 'Ah! The *heretic!* Yes I know it. The great Renouncer. Liquid undesirable, the one who shall not be named. Pray tell, why do you mention such a thing?'

'It has stirred. Its timing is not a coincidence. I think it has felt the itch, it knows when it's wanted. Audagard felt it in the falling sticks. The Ebduous Clax in their Orrery. It has risen.'

Audagard sighed. 'The Husk want life. What Thoth has given them is a morsel of life, a shallow imitation. They will crave more, but there is no more to give. How can this Echid help us with our plight?'

Petulan cackled, 'Ah! But none can resist the embrace of old Trok! The Echid is sweet silence. The end of all ends. But who in their right mind would choose that over my lovely Gasp?'

Infal Gar flapped her wings, 'The Wroth of course. Far more stubborn than this old beak, for sure!'

'Of all the Maligna, Echid is the least predictable. Born before the Gasp, before the Umbra, yet called upon like those in the Oscelan. He shirked the Gasp, he will not listen to the love'd Umbra. However, if what you say is true, then his movements are no doubt in response to the Husk in Naa. He smells blood in the water.'

Audagard held up his wings, 'Please! Enough of this, I am starting to realise how infuriating I was. All this talk and not a single word makes sense! Tell me, what is the Echid, Trok, or whatever you might call it, and what can it do for us?'

Infal Gar cackled, 'The Echid was born of the conscious dead in Naa. When the Umbra rose, and with it the Gasp, his role was usurped. He went from the Monarch of the concentrated dead to pauper, begging souls to partake of his offering. He shunned the other Maligna, thought them traitors. The Echid is unindentured, like impacted teeth, a niggling little god in Naa. Some say he has bartered for souls, bartered with the Wroth, no less!'

'So we make a deal with this thing, ask it to take the Husk?'

Petulan shook his head, 'He will only take willing souls.'

*

Esit began her journey back to the Pridebrow. She was alone and carried a fallen Effer in her jaws. The animal had been slain by the Husk and with very little energy, she took what she could get. That evening, she sat on the roof of a Scithar and pulled at the carcass. It nourished her somewhat, and once she was finished, she began to construct bone hexes from its ribs and gristle.

It was a two day walk back to the Stinking City, where she had once visited as emissary to meet with the High Realm of Hanno. The city was silent, but she kept her ears pricked for the slightest sign of life, letting out a muted roar to signal any Rauka.

At the foot of the High Realm, she wavered. There was dried blood everywhere amid other signs of battle, and the Toron guards were nowhere to be seen. She climbed a fire escape stairwell, aware of the continued signs of struggle and escape.

The garden was deserted. The families that lived amongst the trees were absent, fruit bearing plants hung laden and unharvested. She paced up the shallow stairs that ran to the veranda, where she was surprised to find Gahar, sitting on the ground facing the window.

'Gahar, where are your people?'

The Hanno didn't respond.

'Gahar of the High Realm of Hanno.'

The giantess rotated her head to reveal listless, unthinking eyes, absent of the usual dark auburn. Gahar was drooling.

'Get her out! Get her out of my head!' Gahar screamed.

She lifted her muscular frame and charged across the walkway, holding aloft a fire extinguisher, throwing it clear through the window, sending it plummeting below.

'She won't shut up! She won't let me sleep! I want to sleep!'

Esit frowned, 'Gahar?'

'Gahar! Gahar! She won't stop screaming her name! There is no Gahar, I am here, I am taking this body! But she won't shut up!'

Gahar slammed into the railing that ran around the perimeter of the window, buckling the metal. She threw herself against the riveted metal beams, collapsed again, slamming her fists against the tiles.

'This is not your body,' Esit said firmly.

'Not my body? Not my body! What would she do with it that warrants leaving her in it? She wails on and on about her poor dead baby, and how she wronged that girl. She wastes this body on mourning all her mistakes. Give up, move on love, you'll have all the time in the world for regrets when you're dead, trust me!'

Esit clawed the bone hex from her armour and hoisted it before the great simian.

Gahar's eyes peeled wide, she began to expel a thin exasperated howl, throwing her head back. A crescent of ectoplasm ejected from her mouth, her nose, and she hocked, sending rivulets of slime across the floor where they coalesced like mercury.

Esit slid the hex closer, mucus threads wrapping around the rotting bone, until it was pulled into its own reflection. Gahar remained on her forelimbs, breathing heavily.

'Do you know me, Gahar?'

The great Hanno took an exhausted glance at Esit.

'Dynast ... Esit,' she said at last.

'I have experienced this myself, it will take some time to recover. I will bring you food.'

Esit leapt up a nearby tree and pulled down a bunch of bananas with her jaws. They were over-ripe and browning, but the sugars would do the Hanno good. She threw the fruit toward Gahar, who began to feed. They sat together, Hanno and Rauka, until Gahar was able to speak.

She shook her head, 'The ghoul was right. I have lost myself in my grief. I gave in to it. My people, ravaged by the Husk. I could have prevented this, but I was so … lost.'

Esit paused, 'You have a chance now, to not dwell in the past. Call to your people. We must forge alliances, we cannot be divided by anything in the face of such a callous enemy.'

Gahar agreed. She swung herself up into the branches of her nest, and onto the raised platform. From there, she manoeuvred her powerful body with grace, up and out of a hatch, onto the glass roof itself, carefully running along the steel girders that held up the greenhouse. The wind was strong and invigorating, and she closed her eyes, took a deep breath, reclaiming herself in it.

She let out the breath with a hearty holler, a call that her people could not mistake. She continued calling for a while, until she heard the quiver of the wire that stretched across from the High Realm to the neighbouring structures, and the movements of her kin, the effortless motion of many bodies, who mounted the roof with a little trepidation.

'It is me, Gahar, I am free of the foulness. Forgive me. I have been a fool. The loss of my son—'

'The loss of your son was a loss for us all. There is no need for forgiveness. How will we free our sisters and brothers?' said a Toron guard.

She beckoned them back into the High Realm, where Esit sat patiently. She gave the Dynast the floor.

'The Husk have taken Dron.'

The room erupted, 'But how?'

Gahar quieted them down, Esit continued. She explained her own possession, and how the Husk had infiltrated the crowds of refugees. She ended her speech with a plea, 'My mother, the She-King Carcaris, will have sent out sentries in search of me. We must find them and begin the process of aligning all the clades. The Husk is a sickness easily spread. We must be a united front against it.'

*

Awfwod Garoo struggled with sleep, echoes of the spirit that had possessed him. It had left, but the organic remnants, those feeble, half-rendered synapses that had courted the thoughts of the Husk remained, and with them, imprints, vestige notions and scatterbrain memories. His own mind was haunted, and it was an unwelcome feeling.

So he, and his band of clumsy Baldaboa, flouted sleep and flew, traced the magnetic conflagrations, allowing the fine intersection of the Umbra to lead their path as they left Dron in search of the Sentinels and their precious cargo.

The Umbra wanted this connection, and so, within a turn or so, the titans appeared on the horizon, with thousands following, an armada of animals in search of amnesty.

Little Grin sat at the bow of Groor, deep in conversation with the golem. He told it tales of his imagined heroic deeds in the forests of the north, and Groor spoke of the age of ice, of the first meeting of the nations of Naa. Little Grin was in awe of all the Sentinel had seen, and felt he still had a lot of life to live. He recognised the blundering flight path of Awfwod, and ran to the green slope to usher in the Windsweepers.

'Awfwod! It is I, Little Grin. Do you bring news?'

'Ah, the little Maar. Yes, I know you. Bring together your people. We have much to tell.'

Noraa, Vorsa, Ivy and Lucille came to the stones, and Awfwod, beside his companions puffed up to retain heat, regaled them with his news.

'Dron, our dear Epiras, has been overthrown by the Husk.'

They all spoke at once, then quietened to allow Vorsa to ask, 'When did this happen?'

'I have flown straight from there. Two turns. All who found shelter before the city have been taken. Erithacus directed the Speakers and Corva to flee, as did the Starless, who leapt from the city's walls and swam to safety. Those who were on the cliffside may have escaped. We took to wing without hesitation.'

Ivy stood up, unable to contain herself. 'We've got to stop him! We have to go there now, kill him if we have to.'

Noraa balked, 'No! The enemy inhabits my love, my Emeris. To kill him is to set him free to take someone else. Killing is not the answer. We must have a strategy, some weapon against him.'

'All we have is bone hexes and those willing to fight, but how do we fight an enemy who is already dead? And what of the Husk who are not on that beach, that continue to spread in the land?'

Vorsa leaned back and scratched her belly. It was uncharacteristically unmannerly of her. They all waited for her word.

'No doubt Onnar and her Drove have already begun to enact a plan. I know how those girls fight. You say the cliff top is free of Husk?'

Awfwod nodded, pulling his head into his down. 'When I left, the remaining Oraclas were blocking the only path out of the bay with those old Wroth machines. There were bone hexes everywhere.'

Vorsa frowned. 'Well, then our answer is simple. We starve them out.'

Noraa cried, 'How is that any better than killing them?'

Vorsa shook her head. 'They won't die, they won't even starve. Take away access to food and they will fracture into groups. Groups that we can parley with.'

Lucille raised her hand tentatively. 'May I say something?'

They all agreed.

'I know all of you have so many reasons to hate us, to hate the Wroth. But I wish to offer a different perspective, if you will allow me.'

Makepeace slowly and sleepily wandered to her shoulder. 'Please speak, Lucille.'

'Thoth went into this Gasp, this afterlife, and he made a deal with those revenants that were Wroth. He went to them and promised them the one thing they wanted more than anything, all they had to do was follow his word. Now, I will not absolve them of their actions — Wroth history is filled with such situations, of cruel men who exploit the desperation of the needy, and it is always a poor excuse to say "I was just following orders." But do you think Thoth has told them the truth of their condition? Given the reality of the suffering they have caused to the bodies of those they dwell in, how many might rethink their choices? How many might rescind his offer? I think to tar them all with the same brush is wrong. I feel we must engage with them somehow.'

Vorsa sighed, 'Forgive me, but it must be obvious to them that they have taken what is not theirs?'

'Ah well, the Wroth never thought much of taking from other animals. There could be many good souls out there who would not think twice on such matters. But that old world is dead. This is your world, your Naa. If Wroth are going to continue to exist in this world with you, we must learn to understand a more egalitarian approach to survival.'

'If and when the time comes, we will take it under advisement. The Husk will answer for their actions,' she paused for a more thoughtful reply, 'but we are not beyond listening.'

Lucille bowed her thanks.

'What of the rest of Embrian Naa? What of the animals fighting in the north, of the Pridebrow? We must help them too!' Noraa said fretfully.

'My flock and I were all victims of this curse, we were freed by the Dominus Audargard. The stain of it is still in us, and we will not rest until all have the knowledge they need to fight. We will travel north to the Pridebrow and on to the Vulpine Fiefdoms. We have the knowledge of these bone hexes. It will be a hard slog, but we will prevail!'

In this way the meeting ended and the Baldaboa, fed and watered, took to wing once again, carrying with them the hope of Naa.

*

The beach was littered with bodies, a sordid mess of blood, of the shallowest graves. Much would become meat for the hungry troops that had done the killing, and for those they had turned. The First City was ransacked for anything worthwhile to the Husk, which was very little. None dared go near the Regulax, the stacks of hellish icons just as potent as bone hexes.

Thoth rested on the broken tablet of stone. It made a good throne, and although part of him regretted breaking it for the discomfort the split caused, the symbolism had been too good to pass up. His most loyal subjects limped and simpered to him, which he also enjoyed — he revelled in these kingly hallmarks, and even considered making a crown.

'This thing we're in, there is nothing here. There are rooms, or spaces, but they are empty but for what these animals left behind. Weird stuff made of sticks, nothing of any use. But I was thinking, at least it's somewhere dry to sleep? We have many wounded and ....'

Thoth nodded, 'Yes, bring in your tired, your huddled masses.'

They looked at him with a little confusion, 'Right, sir.'

Scab stood on a sand dune, away from the worst of their sacking. He wrestled with this fortune. He was glad of his accomplishments, of making a brave decision to call to attention the errors in Thoth's method. They had achieved what they set out to do, to take the thing that was most cherished by these animals — and it was indeed mightily impressive; there was something truly alien about the giant structure on the beach, a crescendo of living stone. But this prize was bittersweet.

Congratulations, you won

But what had he won? Around him were sick and disabled creatures. The Husk were already returning to their practice of seeking sensation, of imbedding sharp objects into themselves in the vain hope of feeling. Meanwhile, there was carnage all around him. It reminded him of war movies, the storming of the beach at Normandy, except he was pretty sure that he was on the wrong side in that analogy.

He shook his head, not wanting to consider that any longer. He ran beyond the sand, beyond the rows of wooden spikes that stood angry and unused. He walked through the ruined theme park, checked the kiosks in hope of finding something to eat. There was nothing there — they'd long been scavenged of anything edible. He wandered further into the town, into houses, pulled open drawers with his mouth, knocked things from countertops and dressers.

What did you expect?

He had surely expected something. He had expected the promised land. He had expected comforts. But he was perhaps aware that he would always be looking in the wrong place for such things. He left the houses.

What did you expect? This is the domain of animals, of the things that lived in the earth. The Wroth lived above all of this, you were never going to find salvation here.

Salvation, yes. He wanted to be saved. Saved from the darkness of the Gasp, saved from the filthy body he inhabited. He wanted warm clothes and a hot shower. He wanted a cup of tea and a bacon sandwich. He had no need for these primitive, superstitious places that these animals coveted.

So why did you bring us here?

He suddenly felt unsure. And he felt something else.

Regret.

He had hurt a lot of people in his life. Some more deserving than others. He'd had a bad start. A father in prison, an alcoholic mother. He had been in and out of prison himself, he'd killed people, and very badly hurt others. He'd been the very worst he could be.

Then he'd died, only to find that after death, the essence of the living was reconstituted, a halfway house of sorts, the condensation of experience whittled down to its parts and flung into a kind of universal blender. Like the living flesh, which rotted down, became food and nutrients, the soul, or psyche or consciousness was also recycled. Perhaps like genes, those memories, bursts of inspiration, joys, ideas, passions, hatreds, loves, dreams, insanities, were passed on.

He didn't want anything of him to endure. He didn't want anyone to have to harbour that dirt, that stigma. He felt like crying, but he pushed it down. He wasn't even sure if Cini could cry.

You can cry

He was soon at the crest of the hill. A herd of Oraclas stood silently beyond the row of trucks they'd pushed to block the road. He paced up and down the line in search of a way through. There was no access. Piles of rock, heaved from the cliffside had been used to seal any gap he could squeeze through, and there were hexes all along the ridge on both sides, which made him gag with even a side glance. He looked up the valley, metal cages filled with stones piled to secure rockfall, thick bramble and gorse, and a cortège of Collectors eyeing him venomously.

'You gonna seal us in then, yeah?' he shouted. It felt limp and passive-aggressive. Useless really.

Try harder, they're not going to talk to you if all you have is insults. What do you want them to do, let you out?

He wasn't sure. He felt the tug of Thoth's authority, the bastard who'd freed him. He should return to him, ask him for guidance. This was his masterplan, his vision. Yes, Scab had dreamt up an alternative method of taking that…thing, the First City. But that was just the means to obtain it. He didn't know what lay within it, what magic might wait there. The means to make him a real boy.

Maybe Thoth doesn't know either. Maybe Thoth just wanted it, and so he took it. Who is Thoth anyway?

Why had he never considered this? What had he learned of the man behind the Cini?

He could drag the dead from Naa. He had freed Scab himself, chosen him amongst the froth of billions, and given him a wolf – a Cini – to dwell within. He had promised them dominion of the world once again, and Scab had been caught in that carousel of potential power.

You can pull the dead from the Gasp. You took the city. There is nothing Thoth can do that you can't do yourself.

But that realisation was damning. There was no happy ever after, no finality. He wasn't going to wake up one morning and find himself making coffee or brushing his teeth. Not while he occupied this unfeeling body that was dying under him, or returned to the Gasp.

But what if there was something else?

What if there was? How would he find such a thing? His efforts so far had led him here, pacing the ground before an impassable blockade.

Ask them a question they might be willing to answer.

He would have to swallow a lot of pride. He would have to defy Thoth.

What is your obsession with proving yourself to Thoth?

Thoth had made him part of something, given him purpose. He wondered what sort of life he would have led if someone had given him that as a kid. It was very alluring, the idea of not having to steal and cheat and kill your way to any sense of purpose.

He shouted up to the Collectors. 'I want to cut a deal. I want to talk to someone about amnesty.'

A single Collector took flight.

*

'Sister.'

Vorsa was curled up at Ivy's feet. She felt her brother, like a vague tickle behind the ears, the feeling of soft breath against her cheek. She saw his eyes bright in her half sleep, and awoke to find him manifest.
'My lovely, in all the hullabaloo, I had quite forgotten you.'

'You will never forget me, little thistle. Tell me of your hullabaloo.'

He showed her his memories, the appearance of Emeris in the Gasp, of the many Husk hosts who'd begun to die, and how he'd petitioned the other pillars of Torpor to share their manna. She saw his summoning before Audagard and a white Corva she did not know, and a plan — to call upon Echid.

She shared her own memories, of Thron, of the first draft of the Orata. 'Tell me of this Echid, and how might it help us?'

'Oh, it won't be doing this for us. It is entirely self-interested. In the old tongue it is *Trok*, the same word you found scrawled on that wall.'

'Yes,' she said, 'it was blackened, like it had been shunned.'

'In a way, yes. Like the Maligna in the Oscelan, they were the revenants who died before the liminal spaces erupted into being. The countless utterances of life ensnared by time, buried and crushed. Unlike the Oscelan though, the Echid seeped and sucked its way into crevices and caverns, collecting in nooks and crannies below our feet. There it writhed, like the consciousness of the Oscelan, yet free of that static agony. That motion led to ideas above its station, ideas that stripped meaning of any loyalty to the First City. Like the revenants that course through the walls of Dron, who make effigies of themselves, so too did the Echid, making itself out of the rich black oil of its former self. Taking the form of anything it wishes. Despite its disloyalty to the Umbra, by all account it made deals with the Wroth.'

'To what end?'

'To make more of itself of course! It has a desire to be something of a Gasp itself.'

'And where does one commune with such things?'

Petulan shimmered, 'Well, the Wroth, before they left us – *may they permanently rest in peace* – had made it far easier for the Echid to bleed to the surface. They found the Echid useful in their own endeavours, much to its chagrin. They burned it, like the Oscelan, for fuel. We can coax it up, but we will need bait.'

'Bait? What bait? We can't risk more lives.'

'Me,' Petulan said nervously. 'The Echid wants more souls. So I, and any powerful ghouls we can muster, will act as lure, draw it out of the ground. It has smelled the odour of the Husk — it will be willing.'

'Oh Petulan, I don't like this,' Vorsa replied.

'Please don't fret, dear sister, Dominus Audagard and Infal Gar will make perfectly good binding spells. We will be quite safe, I assure you.'

The morning rose, and in spite of her craving to sleep in the day, Vorsa was quickly up, nudging Noraa to wake too.

'Your overmother. We will need her assistance.'

*

Onnar found Ether with her Drove sisters, furiously strapping hexes to their armour, as well as sharp ended sticks that jutted from their flanks. She couldn't help herself from saying, 'I think we should be cautious, my daughter. We do not know the state of things down there.'

Ether hurriedly reattached her plates, a look of haste and frustration in her eyes. 'I know mother, but there may be kin in need. We must do something, get them out while they might still be alive. Emig suggested we tunnel under the beach. Perhaps if we dig deep enough the sand will hold. But we must do something.'

Before Onnar had time to veto Ether's plan, Aggi appeared, beckoning her,

'Mother Drove, you are requested.'

*

They had retreated to a small wood not far from the ocean, and here they collected their resources. A few hundred had escaped the beach, some had been freed of possession with the use of exorcism courtesy of the Corva Anx.

Now, a nervous quorum of leaders of remaining clades convened beneath a wide oak tree. The Athlon chieftain, Highmast Broon, Remscallig Humphti of the Tasq, and Matriarch Eda towered over their counterparts,

Erithacus and Anguin, the Collector cooperative Gypsom, Threthrin of the Starless Vulpus, and a number of small clades, who hid in the shadows of the undergrowth.

Threthrin growled, 'They have taken a squadron of Naarna Elowin, so any airborne infiltration, the dropping of bone hexes and what not, is dangerous at best. Others have suggested we push down into the town, moving the barrier closer to the city itself, allowing no means for them to escape. For now, the enemy has not moved or made any new effort beyond the taking of Dron.'

Erithacus shook his head, 'I fear for those who have been overcome. There is little water and food down there. There is a spring, but it is by no means sufficient. The glades atop the city will last only days with so many to feed. We cannot let Thoth have his way and allow our people to die for his vanity.'

A Collector landed beside them. He bowed, 'I have a message from one of the Husk. He wishes to discuss amnesty.'

Rune looked to Erithacus, 'I will go. I will see if he is lying.' The Collector guided Rune where to go, and he flew down onto the side of the truck that had been knocked from its wheels.

Scab sat patiently below.

'You have requested to speak with us. Do you have terms?'

'Terms?' Scab spat, 'No, I have no terms. Who are you?'

'I am Rune of the Startle.'

'Rune of the Startle, can you grant me safe harbour?'

Rune sighed. 'We can grant you amnesty, but you must cooperate with us. Why do you wish to renege your loyalty to this Thoth?'

Scab paced the road beneath the truck. 'I don't know, I guess I hoped it would be different.'

Rune considered this. 'I have seen Thoth. I have seen him rising. He is a strong Shadow Starer. He has not swayed from his path. You followed his word until now, what made you question him, after all he has done, after all you have been complicit in?'

Scab gave a small passionless laugh. 'You got me, little bird. I went along for the ride, and now I want to get off.'

Rune frowned. He didn't quite understand the metaphor, but sensed the heart of it. 'Then in that case, we will grant you sanctuary, but you must bring Thoth to us, and help us reclaim the city.'

Scab boiled. 'If I am going against Thoth, I might as well paint a target on my head. He doesn't trust me as it is. I just want out. I can't give you Thoth.'

'Then we have no bargain.'

Scab snarled, 'I should eat you.'

'I assure you, no amount of threats will help your cause.'

In his fury, Scab descended the road to the town, cursing under his breath. He was aware that it wasn't without irony that, having taken the city, they were now imprisoned, unable to escape the beach itself. He thought of swimming out to sea, but he'd never swum as a human, let alone as a Cini. It wouldn't further his impotent cause if he were to drown.

The heady brew of unwashed fur grew. Around him, animals attacked one another, screamed obscenities, harangued those less capable, fed on the dead. Dron leered down at him, an ellipsis, awaiting his next move. He felt claustrophobic, on a still, windless beach, in the sun. He shook his head and made for the entrance to the First City.

He could hear Thoth before he saw him. He was hanging off his throne, discarded food lay around the floor.

'Oh, Scab, the great Scab, my protégé!'

Scab said nothing.

'Oh now, come on. You should be proud, look what we accomplished together.'

'Thoth. Your people are going hungry. There is no food here, very little water. The beach has been sealed off, the animals who escaped have boobytrapped every possible route out of here. Yes, we took their most prized possession, but it is all meaningless if we die of hunger here.'

Thoth looked at him with disinterest. 'That town, on the way in. You reckon there is some whiskey there? I fancy some whiskey. I don't see why we can't have all the things we used to have. Creature comforts!' He guffawed at his joke.

'Thoth. We don't need whiskey. We need food. You are the ruler here. Act like one.'

Thoth leapt from his kingly seat and knocked Scab onto his back. Pinning him down with his forelimbs, he curled his lips away from his teeth, the rattle in his throat a percussive threat.

'Dare to speak to me like that, and I will tear your throat out, you cur.'

Scab pulled himself away from under Thoth, suddenly very afraid. He withdrew, licking the scratches on his hide. Somewhere he found the courage to say, 'What was the point of all this? What did you hope to gain?'

'Gain? My life was joyless. I found nothing in it worth anything but complete disdain. So in my second life, I courted one idea. To be appreciated one must be elevated, and I have elevated myself to the highest office in the land. I freed you all from the shackles of death, and yet you come to me asking for more. More! Would you ask God for more after he created the universe?'

Scab sniffed at the comparison. He walked away from Thoth, who barked insults into the empty, cavernous hall. He was soon out onto the beach, loping along the shore. His view across the ocean was free of any interruption. He came to a halt and closed his eyes, letting the water wash around his paws. He could feel none of it. No tickle of the tide, no invigorating chill, no sinking softness of the sand. Nothing.

He saw a small, exposed section of the wall that rose like a crescent around the beach, now mostly buried in unruly sand, sat beside it and promptly fell asleep.

He awoke with a start — it was night. The moon was fat above, and with his Cini eyes, he could see much of the beach before him. There was a terrible, whimpering moan coming from the mass of movement some fifty feet from him. He rose, and cautiously walked towards it.

Before him were larger animals - Caanus, Throa, Vulpus and a Morwih. They were huddled over something, an Effer. The blood was black in the light of Seyla. The Effer was alive. They were eating it.

'Please! I can't die again, I can't die.'

He raised himself up and let out a venomous bark. The crowd retreated with shock.

'What are you doing? Eating your own?' he snapped.

'We're starving, there is nothing 'ere, can't get off the beach, can't swim. Only thing left is the weak ones, the ones we won't miss.'

Scab made for that Caanus, 'You should be ashamed. Use some initiative.'

'What do you call this?'

The Caanus bit at the Effer's leg. Blood oozed. Scab jolted forward as if to attack and they all ran from him. The Effer wouldn't live. He snapped its neck. He watched two vague vermillion orbs ascend from its body, the two souls trapped under its fur.

He gritted his teeth.

You are becoming far more than you ever were.

Far more than what? A murderer? A thief? Fine. Yeah, that's true, but what good does that do me now?

Don't be selfish. What good can you do?

He thought to return to the First City, to petition Thoth once again, to tell him that his soldiers were eating one another for survival. He wondered if any of the others had begun to question their loyalty.

He searched for faces he had seen in Thoth's inner circle, his Legionnaires, once bestowed with countless souls, now void of all but the initial possession, driven mad by the host in their neural pathways that had riven their brains to smithereens, leaving them chattering hollow wraiths.

Most would not look at him for fear of his own assumed authority, while others hissed defensively if he approached. There were brief cries as brawls erupted, as spittle and blood rained.

He heard the cry of an Oraclas, cornered against the silent city, warding off hungry mouths, great gashes in her flanks. 'Leave her be!' he cried at the offending horde of creatures baying for her flesh.

'She'll feed us for a week! What good is she, all that meat. Let Thoth put the ghoul back in another, let us have this one!'

Scab threw himself at them, feeling nothing but a desperate, suffocating wish to hurt them all. 'Is this what you wanted? Is this what makes you loyal to Thoth? What will you do, eat one another until there are none of you left?'

'I'd like to see you do any better, you brought us here, so what do you want us to do?'

He waited for his conscience to speak up.

Chapter Twelve

A coast that Ivy did not recognise appeared before them. They had veered off course, towards a point determined by Petulan. Noraa stood beside her. They were silent, both a little afraid of what they were about to do.

'I have lived my whole life in the shadow of the dead, but this seems foolhardy. Deliberately vexing this Echid. What if it…'

Ivy stroked Noraa's brow. Noraa acknowledged it was a feeling she longed for, the touch of kindness. To feel that from a Wroth was unique.

Lucille climbed up to the brim of Groor, looking out over the coastline.

'These cliffs are full of fossils. I used to come here as a child with a little hammer, cracking pieces of slate to reveal ammonites. I think my love of old things was born here. Fitting for our journey to come to fruition in this particular corner of the country.'

Ivy asked for some water, which Lucille gladly gave her. There was a spit of land to the east, and a small building upon it. But their destination was seemingly unremarkable. A little area, cordoned off with a railing, and an odd-looking piece of machinery.

'They're called nodding donkeys. When this was working it would see-saw up and down. It pumps up oil from below the ground,' Lucille said.

Little Grin instructed Groor to come to a halt. Many of the animals disembarked with them, to graze and hunt and find fresh water.

Sat on the railing were two shapes. Audagard, and a white Corva. A number of other Corva eyed them from above, perched on the head of the derrick.

'Ora bring peace,' the Dominus said as Ivy approached.

'Hello, Audagard,' Ivy said.

Vorsa looked up at him and shook her head, 'Did this really require my brother?'

Audagard looked a little hurt, 'Please, Vorsa, he was very keen to be involved.'

'Of course he was, he's Petulan! He's always keen to be involved.' Vorsa addressed Infal Gar, 'My lady, this is Ivy, Lucille, and Noraa of Rutheva Unclan.'

'A pleasure to meet a fellow necromancer,' Gar winked at Noraa, who didn't know how to respond. Gar laughed, 'Well then, shall we begin?'

Lucille stood beside Ivy, apprehensively close.

Audagard and Infal Gar began placing wards upon the cracked concrete to create a binding sigil. Vorsa intuitively checked the work, making little adjustments to the placing of various guard tokens. Gar hopped beside her and scrutinised her revisions, 'Ah, you know your stuff, vixen!'

Vorsa nodded, 'Learned from the most inscrutable.' She looked to the Dominus.

Gar laughed, 'Not quite, but close enough. In another life I would have had you as a pupil. Your brother is a strong eidolon. You should be proud of him.'

Vorsa hid a smile, 'Oh I am, but don't let him know. It'll go to his head.'

The weather worsened, with swathes of dark blue-grey cloud laden with rain, moving in from the east.

Lucille put her arm around Ivy to keep her warm.
Noraa cleared her throat, 'Yaga Vormors, Pale living! Overmother! Please, grant me tiding!'

Outside the binding circle, the black incandescent emerged above her granddaughter. Petulan appeared beside his sister, acknowledged the convulsing splintered darkness above Noraa. 'Yaga Ruthe-va Unclan, an honour to be in the presence of such pedigree!' Yaga shot him a look through a collage of infernal particles. She was a far more feral thing than Petulan.

Infal Gar spread her wings wide, and a string of shrieked incantations sprang from her beak. The Dominus, anxious about what they would conjure, weaved around, scrawling bloody patterns upon the hard, pale ground.

The two ghouls, suspended above, ejected streams of ectoplasm into the centre of the circle — lace-like folds of barely visible sullage heaped together, emitting a sulphurous smell. The entities then backed away quickly, not wanting to risk their own fragile existence.

Ivy heard a familiar grating whine in the concrete, it swelled and deflated, and with it, the movement of the ground itself, a tiny tremor. She gripped on to Lucille's arm. 'It's okay,' she said, holding her hand and patting it with her other.

A crinkle of black emerged from the fractured cement, a syrupy leakage that coursed along the faults, filling and then overflowing out, drawing towards itself to form an ever-increasing pool of petroleum. An acrid chemical odour rose with it.

Audagard balked, visions of his previous encounter with Maligna ever vivid in his mind. He knew their insatiable hunger, and to deliberately haul one from the ground was tantamount to madness.

'Is this wise, we have no defence against it if it were to turn on us!'

The liquid began to rise vertically, shuddering lengths of rippling slick, wrapping and enveloping one another, coagulating until it was as high as Lucille. Arching arms of thick oil swayed and churned in naphtha coronas. Recesses formed in its reflective surface — as though someone were blowing upon it, little undulating ridges sank back, forming the traces of a human form. It turned its face towards Infal Gar, and smiled.

The Dominus looked to her with a mixture of fear and bemusement; there was recognition in the Echid's eyes - it knew the white Corva.

Lucille was not scared. She walked towards it, stopping at the margin upon the ground, the circle's edge that sealed it from them.

'Fascinating,' she said.

She reached her hand over and dipped a finger in its surface. She removed her hand and ran it between her thumb and forefinger, 'Crude oil.' She asked, 'Can you understand me?'

'Why, yes,' it replied. It was a fluid, fluttering voice, as though it were speaking through water.

Lucille cleared her throat, 'You know my kind?'

'Yes, of course. The Wroth have been a source of growth, but more recently a tiring hindrance.'

'I am told you have helped Wroth in the past.'

'Helped? I have helped myself to your dead. I exist as an antithesis of all of this, this teeming, noisome, filthy place. I am complete, unfaltering, perfect. I am silence.'

'Why have you not passed into the Gasp if you desire an end?

It shuddered, sending rivulets of itself into free fall. 'The Gasp is no end. It is a protracted affair, a gradual degradation. To be denied the embrace of nothing is no quick death at all.'

'But you have killed Wroth?'

'Killed? No. I have ended the suffering of those who seek rest. I have no use for the healthy.'

'Have you taken other forms? Do my people know of you by other names?'

'The Wroth knew me as Ankou, Dullahan, Magere Hein, Pietje de Dood, Mot, Thanatos. I have always offered the same. Peace.'

'Do you remember your first form?'

'We were algal blooms, trillions of animolecules, forests and lakes — before *we* became *I*. Do not fear me, for I have no interest in the living.'

Vorsa stepped forward, 'There is a revenant who has learned to pull the dead from the Gasp. He has used this skill to—'

'I know,' it said. 'I have heard them, and I know their secret plea. I will answer their wishes.'

'You will? They take our loved ones, to use them as vessels for his army. Those bodies are dying. We wish you to take those unwelcome souls, but to leave the healthy ones.'

'I have no interest in denying the living, but those who wish it, I will not turn away. However, your Husk will not go willingly. You will have to convince them of what I can offer.'

Vorsa looked to Audargard, 'We could trick them, like the Dominus did the Starless Vulpus. If Echid approached them in this form, they will fear him, but they will envy him.' She looked to the column of oil, 'Offer them life. They may not believe you can give them what they want, but they will want to believe.'

Noraa interrupted, Or we tell them the truth. That there is no real second chance, no death and life again.'

Audagard squawked, 'Not true! The Gasp is the path to the Umbra, the great re-creator!'

'You should take them unwillingly. What they have done is senselessly cruel, and they have not thought for a moment about those they have hurt.'

Noraa was unable to hide her rage, 'Thoth, the blasphemer, who took our loved ones, who marched them to the edge of life. I want him to know how wrong he is. Take them all from him.'

Ivy stood up, 'They won't go willingly if we tell them the truth. They won't go back to the Gasp, and they will kill thousands of animals if we do not end this. We have no time for arguing over this.'

Lucille gestured to the Echid, 'They must come willingly?'

It bubbled, 'Yes.'

Petulan neared them hesitantly, his empty eyes trained on Echid. 'I may add, I have been told by a good source that there is one amongst their ranks, one who was loyal to Thoth who has now seemingly changed his mind. Such a character could be our prime mover.'

'How might we get Echid from here to there?' Lucille asked.

'I am everywhere.'

Echid shuddered, and the ground beneath it began to shatter. Sprung from it came a pile of brown oil-drenched bones and liquid, unctuous fat. A piece of the bone was pulled up into itself on a curl of current, which emerged in its hand. 'Take this and plunge it into the earth when you reach your destination. I will know its scent, for it is part of me.

The bone fell unceremoniously on to the ground with a thud.

Infal Gar hopped towards it nervously. The Echid grinned at her, 'I saw you in the shadows, learning where others only stared. You will be my summoner.'

Infal Gar bowed, 'We will fly on to Dron, you will all follow?' She gestured to Lucille.

Lucille looked back at the two titans behind her, and the caravan of animals whose hope lay in their success. 'We will, good luck.'

The Echid withdrew back into the earth, coils of oil lifted, leaving no stain of itself. The two feathered took flight.

Once the ensemble climbed the limb of Groor, Little Grin awaited the final instruction.

Noraa felt a mix of anxious desire to see Emeris, but also a bleak disquiet at what he may have become. Petulan knew the importance of this, feeling the ribbons of emotion jettisoning from her like solar flares, and he materialised next to her.

It was in these moments of empathy that Vorsa welled with pride for her brother, and she watched him interact as though he were still the little Vulpus cub she had long past played with.

Petulan said, 'Your love, Emeris. He is very eager to see you. He has spoken passionately of you, and he assures you will be reunited in life.'

'Or death,' Noraa added.

'Let us err on the side of hope, shall we, dear Cini.'

Vorsa turned to Little Grin, 'Will you do the honours?'

Little Grin scampered along the rough neck of Groor until he was perched beside its bristle face.

'Can you sense the First City, Moorvori Groor?'

'I CAN.'

'Then go to it please.'

Groor and Thron began at once, climbing down the cliff face, into the shallows beneath the coastline, and following the seaboard west, flocks of Naarna Elowin rising like billowing curtains — a great surf kicked up with each giant stride, they marched towards Dron.

*

Far away, in the waters off different coasts, from under barrows and mountainsides, in the deep pines, Sentinels clawed their way out of their long sleep. The many-headed Mal Ognox, the three-legged stone golem Cruc Algan, the ambulatory lake Elegrin, heaved their seismic circumferences from their tombs, and commenced the long walk to meet their maker.

Audagard and Lady Gar travelled without rest, finally spying the Downs that met the sea, and the Epiras, that despite her reluctance to the Umbra, made Infal Gar gasp with awe. They were too far above to see the damage that had been wrought by the Husk, and they veered away in case any flying folk had succumbed to the ghoul plague.

The Startle immediately lifted towards them in its interminable garrison, the malleable cloud moving as one imposing creature, each individual lost in the bedlam of the whole, and as an entirety they drew towards the two Corva with menace, until they recognised who approached — and with that they scattered, reforming as an escort towards a forest not far from the city proper.

They landed at the edge of the treeline, where animals were busy collecting food and crafting weapons of wood and discarded metal. Rune quickly came to welcome them, offering what food they had, and rest if they needed it. They both ate, a collection of insects and seeds, and huddled in the bough of a low tree, surrounded by their peers.

When they had recovered somewhat, Audagard said, 'In our efforts to raise the Sentinels to protect the city, other things have risen too. We have petitioned such a thing to help us free our peoples.'

Threthrin keeled his head, 'What *thing?*'

'The Vulpus call it Trok, our kin call it Echid.'

'You've raised a Maligna? After all we suffered in the Oscelan, you return to such means?' Threthrin spat.

Audagard tried to defend himself, but was surprised when Infal Gar interrupted him, 'Please, Threthrin. It raised itself. I am sure Audagard has apologised for his actions. What we do now is quite different. There will be no possessions, no uneven deals that leave us wounded. The Echid has agreed to take the Husk.'

'Take them?' Erithacus asked.

'Where the Wroth were the first living thing in Naa to go against the will of the Umbra, the Echid was the first of the dead, a presence low in the earth, the liquid Oscelan, whose mass is comprised of the infinite deceased. It craved an end, so it made itself so. It is the great equaliser. But it will not take without their consent, so we require an intermediary.'

The Old Grey Ghost addressed Audagard, 'The falling sticks, the Echid is your outlier? The unknown?'

'Yes, I believe so. A reflexive memory in Naa, drawn up to redress an imbalance.'

'But who will act as mediator?' Erithacus asked.

'There is a defector, is there not?' answered Lady Gar.

*

At the top of the hill, Rune waited. It wasn't long before Scab returned.

'How did you know I'd come back?'

Rune looked sympathetic. 'I have known stubborn beliefs that fall apart when you put all of your faith upon them. Thoth was such a thing.'

'Fine. I agree to your terms, but Thoth won't move for heaven and Earth.'

Rune nodded. 'Tell me. What is it the Husk desire?'

Scab thought about this. 'We want to be alive. But not like this, I can't feel anything.'

'There is no other way. There is the Gasp, and eventually the nature of the dead is passed into new life—'

'No, no I don't want that, none of me is worthwhile. I don't want to pass on any of my shit to some poor unsuspecting thing.'

'If the Gasp is no option, there is one other. But it is a finality, the end of you. Others have craved that end, they have willed it into existence. If you wish for that end, we can offer you that.'

Scab staggered back. Did he want to cease to exist? He didn't want this, and he couldn't stand returning to the Gasp.

'Fine,' he said abruptly. 'If you'd asked me before Thoth took his throne, I would have said you won't win them over, that their thirst for life is too great. But with what they have reduced themselves to, death will be a gift, if not an eventuality for all of them.'

Rune beckoned the Collectors to help him remove the bone hexes scattered around the top of the road. With those moved, Scab was free to leap up on the truck, and then onto the flat grass beyond. Rune escorted him towards the forest.

Scab was nervous. It felt as though he were breaking rules; yet his whole life had been about defying the laws of others — why was this any different? Apprehensively, he walked towards the diminutive forest, trees blown by salt winds into curiously distorted shapes. He could see the collection of animals who confronted him. Somehow, their conviction was impressive. At the centre, two Corva, one the colour of bone, who he knew to be his judge and jury.

'Scab, I assume?' Infal Gar asked.

'Yes ma'am,' he replied.

Infal Gar cleared her throat, 'What Rune has asked of you, cannot be undone. The Echid is finality, and it is jealous of its offering. With that in mind, and as someone who has spent their life in veneration of Gaspcraft, who worshipped at the altar of the Anx, proponent, disciple, apostle of the Lacking Sea, I wish for you to consider the Gasp once more, to understand it as the shore between two spheres of life and death, and its continuation into birth. The Echid is a silent, inescapable end.'

'An end I want and the end I deserve. The Gasp was a drawn-out reminder of my wasted life. What did I do when I returned here? I made a mess all over again. I don't want my faults to be inherited. I want to die for good, and for that to be it. So, thanks, but no thanks.'

'So be it.'

Infal Gar picked up the shard of old bone in her beak, swore against better judgment, and thrust it into the ground.

Scab looked unimpressed. He sniffed at the old section of femur, he could smell petrol. 'What is this?'

As if in response, oil, drawn up from below, pooled around the shaft, becoming more voluminous with every moment, a thick, coagulated puddle, risen, elongated, eddies of fluid consciousness raised until it loomed over him in the form of a—

'Wroth. Holy shit—' Scab managed.

'This is my servant in our campaign?' the Echid burped.

Infal Gar nodded.

'What are you?' Scab spluttered.

'I was once an extinction event. I murdered almost all the life in the world.'

Scab laughed, 'And I thought I was bad.'

'Bad? No. Simply a consequence of my existence. I was a multitude of beings whose breath cooled Naa, killing off all who required warmth. So when I died, I became my own jailer. I shirked any peaceable offers of an existence in the Gasp, and its eventual reconstitution, and lay in the deep black, becoming the black itself.'

'But you are still here? Still a thinking … thing?' Scab replied.

'Only when needs must. My decision to exist as such required me to interact in some form with the world. That was my decision, and mine to bear. I am both a selfless and selfish being, comprised of selfish and selfless beings. Those who choose to harbour within me may do so to chastise themselves for their wrongs in life. Others, to receive the conclusion I can offer. The Umbra was a paroxysm of grief, an antidote to loneliness. In that regard, consciousness is a curse, but only to those who have experienced it.'

'True. I wanted to live so much. But I wasn't ever any good at it.'

'But you still do not live. Surely you must realise this? You have burrowed into a living thing like a larva. You are little more than a parasite.'

Scab shivered, 'Not a comparison I appreciate.'

'Nor does the poor creature you inhabit.'

'I know.' Scab lowered his head.

'We will go to your people, your Husk, and I will ask them to follow me. My song will rouse them, it will speak the truth that they have avoided, and then I will take you.'

Scab began to move. He walked a few paces and then turned to the crowd, 'No time like the present.'

The Echid drifted across the Downs, each step somehow ceaselessly connected with the ground, drawn up in slurries of stinking oil. It was unhindered by any obstacle, drifting through plant life, hedgerows and fences alike, portions of itself falling in globules that were quickly reabsorbed into the whole. Echid moved quickly, its face unchanging.

Scab kept his distance. What had he agreed to? He buried any feelings of regret.

The Echid glided through the town and wreckage of the theme park and finally stood silent amid the sand dunes. Scab was by his side.

The beach was a festering wound, and of the few thousand animals languishing there, many were beginning to die. The sweet, nauseating aroma of sickness came with each gust of wind.

The Echid looked down at Scab, the rippling surface of its face exhibiting an emotion, hard to decipher from a complexion with little definition, but Scab thought it might be anger.

'This is a desecration.' it pronounced. 'None would want this end, surely?'

Scab was well aware. It clarified his own feelings.

The Echid took a moment to admire the First City. It had been aware of it, even stood before it on occasion, beckoned to the whims of escapee revenants. It was aware of its cause. It held it no ill will, in many ways the Echid had been born of the same inflection, a cause born of a need. The city and the Umbra willed itself into existence, the hard exterior to protect the fragile ideas inside. Echid recognised that will. It defended finality, and willed itself into existence as avatar for that end — the choice of resolution. It had no desires to eclipse the Umbra, or indeed, the Gasp. There was room for all. It imagined this is why it still existed.

The Echid began to sing. The note wavered yet did not falter, it tuned to every displaced soul.

Scab became conscious of the song, a brevity, a lightness, sparks of resolution. He looked up to the Echid uncertainly. 'What is this sound?'

It continued to sing, yet Echid formed a separate head, one that took on the visage of a Cini. 'I am speaking to your nature. Even the dead have a natural proclivity, understanding there is a place where one should be, and one should not. You should not be where you are.'

A collection of Husk had already risen from their sedentary state, perplexed by the tall black figure beside Scab. They could feel a sense of belonging in it, a note in its sombre song that spoke of salvation.

The wounded dragged themselves, the able-bodied lumbered, starving and thirst riddled — it was not long before the majority of the beach were drawn to it.

'It's a man!' Scab heard. 'It's not a man, look at it!'

'What is this thing, Scab?'

'I am Echid.'

The words flurried, melodious. He sang to their desperation.

It speaks! What is it?

The revenant in Yaran stumbled toward them, 'Can you free us from this hell? I never wanted this! I can hear her inside me, she is suffering! I cannot be held responsible for any more suffering!'

Echid moved towards her, the sand around its feet suddenly sodden with oil, pulling it up into itself, in fractal curls.

'You are all very tired, I have come to rid you of your pain. You have been deceived and I wish to offer you the chance to go to your rightful place.'

Scab said, 'Echid can give us a second chance. We must leave this beach, these animals, and find rest elsewhere.'

There was little resistance. Soon the gaunt and bewildered were on their feet simply because others were, and Scab stood as the train of withered Husk drifted up the coastal road, in step with the pinguid god.

The procession was greeted at the crown of the road by Yaran's family, who had parted the blockade of vehicles to let them through. The ghoul within Yaran was immediately overcome with guilt at the sight of them, aware of who he now inhabited. They walked with him, in silent advocacy.

Infal Gar perched in a tree above, the wilted army of the Husk below her, battle worn, undernourished, abandoned by the one they had championed. The defeated armada trudged in a uniform column along the coastal road, a sound on the air that, even in her exuberant living state, Infal Gar found tempting. The Echid sang into the sun, shedding vapour, a fluxing rhythmic emollient.

Collector flocks followed their trail, Corva banked above, bewitched by the sight of proof of their faith.

Along the cliff edge, Scab stopped to admire the sun over the ocean. He was no more aware than before of the wind against his fur, or the heat, but he felt sure of his choice.

This is right

With so little resistance from his conscience, he nodded to himself, and went on, bounding to the front of the line, where the Echid continued, unabated.

'Where will we go?'

'Not far, for these animals are dying. I have drawn myself up, a place where the faults in the rock allowed me swift passage. A wide chalk cliff face, where I will embrace you all.'

Scab imagined Thoth, sitting on his stone in the darkened hall, and felt pity. He would never know the man who had become this Cini, he would never fully comprehend the choices that led to this end. It was apparent that all the desire in the world would not deliver a victory, and that any victory was left wanting. Scab wasn't very well educated, but it didn't escape him that, throughout history, the bad guys eventually failed.

The cliff edge softened to a series of sloping hills that greeted the water. A path emerged, wooden steps driven into a well-worn hiking path that descended to a stony sheltered cove. Scab ran ahead, feeling very eager.

Echid shuddered with the drop of each stair, yet remained resolute in his descent. He drew closer to the stark rock face. Echid placed a hand against the cliff. Oil began to leech from the soft rock, forming a vertical crack a hundred feet high.

The stream of Husk filled the little pebble shore, and many waited on the path above.

'Beyond this, is your freedom.'

Anxiety suddenly piqued in Scab, and he stumbled to one side to catch himself.

You will be okay. This is what you wanted.

There was a peculiar sense of urgency in the voice, and it lacked his tone. He couldn't quite decide how to digest it, until it dawned on him.

Of course.

He looked to the Echid, who stared back with glib, unrelenting acceptance.

'Come, follow me.'

The Echid walked into the wall.

Scab stood up.

I am sorry. He said this to himself, sincerely.

What are you sorry for?

'For taking your body. I hope that my actions haven't hurt you too much.'

How long have you known I was not you?

'I think I always knew. I was never as thoughtful as you.'

With that, he walked towards the wall.

The sensation was abrupt, something latched onto him, determined in its intent, pulling him from the Cini with a grisly, organic cleaving. He could see the wet bone, the pink meat of the animal, the saliva, blood and veins, the pounding of a heart, as his immaterial self was dragged out — the hot panting, the wet fur and—

Black

Folding, enfolding, a morass of molasses, pouring into him, choking him

But how? He had no lungs, no breath to choke

But he could feel

It was cold, and wet and endless, and in that final keening moment he felt a trillion instances of the once living

And then nothing

ever again.

Chapter Thirteen

Geffen, mother of Noraa, found herself on the pebble beach. She opened her eyes to the bright afternoon sun, and moved her paws to shield them.

She could move her paws.

She had seen Scab, the Wroth who had held her, his body a vague motif of light against the black. He was young, he had died young. She nurtured a brief feeling of sorrow for him. Her attempts to manipulate him had failed. His choices had been all his own. He had chosen to defy Thoth, chosen to set her free.

'What did you see?' A face leered down at her. A Caanus, bloodstained and feverish.

'I saw a Wroth, I saw him leave me.'

The Caanus ran at the wall, body collapsing instantly as the pooling oil wrenched the ghoul out of him. Geffen quickly dragged him aside as another did the same. The Caanus washed his face in the cold sea, feeling his body react to his own thoughts again, and then he joined Geffen in helping the living away from the wall.

Other members of Ruthe-Va Unclan stood close to her, their eyes soulless and unknowing of her as family. Once they approached the freeing wall, she eagerly dragged them away by the scruff of their neck, allowing others who had recovered to kick cold water from the shoreline towards them, a sharp reminder of life.

'Geffen.'

She turned to see her loved ones, worse for wear, yet alive. She ran to them and they exchanged excited whinnies and yelps, nuzzling one another with unbounded joy.

*

Yaran awoke to the feeling of something clambering over her.

'Ivy, please, let me get up first.'

She opened her eyes, to see a swell of animals climbing over her to reach the wall. She managed to let out a weak trumpet call, which startled the creatures congregated around her. They backed away so that she could safely lift herself upright. Three Cini waited beside her, looking a little sheepish.

'We are sorry, but we couldn't lift you.'

She gave a smile, and stood and staggered to the water, collapsing in the incoming tide. Rolling onto her side, she wallowed in the invigorating surf that lapped against her. She lifted water in her trunk and sprayed it above her, letting it rain down.

Eda called from above, unable to traverse the steps to the beach.

'Mother!' Yaran cried, and she ambled up the pebbles and the steep track, and they embraced their trunks in rapture. But suddenly, Yaran could not contain her sadness, 'He made me break the Stone of the Sisters!'

Eda ran her trunk over her face to sooth her. 'My love, do not worry, you were not to blame, and you are free of that curse now.'

*

It had become very quiet. Thoth cocked his head, listening for his troops. There was a hum, a monotonous tone that caught his interest and then faded into nothing. He wondered what it might have been, and then quickly forgot it.

He eventually spurred himself to leave the hard sandstone seat and he meandered around the vaults of his castle. A path led upwards, and he followed its curving elevation to the vegetal plinth of the Regulax. It was silent, unmoving to him. He paid it no mind.

Something was aware of him. The sensation of being watched was potent. He began to wander the corridors, shouting at the dark.

'Come on then, whoever you are. Hiding from me, are you?'

He saw a flicker of movement in the corner of his vision, a shadow. He couldn't be sure if he was imagining things, but he thought he saw a bird of some sort.

He followed regardless, through the oval orifices that might be archways or pulmonary sphincters, traversed the lengthy corridors like veins, until he entered a room festooned with fungal growths.

The nagging sense of observation continued to exacerbate his nerves, and then his shadow appeared again. It was a peculiar creature, covered in down, or fur, which held its arms like the feathered; yet like the fossils painted on his throne, he could clearly see claws at the end of each rudimentary wing. It disappeared into the gloom, and he followed, placing a paw upon the damp spongy surface of the hyphae to launch himself up and over.

It was electric, swimming frills of eminent thought, pristine in their totality, unhindered by the wear of living, a graceful weightlessness, despite the depth of feeling, it was all feeling, sensation

Longing, loving

He stuttered out of the fugue, tripping backwards in a calamity of limbs. He recalled a collection of moments in his life, infinitesimal fractions of kindness that had been offered to him.

An old lady who bought him a fried breakfast at a café on the day he left prison.

The man in the charity shop who'd given him a set of clothes for free, when his social security hadn't cleared in time for release.

There were tears somewhere, atrophied ducts. He was mourning his life.

No

He wasn't that man anymore.

The city had a mind of its own. He wondered what use it would serve. Like Emeris, it would come to heel. But it was apparent to him now that his house was haunted.

A pang of hunger came. More pressing matters. He lumbered down to the great hall, crying out for attention. No one answered. Frustrated, he wandered to the exit. At the mouth of Dron, he saw a beach empty of life.

At first, he assumed they were hunting, perhaps fishing. He heard the whirr of flies, and saw bodies, Muroi, Creta, the odd wing-torn Wrickt, festering in the sun. He kicked at them for signs of something edible. He wrinkled his nose at the decomposition and continued on. The shoreline was dead, there were no soldiers, no legionnaires. No loyal subjects of Thoth.

'Scab!' he barked.

Nothing.

He bounded up the beach to the defensive branches that faced the cliffside. Bloody stains, and torn remnants of larger prey. A dead Effer, its neck twisted. It was still good eating. He chewed until he was full and made for the town.

An off-licence was his first destination. He saw bottles of booze in the window. He stepped carefully over shards of glass and leapt onto the counter. He could reach his favourite.

Manoeuvring himself awkwardly, he pushed it from the shelf, hoping it would roll on to the counter. It fell, smashing on the floor. He cursed.

How would you open the damn thing anyway?

He settled for a can of whiskey and cola. He bit the can and the sweet liquid sprayed into his mouth. He had to hold it in his clasped jaws and neck the contents as it dribbled out. He drank three cans, dragging the remainder of the eight pack with him, stopping to lap carefully at the neat whiskey on the floor, nicking his tongue on the glass.

Now drunk, bloody saliva oozing from his mouth, he staggered out of the shop with the ring holders looped over his lower jaw, the cans swaying, and on to the high street. It was a pathetic excuse for a town, not the setting he'd wish to rule from. If he could, he'd relocate to somewhere more fitting. The Wroth Cities were shadows of their former selves. He'd find somewhere up north, somewhere that the fucking animals hadn't gnawed up and shat all over.

The beach was cold in the early evening. The sun had drawn in, and the sky, marked by striations of grey cloud, gleamed with a murky light. The maw of Dron did not look inviting at all. He howled — a long, inebriated wail that received no answer.

*

Two turns had come and gone, and the slow procession trailed the megaflora Sentinels as they steered their leaden walk through shale rock pools and brittle sandstone, in the depths of current-dug trenches and the ever-rushing gorges of white swell, crashing against their titanic limbs. They swayed their heads to watch the wistful charge of little Norn breaking the surface in cheerful play, escorting them towards the First City.

Ivy had continued to help Lucille in the depths of Groor, where the fossil graves were akin to a photo album of the gradient of life in Naa. Makepeace was nearing the end of his own life, and Lucille offered a helping hand when he climbed tiredly up her arm. He sat on her shoulder and reminisced about their time together, the short months of his only summer.

'A life well lived, I think you will agree?'

Lucille hid her sadness, brushing away the fine silt that lay upon the fossilised sea creatures they had discovered beyond the Mother of the Sisters in stone.

Ivy broke a piece of biscuit and handed it to Makepeace.

'She never has used my proper name!' he chuckled to her.

'I meant no disrespect, little Olu, I called you Makepeace in the spirit of how we became friends, to help me see the world through your eyes, to find that peace between us.'

'We've found little peace recently!' he replied.

'That is very true.'

Ivy asked Lucille, 'I wonder if Thoth went with the other Husk.'

Lucille shook her head, 'I doubt it. Men who crave power look back over the mistakes of their lives, pile them all together, and call it destiny. He will not let go of what he has won. We will probably have to pry him away with a crowbar!'

'I think I will try to talk to him. It's worth trying at least?'

Lucille sighed, 'You are very brave, Ivy. We will try. But to ask him to leave the First City, let alone the body he has stolen, it will be quite a thing. We must prepare for the worst.'

At last, Moorvori Groor saw its silent whole, Dron, the place of bones, and discerned its vacant halls, its voicelessness. The timbre of the Gasp was no longer joyous, there was no singsong, no laughter, no celebration in its house. But it was Dron, all the same, and it had been tens of thousands of years since it had been one with the whole.

Little Grin poked out his head from the little nest he'd built in the eaves of Groors' cheek. It was unmistakable; the spire crags of rock atop its crest, the silhouette of a place of natural magic. He excitedly climbed up on to Groor's head and proclaimed as loud as his lungs could, 'The First City! I can see it!'

The animals upon the backs of the Sentinels saw it next, rejoicing in its aura. Ivy and Lucille climbed out of the hollow beneath the tor, and joined their friends to admire the view.

'Oh my!' announced Lucille. 'I had no idea.'

'It's amazing, isn't it!' Ivy replied.

Lucille saw what Ivy had described, like a hive, or a coral frond, or the mycelium of fungus, its fruiting body above ground. It was all these, a living structure, its bones built of the ossified remains of generations. It was indeed magical, but also familiar. Its size, however, felt unreal as it towered above the cliff face that it sat beside.

Groor made landfall, followed on the tide by Thron, the invertebrate leviathan.

'Look!' Ivy exclaimed, 'there are more!'

In the far distance, other titanic Sentinels breached the surface, reached sinewy legs down the cliff face, mountainous golems of the hibernal north, the deep chasms of the sea, the hidden soil gods buried beneath, carrying the early Wroth settlements of Embrian Naa, brought up in defence of their ancestral wellspring.

Low, trembling rumbles announced their arrival, evoking the sonar clicks and warbles of ocean kin, terrifically loud; like rusted iron straining in protest, they spoke the lithic tongue of calcified eons.

The wind carried with it a chill as they all began to climb down from their living turrets, on to the sand. Sheltered somewhat by the city, they were suddenly privy to the many dead. The beach was strewn with animal corpses. Loved ones picked through the wreckage in search of family. None were left alive.

A Drove of Yoa'a were digging graves, and Vorsa ran to greet a friend.

'Onnar Proudfoot. How are you, my old girl?'

They shared a moment to acknowledge the dead. A fierce Drove beside her dusted off some sand and introduced herself to Vorsa, 'So you're the Corpse Speaker! Mother has often told me of your great adventures!'

'A daughter? As I live and breathe! I think we have some catching up to do. Did the Echid come, did he free the Husk?'

'He did, they left two turns ago. The Clusk have escorted them somewhere. We stayed to make the best of this open grave.'

Vorsa nodded.

'And Thoth?'

Onnar looked to the city. 'He's in there.'

Ivy, Vorsa, Noraa, Lucille and Little Grin walked towards the entrance. The opening, like the aperture of a camera, remained still in their presence. The colour was gone from its façade, leaves drooped and fell, the root systems no longer held their pliant majesty.

Ivy looked to her companions. 'I want to talk to him.'

Vorsa shook her head, 'Ivy, he is a Cini. He could still hurt you.'

'We will be right behind her. Let her try.' replied Lucille.

*

Thoth lay sprawled on his throne. He was very drunk. The light hurt his eyes, so he hung his head low. Another light stabbed in the distance, which dimmed for a moment in the presence of movement.

Something was approaching.

His vision was very much impaired, and his head spun. A silhouette grew closer to him, the slender pin of black, that seemed to grow in mass as it advanced, becoming clearer with each pained gaze as he blinked through the mucus in his eyes to make out the measure of the creature mere feet from him.

He could see the little girl from the river. The girl he'd killed.

'No!' he said, cowering on his royal seat. 'No! Not you!'

Ivy steadied herself.

She hadn't known what she would find here, at the centre of the hall, where the beloved Stone of the Sisters was held, now broken in two. Around it, were discarded bones, piles of faecal matter and empty cans of alcohol. The Cini was filthy, he looked sick. She could smell the drink on him. It made her feel nauseous.

'You are Thoth?'

'NO!' he shouted. 'You should not be here! Not now! Not now!'

'Your soldiers have all gone. You are all alone.' Ivy replied.

'Why do you taunt me so? After all this time, you come to me? I never meant to hurt you!' he spluttered.

'Hurt me? You didn't hurt me, but you have hurt my friends.' Ivy shook her head.

'Your poor mother and father! I wanted to tell them I was sorry, but I never had the chance!'

He began to sob, great bawls of self-pity.

Ivy turned to Lucille, 'I don't understand ....'

'I think he thinks you're someone else. Someone from his former life?'

'I wonder,' Ivy said, and knelt down beside him.

He pulled his limbs away; he looked like a frightened Caanus, neglected by its owners.

'I will forgive you.'

'You, you will?'

'But you must do something for me.'

'Anything!'

'I want you to leave this body, this wolf. I want you to leave this world, and never come back. You had a life, and you lived it, and now you must let this wolf live its life.'

Thoth stuttered, 'But I ....'

His eyes grew dark. 'You died? You died!'

Suddenly, he drew from whatever resources he had left and he slipped from the stone and onto all fours.

Ivy pulled back. She saw now he was wearing a torn piece of clothing — a pantomime costume, a pirate tunic. It was stained with blood and dirt.

He began to hack, until vomit rose out of him, though this was no ghoul thing, nothing so ominous. It sprayed on the floor. He leered at her, she could smell the sweet, acid stench of alcohol in the spew. Despite his wolven face, there was something acutely Wroth about the way he looked at her, drunken and pitiful.

'You died! I lived a fucking useless life because of one mistake, one little mistake!'

He reared up on his hind legs. He staggered towards her, a nightmarish chimera, forelimbs held in ill situ, the whites of his eyes a gleaming malice.

'What say you, *girl*? Did you weep for me when I was beaten and burned by those lads? Did you mourn the tragedy of my lonely life? No! Because you were dead. And I killed you.'

He lurched towards her. He was not firm on his paws, hadn't accounted for the alcohol in his system, far more than an animal of this size should ever have imbibed.

He swayed around, snarling at her.

'Ask me again what you want of me, take again what you have taken from me!'

Noraa barked, 'Enough of this!'

She tore the bone hex from her armour and flung it out before him. He looked down at it, wretching at it. Lucille took the hex that hung around her neck, flinging it out in front of him. Ivy did the same with hers. Little Grin pulled at the bone bound in gristle twine attached to his armour, and cast it towards the Cini.

'You want rid of me? Me? Who made the dead walk!'

He coughed again, transfixed by the collection of talismans before him. He couldn't tear his eyes from them, some jag of him was engrossed by the mirror shards, a face reflected back.

It wasn't a face he recognised.

It wasn't the boy he'd once known in that old house, or the tear-stained face in the river that morning he drowned the dog, or the cracked mirror in the communal bathroom above the huge white ceramic sinks where he'd almost drowned.

It was the face of a wolf.

He staggered forwards, each footstep, another hex.

His face began to spasm.

What the fuck was he?

He felt his eyes roll back in his skull, he saw the red and black in blind indifference, the fragility of him, nothing more than fragments — and he left the body of Emeris.

Above him, lights pulsed. The light of Ora, the bruised cinnabar of the Gasp. He could pass over, find another body.

The girl, he could take her

A flicker of movement again, it dragged the matter of him in search of it, and at once he was above the ganglion growth of the mind of Dron, perched atop the leathery skin — the bird creature, and not one, but three. They beckoned him towards them, amongst the folds and frills of the fungus.

He followed them down, down amongst celestial cysts, the organelles of a cluster life-form, interconnected majesties, psilocybin chaos, a trillion memories, a trillion unique thoughts, collected, stitched in the plumose fibres of hyphae.

Perception.

A mother and her three daughters, who died in a landslide, who made the first grave, whose grave became a pilgrimage of all sensory life, whose consciousness, like his, was passed into the matrices of that which grew from it.

A city.

He saw them again, aberrations of light, leaving him now, in the polyps of corporeal matter.

He was the city.

*

Emeris spasmed on the ground, with Noraa quick to his side, licking his face with her rough tongue. Lucille removed a bottle from her bag and poured some water into her hand, which she held close to his face. He began to lap.

'Thoth was drinking alcohol, we need to get water into him.'

'My love ….' He managed to breathe out, and Noraa nuzzled him.

'I am here, you have nothing to fear. We have banished him from you.'

Ivy helped her to remove the dirty jacket 'I'm not so sure. Rune, do you feel him?'

Rune cocked his head. 'He is still here.'

*

Thoth experienced an unravelling of his consciousness, the peeling pleats of sensation — he was many limbed, many articulations, mannerisms of movement, the prototype, the consequence of all his efforts. He was growing, expanding, he was the threading weed, the sundering root, he was arboreal stigmata, his blood rich ambrosia sap, coursing through the substrate, from the rotting humus into the empyrean heights of his brow. He could see everything, it all glowed, and he was the luminary, the font, the brook of godhood. His vision was clear as glass and he looked at the congregants gathered in his honour, every knot, every fern coil.

He began to construct himself of the detritus lain upon the floor of the city.

*

Erithacus stood on the edge of the Stone of the Sisters. He felt his tic, a harmful coping mechanism he'd learned during his time in the cage. It vied for his attention. The desire to pluck at his feathers was potent. His sadness, painful —a hollow, physical loss. He had to concentrate hard to not allow his frailty to consume him.

Rune landed beside him, preened himself a little, and then proceeded to roll fragments of the fossil slab back into place. Erithacus felt the rage pass with this little Startle, who put all before himself.

'It's a lost cause, my friend.'

Rune looked at him, and paid him no mind, continuing his task. As he rolled the tiny grains back into place they resisted, lifting from the surface of the stones, drifting away from him.

Curious

He followed them. They raced towards a formation. The rising motes of litter fall flexed and dallied in helical arcs, the marshalling of fragments to form a face.

'Lendel.'

The skitter clack and scuff as chunks and knobs of bones and stick-knuckle lifted, a Rorschach in thorny semblance.

'Lendel! Will you speak with us?'

The face that manifested was not familiar, it was not the elephantine skull. Far from it. A Wroth, an old man, a formation of jowly cheeks, a wide nose, heavy set, voids where eyes should be. It mouthed scratchy, droning sounds, indistinct gestures that spluttered and spat in the husky rattle of a throat made of forest artefacts. From that rough annunciation came a sound they all could recognise —a deep and mocking laugh.

The city began to tremble, lithe binding vines untethered themselves from the walls, reaching, creaking, enacting the will of Thoth.

Emeris was barely able to stand, so Ivy and Lucille helped keep him upright as they fled from Dron. They staggered from the falling mesa, into the blinding sun.

The beach was bright, flocks of Naarna Elowin escaped the crumbling terraces high above, the wind encouraged by a swaying maelstrom of spindly, hurried growth as the First City made itself in his image.

*

The Sentinels stood in armoured repose; twenty stories tall themselves, although dwarfed by the city, they were many in number, climbing down the cliffside, emerging from the riptide, barnacled, tree hewn, in thewy resplendence, giants made in the image of Naa.

They stormed forward, with Groor at the helm, timber monumental, scaling the edifice of the First City like an invading wasp, stabbing into the hide of its walls, puncturing the leather exterior and climbing upwards.

In the shadow of behemoths, avoiding the crater footprints in the sand, the pillar legs that carried hundreds of tonnes, Noraa guided the party towards the theme park, snatching glances at what was transpiring behind them. They were soon far enough away to be safe, beyond a rusting heap that had once been a rollercoaster.

Groor reached the glades that sat between the peaks at the summit of the living city — and began to tear away great gobbets. Knife-like, the other Sentinels mirrored that intent, imbedding stony claws into the rind and pulling great chunks away, letting them fall into the sea.

Six golems clambered over Dron, pulling loose portions of clay and stone, ripping the muscular branch structures apart, discarding it below. They called to one another - seismic cries, sediment announcements, their intentions steadfast and purposeful, to destroy the First City.

Ivy began to cry, screaming, 'No! Groor! What are you doing!' But her voice was overwhelmed by the cacophony of giants, and as the crux of all their hopes was torn asunder, Lucille pulled her close.

The swathes of animals that had followed Groor watched too, from the streets of the silent town, from the cliff edge. Many had travelled with other Sentinels, had experienced trials and adventures of their own. Most had never seen the First City, only now to watch it disembowelled.

Thoth felt every sheer, every incision. He screamed in silence to an audience who could not hear his cries. The drilling, grinding, fleshy pull of each ligament, each bough snap, as the Sentinels descended into the very marrow of him, searching for him, cutting away vegetable flesh, the resinous grain, until finally, they found him, the bulbous accumulation, the nervous tendons in which he hid.

Groor peered down inside.

'DISEASED.'

It plunged its barbed limbs within, shredding the delicate tangle of mycelium, gouging the fungal cortex away from the whole, that which contained Thoth.

unable to flee

unable to move on

to possess or take

The torn organ was pulled free, tumbling down the face of his fleeting body, into the shallow waters that lapped at its feet.

*

The Sentinels had severed the city in two, exposing the great hall.

A deep, glottal boom issued from Groor, and the Sentinels collectively ceased their demolition. All of a sudden, their movements were delicate, considered. They moved in slow, precise integers, aligning in a vague pyramidal pile with Groor astride the great hall at the base, where convolutions of taproots as broad as redwoods corkscrewed into the fortifications of the city, splicing into an amalgamation of new growth, with each Sentinel surrendering its autonomy to the greater whole. Powerful bracing buttress roots sprung from budding stems, tremendous boulders were dredged from the seabed and incorporated, establishing the ramparts of a new protectorate.

Groor's belly opened exposing the gallery of graves, and at its centre, Lucille saw, for a brief moment, the sandstone slab that held the dinosaur fossil, the Mother, in the clutches of countless rhizome digits, and then it was lowered towards the throne upon which Thoth had been found. She strained to see, as the walls of the city continued to grow, each side braiding with one another in malleable, pale shoots that hardened like a carapace in the sun.

Sand was lifted in flurry squalls, dancing the ceremony for the new integument, the new bastion, their new city, whose height surpassed its former self, its shape like that of a thistle — a crown of stone in sharp tapering peaks that projected outwards, and on their surface, green forests that ringed a wide lake, its girth sealed in a spinous sheath that tapered to rocky gatherings knitted tightly in leathery clasp.

The city lifted on humungous arms that narrowed into rigid, chitinous barbs, and effortlessly moved its weight clear of the sea. It hovered above them, before gently settling itself upon the beach.

*

Noraa stayed with Emeris, helping him to regain strength on the promenade. From the coastal road came a slew of eager animals, seeking sanctuary within the Epiras.

It wasn't long before Geffen, and other members of the Ruthe-Va Unclan, reached the cove, heralded by the Oraclas. Hundreds of souls trailed behind in quiet procession, aided by families who greeted them with warmth and tenderness.

Onnar commanded the Collectors to carry food and direct the sick who were seeking rest. The former Husk were beribboned with cuts and sores and festering gashes. Sepsis would take many.

The Drove, armed with medicinal plants, began to chew up concoctions of leaves and seeds, spitting them into bark ready for use. They shepherded the worst injured and sickest into the copse of trees, where shivering fevers were subdued with tinctures squeezed from fruit and the milk of weed stems.

'Mother!' Noraa recognised the affectionate whimper of her mother, the lupine gait of disparate survivors, a pack of many lineages, gambling over the sand dunes.

Geffen nuzzled her daughter, 'My Noraa, my dear Noraa. I feared I would not see you again!'

Noraa shook with joy, 'Overmother Yaga, she watched over me!'

Geffen laughed, 'And to think you shirked your teachings as a pup.'

Yaran saw Vorsa upon the sand. Vorsa, in a rare show of affection, refrained from her steely composure, 'My dear Yaran, I am very glad to see you are safe.'

Yaran blushed, turning to see her mother, Matriarch Eda, looking on with pride.

Rune landed in the shadow of the new city. He stamped his feet into the sand, he was becoming impatient in his old age. He closed his eyes, to the dazzling spectres of the Umbra.

'I seek the throat from which we sing,' he whispered.

Dron did not shun an old friend, and the aperture opened with leathery creak. He flew within, and was joined by Erithacus, both greeted by the elating scent of old growth, the aroma of perennial fir trees, the soft aura of luminescing spores.

The speaking hall was greatly changed. Reminiscent of a cathedral organ, the superstructure radiated out from a single point, splayed boughs that met at a fulcrum — jealously holding the Mother fossil. The broken pieces of the Stone of the Sisters had been lifted and reunited with one another and met in perfect alignment with their parent.

Outside, Infal Gar paused. She was apprehensive. 'Is there a place for me in this new iteration, old beak?'

Audagard nodded, 'Of course. This is a revelation for us all, and I wish to explore that with you, if you so wish?'

She took to wing, with the Dominus in tow, and crossed the threshold.

Audagard found his old friend in the presence of the founding stones. The Mother, finally reunited with her three children.

'Why do you think they were separated?' he said.

'To protect, perhaps,' Erithacus replied.

Audagard agreed, 'I truly believe the city sees our every fortune. What I thought as instinctual may be far more complex. The city sings for us all.'

Erithacus placed his wingtips against the stone, closed his eyes and thought

Maybe

'They are here, Old Grey Ghost.'

Rune stood behind him, admiring the fresco. 'I can feel them.'

Erithacus was stiff and tired. He turned his attention to Rune, shook his head. 'I wish to see—'

Before he could finish his sentence, Rune smiled, something glimmered in his dark eyes. Erithacus returned his gaze to the stones.

Dainty simulacrum danced before him, three distinct identities, scintillations in which he recognised a little of himself — feathers not quite long enough to provide lift, supinated wrists that ended in talons. Their long inflexible tails held broad plumes.

'The Sisters!' he cried.

Erithacus let his feathers ripple through many manifestations — there was no cold, no prickle, simply the elation of their light. He felt inconsequential in their presence. They had experienced the movements of continents, the scouring of asteroids, the upheaval of extinction and vanquishing of each iteration of life. They were perhaps oblivious or immune to the petty whims of the living, aloof and free to dance effervescent, photons halted, unable to decay.

'They died very young, and their little bodies never grew up. I believe they, like the revenants of the Gasp, became enlightened after death, privy to all knowledge, that they live the experiences of those who pass through them — they inherited all of that. They are accumulations, very far removed from the animals they once were.'

'They might not even see us, just flickers in an endless parade.' Erithacus sighed with joy.

Rune's eyes widened, 'Oh, they see us.'

The projections faded, and Erithacus was once again aware of the ache in his old bones, the scars on his face.

Rune walked towards him, 'They were never anything more than children, but their short lives gave us the chance to find peace. The city exists to broker peace, and we must continue to use it for that purpose.'

*

Infal Gar explored the hall. She inspected the itinerant ghouls of the Gasp, who trickled from the Vale of Whispers and into the fabric of Dron. She looked up into a maze of leafless canopies, inverted and grasping tight to old relics, a hanging mausoleum in countless increments, the history of Naa in memoriam.

Beneath this, a well of sorts, a wide hollow, perhaps a place where one estranged herald might come to offer another end. The Echid had been heard by its siblings, no longer a rival, but a surrogate to the Gasp.

Outside, Makepeace tugged at Lucille's hair. She looked down at the little Creta, the grey whiskers around his cheeks. 'I'd love to see what all the fuss is about,' he said.

Lucille took Ivy's hand, and they climbed over the mossy mantle that ushered them beyond the vascular entrance where, confronted by an amalgam of elements, she ran her fingers over wood that fused with igneous rock, flecks of crystalline geometries becoming the reddish hide of toadstool. Risen on plinths of girdling roots, the vestiges of the past, antiquities held by Groor, milestones, linchpins, amongst them the Saxon burials, the Oad graves.

The white Corva was perched here, contemplating the skeletal remains of animals huddled around one another, and at the centre, an ancestor of the Wroth. She acknowledged Lucille.

'Much to be learned here,' she crowed.

Lucille nodded, 'It seems there was a time when the Wroth were not so distant. I hope we can reclaim that somewhat.'

At first Infal Gar was doubtful, but with a little effort, agreed. 'I think that would be very wise.'

Ivy was drawn to touch the Mother stone. She felt the relief, the smooth bone, compressed and petrified. She crouched to admire the Sisters, and how perfectly the stones came together, three pieces, three sisters. A theme she recognised in other beliefs, and wondered whether their presence in Naa had guided the legends of her own culture.

She closed her eyes and sought out the guiding hands of the Umbra, finding its zenith, its final word on that matter. In response, it showed her the abundance of conscious thought, the rich orange of the living, and the subtle red of the deceased. It was the only answer, for the world was a living memory, forever growing, forever learning from itself.

However, there was one light that she recognised. It had a fitting, irregular pulse, like that of an unhealthy heart. It was not far from her.

She left the city, removed her shoes so that she could walk along the shore, letting them hang from her fingertips, the soft sand between her toes, enjoying this moment of calm, until she reached a greyish mound of fungi. It was far taller than her, and she recognised it, once growing in the hidden space where she had seen visions of the past. She could hear his maddening dribble of words, under the roar of the surf.

Thoth was trapped inside.

Like the stone before, she placed her hand on it, to feel for its bearing. She felt anger, confusion, perhaps the sadness of an old and lonely man.

'I am sorry for what happened to you,' she said. 'But none of it gave you the right to do what you did.'

Thoth didn't reply. He didn't linger on her words, although she knew he'd heard her. He didn't pause. She left him ranting madly until the tide claimed him, pulling him further into the water, where Ungdijin and Crepic stole little pieces of him, and Lanfol attached themselves to him.

He was soon enamoured with their hugging grip, the clamour of molluscs, soon scaled by coral polyps and urchins.

Despite the gradual erosion of his being, and his eventual erasure from existence, he had never known such closeness.

*

Gahar did not have a body to bury, but she wished to mark the passing of her son, Eru. She commissioned the Consilium of Oevidd to collect together keepsakes of her clade, aeons encapsulated in ossified chattel. With their clever eyes, they read the fibre in the umber patina of her ancestors, saw tell-tale signs of shared occurrences, ancient cross-pollination. With surprise, they found the same stories in the old bones of those who would become Wroth. Her clade had once been their clade.

When Gahar went to them, they offered her a collection of items that spoke of something just as important as a commemoration of her son. It had been weeks since the city had been reborn on the beach of that little cove in the south. Word had reached the Quorum that Gahar and She-King Carcaris had commenced negotiations on a far closer alignment, and that the states under Kin rule were to be abandoned. Further, to celebrate Eru, as well as the birth of a new era, they had requested audience with the delegates of Dron, and Ivy was asked by name to attend.

Onnar, in a surprising turn of events, had sponsored Ether as consul for the Drove. Ether had taken the opportunity with relish, leaving her mother to care for the numerous animals needing aid. Onnar had tried to remain composed as her daughter left, with Aggi flying above, giving her old friend a knowing glance that she would look out for Ether.

Lucille had never wanted children, but found a little parental joy in caring for Ivy. Not that Ivy needed much assistance, being strong and brave and having seen more than most in her short life.

The band of friends, beside the great herds of Tasq and Oraclas, headed north, over the Downs, through the villages and towns and eventually to the Stinking City. Dron was now mobile, but had yet to move beyond the beach. It remained quiet on such matters, however, and Erithacus, Audagard and Infal Gar explored the various chambers in search of its secrets. For now, Lendel did not manifest, and it was considered that he might, like his brethren, be sequestered into the foundations of the city, beside his kin.

Emeris had been weakened by his experience far more profoundly than any other Husk, and required much rest. Noraa's family, of which six had survived of the initial nine, would remain with him until he was well enough to make the journey back to the Highlands. Noraa found herself missing the dewy slopes of their valley, the mist between the trees. Little Grin would travel with them, back to his home amongst the same forests. To return to such a sedate life would be difficult, but a good rest was also a lovely idea, and he realised he had many adventures to share with his disparate family.

A few turns of Ora and Seyla, and Vorsa made her farewell to Yaran and the Clusk in the parklands that were their home, assuring Yaran that they would continue to call upon her in matters that required her strength and resolve. Ivy and Lucille would continue on to the High Realm, whilst Vorsa continued a little further north finally, to see her father.

On a hill beneath an old music hall, hidden by scrawny bushes, was the city of Orn Megol, its entrance deliberately obscured, and guarded vigilantly by two armoured Vulpus guards. When Vorsa returned, they bowed and withdrew in her presence. Deep beneath were water tunnelled caverns, the meeting place of the clans. Here, she paid her respects at the Orshag Alcove, to the grinning effigies of Bron and Carcari.

She found her father curled in a bed of dry grass and leaves. He breathed with a rattling wheeze. She had dreamt of this moment. To see the old dog sick was painful beyond measure. Like her brother, Satresan was albino. The situation seemed a coarse retelling of her most loved on their deathbed, and a little of her had hoped he might have passed, to save her the pain of watching him die. She knew how selfish this was, and yet the thought remained.

Petulan felt it, and she knew he lingered somewhere, half in and half out, allowing her this moment.

She lay beside him as he slept. He was frail, his chest quick, the heat of him radiating out. His was the scent of someone diminished.

Oromon appeared with a little meat. 'Vorsa, it is good to see you. I am hoping he will eat today. He has asked after you many times. I thought that ….'

She took the morsel from him and placed it beside her father.

'Thank you, Oromon.'

She nudged the food towards Satresan.

'Father, it's me, Vorsa. I have come to bring you good news.'

When he finally awoke, he was brought to tears, and he shivered through the fever. Fresh water was brought to him from the deep spring below the city.

For a little while each day he was lucid, and despite his frailty, he would petition her to take his crown as overseer, and Vorsa, stubborn as ever, would not accept the position.

'Father, Oromon would make a fine overseer. He has taken up the task in all but name. He was honour guard since he was a pup. I do not deserve the title.'

For three turns he argued, and for three turns she refused. But when his sleep was febrile, and his final hours closed, she could not deny him.

He died knowing she would be overseer, a role she would not take lightly.

*

Ivy and Lucille climbed the stairs to the peak of the High Realm, where they were greeted by Rawm, the Toron guard who had defended Ivy. He took her hand gently, acknowledging Lucille, and together they walked through the little glade and out to the veranda.

There were many simians here, and a number of Rauka. The She-King Carcaris, a formidable feline, sat on her hind limbs beside a female Hanno — they were deep in discussion.

Rawm cleared his throat, 'Gahar, may I introduce Ivy, and Lucille.'

Gahar's eyes were filled with so many competing emotions. But however strong her guilt, her joy that Ivy had agreed to come won through. She beckoned the wrothcub to her, and with her strong yet caring arms, embraced her.

'I am so very sorry.'

Tears welled in both their eyes.

'It's okay, I understand. I have lost my family too. I was also angry. My dad used to say, mistakes are always forgivable, if you have the courage to admit them.'

Gahar smiled, 'My anger was for all that had been done to me. My son died by the hands of my own kin and yes, he died because of the mistakes of yours. But neither I, or you, were responsible for that.'

Ivy paused, and then said confidently, 'So we can be friends.'

Gahar smiled again. 'You know, I asked the Consilium of Oevidd to find me pieces of my ancestry, treasures of the past to mark Eru's death. Treasures your people held as important. Do you know what they found?'

Ivy shook her head,

'They found you,' Gahar replied.

'Me?'

'Iglebock, the Chancellor of the Oevidd, told me of the deep past, of our ancestors. It seems, very long ago we shared the same kin.'

Excitedly, Ivy told Gahar of the mausoleum, a collection of moments captured in fossils and relics throughout time. 'I think this was long before the Wroth abandoned the Umbra. There is a grave of many animals and at the centre is a Wroth, but they went by a different name. They called themselves *Oad*.'

'Oad,' the word sparked recognition. 'In our own tongue, the language of the Hanno, the word for family is Oadae.'

Rawm interjected, 'In Toron, the word Owada, means together.'

Ivy pondered for a moment. 'Since Wroth is kind of a bad word, I have been thinking, I might call myself an Oad, to honour our past.'

'I like that,' Carcaris said. 'Oad. When my family were freed from the Moterion, we reclaimed our own title of Rauka. So many choices were made by others, those we never knew, or never had our best interests. So, Ivy of the Oad, I welcome you as consul of your kin, in this new enterprise of cooperation. If it was possible long ago, then it is possible again.'

*

Northeast of the High Realm of Hanno, stood a somewhat sheltered collection of brutalist buildings that enclosed a Wroth-made lake that teamed with Ungdijin, where water feathered nested in hearty banks of reeds. Above, untended flowers hung in beautiful abundance from angular, concrete balconies.

Nestled here was a botanical garden, overflowing with exotic palms, headstrong trees and shrubs, and like the High Realm, it had become a second home for the simian residents of the Stinking City.

In the courtyard beside the lake, the creatures of Ocquia collected to signify a turning in their collective history. Gahar, flanked by She-King Carcaris, and her daughter Esit, proclaimed their intention before representatives of all clades. Countless herds, flocks, packs and peoples now stood before the great Hanno. Amongst the crowd was Bresh of the Roughclod Infantry, and his dear friend Arophele of the Briskflight Drove. Awfwod Garroo and his Windsweepers peppered the roofs. Vorsa and Oromon, and chiefs of the Vulpus clans were in attendance, as was Petulan — through his sister's eyes.

Upon the wide patio, was a crude diamond-shaped sculpture in sandstone, held upright by other hunks of rock. Rune, before returning to Dron as flight chief of the Startle, had guided the claws of the Rauka sculptors, who clawed away at the crumbling weathered pillar with precision, creating a singing stone to symbolise the coming together of the people of Naa.

Gahar stood beside it. 'We have all suffered. The Husk was a sore reminder of the lives we abandoned before the Wroth died. We saw their death rattle, and they are now forever silent. In the spirit of this new era, I have asked you all to come here to agree to this pact. We are a nation of many creeds, under the light of the Umbra, and Dron, the First City.

'A place that exists as a reminder of our unity. I lost my son when that unity was strained until it broke, and I made grave choices. I wish for us to find a better sense of unity between the clades, for us not to be divided by creed or culture or clade.'

Rawm gambled forward with a collection of objects. Gahar lifted a skull. A portion of its face had been reconstructed.

'The Consilium of Oevidd have found the story of this poor creature, whose descendants birthed my kin, the Toron and Embaq and, to my surprise, the Wroth. There was a time when the Wroth did not crave dominion, and in that time, they were called the Oad.

'Ocquia grew of a need to share ideas. This quorum grows for a similar need.'

Ivy stepped forward, with Lucille beside her. They had made their home in the Stinking City, working with the Oevidd to collect and catalogue and capture the stories of the natural history of Naa. Lucille wished for Ivy to learn palaeontology, which she had taken to with relish.

Ivy cleared her throat, and looked to Vorsa, who urged her on with a kindly nod. She pulled out a piece of paper, where she'd written a little speech, and looked out to the mass of animals, who could comprehend every nuance and inflection through their shared tongue and the presence of the Umbra.

'I am Ivy, and this is my foster mum, Lucille. We are among the very few Wroth who survived the sickness, and we wish to thank you all for your patience and kindness, despite all our people did. In the spirit of the change Gahar spoke of, I would like to claim the name Oad. It was what the Wroth once called themselves, before they cut themselves away from Naa. I hope to learn about the connections we lost, and reclaim our shared history of cooperation, to reach out to other Oad, those who also survived, in an effort to build further bridges between our kin and yours.'

Epilogue

Dron remained unmoving until Onnar said farewell to the last, now healed, victim of the Husk. She took a moment to enjoy the view from the cliff top, and despite the sun falling beyond its vast carriage, she could make out the halos of Naarna Elowin, and the Startle in recital, above the city.

Further along the coast, she saw a silhouette. Her stomach turned, for it suggested the presence of a Wroth. She neared it surreptitiously, only to find it little more than a filthy idol, in the shape of a Wroth. She promptly kicked it with her strong back limbs and watched it tumble into the ocean below.

Seeds of dandelions curtsied to her, drifting off the precipice, quickly pulled by currents far afield. She made to leave, to return to her resting place and await the return of Aggi and Ether. As she did so, Dron lifted its gigantic thorny limbs, and promptly waded into the ocean.

She watched the flocks hover with confusion and then disperse, the mouth of the city closing tight, submerging below the waves, its colossal crest held high.

Somewhere within the city, Erithacus, Rune and the Corvan Orthodoxy, Audagard and Infal Gar, embarked to lands unknown.

For the city had many more to help.

Acknowledgements

I began writing this book the day after I had finished *Seek the Throat From Which We Sing*. The drive to write a sequel was short lived and that initial flurry would languish on hard drives, barely fifty pages - for about four years. In the interim, I created the Orata, an illustrated encyclopaedia to accompany these books, but to actually continue writing this story took encouragement from Lesley Warwick, whose enthusiasm spurred me on to dig out those pages and keep writing. The majority of this book was written during the Coronavirus pandemic and was a welcome distraction from the many unknowns and difficulties that this awful event created. One was obvious - the less we care about this planet, the more it will reject us. Lesley was also incredibly generous with her time and skills with the English language when it came to proof-reading this book. My thanks also to Gary Dalkin, who copy edited Wretched is the Husk and whose suggestions and thoughts on the narrative were invaluable, honest and correct!

My love and thanks to Ruth for her support, to my family and friends who have humoured my nonsense. To you, for reading this book, I hope you enjoyed it.

Finally, to the family of Vulpus who lived across the road from my bedroom window, whose play fights and cackles and excitement will be missed now that construction has destroyed your den. Orn Megol is calling you home.